Early Praise for *This Side of Providence*

"Luminous, heartbreaking, and profoundly redemptive, *This Side of Providence* is a hauntingly beautiful novel about the unbreakable bonds between a wounded mother and the children she tries to love. In original, poetic, and surprisingly operatic prose, Harper brings her distinct blend of clarity and compassion to these wonderful pages, echoing the structural ingenuity of William Faulkner and the passionate intelligence of James Baldwin. A must read."

> — Rebecca Walker, author of *Adé: A Love Story*

"So beautifully written and incredibly compelling that I found myself not wanting to do anything but sit inside this world until everyone turned out all right. Rachel Harper is a stunning writer."

> — Jacqueline Woodson, National Book Award-winning author of *Brown Girl Dreaming* and *Miracle's Boys*

"A truly remarkable novel. Rachel Harper writes with jagged grace and unflinching courage—a willingness to confront fear and pain through characters beautifully alive with feeling, truth, and compassion."

> — Scott O'Connor, author of *Half World* and *Untouchable*

"*This Side of Providence* is sung by many voices, some achingly youthful, some wise, some wizened, who sing of desperation, who sing for compassion, who sing from the margins the long song of family. Harper's great achievement is that of choirmaster, keeping the arrangement of voices honest and clear, and somehow pitched toward love."

> — Justin Torres, author of *We the Animals*

"Survival, forgiveness, belonging, addiction: Rachel Harper guides readers along the knife-edge lives of her characters with silken pacing and muscular prose. With deep empathy and intellect, she paints a universal story of honest, imperfect love, and hard-won family. This gorgeous book balances the gritty with the good-hearted, reminding us that only what is dark and difficult can give rise to redemption."

— Neela Vaswani, author of *You Have Given Me a Country*

"Here is a novel that can save lives. Harper holds no bars about the dangers of addiction and poverty, yet offers hope for the near-miraculous ability of courageous young people, guided by dedicated teachers, to survive and flourish as unique and valuable individuals. Readers will root not only for struggling children, but also feel compassion for the flawed adults whose lives are spinning out of control. With unflinching honesty and unlimited love, Harper tells it like it is in many of our cities, and how it can be better. I'll never forget these characters or this novel."

— Sena Jeter Naslund, author of *Ahab's Wife*

"Rachel Harper is a channeler of voices, an inhabiter of bodies, an invoker of spirits. In this exquisitely braided narrative, she trusts her characters to tell their own stories, and grants each of them their own broken poetry. A stunning achievement—I did not want this novel to end, but when it did, I felt a rush of cathartic joy."

— K.L. Cook, author of *The Girl from Charnelle* and *Love Songs for the Quarantined*

"An ambitious, beautifully written, heartfelt novel that demonstrates the centrality of family under the most arduous of conditions."

— Jervey Tervalon, author of *Understand This* and *Monster's Chef*

Praise for *Brass Ankle Blues*

"*Brass Ankle Blues* is a beautiful debut...full of humanity and elusive shocks of recognition. It gracefully explores the fissures and possibilities that all young selves experience. This is a marvelous novel."
— *The Providence Journal*

"The family tensions, poignant discoveries, and richly evoked setting should help this find a broad audience."
— *Booklist*

"Rachel Harper's fierce debut is a tender, passionate, and moving read. A clear window onto a world rarely seen in contemporary fiction."
— Shay Youngblood, author of *Soul Kiss*

Also by Rachel M. Harper

Brass Ankle Blues

This Side of Providence

a novel

RACHEL M. HARPER

PROSPECT
·PARK·
BOOKS

Published by Prospect Park Books
2359 Lincoln Avenue
Altadena, California 91001
PROSPECT
·PARK·   www.prospectparkbooks.com
BOOKS

Distributed by Consortium Book Sales & Distribution
www.cbsd.com

Library of Congress Cataloging-in-Publication Data

Harper, Rachel M., 1972-
  This side of Providence / Rachel M. Harper.
    pages ; cm
  ISBN 978-1-938849-76-3 (softcover : acid-free paper)
 1. Puerto Ricans--Rhode Island--Providence--Fiction. 2. Single mothers--Fiction. 3. Heroin abuse--Fiction. 4. Domestic fiction. I. Title.
PS3608.A7747T48 2016
813'.6--dc23
                                    2015033178ISBN 978-1-938849-76-3

Cover design by Nicole Caputo.
Cover photography by Nic Skerten/Trevillion Images.
Layout by Amy Inouye, Future Studio.
Printed in the United States of America.

for my children

What in me is dark
Illumine, what is low raise and support,
That to the height of this great argument
I may assert eternal Providence,
And justify the ways of God to men.

— John Milton,
Paradise Lost

Arcelia

Before they knock down the door, I run. I'm wearing flip-flops, men's pajama bottoms, and a tank top with no bra. My sunglasses on the top of my head. I grab my baby and tuck her under my arm like a purse. She's one of the few things I own, and unlike everything else in my possession, I never lost or broke her.

I hear them enter the apartment—the front door cracks, their voices boom—but I'm gone before they catch me. Out the back window and down the alley before I know where I'm running to. Doctors always say I'm too skinny but you'll never catch me with my hips stuck in no window—even them small ones they put in basements—and I can still outrun almost any man, even in sandals and with a baby in my arm and a dope habit that keeps me shooting almost ten bags a day.

My baby's three now—not a baby anymore—and if I put her down she could run alongside me, but I hold her instead, to keep her close to my body, and to remind myself that I still have something to hold onto. Besides, what kind of mother lets her little girl run from the police? I don't know a lot of things, but I know that ain't right.

Me, I'm always running. So quick my feet don't seem to touch the ground. I hear the sound, though, the slap of my sandals on the pavement as I run down Manton Avenue in the rain. It sounds loud and quick like a machine gun. I am not a gun, but sometimes I feel like a bullet. Fast. Unstoppable. Deadly. I used to think I could outrun a bullet, when I was a child and I still believed in things I couldn't see. Like the truth, love, and forgiveness. Today I believe in only the things I can feel: hunger, pain, my beating heart.

I don't remember most of my childhood. I got a few memories from when my mother was alive, but not as many as I should. Only a few are clear. The rest are faint and jumbled, like the lines of a long and complicated joke that ends without a punch line. Or that never ends.

I see flashes all the time. Real quick, like a movie preview. They jump into my head and jump out, quick as they came. I try to control them, but I can't. They're not mine. They come so often they don't belong to me. It's like I'm watching TV without the sound. Like I'm remembering somebody else's life. There's a kid in most of them—me, I guess—but I don't recognize her. I try not to look her in the eyes. There's a man with her, or sometimes a boy, but he is always someone she knows. He looks kind, but he is not kind. Sometimes he smiles at the girl, but she never smiles back. She is always trying to escape, or looking for a place to hide.

When the rain stops and darkness comes, I'm still running. My baby girl is asleep in my arms, her breath a whisper on my neck. The high gone, she's now too much to carry. My arms and legs burn. I cut through the parking lot behind Atlantic Mills, hoping to lose the cops before my legs give out. I been running my whole life—either to people or away from them—and I don't really know where to go anymore. All the streets look the same and I wonder if I'm lost. Not sure it matters, as long as I keep moving. All roads got to end somewhere.

I run up an alleyway where two men are working under the hood of an old Buick. The car looks familiar but they don't. My legs continue to move, purely on instinct. I hear music from inside the car, the radio playing a Spanish song about a bird that follows a balloon all the way to the sun. The old man whistles the tune, and the younger one sings so softly I can't even tell if he knows the words.

They don't stop to look up as I sprint past them, as if I'm so fast they can't see me.

As if I'm invisible.

Cristo

On the streets I hear a lot of stories, but I'm telling this one because it's mine and it's the only one I know by heart. My teacher says storytellers use their imaginations and don't always stick to the truth, but I don't like when people lie all the time. So I'm planning on telling the whole truth here. Just as I see it. Just as I remember it.

My name is Cristoval Luna Perez, but everybody calls me Cristo for short. In case you don't speak Spanish that means Christ. Sometimes it makes me feel special, but most of the time I think it's just my name. I'm supposed to be Catholic, just because I'm Puerto Rican, but I don't believe in God. I don't really believe in anything I can't see, which means I don't believe in Santa Claus, the Easter bunny, or my father.

It's Thursday afternoon and if I was in class right now I'd be practicing my multiplication tables in a math notebook I share with two other kids. Instead, I'm sitting on an old wooden bench in the hallway outside the principal's office. Unless they expel me, I'm in the fourth grade at Hartford Avenue Elementary School, a huge yellow-brick building that looks like a prison. It used to be the pride of Olneyville, which it says on a plaque in the gym, but then a bunch of Spanish kids moved into the neighborhood and all the good teachers quit. Last year they took out all the grass and made the playground a big slab of concrete, giving the gang bangers a better surface to tag. They also put up a chain-link fence taller than the biggest kid in school, supposedly to keep the stray dogs out. That's when it started to feel like lock-up.

I live on the west side of Providence, which is the capital city of Rhode Island, which is the smallest state in America. I learned all that last year, in Mr. Clauser's class, but I'm not sure I believe it. They teach a lot of things I have trouble believing, like how this neighborhood used to be a big old apple orchard, and how when black people first came to this country they were in chains. This year I'm in Miss Valentín's bilingual class, and if there is a God I won't ever have another teacher in my life. When I tell her that she says, "God didn't make me a good teacher, my education did." She's always saying stuff like that, about how school can save you from being poor, but I don't understand how when almost all the kids in my class are on welfare and I have to walk by a crack house and two projects just to get here.

I'm supposed to be in the fifth grade but I don't read so good, especially in English, and I don't always pay attention like I should. I don't speak that good either, but I can usually understand movies and those guys in the street who yell about women and the lottery. Teacher says I can transfer to Regular Ed once I pass some test, but I want to stay in her class because everybody's poor enough to get free breakfast *and* lunch, and during music hour we all vote for salsa. They call it *Bilingual*, which is a fancy way of saying everybody in my class speaks Spanish, and even though we all come from a whole bunch of different countries, nobody thinks they're American.

The overhead light in the hallway is busted so I'm sitting in the half-dark. I've been waiting here for most of the morning, with nothing to do but listen to the secretaries talk about their diets and watch the seconds click by on an old wall clock locked up in a cage. Fuck if I know what that clock ever did wrong. I, on the other hand, got caught trying to flush David Delario's allergy pills down the toilet. I would have done it too, but those old toilets can barely flush the water. It don't make sense that David's not sitting next to me on this bench, since he was the one who started it by calling me a Spic and saying my girlfriend's so poor she reuses her toilet paper. He might be twice my size but I still punched him in the head and tore off his backpack and stomped on it till I felt something break inside. You can't talk shit about my girl and expect me to just sit there. Not gonna happen. Mami didn't teach me everything, but she did show me how to win a fight everybody thinks I should lose.

I coulda gone right home, but they can't find anyone to come pick me up. The school's been calling the house all day and nobody's answering. Which is weird since there's always somebody home in that apartment, even if I don't know who they are. Mami brings home strangers like some people bring home stray cats. She's always trying to help someone out, as if she don't have enough to do already, taking care of three kids and half the weirdos in the neighborhood. Not to mention herself. So now I gotta sit here and wait for her to come sign me out, even though if I wasn't in trouble they wouldn't care about how or even if I got home. That's public school for you; can't get nothing for free.

At 2:45 they give up and write Mami a note about what happened and ask me to bring it home. Yeah, right. That's like those kids who bring their father his belt so he can whip them with it. What Mami don't know won't hurt her, or in this case, me. She usually don't hit, yelling's more her thing, but sometimes she grabs my ear too hard or twists the skin on my arm till it's red like a sunburn. Sometimes it's worth it because later, when she's calmed down, she sits me in her lap and rubs coconut oil onto the mark and holds me like she's never held anyone else on earth. Sometimes it sounds like she's crying but no tears ever fall.

By the time I make it outside my bus is gone and I have to walk home alone. It pisses me off because I'm only wearing a T-shirt and it's raining, nothing heavy, just a soft spit-like rain that tells you summer's not quite here yet. I don't really mind walking, but I like riding the bus because I get to sit next to Krystal and hold her hand without anybody seeing us. In the winter she used to let me keep my hand inside her mittens to get warm. I know my fingers were ice cold but she didn't complain. That's when we started going out. If I was older or had any money I'd have to take her places and buy her food and jewelry and other things girls like to make her feel special, but for now we just sit together on the bus and pass notes in class that usually just say "hi."

I first noticed her because she has long curly hair that goes halfway down her back and she never ties it up like the other girls, not even in P.E. She says she likes me because I talk when I'm not supposed to and I got green eyes like the men on soap operas. People always ask me if they're fake since Puerto Ricans aren't supposed to have green eyes. I say I wish they were darker so I wouldn't have to squint in the sun and answer dumb questions all the time. What they don't know is that I got them from my mother, and if she ain't Puerto Rican then nobody is. I know she thinks they're the only nice thing she ever gave me, even when she looks at them and says they're too pretty to waste on a boy.

I walk the long way home, instead of taking the shortcut over Route 6, since I'm by myself and gotta avoid the white kids that hang out by the water tower and smoke cigarette butts and stick up for their own like that punk David Delario. Halfway down Hartford Avenue it starts raining harder, so I stop by the projects to visit my best friend César and maybe borrow a jacket for the walk home. He's smaller than me, around the size of my little sister Luz, but his uncle Antonio gave him free run of his closet when he got a new girlfriend and she refused to touch anything that some other girl had touched before her. Most of the clothes I got used to be Antonio's, including the Yankees shirt I'm wearing right now and a pair of jeans so big I have to tie an extension cord around my waist just to keep them up.

When I pass César's apartment the door is wide open and I can hear his grandmother yelling at him to stop tracking mud into the house. She's a big woman, about the same size as Teacher, and she grabs his arm and drags him to the front door like he's no bigger than a five-pound bag of rice. He says something I can't understand but it doesn't seem to matter to her. She tears his sneakers right off and throws them out into the rain. Then she smacks him across the face. His head flops onto his chest like a rag doll and he doesn't even try to protect himself. I wonder how his grandmother can hit a kid who only comes up to her waist. At school the kids call him Elmo since he's got a wild patch of curly red hair and strangers are always asking him how an Irish kid can speak Spanish so well. He always says the same thing, "I guess it's the luck of the Irish," and then we both crack up, even though we don't know anything about the Irish or being lucky.

His grandmother smacks him again, on the other cheek this time, and I watch him wipe his eyes with the back of his hand, pretending not to cry. Before he can see me his grandmother slams the door, erasing both of them from my view. Like if I can't see it, I won't know what goes on inside. I keep walking, telling myself that next time somebody calls him Elmo I'm gonna punch them in the face. My chest starts to feel tight, like when you hold your breath too long, and when I get under the highway overpass I let out a huge scream. It echoes in a dozen voices I don't even recognize. My heart stops for a second, and then starts to beat fast again, but I don't feel better.

It's dry under the overpass, but it smells like pigeon shit and homeless people—no place I want to hang out for long. A lady with a face so dirty I can't even tell what color she is climbs up the cement hill in worn-out tennis shoes three sizes too big. She slips under the railing at the top and disappears into the darkness. The sound of coughing echoes through the overpass, so loud I duck on instinct. Crouch low like an animal. I run my fingers across the stubble on my head, a habit I picked up after I started buzzing it. I like the way it feels against my fingertips, like petting a shaved dog. The first time Mami cut it all off was to get rid of lice, but I kept the clippers she borrowed from school so I could trim it once a week—just like the black guys at the barbershop on Broad Street told me to, so I could hold onto that feeling. Sometimes I want to let it grow out, to see how big of an Afro I could have. I don't really remember having long hair, but I've seen baby pictures where it's so curly I look like I'm Dominican. Mami begs me to grow it out all the time, to look like her little boy again, but no matter what I promise her, I'm in front of the bathroom mirror buzzing it off again when Saturday morning comes.

The cars on Manton are backed up like it's a parade, half waiting in line for the Dunkin' Donuts drive-thru, half going to the flea market. If I had a few dollars I'd buy Mami an iced coffee, extra cream no sugar, but instead I walk through the flea market. No matter who's working the booths they're always selling the same stuff: Nike rip-offs in extra-large sizes, twelve-packs of tube socks with the stitching all crooked, fake leather suitcases with broken wheels. One suitcase is so big I could crawl inside and it could take me anywhere. We don't go on trips no more, not since moving up here from the Bronx almost five years ago. Mami always says she's never going home again, but I'm not sure what she means. If home ain't where you live, where is it?

A small table in the corner is selling a bunch of stuff with the Puerto Rican flag on it. I grab a key chain and stuff it in my pocket before the guy can see me. I don't even have a set of keys, since the lock on the front door is busted and we only use the chain lock at night, but it's nice to feel it in my pocket, to hold something no one else has held before.

I cut across the parking lot and down a side street, passing the outdoor pool I spent every day floating in last summer. It should be opening for the season next week, but some kid drowned last Labor Day and they shut it down for good. There's a chain-link fence surrounding it, the bottom curled up from years of people sneaking in after dark. Like all the fences in this neighborhood, it can't keep nothing in or out. A piece of plywood covers the old sign, with the word CLOSED spray-painted in large black letters across it. I read the sign out loud, just for practice.

"Closed." *Cerrado.*

I rest my head against the sign and stare into the empty pool, its bottom covered with rotting leaves. Where does all the water go when they drain a pool this big? There used to be tiles on the sloped part of the floor, blue and white stripes like the flag of a country I'll never visit, but now they're gone. I wonder if they got washed away with all the water. I remember doing handstands on that floor last summer, how smooth the tiles were against my fingertips, and how quiet it was under the water, so quiet I always worried I'd busted my eardrums and would come back up deaf. Teacher says they'll probably turn the pool into a playground one day but for now we have to walk by and stare at this empty shell. It must be like staring at a boarded-up house you used to live in, or a picture of a dead person you used to love.

A bird circles overhead but never lands. It watches me like it knows something I don't. I whistle at the bird and it screeches in response, landing on the roof of a nearby building.

Last week Teacher took me to the indoor pool at the Y for my birthday. She said I could do anything I wanted and I said I wanted to dive into a pool so big I couldn't touch the bottom. They put a blow-up dinosaur in the deep end and all the kids climbed it like a mountain and jumped off into their parents' arms. Teacher sat at the edge with a T-shirt over her bathing suit and only put her feet in the water. Her legs were soft and white like marshmallows. I tried to get her to come in but she kept saying "no thanks," so I finally splashed her till she was all wet. She pretended to be upset but really she wasn't. On the way home we stopped at a Del's Lemonade truck and got frozen lemonade with chunks of real lemon peel in it. Teacher smiled when I told her it was the best birthday I could remember. She looked like a little girl with her hair all wet and slicked back and I thought of punching all the kids at school who call her Señorita Gordita, because even if she is fat, she's still the prettiest teacher at our school.

I asked her if we could do it again sometime and she said sure, but when I said I wanted to bring César she said she wasn't really supposed to be taking me there so it should just be our secret. Otherwise she might get in trouble for showing me special treatment. During school most teachers say they want to help you out, but when the bell rings they act like they can't see you on the way to their fancy cars. Teacher ain't like that. She acts the same, inside and outside, and I know she's gonna be there if I really need her. Maybe it's because we're both Puerto Rican or maybe she misses a nephew she used to have back in New York, but all I know is she treats me like I'm special, even when I'm pissed off and saying things I don't mean and everybody else is scared to go near me. I guess it's kinda like family except she doesn't hit me or yell for no reason and she hugs me when I say I'm sorry, even when I've broken something that can't be fixed.

Thunder booms in the distance, and the rain starts to fall harder. The storm clouds are so dark they're almost black and they hang over the city like smoke. Mami hates being out in the rain so I start to wonder where she could be. Not worry, just wonder. What could make her leave the house in weather like this?

I decide to keep reading signs for the rest of the walk home, just to practice. *Anthony's Drugs; Apartment for Rent; Tenares: Spanish and American Foods; Calvino's Auto Repair; Bill's Liquor Mart.* I never noticed there were so many words on the street. A bright yellow sheet of paper stapled to a telephone pole says, "Need Clean Needles?" with an address and phone number for a place called ENCORE. When I was in third grade I found that same piece of paper in Mami's room and when I asked her about it she said she grabbed it for one of the guys in the neighborhood who hurt his back on a construction job and got hooked on painkillers. When I asked her what the needles were for she said the medicine gets into his body faster if he puts it straight into his veins but that I should never do that, even if I was in a lot of pain and thought I was gonna die. She said using needles like that was a lot like dying. I know she was talking about that construction guy, but later I figured out she was talking about herself, too. Her veins are always bruised and she's got marks on her arms like the other junkies she tells me to stay away from. Luz don't want to know, but I asked Mami straight out one day and all she said was there are things a son shouldn't know about his mother. That's what she's like—she won't lie to your face, but she won't always tell you the truth either.

But for real, Mami don't have to worry about me and needles. I still turn away when I have to get a shot or when they prick my finger for blood at the clinic. Sometimes I think I want a tattoo, when I see the men in my neighborhood with fancy dragons painted across their backs, but then they tell you how they spent half a day with some guy jabbing at their skin over and over again and it kind of makes me sick. Mami says I can get one when I'm fifteen but I don't think it would look too cool to faint in the middle of it and have to get carried out on a stretcher.

I pass the liquor store, where the guys in hoodies who are usually standing on the corner are now huddled together inside, scared of nothing in this world but the rain. The windows are filled with fluorescent signs: *Liquor Sold Here; Open Late Nites; Cigarettes: $2.99; Lottery: 25 Mil.* The Gonzalez taxi drives by and parks in front of the store. Mr. Gonzalez gets out and calls to me.

"Hey kid, give me a number."

"*Veintiseis,*" I tell him, the same number I say every time he asks. "Twenty-six."

"Okay," he says, walking into the store. "I'll buy you a cheeseburger if I win."

He's been saying that twice a week for over a year now and I've never even gotten a potato chip out of him. He either lies a lot or he loses a lot. I'm not that good at math, but if he'd saved all that money he spent on tickets I bet he coulda bought me a hundred cheeseburgers by now. But most adults ain't smart when it comes to money. If they got it they spend it, and if they don't got it they sit around thinking about how they'd spend it if they did get it. Seems kind of stupid to me.

A few blocks later I pass a church whose name I can't pronounce. Saint Ignacio de Baptiste, Church of the Immaculate Heart. There's a statue of a man in front, his right hand holding a book while the left one is empty, palm opened to the sky. I've walked by it for years without a second look, but today something makes me stop. He doesn't have any eyes, but he still seems to be looking at me. When I walk over to him I feel tiny, like how César must feel next to his grandmother. The sign at his feet says he's been here since 1862 and all I think is, how can anything be that old?

His hair is long and it floats down his back in a wave, just like Teacher's. It looks like it's tied with a ribbon and I wonder why they made him look like a girl. It musta taken a long time to carve a statue that big. They used some type of brown metal, copper or brass maybe, which sounds hollow when the rainwater hits it. It's raining hard now, and it sounds like pebbles are falling out of the sky. My arms are covered with droplets of water that make them shine, like my skin is made from coins. I touch the edge of the statue's hand, which is the same color brown as my own. He feels hard like cement, and it's easy to picture him standing here in another hundred years. Sometime I wish I could live as long as a statue, but other days I wonder if I'm even gonna make it to eighteen.

There's a half-empty bottle of Pepsi on the ledge next to the statue, the sides wet like it's been sitting in the rain all day. I pick it up and shake it to see how much fizz is left. The bottle is still cold, so I open it and take a small sip, trying to figure out why someone left it behind. It tastes fine, so I take another sip. My stomach feels hollow like that statue, since I missed lunch sitting outside the principal's office all day. I keep drinking until my belly fills up and my throat starts to burn from the bubbles.

I catch my reflection in the puddle of water collecting at the foot of the statue. Even with my hair cut short I look like a little boy. It makes me smile since on the inside I feel old like those men who sit on park benches and talk on and on about their childhoods. Mami is right. I do look like her when I smile. Even though she's too skinny and her hair is dyed a color no Puerto Rican would ever have, she's still a pretty lady. I wonder what that makes me.

I tuck the Pepsi bottle into my backpack, which is empty except for a pencil box and a spiral notebook I never use, and put it back on my shoulders. It's heavy now, and I'm glad I'm almost home. I sneak another look at my reflection, trying to recognize this kid who looks so young but is old enough to walk home alone and have nobody waiting when he gets there.

I keep on walking, reading the street signs when I'm close. *Olympia. Penelope. Rose.* The streets over here sound a lot prettier than they look. The gutters are always filled with crap—broken glass, gravel, pieces of rotten wood—and the sidewalks are so dirty you can't even walk in some places. Today there's a diaper, four empty beer bottles, a stepped-on hamburger, cigarette butts, a wall clock with no hands, pizza boxes, and a jacket with the sleeves torn off—and that's just one corner. Even in the rain, nothing gets clean. I don't mean to complain, but a lot of the houses look cheap, like they're made out of plastic, and they're all bunched together right on the street since nobody has a frontyard. Every house was cut into three or four apartments, with at least five people in each one, so there's always a kid around to play with. There's no grass in anybody's backyard, just dirt lots that somebody's uncle turns into an auto shop every summer, and on rainy days like this you can use the junked cars as forts and hide out there for hours.

Sophia. I finally get to my street. Our house is a triple-decker with yellow vinyl siding that's starting to rot and a blanket taped over the front window that I broke with a miss-kicked dodge ball I stole from the Rec Center last fall. All the rooms in our apartment are small and I have to share a bedroom with my two little sisters, but it's better than the projects. At least that's what Mami said when we moved here with her ex-boyfriend Scottie last summer.

"At least he got us out of the projects," she said, tying her hair into a loose knot like she does when she hasn't cut it in a long time. "Don't say he never did nothing for you."

He did a lot for me, I wanted to say, and I've got the scars to prove it. Instead I told her that I liked it here because if I ever had to jump out the window there's a row of bushes around the house to break my fall. I remember her laughing when I said it, but then later I found her leaning out the window, checking to see how far the drop was.

When I come around the corner I see the cop car. It's white, like a powdered doughnut, with *City of Providence Police* written on the side in fancy black letters. Pretty, like a teacher's handwriting. The cruiser sits in the middle of the street, as if the engine just died while they were driving by my house. What hits me first is how new the car looks, like it just came off the lot. Nothing stays white for long in this neighborhood. The car is empty when I pass it, but I can hear static coming from the radio and some guy's voice cutting in and out like when you're talking on a cheap cordless phone. You'd think the cops could afford a radio that works.

When I get to the driveway I finally see them, standing together as stiff as soldiers.

"You live here?" The big one speaks first.

"Yeah."

"On the first floor?"

"Yeah."

"You know where your mom is?"

I shrug and keep walking toward the back door.

"Didn't she ever tell you not to walk away from a police officer?"

I try to climb up the back steps but the smaller cop gets in my way.

"Hang on a sec, kid. We're just trying to find out where your mom is."

"I told you I don't know." I put my hands in my pockets, touching the stolen key chain.

"What you got in those pockets?" He stares at me with blue eyes so pale they seem to have no color.

"Nothing."

"Are you lying to me?" He grabs my arm but I dig my hands in deeper.

He's chewing mint-flavored gum, and his breath on my face makes me blink. My heart is beating so fast I feel like he can see it knocking against the wall of my chest. I take a deep breath, make a fist around the key chain, and remind myself that they don't have anything on me yet. In this country, you're still innocent until they prove you guilty.

"Mike, leave the kid alone. He doesn't know anything." The big cop fixes his hat, which pours rainwater onto his shoulder when he tilts it back. The water runs onto his name tag, blurring the letters of his name.

The smaller cop squeezes my arm before letting go. His grip leaves a mark on my wrist, which starts to darken right away. I refuse to rub the spot in front of them, even though it hurts enough to leave a bruise.

He pulls a Polaroid from his shirt pocket.

"You ever seen this guy before?"

I take a deep breath as my heartbeat returns to normal. I look at the photo. It's blurry, and the guy's hiding his face, but I recognize him from the car wash on Valley and maybe once or twice in my living room late at night.

"Nope." I shake my head.

"He's got a tattoo across his neck that says CUT HERE with a dotted line under it."

"Never seen him."

The cop puts the picture away. Then he smiles, one of those evil smiles that mean they want to kick your ass. "Tell your mom we'll be back. If you ever see her again."

Then he laughs and the bigger cop shakes his head. While they're walking away I hear one of them say, "If that dyke was smart she'd never come back."

I walk into the apartment and close the door behind me, my fist still tight around the key chain. I open my hand and see the center of my palm marked with the imprint of the flag. My hand aches as the blood returns to my fingertips.

The lights in the kitchen are on, and the radio hums in the corner. I feel the emptiness in the rooms, but I still look for her, checking the bathroom first. The water in the sink is running and the towels are still wet. My baby sister's dolls are in the middle of the floor.

"Mami?" My voice is barely a whisper. I get no response, so I keep searching for more clues. The window is half open, the floor below it wet with rain. She was here and now she's gone. I pick up the dolls and put them in Trini's crib. I turn off the water and close the bathroom window. Mami's charm bracelet is sitting on the windowsill. It must have fallen off as she made her escape. I pick it up and clip it to the ring on the key chain, as if it was a key. The charms sparkle in my hand like stars.

◆ ❖ ◆

She comes home a few hours later, after the sun sets and the sky is completely dark. I guess she ain't very smart. I'm in the living room with all the lights off, watching TV under a blanket so it looks like nobody's home.

She walks into the room without saying a word, Trini asleep in her arms. Mami looks like she's wearing her pajamas, like she should be in bed. Her eye makeup is smeared like she's been crying.

"*Vamos, mijo*," she says softly. "We're going to stay with Chino tonight."

I stand up. "The cops were here," I tell her.

"I know," she says. She doesn't turn on the lights or put Trini down. "You talk to them?"

"No. I told them you weren't home."

"Good boy." She rubs my head as she walks by. She smells like cigarettes and burnt coffee. "Hurry, go get Luz. Lucho's gonna be here soon."

She grabs some clothes from a laundry basket in the middle of the room. "You seen that army bag I keep in the back closet?"

I lift up the bag, already completely filled.

"I packed already. For me and the girls." I can feel her looking at me in the dark. She smiles. "I was gonna pack for you but I wasn't sure what you needed."

"*Nada*," she says. She throws a few T-shirts over her shoulder. They rest on her collarbone, which sticks out so much it looks broken. She's skinny and shapeless like a child.

"Go now. Get your sister. *Rapido*." She keeps telling me to move fast but she moves slow, like she's trying to walk through water.

I go next door and get Luz from the neighbor lady who sometimes watches Trini during the day. She has a set of encyclopedias just like at the library, so Luz always disappears over there whenever no one's looking, which is pretty much all the time. I'm only gone three minutes, but when we get back Mami is leaning against the kitchen wall with her arm over her face. Trini's laid out on the couch, still sleeping.

"Mami?" I touch her arm.

"What?" She opens her eyes. She looks at me like she's trying to figure out who I am.

"Is Lucho here yet?" I ask her.

She looks around the room. "No."

I pick up the army bag. It's heavy, like there's a body inside. "You ready?" I ask her. She nods, but I can see that she still hasn't packed anything for herself.

Luz sits down at the kitchen table. She opens the book in her hand, even though there's not enough light to read. She won't look Mami in the eye. Trini wakes up and stumbles into the kitchen like a drunk.

"*Tengo hambre*," she says in a soft voice. Sometimes I think she sounds like how a hummingbird would sound if they could talk.

"No," Mami says. "*Necesita esperar.*"

"We can eat when we get to Chino's," I tell her. Trini starts to cry. Mami stares at her, looking pissed. She opens her mouth, but then closes it without saying a word. Trini cries harder. Mami pulls out her ponytail, snapping the rubber band around her wrist to wake herself up. She shakes her head like a dog. Her hair flies around in long, blonde strands like spaghetti.

"Sit," Mami says, pushing Trini into a chair. "*Callate.*"

She gets Trini a plate of rice and beans left over from my birthday party. Luz smoothes the hair away from Trini's face to calm her down, something she's done since Trini was a baby. While the food is warming in the oven Mami gives her a cold pork chop, which she holds in her hand like a chicken wing, nibbling on the edges. I stand in the corner, letting the army bag hold me up.

Mami keeps looking out the window. She lays her head against the glass. Raindrops splatter across the windowpane and the reflection on her face makes her skin look blistered. She looks like a monster. I wonder how dark the room would have to be for her to look pretty again.

We hear footsteps on the front porch.

"Good, she's here," Mami says. She closes her eyes.

But she's wrong.

The cops enter quickly, their flashlights streaking the dark. Something falls to the ground and shatters. Trini screams. All at once the lights turn on. This time Mami don't run. She stares at them with a look that says, *What took you so long?* They handcuff her right in front of me. She sucks in her breath as the metal digs into her skin. It looks too tight, like her wrists are going to snap off any second and the cuffs are gonna drop to the ground and then she's gonna be free.

I follow them into the hallway as they drag Mami away by her handcuffs. I'm yelling but not really making any sense and the cops are telling me to go back inside. Mami tells me to calm down and shut my mouth so they don't take me with her.

"He's just a boy," she yells to whoever will listen. "*El no sabe nada.*"

She's right, I don't know anything.

I try to jump on the smaller cop's back but I keep sliding off his uniform. The bigger cop picks me up off the floor and sets me down gently like a flowerpot. Like I could break or get him dirty.

"Your mom's in trouble, son. She's sick, and we're going to help her get better, okay?"

"Fuck you." I try to kick him but my foot slips and I end up kicking the wall instead. The plaster cracks in the shape of a broken star.

When he lets go of me I run outside and watch the small one walk Mami to the police car. She trips over a rollerblade and loses a sandal. The next-door neighbors are on their front porch but nobody says anything. When I get to the street he's putting her in the backseat. She looks like she's crying but I don't see any tears. I run up and grab her around the waist. Her hands are tied so she can't hug me back. I feel her kiss the top of my head, hard, like she's planting a seed under my skin.

"*Los aviones,*" she whispers into my hair. "*Los regalos estan con los aviones.*"

The presents are with the birds. I have no idea what she's talking about.

The cop palms her head like a basketball and shoves her inside the car. He slams the door. I try to give her the sandal but the back door won't open. She smiles at me and turns away.

I take off my backpack and throw it at the cop. He knocks it to the ground and the Pepsi bottle breaks inside, spilling the soda onto the street. It mixes with the rainwater and washes some of the broken glass into the gutter. The rain falls steady and hard, soaking my shirt in seconds. Droplets fall from my face like tears, but I'm not crying. I am too angry to cry. I can see my sisters in the living room window, staring down at us. Trini is screaming while Luz tries to pull her back from the glass.

I see Lucho in the driveway, standing next to a lady with

a badge around her neck who keeps saying she works for the state. She calls my name but I look away. I hear the lady ask Lucho if she's my father. When I look back Lucho is shaking her head with a smile on her face. The lady has a file in her hand like at the doctor's office. Lucho pulls out her wallet and hands the lady her ID. The lady wipes it on her jacket a few times, trying to clear off the rain.

As the police car pulls away, I watch Mami through the back window, like I've watched lots of people leaving our neighborhood. She looks small, like a child, and I wonder if they put on her seat belt. I know it's her, but already she don't look like my mother. She leans her head against the window as if she's going to sleep. Her hair falls like a shadow across her face. By the time they turn onto Manton, I don't even recognize her.

I'm telling this story because nobody else will.

Arcelia

I don't remember much about the precinct, except those asshole cops ask a lot of questions, and I don't feel like talking.
Which is rare for me, 'cause usually you can't get me to shut up.
Turns out they have everything they need to keep me locked up
for a few years—two bricks as evidence and a few of my clients—
but the lawyer they get me says if I plead guilty they'll reduce it
down to possession and I'll only get nine months. With good
behavior I could be out in six. He says it like I should be happy.
Like six months is easy to do. The longest I been in one place
since I left Puerto Rico is four months, and that was only 'cause
I was pregnant. And I thought I was in love. They were both
dead by the fifth month.

I guess they popped some john I used to score with, and
he gave me up. That's the problem with this business: no loyalty. I suppose it had to happen—sooner or later everybody gets
busted—and really I had a pretty good run, almost three years of
using, selling, and working the streets without so much as a cop
looking at me sideways. I think you could say I was better than
average. About time I excelled at something.

I ain't gonna lie—I done some pretty bad shit. But who
hasn't? If you got any imagination and you live long enough,
you're bound to break a rule or two. Everybody lies to someone—their doctor, their kids, their priest—and some of us lie to
all three. But I never been very good at lying. I'm really good
at screwing up, but not very good at covering up. I guess we all
have our weak spots.

My first night at the ACI isn't like I expected. It's quiet, and the building feels abandoned, like everybody just ran outside for a fire alarm. The guards don't say much, and neither do the other ladies, and I'm grateful for the silence. In prison movies you always see the inmates fucking with the new guy, but maybe that's only for the men 'cause nobody fucks with me the first night. Like they don't want to mess with you till they know how crazy you are. Pretty soon they'll see I'm crazy no matter what. Crazy clean. Crazy high. Crazy locked up. Crazy free.

They must know it, too, 'cause they send me to the sick ward first thing. A nurse twice my size walks me there when I'm still in my street clothes. She don't say anything and she don't look me in the eyes. When we go through a set of locked doors, she holds my shoulder like I'm an old lady and she's helping me cross the street. She rubs an old burn scar on my wrist and asks if it still hurts.

"I can't feel anything," I tell her.

The room they give me is small and cold like they got the AC running. There's nothing on the walls, and the only furniture in the room is a bed on a metal frame. It's close to the ground, like a child's bed, and the mattress is covered in a thick plastic that squeaks when I sit down. The toilet is in the corner, behind a half wall. It's metal, and the toilet seat is missing, and all of a sudden it hits me—I'm locked up. Seeing that toilet finally makes it real.

"You're lucky," the nurse says. "Most people don't get their own toilet."

I look at her. I want to say something, but my head hurts too much to speak.

"They must think you're going to need it."

I look out the window, which got no curtains. It's tiny, but it lets in enough light to keep me from sleeping. I can see the edge of a parking lot and a sign that says STAFF. The cars look like toys my son used to line up and forget about. The sun is rising in a gray sky and I watch the trees blow silently in the wind. I wish there weren't any windows, so I could block out everything from the outside.

The nurse finally leaves. I sit on the floor and hug my

knees to my chest. I can feel my last fix wearing off, so I hold my breath and wait for the buzzing to start. My hands twitch. I look at the walls to steady myself. They are the color of my skin, a pale and washed-out gold. My head pulses as I feel them start to close in on me. They must be soundproof, 'cause when I scream, nobody comes.

By lunchtime I think I'm dying. The pain is so big it's like my head can't stretch around it. I'm cold, but I'm also sweating, and when the sheets get all wet it's like lying naked on a frozen lake. But then it switches and all of a sudden I'm hot and thirsty and the covers are like a blanket of sand that suffocates me. My sweat starts to burn my skin like fire ants are crawling out of my hair. I try to scratch them all out but they won't die—it's like they're feeding off my sweat—and even when I pull them out one by one and flush them down the toilet, they keep coming.

There's a bucket for me to puke in, and when it's full someone dumps it out and brings it back to me empty. It's rinsed, but it still smells like death. I sit on the toilet for what seems like hours. I hear songs in my head from my childhood, things my mother used to sing to put me to sleep. I hear my children laughing. I try to picture their faces, but I can't see past the pain: a bright orange wave crashing into the sand. Everything in me screams, *I want to go home.*

Then something changes. I want to die but I can't—I won't—'cause something in my body won't let me quit. It's not going to stop, I think to myself. The rest of my life is going to be like this. No end to the crazy heat and ice, the dizziness, the vomiting up of everything I eat and even bits of food I only think about eating. Every time I pass out—every time I think it's over and I'm already in the next world trying to lie, cheat, or steal my way into heaven—I wake up and realize I'm only sleeping and the pain is still there and I haven't been let go and I'm not free. I keep thinking, *I'm not strong enough for this, I'm not strong enough to live through this,* but my body just won't quit.

On the third day I know it's time to stop. I give in to the pain and let it just run over me, till it fills every corner of my useless body and spills onto the floor around me. I guess I was hoping it would happen all at once—that one wave would come and just drown me—but it keeps coming back and coming back and coming back until it's done. I thought it would beat me until I died, but when it's over I'm still alive and I don't think that means I'm brave or strong but I guess it proves I can endure almost anything—even life.

A week later they transfer me to my regular room and now I'm just like any other woman in here. I have to get up for bed check and do my daily jobs and meet with counselors and try to deal with the fact that I'm in prison, and that I don't have control over my body. I can't just walk outside, take a shower, have sex, shoot up, or see my kids whenever I want to. I won't be able to do any of those things for the next nine months. The length of a school year. The time it takes to grow a baby to be strong enough for the outside world.

◆ ❖ ◆

After a few weeks they take me to the infirmary and a social worker tells me they're going to test me for HIV and Hepatitis C. I tell her they don't need to bother with the Hep C 'cause I already know I have it from when I lost my last baby. I didn't even know I was pregnant but I started to bleed real bad and the doctor at the clinic said I was miscarrying. Turns out he was only a medical student. I asked him if it was from the drugs and he said maybe, but my liver was also sick and my diet wasn't too good and we'd never really know what went wrong. He said he wasn't surprised about the Hep C 'cause almost all junkies get it eventually, since bleaching needles won't kill the virus. He told me I should use the needle exchange so I could at least get my own needles even if I couldn't stop using.

The social worker doesn't look at me. She puts down her coffee and takes a deep breath. Her pants are tight at the waist. She looks tired. The color of her fingernail polish matches her lipstick, a purple as dark as an eggplant. If she would smile, she could erase ten years and be pretty again. I want to tell her that, but I don't want to break the silence.

She puts a new legal pad and a pencil in the middle of her desk. Then she puts on her eyeglasses and starts reading from a long list of questions.

"Did you ever try to get treatment for the Hep C?"

"They said I couldn't because I was still using."

"Did you ever try to stop?"

"A few times. Never lasted more than forty-eight hours."

She writes something down on the pad. "So this is the first time you've been clean in how long?"

I shrug. "I guess around three years."

She nods. "And how does it feel?"

"Like shit."

She looks down. "That's to be expected." She circles something in my file. "We'll need to do a blood test to find out how your liver's doing. Maybe now that you're clean you can actually get some help." She crosses her hands on the desk. "Now what about HIV?"

"What you mean?"

"AIDS. Have you ever been tested?"

I shake my head. "Nope."

"Do you think you're at risk?"

I shrug. "Ain't everybody?"

"If you practice unsafe sex and share needles, yes."

"So I guess I am."

She hands me a form and tells me to sign at the bottom if I give my consent. When I take a long time reading it she asks me if I need the Spanish version. I shake my head. Either way I know all it says is that I don't have any rights.

She starts to fill in the testing form, but when she gets to my birthday she looks up from the file. "It says here that you were born in 1969?"

"Yeah."

"But that means you're only...twenty-nine."

I nod. "Thirty this winter."

She looks at my hands, the fingertips yellow from cigarettes and bleach, and then looks away. People always think I look older than I am. When I was a kid I liked it 'cause it helped me get into bars when I shoulda been going to school.

"Still got my whole life ahead of me." I laugh, trying to make her feel better, but the lady won't even smile.

A nurse comes in with a needle and a fat rubber band and tries to find a decent vein to draw blood. My left arm is shot from using and my right one is half-covered by a burn that never healed right, so she ends up using a vein in my thigh. I stop myself from telling her that I've had to use that one, too. Shot some bad shit from Philly that was laced with coke and kept me up two nights. It's a useless talent, but I can remember the specifics of almost every time I've used—where I bought it, where I shot it, how long the high lasted—like how my husband used to memorize baseball stats.

After she draws more blood than I knew I had, she labels the vials with numbers from my file and leaves without saying a word. The social worker speaks once we're alone again.

"We'll have the results in two weeks. They'll bring you back here to meet with me and then we'll go over what it means together. In the meantime, I can give you some literature on HIV prevention."

"I thought it was an AIDS test."

"We're testing you for HIV, which is the virus that causes AIDS. There is no actual test for AIDS."

"So how do you know if I got it?"

"If you're HIV positive we'll get you meds so you can stay healthy. Hopefully you won't get AIDS." She rubs her eyes, like this conversation is exhausting her. "I know it's a lot of information to take in at once. Do you have any other questions?"

I want to laugh or scream in her stupid face. Instead, I lean forward in my chair. Our eyes lock.

"Just tell me the truth—you think I got it?"

She looks at me. We seem to see each other for the first time.

"You'd be a lot sicker if you had AIDS," she says.

She takes off her glasses; they hang from a chain around her neck. I reach for my own necklace, a gold cross my mother gave me before she died, forgetting that the guards took it off when they checked me in. I rub my fingers against the bare skin, as if I could somehow make it reappear.

She leans in closer. Her voice is softer when she finally speaks, like she's apologizing. "I'll tell you what I tell everyone,

Arcelia. Your body already knows if you have HIV. Now we're going to find out. All you can do is hope for the best while you prepare for the worst."

I want to ask her what that means, but I don't. I'm done talking for now. Nobody in here knows me, and I want to keep it that way. When I die I don't want to leave anything behind. Except my children. Those three are the only thing that's gonna outlast me. The only proof I was ever here.

On my way out she hands me a stack of orange and blue pamphlets covered with cartoon drawings of rubbers and needles. The one on top says, "HIV: What Every Woman Needs to Know." Underneath it another one says, "Ten Things You Can Do to Avoid HIV." I tuck them into my pocket and wait for a guard to come get me, wondering if it's already too late.

◆ ❖ ◆

I been clean for two weeks but I still feel like shit. That's the problem with being clean—you feel everything. Fuck detox. I'm still looking to score every chance I get. Mostly 'cause it gives me something to do every day. Word is the men still shoot up in here, with needles stolen from the infirmary and a hollowed-out ballpoint pen. But not the women. All we can get is cheap liquor and the occasional joint, in exchange for making friends with the guards. But I realize right away that ain't for me. I had enough sex on the outside, I don't need to be fucking no uniforms. I keep to myself, smile at the right time, and get all the cigarettes I could ever smoke from the butches who say I look like their daughters. Then I trade the extras for candy bars, gum, and lollipops. In here sugar's the real drug, as valuable as dope, and just as easy to get hooked on.

It's all a waste anyway. Who wants to have things that feel or taste good? All it does is make you want more, and there's no point wanting something you can't have. So most days I don't bother wanting anything—not my freedom, my children, or my girlfriend. Not my home. Instead, I think about what I can get. Time. Peace. Silence. But it's all a lie anyway. I don't want any of that. What's a junkie need peace for? Or time. We want time to stop.

But time don't stop in here. It goes on and on forever, like when you're a little kid and every day is the same. Three weeks in and I'm done counting time. Done being inside my own head. Done being in prison. Some of the ladies knit or do crossword puzzles, but not me. I don't have hobbies. I've never really done anything in my life other than being a kid and a mother and now that I'm neither, I don't know what to do with myself. How to be myself.

Most of the books in the common room are from the men's prison, with far-out stories and all those crazy sci-fi names. There's one romance novel that everybody fights over, but when it's finally my turn I see there aren't any pictures so I give it to the next girl without reading it. One of my bunkmates—an older white lady who was here for five years 'cause she killed someone drunk driving—spends her whole day reading magazines. When they finally let her out she leaves behind a stack that's taller than I am. Most of them are about decorating your home and firming up your thighs, but there's a few about food and cooking I like to look at over and over again.

When I first got married I used to cook with my husband's mother, simple things like arroz con pollo and *pasteles*. Seeing pictures of all that fancy food—all those perfect fruits and vegetables—makes me miss those days. We never cooked anything that looked like it should be in a magazine, but it was still nice to take the time to make something pretty. Sometimes I cook for the holidays—with free turkeys from the needle exchange—but I stopped cooking for real when I left Puerto Rico. The food don't taste as good here. Nothing in America tastes like home.

After that old white lady leaves I move all her magazines to the common room, except for one—the holiday issue of *Gourmet* from a few years back. I hide it under my bed like a dirty magazine. I want something to be just mine. At night I tuck it inside a book so nobody can see the cover and I look at all the pictures, fantasizing about the food like it's sex. One night I tear out a few of my favorites and glue them to the wall with chewing gum. The other ladies put up pictures of their kids, but I can't.

I don't want to look at them yet. Not from in here. I don't want my kids to touch these walls, not even in a photograph.

◆ ❖ ◆

The first letter I get is from Cristo's teacher. Why the hell is she writing to me? We ain't friends. She don't even know me. She knows my children, but she ain't no friend of mine. I want to throw it away, but she sent pictures of the kids and a copy of Cristo's report card. I hide the pictures under my pillow without even looking at them, but the report card goes on the wall for everybody to see. She says he's smart, my sweet boy, one of the smartest kids in her class, and he could be on the regular track if he did all his homework and showed up on time. She wants to know if I encourage him. If I ask to see his school projects. If I sit and read stories with him.

Who encouraged *me*, lady? Who read *me* stories? She thinks she gets me 'cause we're both Puerto Rican, but she don't get anything about me. She don't know how much I think of him. How I wake up at night with his name in my mouth. See his goofy grin in the mirror, his bright eyes looking just like mine. Every day I pray he finds what I hid for him. I want to ask him about it on the phone, but I can't risk getting caught. Cristo is a smart boy. He listens to me. He'll know where to find what I left for him. He knows me better than anyone.

When I first started using I was living in the Bronx with my cousin Chino and one day he caught me shooting up in the bathroom. He was pissed and he yelled at me for a while but at the end of the fight he just sat on the toilet and cried. He wouldn't look at me, but he kept saying, "Why you wanna die?" over and over again. I didn't say anything but I remember thinking, what's he talking about? I don't want to die. I want to live. I want to live the most, the highest, the hardest.

Don't nobody want to die.

SHE SEES a girl holding a broken lantern. The girl is alone. She stands in front of a house with no doors. A small house, filled with people she loves. A wind chime blows in the warm breeze. The sound like coins dropped in an empty glass. There is a porch swing, slowly rocking in the heat. Her father comes out of the house. The girl cannot see him, but she smells his cigar. She feels the heat of it near her arm, as if it was burning her skin. He touches her shoulder. "Hija," he says softly. She holds her breath. He has been crying. She doesn't turn around. She refuses to move. Her mother is dead. She no longer wants to be alive.

Miss Valentín

The first time I saw Cristo's mother she was getting out of a pickup truck, tucking a twenty-dollar bill into her bra. It was March and she was wearing shorts and a tank top. I was picking Cristo up to take him to the park. She walked up to my car slowly, reeking of liquor and some sour smell I didn't recognize. She looked at me like she knew who I was, not because I was her son's teacher, but because she could tell things about a person by looking at them in the right light. As I rolled down the window she leaned into it, pushing against the glass like she wanted to test its strength, or her own. Then she asked me to take her for a ride.

I didn't take her up on the offer, then or any other time. Cristo is the only person I ever pick up from that house. I've asked him to invite his sister Luz to join us on some of our outings, but he always tells me she's busy. I can't imagine that a nine-year-old has that much to do. She reminds me of myself at that age, except her head is in a book while mine was always in a box of cookies.

When Cristo comes back to school after his mother gets arrested he acts like nothing happened. When I ask him in the morning how he's doing he says, "Fine," and when I ask him after lunch he says, "Seriously, I'm fine," and when I keep him after school to ask him again he says, "I'm not the one they locked up." He tells me they're going to stay in the same apartment and that his mother's friend Lucho is going to take care of them, be their official guardian. I've never met Lucho, but I saw her once, standing on the corner with a pack of men twice her size, and she was the one who looked scary.

"Are you okay with that?" I sit down at my desk. My knees often hurt after standing all day, something my mother tells me will change if I lose a little weight.

Cristo shrugs. I ask him if he wants to sit down but he keeps standing. He's short for his age, so we're about eye-level. He has the prettiest eyes, bright green like a gecko. I always thought my own son would have eyes like that, since half the men in my family have light skin and green eyes, a combination that gets them the best jobs and the richest women in New York and Puerto Rico.

"How well do you know her?"

"She sleeps over sometimes. Mami says having her there makes her feel better. Or safer." He shrugs again, which makes his backpack slip off his shoulder. "Or something like that."

I stop myself from fixing his backpack and remind myself that I am only his teacher, not his mother. "Do you like her?"

"Yeah, she's all right." He rocks back and forth on his feet. His sneakers are too big, which causes half his foot to slip out. He slides it right back in and keeps rocking.

"How long have they been friends, she and your mom?"

"Don't know. A couple of months maybe. Since she got out of prison."

"Lucho was in prison?" I try to keep my voice from rising. After four years at this school, the word prison should no longer shock me.

"She stabbed a guy who was trying to steal her pit bull."

I nod and try to stay calm. Sometimes I think I should have trained as a social worker to do this job. "Does she get mad a lot?"

He shakes his head. "I think she stopped fighting after that. She's real quiet now. I usually forget she's in the house." He finally fixes his backpack. "She's different from the rest 'cause I could never forget they were there, even when I tried."

A car horn honks and I glance outside. The tops of the trees are just visible through my windows, their bright green leaves adding a splash of color to my normally dreary view.

I stand and walk toward the windows. In the distance, I see smokestacks from the power plant and the pitched rooftops of hundred-year-old houses that should have fallen years ago. I see the old water tower, which hasn't worked in decades but is too expensive to tear down, so the city just ignores it. And I see the twin striped towers of Atlantic Mills, an old warehouse filled with God knows what. When I first moved to Providence almost ten years ago, to go to a college that cost more each year than my parents made at both their jobs, I never saw this view. I lived on the east side, in ivy-clad brick dorms and restored Victorians that had views from every window, but never showed me this side of Providence.

"Can I go now, Teacher?"

When I turn around he is standing in the door to my classroom. I release the blinds slowly, blocking out the afternoon sun. In the darkness, his features blur and he could now be one of a dozen boys in my class: buzzed head; baggy clothes; empty backpack; and last but not least, a look of desperate indifference that somehow manages to border on contempt. "Sure. But promise to walk home safely."

He smiles. "Only if you promise to drive like a lunatic."

I laugh. "I'm a New Yorker, I always drive like I'm crazy."

"Nah, Teacher. You're Puerto Rican, that's what makes you crazy."

He points at me and winks like an old man making a bad joke. We laugh together, standing on opposite ends of the dimly lit room. He's still laughing as he walks down the hallway. I stand completely still, just listening to the sound of his joy.

◆ ❖ ◆

I drop it after that and he seems to be okay during the last two weeks of school. He does all his work and shows up on time and everything seems fine on the outside. The only real difference is how he is with the other kids. I'm used to him being in the middle of a big group, the one laughing or yelling or singing the loudest, but every day he seems to withdraw a little more. His body shows up, but his spirit seems to be missing.

On the last day of school we have a class party to celebrate the end of the school year. While the other kids eat rice and beans their mothers cooked in huge tinfoil platters, Cristo sits at his desk shuffling cards. Even César, his best friend since the first grade, can't get him to eat a bite of food or play card games with anyone but himself. When their favorite song comes on, César dances alone on the improvised dance floor, his fiery red hair like the flames on a torch, while Cristo deals himself another hand of solitaire. Finally, five minutes before the final bell rings, I announce the last song. Krystal, Cristo's girlfriend for the last three months, walks across the room in front of everyone and asks him to dance. Cristo looks up at her and smiles. Then he tells her no.

Krystal, who is petite and pretty like a porcelain doll, is so new to rejection she doesn't recognize it. She stands next to his desk for the entire three minutes of the song, appearing to wait for him to change his mind. I feel sorry for her, so I turn off the music early. I have a lot of experience with rejection. I put all the desks back into rows and when the bell rings at 2:45 the school year is over.

"Don't forget to take everything out of your desks when you leave," I remind my students, "and check your lockers on the way out. Next time you're back here you'll be in the fifth grade and this won't be your classroom anymore."

I stand by the door and hug every student as they pass me by. "And don't forget to practice your English over the summer. Read every word you see. Go to the library and check out as many books as you can carry. And *speak* to each other. Practice makes perfect."

"Does watching TV count?" César calls out from the back of the line.

"Only if it's educational."

He turns to Marco, the only student in my class who tested out of Bilingual and will start on the regular track in the fall.

"Is Jerry Springer educational?" César asks.

"No," Marco says. "She means like *Sesame Street*."

"Oh." César looks disappointed. "But I learn a lot from talk shows."

"You *are* a talk show," Marco says.

César laughs, hanging on Marco to keep himself up.

"Talk shows are entertainment." I speak loud enough for everyone to hear. "They aren't about real life."

He smiles a toothless smile. "Why not, Teacher? I want my life to be entertainment."

This is the same kid who told me he didn't want a job when he grew up, he just wanted to cash his WIC checks and watch talk shows like his grandmother. I shake my head and pull him into a hug.

"*Ay, Dios mio,*" I say, pinching his cheeks as he pulls away from me. "What am I going to do with you, Señor Martinez?"

"When my grandmother gets mad she says she's gonna put me back in the system. Maybe you should do that, Miss Valentín?"

He's still smiling, oblivious to the implication. I force myself to match his smile.

"No, César. I will never want to do that."

Before I can finish my sentence he's out the door and halfway down the hall, singing "La Cucaracha" to a group of sixth-grade girls at the water fountain. When friends ask me if I'm making a difference I think of moments like these and wonder if I can ever truly help anybody.

It takes several minutes for the room to finally empty, and only then do I notice Cristo sitting in my chair, his feet propped on the desk like he's been waiting all day for me to come find him. The soles of his sneakers are worn through and they look large enough to fit a man.

"You need help cleaning out this desk, Teacher?"

"Maybe. You need help figuring out where your feet belong?"

He drops his feet to the floor. The laces are tied as tight as possible, but the sneakers are still loose. His bare ankles float like buoys in the oversized shoes.

"You got a box?" he says.

I grab a cardboard box from the bookshelf and hand it to him. He begins to take the items off my desk, filling the box.

"You okay?" I ask him.

"Sure. Why not?" He packs my books in gently, as if every one were made of glass.

"Well, you didn't eat during the party."

He shrugs. "Wasn't hungry."

"And you didn't dance with Krystal."

He keeps filling the box.

"Any reason?"

He shrugs again. "Nope. I just didn't feel like it."

"Did something happen between you two?"

He doesn't answer.

"You still like her, don't you?"

"She's all right."

"All right? Last month you passed her notes in every class."

He picks up a snow globe and examines the miniature world inside. He shakes it before placing it into the box. "I just don't have the time anymore."

"For what?" I ask him. "To pass notes? To dance?"

He smiles. "You know what I mean, Teacher. To have a girlfriend or whatever."

"Cristo, come here for a minute."

He walks over and stands next to me, leaning against the desk. "You're eleven," I say, squeezing his shoulder. "You have plenty of time for a girlfriend. What you don't have time for is to carry the weight of the world on your back. Lighten up. Don't be in such a hurry to grow up."

He cocks his head, as if he's trying to hear me better. I know he's listening, that he wants to understand, but I also know I should be talking to someone else. To Lucho or his mother, or God, if that would help—but to someone who could actually do something. Not to a child.

"I'm okay, Teacher. You don't have to worry about me, all right?"

"No, it's not all right. I'm a teacher. I was born to worry, just like a mother."

He touches the leaves on a ficus plant almost his height, pulling a few of the dead ones off. "My mother don't worry."

"*Doesn't* worry," I say, stressing the correct grammar.

He makes a face. "You know what I mean."

I make the face back, mocking him. He laughs, crumbling the dead leaves in his hand.

"How do you know she doesn't worry?" It's an obvious question to ask, yet suddenly I'm not sure I want to know the answer.

He shrugs, and I can see his eyes deciding to move on, to let this, and so many other things, go. "Anyway, school's over now. You're not even my teacher anymore." He smiles as he pulls away from my hand, backing up in those big shoes.

"Wrong. I'm always going to be your teacher. And your friend. I don't care what the calendar says."

"I know, I know. That's why I love you." He looks surprised as the words come out, almost apologetic, and quickly averts his eyes.

I feel my own eyes welling up so I force myself to look away too. I can't let myself cry in front of a student, even if he is the only person aside from my parents to ever say those words to me. He stops to sprinkle the crumbled leaves into the garbage, watching the pieces fall like snow into the bottom of the can.

"See you next year, Teacher." And then he walks out of the room without looking back.

"Don't even think about it, Señor. You're not going the whole summer without seeing me." I follow him to the door, calling after him as he walks away. "I'll take you to the beach one day. Or to a movie, okay?"

"Okay, Teacher. You know where I live." He throws up a hand to wave good-bye, but doesn't turn back around. Seconds later I watch him disappear down the stairwell.

The hallway is deserted, but I still curse my big mouth. I know better than to say that stuff out loud, especially on school grounds. I shouldn't cross those boundaries in the first place, let alone advertise that I have.

Back in my classroom, I finish collecting the rest of my things. When I've boxed it all up and emptied my desk, I run across my desk calendar, the final thing that connects me to this class, and to this year of my life. I've saved each one since I began teaching; eight years filled with parent/teacher conferences, class projects, and birthday parties meticulously scheduled into half-hour time slots. Every year it's the last thing I take out of the room. I look down to see that the second half of June is completely empty, as if no life exists once the school year ends; for me, it's pretty close to the truth. A few words stand out from the neatly scripted entries, a familiar scrawl that cuts across the blank date of June 23rd: "Thanks, Teacher. *Ya te echo de menos.*" I already miss you.

A good teacher should never have favorites, so I guess I haven't been a good teacher. Not since Cristo joined my class. Right or wrong, I favored him from the very beginning. While other kids worry about sitting at the right table at lunch or playing the latest Nintendo game, Cristo wonders who will spend the night in his mother's bed; while they look forward to their parents getting home from work, Cristo will look forward to the day she gets out of prison. Of course he's not the only one who has it tough at home (half my class comes to school without eating breakfast), but there was always something different about him; he seemed to need something specifically from me. Or maybe it was just what I needed to give him.

When the school year started, he interrupted every lesson I tried to teach. He spoke when it was his turn and he spoke when it wasn't. He refused to read out loud, didn't turn in any homework, and walked out of the room without a hall pass. He was always late. I responded appropriately, but I never yelled at him or kicked him out of class. I never sent a note home or sent him to the principal's office. I told him what I expected from him and when he failed to comply, I told him again. I refused to give up or give in.

And then one day it all changed. He came to school on time; he did his homework; he raised his hand when he wanted to talk. He only fought if he was provoked. And he tried to reprimand the other kids if they broke the rules. On the last day before Christmas vacation he came up to my car and gave me a candy cane and apologized for his behavior all fall. He told me that he didn't know that teachers could be people you'd like in your real life. And then he stood there until I gave him a hug.

So that's how it started, with talks after school and rides home if he missed the bus; with hugs in the hallway when I'd catch him punching lockers in frustration; with a shared lunch of grilled cheese sandwiches, cold tater tots, and chocolate milk drunk straight from the carton. After a while we started making plans to meet outside of school. He brought me a note from his mother (no doubt written by Cristo himself) giving me permission to pick him up at his house, so I took him out for pizza, to the movies, and to the park to go sledding after a snowstorm. I took him to church on Easter, and for his birthday we went to the YMCA to swim in the indoor pool since he'd written a story called "The Saddest Day" about how lost he felt when the public pool in his neighborhood closed down.

I know I've crossed the line. I'm breaking rules that could cost me my job. But who else does he have? Who else do I have? I'm not supposed to care this much about a student, to be this involved, but I don't know how to stop. Of course he is not my son. But he is not simply my student. He is another species entirely. Every school has a student like Cristo: a kid who lives on the border between civilization and wilderness. Every school has a teacher like me: a bridge between two worlds. If he's not careful, he'll spend his whole life split in two. If I'm not careful, I'll spend mine holding his together.

◆ ❖ ◆

Once school ends, I spend all my free time trying to convince myself I'm not pregnant. After two weeks of denial, three days of eating nothing but egg rolls and ice cream, and five episodes of *General Hospital* I taped during the week, it's finally time to take a pregnancy test.

I was pregnant once before, during my junior year of high school. I was sixteen years old. The boy lived in the projects where my Tia Sonia and Tio Ernesto lived. I went to their apartment every day after school so I saw him all the time. He was like a cousin to me. I didn't have a crush on him, not in the conventional sense, but I did like him. His eyes were a beautiful shade of green and his hair was shiny and black like licorice. He was quiet and kind to old people, and he always had change for the vending machine. He would buy me peanut M&Ms or

Goobers almost every day and he didn't get mad or tease me when I ate the whole bag. He would simply buy another one.

His name was Alberto, but we all called him Tito. He wasn't handsome. He was small and frail like a middle schooler and I remember him getting carded for cigarettes well after he turned eighteen. One night he told me he'd actually started smoking because he wanted to look older, figuring the nicotine couldn't do anything to stunt his growth that his genes hadn't already achieved. He had thick glasses he never took off, even during the three times we had sex, and kids used to joke that he showered in those glasses. When they teased him he would bend his head and smile and never refute it. His skin was pocked with acne, even on his back, and I remember running my finger over the bumps when he was on top of me, wondering what they looked like in the light, if they hurt, and if he would bleed onto his sheets when he slept shirtless in the summertime.

But I knew he never did. He hid his body as well as I hide mine, in long-sleeved shirts, loose jeans, and puffy ski jackets that doubled his size, making him almost as chubby as me. He used to say he didn't mind that I was fat. *Un poquito gordita*, he would say, hugging me from behind. He used to tell me that he couldn't feel my bones, that I was like a perfect pillow since he could rest on any part of my body and be equally comfortable. We used to spend hours in the playground with the other teenagers, and while they rolled lopsided joints and played Spades on the concrete, we would eat candy bars and talk about the fastest trains in the world or what it would feel like to be stuck on a submarine for two years. Tito laid his head on my soft curves, both of us wishing we had the means to escape from that penned-in playground, by any mode of transportation modern science would allow.

I stood out for a lot of reasons growing up. I played chess instead of playing with dolls. I never learned how to sew or cook, but I knew the rules of baseball by the time I could read. Other girls sang in church and jumped rope in teams of two or three while I played the violin and walked to the corner store all by myself. Food was my constant companion (my first friend, my oldest friend) and the only thing that has never let me down. By the fifth grade I could read equally well in English and Spanish, something even my parents struggled with, and I was on the honor roll for all of junior high. When I was thirteen my homeroom teacher encouraged me to apply to the same college-prep high school she'd gone to, so I rode the subway from Brooklyn into Manhattan (by myself) and took the entrance exam without even telling my parents. At first they didn't want me to go, but when I told them that two presidents had gone there they rushed out and bought me the school uniform. New, not used.

I was comfortable being an outsider, both in my neighborhood and in my own home, but suddenly I wasn't so different from the other Puerto Rican girls I'd grown up with. Sixteen, pregnant, and unmarried; I finally fit in.

Tito wanted to keep the baby. He was a sweet kid and he thought he was doing the right thing. He told me we were going to get married at St. Anne's, that his brother would be his best man, and that we would live in Crown Heights with his grandmother, who had a three-story brownstone and was starting to lose her eyesight. But he never asked me to marry him.

"Will I wear white?" I asked him.

"What?"

"My wedding dress. Will it be white?"

He paused, as if reviewing pictures that had already been filed in a photo album we pulled out on lazy Sunday afternoons when we wanted to reminisce about our youth. His zipped his jacket against the harsh November wind.

"No, of course not. White is for virgins. You can wear yellow or pink or something like that. My mother could probably lend you one of her dresses. You're about the same size."

I smiled, even though I wanted to cry. He was acting like I should be grateful that he had worked everything out. I shook my head.

"We're not getting married, Tito." The only reason I'd even told him I was pregnant was to say it out loud and somehow make it real.

"Yes, we are. We have to. I won't have my son born a bastard."

I looked at him for a long time. His milky green eyes, always magnified by his glasses, seemed larger than usual in that moment, and they were glassy, like he was about to cry. I chose my words carefully.

"This…baby is not your son. He is just a baby. *It* is just a baby." I rested my arm on his shoulder. "And after tomorrow, it won't even be that."

"What are you saying, Vanessa?"

I swallowed the Skittles I was sucking on. "I'm saying that I'm not going to keep this baby. I'm not going to have this baby."

He looked down at the bench we were sitting on. The wind kicked up again, so I huddled closer to him. He backed away.

"An abortion? I don't understand."

"What do you mean you don't understand? What's not to understand?"

He looked around the park, as if wanting to appeal to some other reasonable person. "But I'm the father. I'm going to be a father."

"No, Tito. You're not. Maybe someday, but not right now. Not with me."

He stood up. "What, I'm not good enough for you? 'Cause you go to some fancy school Uptown and you play the violin and read Latin? You think you're better than me."

"No, that's not what I said. You misunderstood." When I touched his arm again he jerked it away.

"Oh no, I understood. I understood perfectly clear."

He took a few steps away from me. I was about to call his name when he came back, leaning down until his mouth was only a few inches from mine.

"I wish I'd never slept with you," he said, his voice filled with a hatred I'd never seen before. "I wish I'd never seen your fat fucking face or touched your fat fucking body. You make me sick."

He slapped me across the face and walked out of the park. The sting from his hand stayed with me for the rest of the afternoon, but the real injury came from his words. That was a blow I am still recovering from.

I saw him a few more times, but we never talked again. He

would glare at me from across the playground, those big green eyes bearing into me like lasers, and when I couldn't take it anymore, when I would turn to face him, he would either look away or look right through me like I didn't exist. I missed him, I missed my friend, but I never tried to approach him again. I knew I was dead to him, just like our baby, and I tried to feel the same way. But I couldn't. Neither one was dead to me. Even now I think about him every day.

I went to the clinic by myself. The weather was cold and clear, but the sun was warm; I remember how hot it felt, shining on the back of my head. I kept my face down as I walked between the buildings on Atlantic Avenue, feeling miles away from my home (though I didn't even have to leave the neighborhood). The procedure was fast. Less than an hour and I was free. The burden of carrying Tito's child, my child, was gone. I felt empty. I did not think of a baby, or even a toddler, when I thought of what I had done. Instead, I pictured an older boy, six or seven, with short brown hair and green eyes, a non-stop talker who liked books and baseball and ice cream sundaes, and when I cried for weeks afterward, that is the child I imagined I'd lost.

I lost my appetite. Barely interested in solid food, I began to shrink. My mother was so proud of the weight I lost. She told me I was beautiful now, that I looked just like her mother, and she let me try on her wedding dress, which she kept boxed in the closet for me to wear one day. She took pictures of me with my father's Polaroid camera, which was usually reserved for shots of our dog, Lucky, and she displayed them proudly on the refrigerator door, held in place with Yankees magnets, until they eventually moved back to Puerto Rico when I graduated from college. I didn't like all the attention—the stares from men on the subway, the whistles from packs of teenaged boys— so I started eating again when the bleeding stopped. I've been eating ever since.

I never told anyone other than Tito that I was pregnant. I've kept the secret for the last fifteen years. I am still keeping it. My son would be fourteen years old today. Almost as old as I was when I got pregnant. Almost a man.

If I'm pregnant now, I will still be a young mother. Not as young as I would've been (and not as young as my own mother), but young enough. Maybe too young. The father, if I am pregnant, lives in Atlanta and works for the CDC. Right after we had sex he told me he had a girlfriend he thought he would marry. We ran into each other at our ten-year college reunion, and after a few glasses of Asti Spumante he invited me to his hotel room. I hadn't seen or talked to him since graduation, and just like Tito, we never actually dated. We were friends with benefits.

I drive to a pharmacy in Cumberland to buy the home pregnancy test. I can't buy one in Providence because being a teacher is like being a politician—someone's always watching. On the drive home I try to imagine calling my parents and telling them I'm pregnant, that it was an accident, and that the baby's father is black. I can't decide which will disappoint them the most. Probably the fact that he's black, even though I have relatives in Puerto Rico who are darker than he is, starting with my mother's own father. But I know how they are about color, how they prayed for me to be pale, with soft wavy hair and green eyes like my father. How happy they were when I came out light and didn't disappoint them.

But this could change everything. Having a baby when I'm not married, not in love or even dating, will permanently alter our relationship. I feel their shame rise up in me: what will I say to my grandmother; to the other teachers (who will notice I no longer drink coffee, sip cheap wine at happy hour, or sneak drags off bummed cigarettes in the teacher's lounge); to the students who ask about my expanding belly and the lack of a ring on my finger? I'm disappointed in myself, so how could I expect my parents to feel any differently?

But sometimes I argue the other side. I have a job, an apartment, and a car. I have a savings account and a retirement fund. Why am I scared of being a mother? I don't need the government to support me, I don't need a man, and I don't need my family. I can do this. If I can handle twenty-five kids a year in the classroom by myself, surely I can handle my own little baby.

When I get home I run to the bathroom with a sense of exhilaration I don't remember having since childhood. I pee on the stick and watch the second hand on the clock tick by in slow motion, waiting for the results. The longest two minutes of my life.

Cristo

The house smells different without Mami. Not better or worse, just different. It smells like somebody else's home. Lucho moved in but she didn't bring anything with her, and Mami didn't take anything away when she left, so it looks exactly the same. But somehow it's not.

I get home early on the last day of school and find the apartment empty. I shouldn't be surprised, but it's weird for the place to be so quiet. I don't think I've ever seen the living room with nobody in it. I'm hungry since I didn't eat at Teacher's party, but there's nothing in the fridge. I check the cookie jar but the money and the WIC checks Mami usually keeps there are gone, so I hope Lucho remembers to stop by the market after work. If not we'll have to eat next door with Miss Wendy and everything she cooks tastes like dish soap and cigarettes. I shoulda said yes when César asked me to hang out after school, but I didn't want to deal with all his questions about Mami and when she's coming back and who's watching us now. I love that kid but sometimes he just doesn't know when to shut up.

I leave the kitchen and try to forget how hungry I am. The sun is shining so bright in my bedroom, I don't even have to turn on the light. A rich lady would use this room as a closet, but we got a bunk bed, a crib, and a dresser taller than I am all jammed inside. We used to have a desk for coloring or homework, but when the baby came we had to get rid of it to fit the crib. But a small room has its good points. When Trini used to wake up in the night because she lost her *chupete*, I could always find it and pop it back into her mouth without even getting out of bed. That's why I took the bottom bunk, so I can be there in the night if she needs me. I used to sleep up top because I'm the oldest and I liked to touch the ceiling, but Luz is pretty worthless at night. She sleeps like a dead person until you wake her up, then she kicks you in the stomach and says she don't remember nothing in the morning.

Even though she's a year younger than me, Luz and I are in the same grade. She's smart, just like my friend Marco, so they moved her to Regular Ed two years ago. We never been in the same class. With the scores she gets and the books she's always reading, I'm surprised she hasn't skipped a grade yet. Some people think we're twins because we're the same size, but I don't think we look that much alike. I look just like Mami and everybody says Luz gets her coloring from my father. I think that's why Mami's so hard on her. She must look at Luz and think no matter how far she goes, she's never gonna really get away from him.

I still call her a baby but Trini is three already and she's the happiest little kid you ever seen. She laughs all the time, like she's always telling herself jokes, and she's got these great dimples when she smiles. She's too old for a crib, but when we moved her into Luz's bed when she was two she kept climbing back in during the night, even though we were using it as a laundry hamper. Eventually we gave up and put her back in the crib. Her hair is so light it's almost blond in the summer and she has a voice just like a bird. She's half Puerto Rican and half question mark because her father don't know where he comes from. Scottie calls himself a mutt, which is what the nuns at the orphanage used to call him and his sister after their parents died in a house fire. He says he don't look like anything but I think he looks like everything. If he changed his accent he could convince you he was from a dozen different countries. He says that's a pain in the ass but to me it seems like fun. Almost like wearing a mask on Halloween—you could be anybody.

When Lucho gets home I turn off the TV and pretend to be reading a book. She walks by me without saying anything and heads to the kitchen. From the doorway I watch her unload a bag of groceries straight into the fridge: a six-pack of beer, three types of milk—regular, chocolate, and coffee—juice boxes, peanut butter, eggs, frozen waffles, cheese, and mayonnaise. Then she puts a few cans of beans, two boxes of cold cereal, a bunch of bananas, and some crackers in the cupboard. She tosses a bag of white bread onto the table and walks out of the room, leaving a trail of aftershave behind her.

What I like about Lucho is that she don't yell; the downside is she sometimes don't talk for days. That kind of silence scares me more than yelling does. Her other problem? She disappears. Just leaves for work in the morning and we don't hear from her for the rest of the weekend. But she always comes back, that's the important thing. She used to do the same thing when Mami was here, something about her needing to breathe different air. At least that's what Mami told me the first time she left.

She also told me Lucho's not just her friend. She's her girlfriend, just like Krystal and me. The men on the corner say it's wrong because somebody has to be the man, but all you gotta do is look at Mami to see that she's happier with Lucho than when Scottie was living with us. When Lucho first started coming over I used to walk into the living room and find them sitting on the couch just looking at each other. The TV was off and they weren't even talking. Mami would smile at me and then go back to looking at Lucho. Luz told me she read in a book that when people are in love they don't have to talk, they just sit and stare at each other and it makes them feel better. I guess I never been in love 'cause I don't ever feel better just by staring at a girl.

I'm sitting at the kitchen table cutting coupons out of a flyer from Star Market when Lucho walks back into the kitchen. She's out of her jumpsuit from work and has on the white tank top and jeans she usually wears. Her hair is cut short and combed straight back so if you didn't notice the sports bra that flattens her chest you might guess she was a man. Sometimes I think she wants people to think that. She sits down in a chair across from me and peels a banana, giving me half.

"You seen your sisters?"

"They're still next door, I think." I stare at the tattoo of two masks on her arm: one happy, one sad. When I asked her about it once she said, "My two faces—never know which one you're gonna get."

"Ain't it dinnertime?" She eats her half in one bite.

"I can go get them," I say, standing to leave.

"Wait," she says, putting her hand on my shoulder. It's the first time she's ever touched me. "I want to talk to you. Alone."

I sit down. My heart pounds loud in my chest.

"Your mom, she's not coming back right away. You know that, right?"

I nod. I keep hearing the last thing Mami said to me, about the presents being with the birds, but I still can't figure out what it means. I think about telling Lucho but she's got enough to worry about.

"She could be gone for a few months, maybe even longer."

I look at the chunk of banana in my hand. It suddenly doesn't seem ripe enough to eat.

"That's a long time to be without your mother." Lucho throws the banana peel into a garbage can with no liner. "Are you okay with that?"

I shrug. "I guess I have to be."

"It's not going to be easy. For you or your sisters."

"But you're here," I say to her.

She looks at me.

"You're here, right?"

"Sure, kid, I'm here. But I'm nobody's mother, you know what I mean?"

"Yeah, sure. Okay."

"And if your sisters ask any questions, you tell the truth, okay? Kids get fucked up when you lie to them." She gets a beer and opens it with a bottle opener that's screwed into the countertop. With her back to me I speak again.

"Hey Lucho...you must like my mom a lot, to do this for her."

She shakes her head and tries to hide a smile. She has a gold cap on her front tooth that makes her look like a gangster. "I don't like your mother, Cristo. Like is for puppies and ice cream sandwiches." She squeezes the neck on her bottle of beer. "I love your mother. I'd do anything for her. I'm not her husband and I'm not her boyfriend, but I'll take care of her better than any man ever has. No prison's going to change that."

Then she walks into the bedroom, using her foot to shut the door behind her.

◆ ❖ ◆

For dinner I make my sisters waffles with peanut butter and honey and fried eggs. Usually Mami won't let me make break-fast for dinner, but Lucho doesn't care what we eat, so long as we clean up right away so the roaches don't come out.

Lucho sleeps through dinner but I wake her up later when the landlord comes by looking for the rent. I've seen him before, walking around the neighborhood by himself, head-phones blaring, but up close he looks like even more of a freak. They say he's an albino, so even though he's black his skin is completely white, and he has these bright blue eyes that look like they run on electricity. It's hard to look at him for long, but once you get past his eyes, it's not too bad. His head is shaved smooth like a cue ball and he has a goatee, perfectly white like it was painted on his face with snow. People say it's the only hair he has on his whole body.

It's eighty-five degrees out but he's wearing a hooded sweat-shirt and cargo pants. Fuck if I know what his real name is but everybody calls him Snowman. I used to think it was mean but now it just makes sense.

Lucho sends us out to play since the days are getting longer and it's still pretty light outside. Luz takes Trini to the sandbox in front of our neighbor's house, but I hang back on the porch, trying to hear their conversation. I can't hear much because Lucho's not talking and this Snowman guy whispers, but I do hear him ask about Mami. Lucho offers him a beer but he says he don't drink. When she offers him a chair he leans against it instead of sitting down. He says that somebody owes him money and I hear the word *evict* several times. Finally Lucho leaves the room, and when she comes back she hands him a stack of money. He folds it into an envelope and says, "I'm sorry," as he takes it, looking like he actually means it. She shakes his hand hard like a man.

"I'll get you the rest," Lucho says, looking him right in the eye.

He smiles and nods and doesn't say anything. I'm surprised she doesn't look pissed. When I see him heading toward the door I back up and try to make it look like I was just walking up the stairs.

"You should be careful on these streets, little man," he says to me as he's leaving. "Some kid just got shot on his front stoop. Right in the projects on Hartford Avenue."

"You mean a drive-by?"

"No, it was an accident. His own uncle shot him. Right in the head, too. That's fucked up."

He leans over to tighten the laces on his Jordans. They look brand new, like he scrubs them every night with a toothbrush. They're almost as white as he is.

"I heard about that," Lucho says. "They were fighting over a parking space and the gun went off. It was a little kid, too, like no more than ten."

"Who was it?" I ask, figuring I know almost all the kids in that project.

"I don't remember his name. Something Spanish. At first the cops thought it was this white kid from Johnston or something because he was a redhead and had all these freckles. But then his grandmother came out and said he lived there with her and that it was her son who shot him."

Redhead. Freckles. Grandmother. My heart is suddenly pounding. "It wasn't César, was it? César Martinez?" My stomach drops as the pieces fall into place.

"I don't know, maybe," Lucho says. "All I remember is the red hair."

"He's short and kind of chubby and he's always saying crazy things." I wish I had a picture of him but we don't even own a camera.

Snowman shrugs. "You should call the hospital if you think it might be your friend."

"I'll call," Lucho says quietly, walking into the house.

"And they say the projects get a bum rap." Snowman takes the porch steps two at a time. "We can't even keep a kid safe in his own frontyard." He puts on his headphones and walks away, shaking his head.

I call out for Luz to bring Trini home. She says, "Just a minute," but keeps playing so I yell back, "Right now," and something in my voice makes her listen. I watch as she lifts Trini out of the sandbox and cleans off her clothes. That sandbox is the most popular toy on our block, but the truth is it's just a pothole. A while back it was small like a box of kitty litter but every winter it gets bigger from all the cars driving over it, and now it's the size of a car itself. A big truck from the city filled it with sand one day, promising to patch it up, but that was two years ago and they still haven't come back.

Luz asks me what's wrong but I don't want to scare her so I say nothing. We go inside and wait for Lucho to get off the phone. When she hangs up she tells me she's sorry. She says the hospital wouldn't tell her anything, so she called her aunt who lives in the projects and she said it was César. She said he's in surgery right now.

"That's good," Lucho says softly. "That he's not dead already." She looks like she's reaching for me, but then she puts her hand on the wall instead, her fingers spread wide. It makes a hollow sound, like it could crumble under her touch.

I shut myself in the bathroom to be alone. It's the only door in the house with a lock that works from the inside. I feel like I'm gonna faint or puke or shit my pants. I close my eyes and the room starts to spin so I grab onto the sink to keep from falling. Everything inside me feels hot and tight. I make a fist and punch the wall. It feels good so I do it again. The second time hurts. And the third. Luz knocks on the door. I hear her call my name but I don't answer.

My hand is throbbing. I turn on the sink and run the cold water over it. It feels nice for a second, but then it starts to burn from being so cold. When both my hands are numb I turn off the water. I hold onto the sink but I can't feel anything. It looks like a toy in my hands. I try to tear it off the wall but it don't move. I wish I was strong enough to break things. When I see my reflection in the mirror I start to cry.

After a while Luz knocks on the door again. She tells me that Teacher's on the phone. I don't want to talk to anyone, not even her, so I don't answer. Luz knocks again, softer this time, and I watch the doorknob turn. The latch is locked so the door doesn't open.

"Damn you, Cristo," Luz says through the closed door. "You're not the only one who's scared."

I'm not scared, I want to yell through the door, but then I look at my face in the mirror and know she's right.

Luz

Ever since César got shot that's all my brother wants to talk about. How great his friend is. Whatever. I'm sorry the kid got shot but truth be told he's annoying, hyperactive, and a bad influence on my brother. Okay, okay, and he's also pretty funny. But to make him out to be a saint? I don't think so. Saints don't leave chewed bubble gum on the doorknob to the girls' bathroom, or stick a wet finger into your ear while you're waiting in the lunch line. I really hope he doesn't die. Then everybody's going to rewrite history and say he was a perfect angel and could have grown up to be president.

They take him to Hasbro Children's Hospital and he ends up staying in the ICU for a week. The doctors perform eight operations in five days and they still can't get the bullet out. They say it's stuck in his scalp, above his right ear, and for now it's better to just leave it there. I don't know about you, but I wouldn't want to walk around with a bullet in my head, thank you very much. But he's still alive so I guess he can't complain. Not that he's saying much of anything. They keep telling us he's not in a coma, he's just unconscious, and they say other funny things like he's "out of the woods" even though it's still "touch and go." It reminds me of hospital scenes in soap operas, which sometimes make me feel like none of this is real. No matter what they say, all I know is this: we can talk to him as much as we want and he still won't respond. Which is a first for César. It must be killing him to be so quiet.

When we get to the hospital Cristo won't even walk into the

room. He stands in the hallway with his hands in his pockets and peeks in through the window. I'm not sure what he's looking at, since most of it's covered up by get-well cards the kids in his class made. At first I think his grandmother put them up, though she isn't the sentimental type, but later I overhear the nurses saying it was their idea. Miss Valentín says it's sweet but I think it's kind of pathetic. César's not even awake yet. And when he is, he's going to have a lot more to worry about than where to hang those silly cards. I bet most of the kids won't even come to visit him.

I stand by the candy machine and try not to be seen. It works for a long time, but then Miss Valentín notices me and asks if I want to see him. I don't, but I don't want her to think I'm a baby so I say, "Yeah." I thought the room would be quiet but it's real loud inside. One machine has a steady, high-pitched beep that sounds like a smoke alarm when the battery's dying. Another one vibrates so much I can feel my teeth shaking. The walls are a blinding white that makes my eyes water like I'm crying even though I'm not. But I bet this room has seen a lot of tears. The only color in the room is from a bright red teddy bear sitting on the windowsill. The bear stares out the window like he's looking for someone to take him away from here.

I glance around the room slowly, looking at César last. He's the smallest thing here except for the teddy bear. I take a deep breath and walk right up to the side of the bed. My sneakers squeak against the floor with each step. No way did I think I would ever hold hands with César Martinez, but his fingertips are peeking out of the covers and they seem like they need to be held. His skin is warm and it feels kind of nice actually, a reminder to me that he's still alive. I know it doesn't really count but I can tell people I've held hands with a boy now, if it ever comes up during Truth-or-Dare at a sleepover. Not that I go to sleepovers. But still.

His head is wrapped in gauze, like a mummy from an old movie, and the tubes coming from his nose and mouth are taped down to his cheek so they won't move. His right eye is covered with a bandage the size of my hand. The left one is bare and it keeps twitching every few seconds like he's about to wake up. I've watched cats sleep and they do the same thing when they dream.

Miss Valentín leans down to whisper in my ear.

"You can talk to him if you want."

"No. That's okay."

She smiles. "The doctors think it might help. For him to hear familiar voices."

I try to think of something to say to him, about how hot it is outside or about the nurse whose fingernails have miniature American flags painted on them, or the fact that it's my birthday tomorrow and I'm finally going to be double digits, but none of it seems very important.

Instead, I turn to Miss Valentín and say, "Look at his eyes. They twitch like a cat who's dreaming."

"That's a good sign," she says. "It means he's healing." She squeezes my shoulder in a half-hug. "Trust me, Luz. Everything's going to be fine."

I nod, even though I'm not sure I believe her. The weight of her hand feels good, like a heavy blanket. She smiles down at me, but I turn away. I'm trying to remember the last time a grownup touched me.

A few minutes later, Cristo finally comes into the room. He sits in the chair next to César's bed and buries his face in his baseball hat. He cries without making a sound. I feel bad but I know I can't comfort him. He's the type of kid who can't even comfort himself. Instead, I grab my book and leave him alone in the room. Even when the cops took my mother away he didn't cry like this. Maybe it's different when it's someone your own age, or someone who might never come home again.

At eight o'clock the nurse goes in and tells him visiting hours are over. She tries to grab his hand, but Cristo jerks away and tells her to leave him alone. Miss Valentín is on the pay phone in the hallway, but as soon as she hears his voice she hangs up. I pretend to keep reading my book, but I'm listening to every word. The nurse tells him to calm down, that she's sure César's going to be all right.

"It's Say-zar, not See-sir," Cristo says, loudly. "How do you expect him to wake up if you're not even calling him the right name?"

The nurse doesn't say anything else. She looks at César's chart, and writes something down before leaving. Miss Valentín thanks her and tells Cristo to get his things. He starts to complain but she gives him a look like my mother used to give us when we said we didn't want to eat rice and beans again for dinner. She takes both our hands and walks us out of the hospital before Cristo can insult anyone else. I can tell from the looks we get that people think she's our mother. It makes me smile, to imagine I have a family that's all together in one place.

That night, after he turns out the lights, I think I can hear Cristo praying. At first I think he's talking to me so I peek over the side of the bunk bed to look down at him. He sleeps on the bottom bunk, mostly because he's afraid of heights and won't admit it. His eyes are closed and he's lying completely still. He's always saying he doesn't believe in God, but under the covers it looks like his hands are clasped together. I watch his lips move in the darkness.

On the street I can hear a man yelling something I don't understand. I lie back in my bed and look at the ceiling. It looks close, but when I reach out my hand to touch it I don't feel anything but air. Cristo's voice startles me.

"I had a dream about César last night. A nightmare."

"What happened?"

"A long time went by and he never woke up."

"How long?"

"A couple of months."

"Did he die?" I turn over in my bed. The mattress is thin and I can feel the coiled-up springs pushing against my backside.

"I just told you, he never woke up."

"Oh," I say. "That's sad."

I look around the tiny room, wondering why it looks so much smaller in the dark. Cristo is quiet for a while so I think he must be asleep. I watch Trini's chest move up and down under the sheet. Her feet poke through the bars of the crib, almost touching Cristo's bed. In a few months she'll be tall enough to reach him.

Suddenly Cristo speaks again.

"But that's not the horrible part."

"It's not?" I lean over the edge to look at him. His eyes are still closed. "What else happened?"

"When they unwrapped the bandages, it was my face. It was me lying dead in that hospital bed." His voice cracks and I hear him take a deep breath. I can feel the bed shaking beneath me.

Without saying anything I climb down from the top bunk and join my brother on his bed. He turns onto his stomach and buries his face in the pillow. I rub his back through the sheet, like I've watched my mother do a hundred times. He doesn't move or say anything. After a while his breathing evens out and I know he's asleep, but I still keep rubbing his back until my hand is numb and I can't feel the difference between his body and mine.

◆ ❖ ◆

I wake up on my birthday to a shopping bag sitting at the end of my bed. *Feliz Cumpleaños* is written on the side of the bag in purple magic marker, my favorite color. Inside I find a new pair of sneakers, a package of tube socks with pink stripes, and a key chain with the Puerto Rican flag on it.

Cristo peeks over the railing, standing halfway up the ladder. "Happy birthday," he whispers. A crooked smile splits his face.

"Thanks."

Trini jumps up and down in her crib, singing a made-up song about birthdays and butterflies that seems to have no tune.

"It's from Mami," Cristo says, "before she went away."

I smile, even though I know it's a lie. I don't bother asking him where he got the money. The sneakers look too big but I try them on anyway. They fit okay with two pairs of socks. Cristo says they'll be perfect come fall and I nod just to agree with him.

"Where's Lucho?" I ask, listening for sounds of her in the other room.

"Gone already." Cristo lifts Trini out of the crib. "She's working a double, remember?"

"Oh." I try to hide my disappointment by chewing on one of my braids.

"But I'm sure she'll bring you a surprise when she comes back. A cake or something." He hands Trini a sippy cup with chocolate milk in it.

"Whatever." I take off the sneakers and put them in the closet so they don't get lost. "I don't need cake."

"Everybody needs cake on their birthday," Cristo says, sitting down to tie his sneakers. "Maybe Scottie will have some for you. He likes cake."

"So? He also likes pit bulls and strippers."

Cristo laughs. "You're crazy, Luz."

I blush, and feel a tickle of pride in my stomach. It's been a long time since I made my brother smile.

"I gotta go call Marco. We're trying to get his *tio* to give us a ride to the hospital." He checks his watch. "Scottie should be here soon, okay?" He kisses Trini on the top of her head. "*Adios, chiquita.* Have fun." She's still blowing him kisses when he walks out the door.

Trini wants frozen waffles for breakfast but since we don't have any I give her the last piece of bread, toasted and covered with cinnamon and sugar. When she asks what it is I tell her it's a Belgian waffle, something I read about in a magazine at the teacher's lounge at school. I find some Cream of Wheat for myself and make it with warm water from the tap.

"When's Scottie coming?" Trini asks later, licking the sugar off the plate like a cat. I think it's weird to call your father by his first name, but what do I know? I don't call my father anything.

I tell her noon, which is the same time he comes every Saturday. It hasn't changed since he moved out. When Scottie lived here he treated us like we were his own. He yelled a lot, but he also gave good piggyback rides and Christmas presents, and would always let me keep the money I found in his pockets. Now he doesn't do any of that stuff anymore. He usually doesn't even come inside, he just pulls his car into the driveway and honks till we bring Trini out to him. If I didn't put the car seat in myself he wouldn't even use one. Which is scary because even when he's not drunk he's a bad driver. He once got a ticket for going sixty-five in a school zone and was crazy enough to say the cop was racist. Which doesn't even make sense because Scottie doesn't look like anything. Nothing bad anyway. He doesn't look black or Puerto Rican or even Mexican. He looks like he could be from anywhere.

After we eat I get Trini ready early. I braid her hair and put her in a new dress our neighbor gave us after her daughter outgrew it. It's a little long because Trini's so tiny, but it makes her look cute, just like a doll. Then I put her in the crib so she won't run around and get dirty. I braid my hair, too, and put on the only nice outfit I own, a light pink Easter dress with matching pumps that my mother bought at the Salvation Army. It's long-sleeved, too hot for this weather, but when I look in the mirror I know it's just right. I look pretty, like one of those models in a fashion magazine, and almost like a grownup. I *am* ten after all, as of this morning. Double digits. All the fingers on my hands.

We're standing outside on the porch when a spray-painted black car pulls up in front of the house. A white guy with a buzz cut and tattoos gets out and leans over the roof.

"Is Celie back yet?"

I shake my head.

"How much more time she got?"

When I don't answer him right away he shuts the driver's door and walks around the car. He takes the steps two at a time. He has a tattoo on his neck of a dotted line and the words CUT HERE. The one on his arm is a big S like the Superman symbol.

"You're her daughter, right?" he asks with a real sweet voice. I nod, taking a few steps back as he gets close to me. I hold Trini's hand tight in mine. "I knew it," he says. "You look just like your mom. Real pretty."

Now I know he's full of it. I don't look anything like my mother. He pulls on Trini's braid and smiles down at her.

"She leave anything for me? Maybe an envelope with my name on it?" He cups his hands around his eyes and looks in through the windows.

"Who are you?"

"Name's Jimmy. We're old friends, me and your mom." He

sticks out his hand, but I don't shake it.

"She never said anything about you."

"Damn." He rubs the stubble on his head. "It was real important, too."

"Sorry. We don't have it."

He walks toward the opened door. "You mind if I look around?" he asks, but he's inside the apartment before I can say anything. Adults always ask a lot of questions, but I never see them stick around to listen to the answers. We follow him into the house and watch him look in the dressers and under the beds. When he doesn't find anything we get bored and go back to the porch to wait for Scottie.

Scottie always honks three times when he pulls into the driveway, announcing his arrival to the whole neighborhood. He drives an old Cadillac, white-gray like pigeon shit. I guess it can go fast but he drives it like he's in a parade. Babies it, like it's the most valuable thing he's got. Scottie thinks he's a big deal because when he was boxing he once knocked out Vinnie Pazienza in the third round. He acts like Muhammad Ali, but really he's just another punk from the streets with quick hands and an even quicker mouth. My father lives in Puerto Rico, but I'm guessing he could live down the block and he still wouldn't come get Cristo and me. My mother says he still loves us, but if that was true, wouldn't he show up himself and say it to my face?

Scottie's a few minutes late, and as usual, he doesn't get out of the car. I stand Trini on the sidewalk while I fix the car seat, fastening the seat belts as tight as I can. Then I buckle her in and smooth out her dress under the straps.

"Hey, beautiful," he says.

I turn around to say thank you, but he's looking at Trini in the rearview mirror. Then he reaches back to tickle her toes. She laughs and kicks her legs, trying to get away from him. I smile at her and kiss her forehead, harder than I should.

"Have fun," I whisper into her ear.

She smiles back at me. "Have fun," she says, her little feet still kicking.

Scottie finally looks over at me.

"Why you all dressed up?"

"It's my birthday," I say. "I'm ten years old today."

"Ten years old?" He lifts his eyebrows like he's impressed. "That's pretty goddamn old. You better watch out, you're almost over the hill."

"Cut it out, Scottie. I'm not *that* old."

"Yeah, I guess you got a few good years left."

I get out of the car and close the door behind me. He rolls down his window.

"Hey, what's the word from your mother?"

I twist one of my braids around my finger. "She called a few times before the phone got cut off. She hates the food."

"How long they keeping her?"

"Lucho says a while. Till Christmas at least."

His face hardens. "She still around?" He bites his fingernail and spits it onto the ground.

"Yeah, she's living with us. Officially."

He shakes his head. "Christ, that's fucked up. I only get my kid on Saturdays but that dyke gets to move right in? She's not even family." He punches the steering wheel and accidentally honks the horn. Through the window I see Trini's whole body jump. I make myself smile when her eyes find mine.

"At least she's got a job," I say, tapping my finger on the glass to make Trini laugh.

"Fuck that. I work."

"I didn't mean you. I just meant...she takes care of things."

"I can take care of things, too. My family and shit. I can do that." He scratches the stubble on his face. "If she gave me a chance I could do that."

I wonder who he means—my mother, Lucho, or the judge that only gave him weekly visitations.

"This ain't right," Scottie says. "I'm gonna have to do something about this." The muscles in his cheek twitch like a firecracker before it pops. He grabs the steering wheel with both hands, squeezing it till his knuckles turn white and start to swell. When he lets it go I watch his hands turn back to normal.

Just then Jimmy comes down the steps, taking three at a time.

"Who the hell is that?" Scottie asks, leaning out the window. "A friend of Mami's."

Scottie gets out of the car and slams the door behind him. He walks over to Jimmy. "What the fuck do you think you're doing?"

"Who the hell are you?" Jimmy asks.

"I'm a royal pain in your ass." Scottie backs Jimmy into his car. "Who are you?"

"Name's Jimmy." Jimmy sticks out his hand to shake, but Scottie knocks it away. "Hey man, chill. I'm not looking for trouble. I'm just looking for what's mine."

Scottie looks toward the house. "And just what in there you think is yours?"

"Arcelia owes me some money." Jimmy looks at me, then back to Scottie. "She was supposed to leave it for me before she got nabbed."

"How much?"

"A couple Gs," Jimmy says.

"Bullshit." Scottie points a finger in Jimmy's face. "I can see in your face you're a fucking liar."

"I'm not lying, man. She owes me two Gs. But right now I'm just looking for one."

Scottie points to his car. "You see that little girl over there? That's my daughter. She lives here." He points to the house. "And I don't ever want to see you over here again, you got that? I don't want you ever talking to those girls, or looking at them, or asking them any questions." He opens the door to Jimmy's car and waits while Jimmy climbs in.

"You know Sandro's Gym on Valley?"

Jimmy shrugs.

"Come by and see me. I'll get you your money." Scottie slams the door shut, locking Jimmy in. "Do yourself a favor and forget this street even exists."

Jimmy nods and turns on his car, blasting a rap song. Scottie shakes his head as he watches the car drive away. He brushes my shoulder as he walks by me, his anger burning my skin.

"Jesus Christ," he says, "what is the world coming to?" He checks the time on a digital watch. "Ah, fuck, I gotta go." He starts his car with a pop and looks over at me. "Take it easy, kid."

He turns the AC on full blast, but doesn't put his seat belt on. I hold onto the car door to keep him from backing up.

"Hey, where you guys going anyway?"

"My sister's making gumbo for dinner. Then to Waterfire if she's good." He smiles at Trini in the rearview mirror before looking back at me. "What about you?"

I look toward the empty house. "They're taking me out. Dinner. A movie. Cake. You know, regular birthday stuff." I shrug, hoping he can't tell that I'm lying.

"Sounds fun," he says. "Too bad you can't come with us."

"Well..." I straighten my dress, trying to iron out a wrinkle with my hand. "Maybe I could ask. If you want me to."

He scratches the stubble on his face and pretends to think about it. "Maybe next time, okay?" He puts the car in reverse and rolls out of the driveway.

"Yeah, sure. Whatever." He's been saying next time for over a year now.

I walk up the driveway, careful to lift the bottom of my dress so it won't drag on the pavement. I'm not used to walking in pumps and I trip over a box of Dunkin' Donut Munchkins someone left on the ground. I feel my face get hot as I rush to stand up quickly. I try to walk as if my knees don't throb from where I hit the sidewalk. Scottie honks the horn, startling me. I look up to see him leaning out the window, while the car rolls steadily forward.

"Hey Luz, smile already—it's your birthday!"

I force myself to wave as he drives away. I see Trini clapping wildly in the backseat, which makes me smile, even though I feel my throat getting tighter and my eyes beginning to water. My body wants to cry but I won't let it. I blink several times and bite the insides of my cheek to distract myself. I drop my head, wishing I could disappear.

"Hey kid, you all right?"

A man's voice, one I recognize but can't name. I turn to see our landlord strolling down the sidewalk. He's wearing a sweatshirt and jeans even though it's eighty degrees out, which makes him stand out more than the color of his skin. Snow-man, a fitting name.

"You okay?" he asks again.

"Yeah. I'm fine." I try to walk around him, but he follows me up the driveway.

"Hey," he calls after me. "You ever see that kid that got shot?"

I stop walking and turn to face him, wondering how he even knows about César.

"You know, that Martinez kid?"

He gestures with the bag in his hand. It's from Circuit City. If the gods were kind it would be my birthday present.

"Yeah, I know him."

He steps toward me. "How's he doing? I heard he was lucky to still be alive."

"Yeah, he is," I say, nodding my head for emphasis.

He looks at me like he wants me to say more.

"He's the same. They're still waiting for him to wake up."

"Oh. Okay." He wraps the bag around his hand, cutting off his circulation. I didn't think his skin could get any whiter, but it does.

"Sometimes it's worse when they wake up," he says. "If they find out they can't walk or whatever."

I try to think of something to say to get this guy to leave. Then he hands me the bag.

"Give him this, will you? When he wakes up." He steps back from me. "If."

I look into the bag. There's a Sony Discman and a bunch of CDs. Prince and Janet Jackson are the only covers I can see through the plastic.

"Okay."

He reaches into his pocket. "And these. I almost forgot." He hands me a package of batteries. Kind of makes me wish I was in the hospital.

"Thanks, kid," he says. "Appreciate it."

I nod and walk into the house. The apartment is hot and stuffy, and it smells like old furniture. I hang the Circuit City bag on the back of the bedroom door. Even if I do give it to him, it's not gonna be on my birthday. I take off the dress I was wearing and change into an old T-shirt and shorts I've had for the last three summers. They're small, but they still fit good enough to wear. I throw the pumps into the back of the closet and swear I will never wear them again. My braids make me feel pretty so I leave them in. I pretend they are gifts and wrap each end with a purple bow.

I hear laughter and the annoying jingle of the ice cream truck as it comes down the street. From the window I can see half the neighborhood run outside and chase it down. A girl and her sister run hand-in-hand down the street, jumping over the pothole we use as a sandbox. There is a part of me that wants to join them, to play in the sun and eat ice cream and laugh. But the bigger part, the one I listen to when I can't hear anything else, tells me to climb into my bed with my book and read in the half-dark, while the rest of the city is lit up like a birthday cake. Not that I've seen one of those in a while. But I still remember what one looks like.

When Cristo gets home he comes into the room without knocking. He stops short when he sees me, obviously startled. He holds his hand over his heart just like our mother used to do.

"Luz, what the fuck? I thought you were going with Trini today."

I keep reading my book. "I didn't feel like it."

"So you're gonna stay home? On your birthday?"

"I don't even like Scottie, or his sister. And I don't like Waterfire. Who wants to sit around staring at burning logs all night?"

Cristo shrugs. "Teacher says it's cool. Like being in church, only you get to listen to music instead of some old guy preaching." He kicks off his sneakers and throws them into the closet.

"Church on a Saturday night? No thank you, very much." I hide my face so he can't tell I'm lying. Miss March, the librarian, goes all the time and she says the best part is the smell, like the whole city is roasting marshmallows in front of a campfire. The only fire I've ever seen was when an old carpet factory burned down on Cranston Avenue, and that smelled like chemicals and death.

He points to the Circuit City bag. "What's that? Scottie get you a present?"

"Please. He never remembered our birthdays when we still lived together." I jump down from my bed and try to snatch the bag from him, but he holds it away from me and peaks inside.

"Damn, a Discman? Who's it from?"

I hesitate. "Snowman." I walk into the kitchen, hoping he forgets about it.

"Shit. I wish it was my birthday," he calls out from the bedroom.

The fridge is empty except for some old take-out containers and a few bottles of root beer. I drink the soda and find some peanut butter crackers in the cupboard. I remind myself that when her shift is over, Lucho will bring us something to eat. Sometimes she forgets to come home, but whenever she shows up, she never forgets to bring food. That, if nothing else, can be counted on.

Miss Valentín comes by at seven to take Cristo to the movies. I've heard of Big Brother or Big Sister programs, but I've never heard of a Big Teacher program. What teacher would want to spend this much time with a student, especially in the summer? And what's so great about my brother anyway? You'd think she'd have her own family to hang out with.

A few minutes after he leaves, while the TV is still warming up and there isn't even a picture yet, Cristo walks back in the house.

"Hurry up," he says, slapping the knob to turn the TV off. "And grab your coat, you know how cold the Showcase gets." He picks a sweatshirt up off the floor. "Here, wear mine."

"What are you talking about?"

"We're gonna miss the previews if you don't get off your ass." He hands me the sweatshirt. "Let's go."

I get off the couch slowly. "You sure? I can come?"

He nods and gestures with his hands. "*Vamos, vamos*. God, why are girls so slow?" He grabs me by the hand and tries to pull me out the door. I jerk my hand free.

"Why are boys so pushy?"

He glares at me and I give him a fake smile, tying the sweatshirt around my waist. I know he's only being nice to me because it's my birthday and there's no one else around who gives a damn. But still, it's pretty nice of him to drag me along. A few months ago he would've left me here without thinking twice, but ever since César got shot he's afraid to leave me home alone. I guess having one of your friends almost die can make you nicer to your sister.

I say, "Thanks," as we walk to the car but I don't think he can hear me over the sound of an ambulance speeding by. Cristo stares after it, like he's checking to see if it's someone we know.

◆ ❖ ◆

The movie Miss Valentín takes us to is a cartoon about this Japanese girl who pretends she's a boy to get into the army and protect her family. It's pretty good but not very realistic. I don't know any girl who cares more about her family than she does about herself. But it's nice to be out of the heat and in a room full of people, even if they're all strangers. We don't usually get to go to the movies because my mother doesn't like big crowds. I like them because you can sit in the dark and forget who you are for a few hours. People think I read a lot because I want to be smart but really it's because I like to forget who I am. The more I read, the longer I can pretend to be somebody else.

When I was little, Cristo used to let me sit on his lap for the whole show. He even let me hold the popcorn. Now he holds the bucket on his lap and doesn't even look over. Every time I take a handful I sneak a look at his face. In the daylight, he never lets me study him like this. A lot of girls think he's handsome, but I think he's too thin, and he has these deep circles under his eyes, just like my mother. His eyes are so green they almost look fake, like the contacts dark-skinned women wear so people will notice them. When he laughs I can see his teeth; half are capped in silver thanks to the milk rot that ruined his smile, and they shimmer like he's chewing on coins. He looks so young in the dark, and happy, like a little kid. Like how he used to look.

He probably never thinks about it, but I remember the exact day when Cristo stopped looking like a little kid. It was a few years ago, when Scottie locked us in our bedroom all day. He had worked a night shift and just wanted to come home and go to sleep, but my mother said she had to go out and he had to watch us. We were all pretty little, Trini wasn't even walking, and they weren't leaving us alone yet. After my mother left Scottie was sitting on the couch falling asleep and we were running all over the place. Finally he said, "Fuck this," and told us to go to our room. Cristo tried to run but Scottie picked him up by the shorts and tossed him into the room. When he tried to sneak out between Scottie's legs, he slapped Cristo across the face.

Once we were all inside he locked the door from the outside with a bike lock. He told us what he was doing and said if we tried to jump out the window he'd beat us all the way back to Puerto Rico. It was summer and it was hot in that room, so hot that it felt like the oven was on. Trini wouldn't stop crying, even when I took off my shirt to fan her with it. After a while Cristo started banging on the door, saying he had to use the bathroom, but Scottie just yelled for him to shut up and piss out the window. Cristo pounded on the door and said that he couldn't, that it was more than that. Chips of paint started to peel off the door where he was hitting it, and the wood began to splinter under his hand. But Scottie didn't come back. Finally Cristo gave up, and he shut himself in the closet and went to the bathroom on the carpeted floor. I watched Trini pick a paint chip off the ground and put it into her mouth, and even though I shouldn't have, I let her keep it since it was the only thing that got her to stop crying.

I didn't have a book to read, so I picked up a pencil, and when I couldn't find any paper, I wrote on the wall. Not a story, I just wrote my name over and over again, scratching letters into the white paint like I was holding a knife. After, I moved the dresser in front of it so I wouldn't have to clean it off, but also because I wanted someone to read it years later and know that I had been there. That I was alive.

When Cristo came out of the closet he didn't say anything

and he didn't look at me. He closed the closet door and sat on the floor in front of it. It must have been a hundred degrees in that room but he wrapped his arms around his knees like he was cold. Eventually we all fell asleep, even though it was the middle of the day, and when Scottie opened the door the whole place was dark and the sun had set. I know because I woke up early and watched it set from the window, wondering how I could see anything so pretty on this side of town.

When Scottie figured out what Cristo did he got all pissed again and forced him to clean it up. Cristo didn't say anything, didn't even fight him, he just got the pail from under the sink and an old rag and went to work scrubbing the carpet. Since Trini was still asleep I helped him, working until our knuckles were raw from rug-burn and it was as clean as it was before, which was really not that clean. Then Scottie made him hand wash his underwear and put them back on.

After that Cristo didn't really talk to me that much and he started playing with older kids in other houses. He stopped giving me rides on his handlebars and he forgot to save me the gum from his Blow Pops. I used to think he stopped loving me after that day, but now I think he stopped loving himself.

After the movie Miss Valentín takes us to Newport Creamery for dessert. We order an ice cream cake in the shape of a whale and they sing "Happy Birthday" to me twice, once in English and once in Spanish. The other people in the restaurant think we're crazy but I don't care because sometimes it feels good to do what you want and not worry about other people. Before I blow out the candles I wish for César to wake up and for my mother to come home soon and for Cristo to be able to sleep through the night and for Trini to never know what it feels like to be forgotten.

I don't make a wish for myself.

SHE SEES the girl lying in a darkened room. Sunlight shines in from the edge of a drawn curtain. The girl can't sleep. She no longer trusts the darkness. She's not safe in this house without her mother. Now it is a house of men: her brothers, her father, the farmer who owns all this land. Even the house they live in. The girl wonders what else he owns. A man crosses the room, his face hidden from view. There is a faint smell of cigarettes and fried pork. The scent of a man who works long hours in a field. The farmer sits down next to her on the bed. He fixes the bow on her dress. Her dress is too small. She closes her eyes. The last thing she sees is her feet on the bed. How small they look, like they belong to a doll. He touches her leg. The girl flinches, as if he had just hit her across the face. The next time he touches her, she doesn't move.

Arcelia

S ometime in July one of the counselors tells me I been clean for forty-five days. I ask her if it still counts, since it's not by choice. She laughs and says being sober is always a choice, even in prison.

I thought it might be different, but prison's just like the streets. You've got your good spots and your bad, your cops and your criminals, your teachers and your preachers. You've got your addicts and your angels, your doctors and your lawyers, your enemies and your best friends. If you know the right people you can get anything in here—drugs, sex, movies, or jewelry. Hell, they'll even give you medicine. That's the real difference between prison and the streets—in here the medicine is free.

They put me on something called AZT about a month ago, and a few other drugs I can't pronounce. They're supposed to help my body fight the HIV. They said I don't have AIDS yet, just HIV, but I still don't get the difference. If they both make you sick, what's it matter what you call it? They told me there's a Spanish-speaking nurse who works overnights and I can sit down with her sometime if I got anymore questions.

When the social worker told me I had it, she asked if I was surprised. I said no, 'cause all those pamphlets they gave me made it seem like I was a perfect match. All I wanted to know was if I'm gonna die. When she said not now I figure that's a good enough answer. Then the nurse came in and started talking about something called my T-cell count, saying how it was 220 and I was on the verge of pneumonia and how I had to get that number up to at least 500. I guess it's like baseball—the good hitters are in the three or four hundreds, but you know you're a superstar if you're batting better than 500. She asked if I had other problems and I told her I get yeast infections all the time. She said that was probably from the virus, too, so now I'm thinking I can blame the HIV for everything—like being broke, shooting dope, and getting locked up for almost a year.

As soon as I start taking the medicine I have to stand in the med line every morning, instead of going to the rec room after breakfast with all the regular girls. They try to keep it private but all my pills are such crazy colors that any idiot would know I'm not taking Vitamin C. They call it a cocktail, but it don't look like any mixed drink I ever seen. And I used to get drunk in some fucked-up bars. The worst thing about it is it makes me have to go to the bathroom all the time. It's real loose, almost like diarrhea and sometimes it burns like I been eating nothing but Chinese food for a week. And bottom line—I'm just not used to shitting that much. Thanks to the dope I was only going a few times a month. I guess I never knew how much money I was saving on toilet paper.

I see the nurses every day, but once a week the doctor comes out here from some big hospital in Providence to check out my blood and see how my body's reacting to the drugs. I ain't seen a doctor this much since I was pregnant—and I missed at least half those appointments. I think a few other girls got it, too, 'cause their pills look pretty much the same as mine and sometimes we fight over the bathroom. We don't talk about it, though. Nobody in here talks about anything they don't have to. One time the counselor asked me if I wanted to go to a support group for women with HIV and I said only if they can cure me. What's the use in talking is how I see it. The damage has already been done.

◆ ❖ ◆

The first people to come visit me here are my cousin Chino and his girlfriend, Kim. Kim's all right—for a white chick with big hair and a Cranston accent—but she's one of those people who always hints at things and never just says what's on her mind. Chino is like a brother to me. He took me in when I showed up in New York with nothing but a baby and a duffel bag and the dream of raising my kids in America.

We sit at a small table in the visitor's room—Chino and Kim next to each other, me on the other side. They bring me *arroz con gandules* and *chuletas* but the guards take it all at the door, pointing to the sign that says: NO FOOD ALLOWED. The only thing they let them bring in is a calendar with pictures of sunsets from all over the world and a light-blue hooded sweatshirt that says "Little Rhody." I'm happy to have something warm since nights get pretty cold in this building, and everybody always says I look good in blue. At first I think there's something wrong with it 'cause it smells weird but then I realize that's just the smell of something new. I'm a grown woman, but I'm still not used to having anything someone else didn't have before me.

Kim talks non-stop—about the weather and her job and how being inside here isn't as bad as it seems from the outside. I want to say, "Try sleeping here," but I stop myself. When I ask about my kids Kim finally gets quiet. Chino looks at her before he answers me.

"They're all right, they're fine." He shrugs. "They're kids, they'll bounce back."

"How's Cristo doing with everything?" For some reason, he's the one I really worry about.

"He's fine, Arcelia, he's the same."

"And the girls?"

"Everybody's good. Lucho, too."

Hearing her name is like a punch in the chest. "How's she doing?" I cross my arms like I'm hugging myself. "I mean, how are things going?"

"We don't see her a lot, Ari, you know how she is."

"I know. That's why I have to ask."

Kim clears her throat. "Last time I stopped by she wasn't around. But the kids said they had just seen her. Within the last day or two."

Chino rubs his hands on his jeans. "She's working a lot but she's still there at night. She promised me she's sleeping there."

He glares at Kim, but she won't look him in the eye.

My stomach tightens like I just got kicked in the gut. "I know she's not perfect, but she signed those papers with the state. She said she would take care of them. I don't think she'd go back on that." My hands are suddenly cold and I try to warm them in my armpits. "I need her to be there, to take care of those kids." And me, I'm thinking, I need her to take care of me.

"Don't worry about it, it's going to be fine. You need to focus on yourself." Chino looks around the room. "Focus on getting out of here. There's nothing you can do from in here anyway."

I look at him. "They're my kids, Chino. I worry about them wherever I am."

He nods and don't say anymore. Kim shuffles in her seat. Her leather jacket squeaks against the plastic, making half the eyes in the room look at her. She don't seem to notice.

"I wish we could help out more. That we could take them, you know? But three kids...that's a lot. And with Chino out of work and without any money from the state, we just can't do it right now."

"I know. I'm not asking you to."

"If it was one or two, maybe we could talk about it. Just the baby or—"

"No, I don't want them split up." I blow on my hands to warm them. "It's too hard."

Chino looks at me. "On who? You or them?"

"What's the difference?" My fingers feel stiff like a doll's, like I'm made out of plastic. "I made that mistake once before. Never again." Chino knows the story so he don't make me say no more. How I left my husband in the middle of the night. How I took Luz—my baby, my little girl—and walked out holding her and the bag I had in my hand. What he don't know is that I never said good-bye to Cristo, I just pressed a flower to his pillow so he could remember how I smelled and kissed his head in the dark.

"It wasn't a mistake, Ari. It was the only choice you had."

I shake my head, not looking in his eyes. "I coulda done it

different."

"It's done now, it's over. No use beating yourself up over something you can't even change." Chino picks a scab on his hand. "And you left him with his father, for God's sake. It's not like you left him on the street corner."

"I still left him."

He licks the scab as it begins to bleed. "It was only six months."

"You say that like it's a sneeze. Try doing that same time in here."

Chino exhales and sits back in his seat. He tries to avoid my eyes but I stare at him. When our eyes finally meet he lifts his eyebrows, a sign that he wants to squash the conversation. All the men in our family do that, but he's the only one who waits for an answer. I shrug, letting him know it's okay.

"Lucho told me she finally paid the phone bill," Chino says with a smirk. "So it should be turned back on soon. Any day now."

"Good. They let me call out once a week. On Sundays. So tell the kids to be home." I squint to block out the harsh fluorescent lights. "You know, if they're not doing anything else."

"The only place they really go is the hospital, to visit Cristo's friend."

"Oh right. I heard about that on the news. How's he doing?" One of the guards gave me a newspaper article when they heard I knew the kid that got shot. I pinned it to my wall but never actually read it.

"All they're saying is that he finally woke up. I don't think he's talking yet, so they don't know how much, you know, brain damage he has or whatever. But he's alive."

"Good. That's good to hear."

Kim leans back in her chair suddenly, making a loud creak that echoes throughout the room. The guard near the window stands up while the others stare at us from the door. One of them holds up her hand, telling us we have five minutes left.

"Oh, to be that boy's mother." Kim shakes her head. "I can't imagine."

"I'd kill someone if they did that to my kid. Accident or

not. Family or not." Anger rises in my chest and makes my whole body hot. My skin feels tight and all I want to do is punch the wall or run along the beach or take the biggest hit of any drug I can find.

"He wouldn't be walking around," Chino says. "I can tell you that much. An eye for a fucking eye."

"Shit. You know that's right."

Chino flexes his bicep, making his tattoo—a picture of the Puerto Rican flag he got on his eighteenth birthday—ripple. I reach out to touch it, but the guard gestures for me to stay put. I take my hand back after squeezing him softly.

"Hey, is that teacher still coming around?"

Chino nods. "She's the one who takes them to the hospital. And to the movies, Cristo said, and sometimes the park." He leans closer to me, his face softening. "It's nice of her to take an interest in him, don't you think? It's good for him."

I nod because I know I'm supposed to, but I feel like saying, "Hell no." So what if she went to college and drives a new Jetta and speaks English without an accent—why does that mean she gets to spend time with my son? I'm his mother. I'm the one who should do those things with him. What does she know about being someone's mother? It's not just about the good times—it's hard fucking work—and you can't just replace someone because they ain't perfect.

After they leave I make a promise to myself that when I get out I'll take him to the park, even if it's twenty degrees and snowing, and I'll take him to the movies, even if we have to sneak into the theater, and I'll be the mother I never was—the one I shoulda been—even if it damn near kills me.

◆ ❖ ◆

I'm still pissed about the teacher when I meet with the social worker later that day. She wants to know why I got a problem with her so I tell her about the letter she sent and how she thinks she knows me. She don't say nothing, just puts a notebook and a pencil on the desk between us. The desk is so high I can't really see her body. She looks like a puppet, her head just floating on top of the chair.

"Write her back," she says, pushing the notebook closer to me.

"Who?"

"Miss Valentín. Do something constructive with your anger and write her back."

I sit back in my chair. "I don't got nothing to say." The plastic is so smooth I almost slip off and fall on the floor. I steady myself while she looks at me.

"That's bullshit," she says, her face turning red. She acts like she's got balls but on the street she'd be scared to talk to me. I laugh at her.

"You think that's funny?"

"I think you're funny," I say, still laughing.

"Why?"

There's a picture on her desk of a family in front of a fake Christmas tree. I can't find her face in the crowd. "All white people are funny."

"Let's keep this about you, Arcelia."

"Me? Okay. I don't write letters."

"Why not? What are you afraid of finding out?"

I pick my fingernails, cleaning out food I don't remember eating. "I'm not afraid of anything."

"Prove it," she says. "Write a letter to someone. Anyone. Your children. Your family. Yourself. I don't care. But say something." She drinks coffee from a Boston Bruins cup. From the look on her face it's cold. "Have the courage to come clean."

"Shit, I been clean for almost two months."

"Come clean about your past. About who you are and what you did to get here." She pushes the notebook toward me again, this time knocking the pencil to the floor.

"That's a lot to write," I say, picking up the pencil.

She smiles. "You've got time."

She pours her coffee into a plant on her windowsill. I was wrong—it was only water. But I was right about it being cold.

"Yep," I say. "Nothing but time to waste."

"It's not a waste if it helps you. That's what therapy is."

I roll the notebook into a tube and tuck it under my arm. I

put the pencil in my hair like a chopstick, the way I see Chinese ladies do it.

"Don't lose that pencil," she says as I'm walking out. "That's worth a lot in here."

Back in my room I unroll the notebook and hide it with the pencil in my magazine. Then I put it all under my bed and don't think about it for the rest of the week. But on Sunday night—after I try for three hours to call my house and nobody ever picks up—I suddenly need it. While the other girls are watching a rerun of *Law & Order*, I go into my room and lie down on the bed and think about what got me here. I want to talk to my kids and I want to talk to Lucho, but I only got myself—then I remember the notebook.

I get it out and write *"Querida Arcelia"* at the top of the page, like I used to write *"Querida Mami"* in my journal after she died. I laugh out loud when I see my name on the page, in the middle of a page as white as snow. When I stop laughing I write *"Quien eres?"* Who are you?

I'm quiet for a long time, thinking about all the ways to answer that question. Finally, I start to write. At first it's a list and then I write in sentences and next thing I know I fill up most of the sheets in that notebook. I tell myself I never have to read it again if I don't want to, but I have to write it down—all of it—without leaving out the bad parts or the parts I don't want to remember. I put it all down, my whole life on a notebook filled with striped paper from the ACI, and then I put it back in the magazine and hide it under my mattress.

When I close my eyes I don't see all the flashes I usually see. The voice in my head—the one I turn off with drinking and drugs and running as fast as I can—is pretty quiet and next thing I know it's morning and they're calling for bed check and I'd actually stayed asleep all night. The first time I did that since I got here in May.

Snowman

rovidence is a dark city. Even when the sun is out you can miss something. Even in the summer when the days are long, some things just never get lit.

I am also dark, but you wouldn't know it to look at me. I'm like a hundred-watt light bulb; I make people squint. They tell me I have a condition called leukoderma, which means I have essentially no pigment in my skin or hair. Translation? I am completely white, except for a few patches of brown on my hands, knees, and elbows. Freaky, huh? But that's not the only thing that makes me different. My eyes are a light blue you would find in the waters of the Caribbean, not on a black kid from South Providence. Toni Morrison was wrong—I have the bluest eyes.

Some people don't know what to do when they see me, so they look away. Others stare at my skin like it's parchment covered by some ancient text they're trying to figure out. A few come right out and ask me what the hell happened to my face. Those are the ones that I talk to.

I don't use the term *albino*. Don't like it. It makes me think of a lab rat or a genetically modified pit bull some gangster would pay a lot of money to lock in a case. I've been called dozens of names in my life—whitey, Casper, ghost, spook, marshmallow, paper-plate, rice-man, milky, vanilla, light bulb, Charmin, Wonder bread, ice cream, tampon, new socks, Elmer's, cotton, goose, coconut, yogurt, sheets, cocaine, sugar, and salt—but the one I like the best, the one I let people call me, is Snowman. It just fits.

When I was a kid I used to love that scene in *Frosty the Snowman* when he got locked in the greenhouse and melted away. Everyone else thought it was sad but I remember thinking it was cool that he could disappear anytime he wanted to, just by going into a warm room. I wanted to have a power like that. So when they started calling me Snowman I let it stick. I didn't beat anyone up and I didn't complain to the teacher. I started answering to it and writing it on my homework till even the principal was calling me Snowman and Dayton Lewis ceased to exist.

Truth be told, I'm an orphan. Been one a long time, way before my momma died. My parents met at a high school dance and married three months later, the day after my momma graduated at the top of her class from Hope High School. After a tour in Vietnam my daddy got a job at the post office. By then my momma was pregnant, so she quit her job at the phone company to wait for her first child to be born. They bought a small house off Elmwood Avenue and she filled the nursery with books she bought at yard sales for a nickel each. It took her the entire pregnancy to get through *Moby Dick*, reading every night to her doting husband and the restless baby, who, even in the womb, would not sleep.

I came early. It was a long and painful labor, one my momma thought she might not endure. When the doctor pulled me out by forceps, she was passed out from a shot of Demerol; my daddy was in the car listening to the Yankees beat the Red Sox in extra innings. I was almost an hour old before I saw either one of my parents. He was gonna name me Junior, Floyd Rutherford Lewis Junior, but when I came out white—or worse, actually, with no color—he told my momma she could call me Dayton after her favorite uncle, the first black undertaker in the state of Rhode Island. He's the one we moved in with after my daddy left, the one who paid for ten years of Catholic school without my momma even asking. He was also the one who left me his entire estate when he died from a heart attack at sixty-five and had no heirs. Left me his house and the business and $37,000 in cash. I still own the house, but I sold the business and used the cash to buy my first rental property.

When my daddy moved out he left me something, too: the set of Lincoln Logs he got for my first birthday and didn't stay around long enough to give me. Momma never let me play with them, but she did take them out to show me every year, cursing his weakness for leaving, and her own for staying behind. They never divorced and she never remarried, but she did have another baby, mostly to prove to herself that there wasn't anything wrong with her, that none of it was her fault. I was twelve when Justin was born, a perfect brown-skinned boy with curly dark hair like my momma's and almond-shaped eyes that made women in the street ask if he was part Eskimo. Momma would smile and deny it, but he could've been for all I knew. I never met his daddy and my momma never spoke his name. She said Justin belonged to both of us, and until the state came and took him away from me, I believed her.

◆ ❖ ◆

When people ask me why I like to walk everywhere, I tell them I like to feel the ground. I like to step where someone else has already walked. Don't matter what type—pavement, sidewalk, grass, cobblestone, brick, or dirt—I'll walk on anything solid. Most of the city's cobblestone streets got paved over by the time I was in high school, but there are still a few spots left downtown and on the east side where the rich people live. Sometimes I walk over the Point Street Bridge just to feel the stones under my feet. I imagine all the tires that have touched them, all the horse's hooves, and it makes me feel like I'm a part of something bigger than I am.

I probably walk about five miles a day, depending on how many jobs I got. I like to work 'cause it keeps me moving. Can't get anything done by sitting in one spot. If anybody asks, I call myself an entrepreneur. They don't usually ask more questions after that. But really I'm just a businessman, and like any good businessman, I've had to diversify. Some of my ventures are legal, like renting vending machines at the high schools, and some are not so legal, like introducing people to the pharmaceuticals of their choice. Just for the record, I'm not a dealer. I'm just the middleman. I find customers for the big dogs and I take a cut. If I was dealing full-time I could bring in two or three grand a day, but I'm not a greedy man. What I am is a smart man, so every dollar I make I put right back into my business. I am also a free man, and I want to keep it that way. To do so, there are six simple rules I have to live by:

1. Don't spend money on flashy cars. (I walk everywhere.)
2. Never talk on a cell phone. (Don't own one.)
3. Never let customers know where you live. (Nobody knows where I live.)
4. Never have a girlfriend. (Last one was in kindergarten.)
5. Always have a job. (Since I was sixteen.)
6. Never use what you're selling. (Not even once.)

In the ten years I've been working I haven't broken a single rule. That's what makes me different from the average dope-slinging joker, and that's why I still got a clean record. The cops might know who I am (I'm not stupid enough to think I blend in) but they don't know what I do, and I plan on keeping it that way. *Can't find what you can't see, can you?*

Out of all my jobs there's only one that feels like constant work: being a landlord. Every day I ask myself why I wanted to take care of something. I never really come up with a good answer, just keep coming back to the idea of permanence. The need to own something. To have something belong to me. I've got six houses now: two in Olneyville, two in Federal Hill, and two in the West End. What's it add up to? Six headaches. I'm not sure if it's the plight of all houses, or just these hundred-year-old Victorians we've got here in New England, but something's always going wrong. Mostly it's a problem with the house, like a busted hot water heater or a leaky roof, but sometimes it's the tenants themselves, fighting over a parking space or somebody's colicky kid or neglecting to pay the rent on time.

I don't want to make it about race, but usually that's what it comes down to. Like most things in America. My white tenants don't bother me much. They usually keep to themselves; don't mess with me and don't mess with anyone else in the house.

Quiet. Predictable. On time. The black folks? Late. Loud. Always complaining. The Spanish? Shit, they're real consistent: something's always broken; someone's always yelling.

The folks on Sophia Street are ridiculous. Ever since the mom got locked up, the first floor's been late with their rent every month. That's three months and counting. Could've collected a lot of late fees if I was an asshole. But I'm not. I feel sorry for those kids. I know what it feels like to be left alone like that, to have to take care of your home when you don't even know how to take care of yourself. It's not their fault they can't pay the rent. But of course, it's not mine either. If I let them miss a month then all the others will think they can get away with it, too. And then it multiplies and next thing you know everyone's living rent-free like this is the projects. Hell no. This is not some government-assisted-everybody-gets-their-own-patio-but-the-hallways-smell-like-piss-and-if-you-don't-keep-your-kids-inside-they'll-get-shot-on-the-front-porch program. Please don't do me like that. This is a legitimate business operation. I rent out clean, comfortable apartments in fully inspected houses for affordable rates. I don't care who you are and I don't care who your momma is—if you can't pay we don't play. It's nothing personal; it's business.

◆ ❖ ◆

By the 15th of August all my tenants are paid up except for the ladies on Sophia Street. I guess the term *ladies* is a stretch. Lucho ain't like no lady I've ever known.

I stop by the apartment first thing in the morning, pissed already. Don't make me come looking for you. I ain't no doctor. I shouldn't have to make house calls.

The boy answers the door in his pajamas. He stares at me without speaking and doesn't invite me in.

"Is Lucho around?" I ask.

He shakes his head. "She's out."

"You know when she'll be back?"

"Uhhh, no." He eats a handful of sugared cereal straight from the box. "She doesn't like me asking a lot of questions, you know? It's not like I'm her mother."

"But she's coming back, right?"

"Of course she's coming back. She lives here." He gestures around the room like I should recognize all her things.

"'Cause nobody's seen her around in the last week. That's a pretty long time to be 'out.'"

He shrugs. "She moves kinda slow."

"Uh huh." I nod my head like I believe him.

He shoves another handful of cereal into his mouth and coughs hard like a smoker. I smell the corn and sugar on his breath. The smell is familiar but I can't place it.

"Who else lives here?" I ask him.

"My sisters."

"How many you got?"

"Two."

"So there's three of you."

He appears to be counting in his head. "Yeah. And Lucho."

"Right, of course. When she's here."

"Right."

He puts the box of cereal down on the floor and wipes his sugary hands on his pajamas. The gesture makes him look like a toddler, and I suddenly think of Justin at that age, how I used to feed him in the mornings when my momma was too sick to get out of bed, the cancer already eating her body from the inside out. It's been twenty years, but I can still see the plastic spoon in his chubby fist, can hear his squeaky voice talking about butterflies and balloons and helicopters that fly so high in the sky, can feel the scratch of the dried milk on his top lip as he leans up to kiss me, saying "Love you, love you," and laughing until he chokes, as if the happiness had come bubbling out of his chest and got caught in his throat.

The boy looks at me. "You all right?"

I shake my head to clear the memory. "She leave you any money for rent?"

"Rent?" He blinks like he can't see me clearly.

"Yeah, it was due two weeks ago."

"How much is it?" He asks like he's about to pull the cash from his pocket.

"Three-fifty."

"Three *hundred* fifty?"

"Don't say it like that, that's a good price. I was doing your mother a favor."

He closes the cereal box. "Lucho didn't leave no money."

"Well, I hope she comes back then. For your sake, kid."

I walk down the driveway, not knowing what to do next. I could evict them, of course, on several grounds, but the process takes months and is a total pain in the ass.

"Hey Snowman, wait up." The kid runs onto the porch to stop me. "Listen, what if I started working for you, so I could pay off the rent?"

"Who said I was hiring?"

"Come on, I'll do anything." He flashes a crooked smile. "And I'm real cheap."

I scratch my chin, like I'm seriously debating. "You got any skills?"

"Like what you mean?"

"Can you fix cars or toilets or refrigerators, anything like that?"

He looks at me like I'm crazy. "I'm eleven," he says.

I shrug. "Hey, you seem like a smart kid."

He thinks for a few seconds. "I can wash and wax a car in fifteen minutes. And I can paint, even with one of those roller things. They taught me how at the Rec Center before it burned down." He stands on the edge of the railing, as if to make himself look taller. "And I'm good with kids and animals. Cats not so much, but dogs like me. And I'm a good runner; I can run all the way to the pineapple on Atwells and back without taking a break."

"See what I mean? Sounds like you've got a lot of skills."

He gives me that crooked grin again. "Any you want to pay me for?"

"I'll have to think about it," I say, already knowing that if I was going to have an assistant this kid would be it.

"Cool," he says, crossing his arms. "Get back to me whenever."

He sounds so serious I have to laugh. "Sure, I'll call you."

His smile turns into a look of panic. "Uhh...we don't have a phone anymore. It's better to just come by."

"Okay," I say, forcing myself to walk away before I agree to something I can't even begin to justify.

Something makes me stop at the end of the driveway and I turn around to see the boy still standing on the porch, his eyes locked on me like he can't bear to see me leave. I think of Justin again, of saying good-bye that final time after our momma died when we were in our second foster home. It was so easy for him to let me go that day; to hug me, to wave, to call out "Love you, love you," and blow me a kiss so hard it could have knocked me over if it was solid. He had the freedom of ignorance, while I was burdened with knowing the truth. Justin was going to a new family, one that wanted to eventually adopt him, but I (fifteen, black, colorless) would be staying in the system indefinitely. No matter what the social workers told me, I knew I would never see him again.

I call to the boy. "Hey kid, tell me something. When was the last time you saw Lucho, for real?"

He's quiet for a minute, deciding if he should tell me the truth.

"About two weeks," he finally says.

There's a flash of something close to heartbreak in his eyes, for just a second, and then it's gone. That look of loss, of a fear and loneliness so great it vanishes the instant it's formed, is so familiar it's like I'm looking at myself as a child. My eyes begin to burn and for a second I think I might cry, which surprises me as much as if I suddenly bent over and vomited onto the sidewalk. I am not a person who cries. Not as a child, and definitely not now. I didn't cry when my daddy left or when my momma died, or when my baby brother, the only person in my life who never looked at me with pity or shame, was taken from me. I never cried for the boy he was, or for the boy I used to be, and I will not cry for the one who stands before me now, as lost and motherless as I am today.

I blink several times and look to the ground. Garbage litters the sidewalk but the spot around my feet is clean. The white of my sneakers stands out against the dull cement, like how my face must stand out in a crowd. I inhale deeply before I look up. The boy stands with his arms at his sides, his hands opened like he's ready to catch whatever the world throws his way. His eyes look straight at me, but I refuse to meet his gaze.

"You've got the job, kid," I say, walking away before I change my mind.

"Thanks, Snowman," he calls out after me, his voice conjuring the boy I'd tried so hard to forget.

◆ ❖ ◆

I start him off with small jobs: hand-delivering letters; picking up weekly checks from tenants on payment plans; running general errands. When I have to fix something in one of the houses I bring him along and try to teach him how to do it. He never runs out of questions, which sometimes makes me regret my decision to hire him, but most days I like having the kid around. He's funny as hell, and since he's small he blends in everywhere and nobody asks any questions about him. And he can translate for me when I want to curse somebody out in Spanish. Ten years ago this whole neighborhood was black and Italian, but now I'd say almost half of it is Spanish of some kind: Puerto Rican, Dominican, Guatemalan, Mexican. They come from all over. This must be what New York felt like in the 1950s. Integration—ain't it a trip.

Cristo promises every day that Lucho will be back. He says she leaves like this all the time, and always comes back. I don't believe him but I let him stay in the apartment with his sisters anyway. Who's it gonna hurt? Better than sending them to DCYF. I've seen what happens to kids in the system and it ain't pretty.

One day I take him with me to install a ceiling fan for an old lady in a third-floor apartment. It's not covered in the lease, which means I don't have to do it, but it's hot as hell this week and I don't want the lady paging me at night to complain. Plus, I've seen on the news how so many old people die during heat waves and I don't want that on my conscience. She lives alone and almost never goes out, probably because she's real heavy and walking up the stairs is too much for her. She says she has kids but I've never seen them around and whenever I do something for her she always feeds me and says I wish I had a son just like you.

As soon as we get there the old lady starts cooking. She says she doesn't mind the oven being on since the kitchen's so hot she can't tell the difference. She brings us lemonade with ice cubes that have melted before I take my first sip. Cristo drinks his down quickly, sucking on the one remaining ice cube like it's a Jolly Rancher. It takes a while to get the old light fixture off, but once that's done I get the new one up pretty quick. Cristo stands on a chair next to my ladder and hands me all the tools before I have to ask for them. He's quiet for most of the job, and then right as I'm hanging the new fan he asks me about my skin color.

"Did something happen to you, for your skin to look like that?"

He hands me the screwdriver, which I use to tighten the blades.

"Nothing happened. I was born like this."

"Does it hurt?"

I laugh. "No, it doesn't hurt. Unless I'm in the sun too long. Then I burn as quick as a match." I screw in the light bulb, then pull on the string to test the lights.

"It must be weird, though, to not look like other black people."

I shrug. "To me it's just normal."

"Do you ever miss being able to blend in?"

"Sure, I guess." I get down from the ladder. "I imagine it's nice to fit in, to disappear into a crowd. But I wouldn't want to always look like everyone else. Then I wouldn't be me." With my back to him, I say something I could never say to his face. "I might look like a freak, but I look like myself, and nobody can take that away from me. Nobody else can be me."

I can feel him looking at the back of my head. I gather up the tools and lock them in my toolbox.

"You don't look like a freak," he says, pausing to choose his words carefully. "You just look different, like you're from the future or something."

I want to laugh but I don't. I can tell he's serious. Like he's been to the future and saw me there.

"I hope you're right," I say, handing him the toolbox. He has to hold it with two hands, but he acts like it's easy. "It's better to look like the future than the past."

He shrugs. "I look like my mother."

"I know," I tell him. "That's a good thing. She's a pretty lady."

"I don't want to look pretty. I want to look tough." He lifts the toolbox, flexing the small muscles in his arms.

A few seconds later I ask him what's more important—to look tough or to be tough—but he never answers me.

I call out to the old lady that we're done and when she comes out she's got a plate of rolls and a pot of spaghetti and meatballs on a serving tray. She sets it on the card table and tells us to hurry up and eat before it gets cold, while she lies on the couch under the ceiling fan and watches *Jeopardy!* I've never seen anyone eat as much as this kid. He even stuffs a few rolls into his pocket when the old lady leaves the room to get more meatballs.

"Here, finish mine." I offer him my plate.

"Nah, I'm good," he says. "I'm bringing these home for my sisters."

I take a sip of my water. "You got enough food at home?"

He shrugs. "We're all right."

"What does that mean?" I push back from the table, having hardly touched my food. I prefer to eat with no witnesses.

"We eat where we can. At the neighbors, at my cousin's house, with Teacher. We make the rounds."

"Well, let me know...if you need anything extra."

"Thanks," he says with his mouth full. "But I'm taking care of it." He gets up from the table and carries our plates into the kitchen like a waiter with years of practice. Then he thanks the old lady and I grab the toolbox and we leave.

We walk a few blocks together and then he splits off down an alley, saying he knows a shortcut home. How can this kid know a route that I don't know? I watch him as he runs away from me, his steps so light it's like he doesn't have a burden in the world. I stand there for a while, hoping he'll turn around to see me there, still watching over him, but he never looks back.

Cristo

It's been three weeks since I seen Lucho and I'm starting to think she's not coming back. All Mami's friends know how to disappear, but they usually come back in a few days, or even a week. Lucho left before, but not for this long. I don't tell anybody, but I'm thinking she's gone for good.

It don't bother me that much, but I think Luz misses her, or maybe she just misses having an adult around. Not that Lucho spent much time with us, but she did buy food and bring home new music once in a while. And having her here meant we weren't alone. I know she's not our family, but it did seem like we were something more than just strangers living in the same house. Maybe something like friends.

With Lucho gone, we run out of money real quick. Luz gives me her Discman to sell at the flea market, but once that money runs out I start stealing food from the Price Rite. It's easy to do if I go when it's real busy because then I get lost between people's legs. I wear an old jacket of Scottie's that's real big so I can hide all the food inside. Even though it's August it's the style to wear winter coats all year round, so nobody questions me. Mostly I take fruit and cans of soup that are small and easy to hide, but I once walked out with a package of tortillas and a dozen eggs tucked into the waist of my pants. I was nervous at first and my hands used to sweat, but it's getting easier with practice. Now I'm pretty good at getting in and out in less than five minutes with my pockets full.

I don't have much time to clean so the house gets dirty pretty quick. Luz does the dishes when we have soap, but mostly I try to steal paper plates so we can just throw them away. Cleaning our clothes is harder because the boxes of laundry soap are way too big for me to sneak out of the store. Lately I've been going through the trash at the Laundromat looking for any leftovers, and when I find some I add it to a collection I got in an old peanut butter jar. The soap ends up looking kind of nasty, because all the colors get mixed up and turn into this brown paste, but it still works good enough. To get quarters I check pay phones or parking meters, and when that doesn't work I steal the tip jar from one of the coffee shops on Federal Hill. Sometimes I get lucky and find a few dollar bills in there, too, and then I can buy a slice of pizza for dinner.

But I'm not always that lucky. Once the guy caught me taking the tip jar and he yelled for me to stop and then grabbed me by the hood of my sweatshirt. I tried to jerk away but I couldn't move so I ended up zipping myself out of the sweatshirt and taking off without it. It sucks because it was my lucky sweatshirt, too. But at least I got the money.

So far my job with Snowman is working out pretty good. He writes down all my hours and puts that against the rent money Mami owes. I don't really know how he's gonna figure it, but I know I worked off at least a week or two of rent already. Mostly I run errands for him in the neighborhood, but a couple of times he took me along to fix things in some of his houses. It was kinda fun to see all the apartments from the inside, because a lot were real different from how they look on the outside. One place had a TV in every room, even the bathroom, and this other guy had a fish tank in the living room that was as tall as the ceiling, with all these huge fish in crazy colors swimming around. Snowman was pissed because he has a policy about no animals, but I thought it was cool as hell, especially when the guy fed them a bunch of minnows right in front of me.

Sometimes Snowman needs me at night and I have to leave my sisters alone in the apartment. When I sneak out I lock the bedroom door behind me, since the lock on the front door is busted. I don't like locking them in like that but I don't want anything to happen to them. Not when I'm gone and they can't protect themselves. Scottie used to lock us in the same way, with a bike lock wrapped around the doorknob, but I don't think he was trying to protect us. He was only looking out for himself. Sometimes I get freaked out because strangers still walk right in the front door, looking for Mami. They come in packs: skinny white guys with long hair and scruffy beards, and ladies who talk real loud, their eyes flying around the room like mosquitoes. They haven't seen her in a few months and don't know she's in jail. They seem real sad when I tell them she's gone, and after a while they leave without ever telling us their names or why they stopped by.

Snowman gave me a pager to wear and he said not to turn it off, even when I go to sleep. He never pages me in the middle of the night, but I'm always ready, just in case. The only time I turn it off is when I go to visit César because the nurse says it messes with the machines that check his heartbeat. He should be getting off those soon and if everything checks out they'll let him come home before school starts. Now that he's awake they make him get out of bed every day and walk a few steps in the hallway. His right eye is still covered by the bandage and he says the left is kind of blurry so he's pretty much doing it blind. Today he's trying to walk from his room to the nurse's station 'cause he gets a lollipop if he makes it the whole way without stopping. Now he says it's his favorite candy, but before he got shot it was bubble gum. The chewing makes his head hurt so he had to stop.

His legs are so skinny and pale they remind me of chopsticks, and he looks like he could splinter with each step. At first he holds onto the wall and shuffles his feet, like how Trini used to when she was learning to walk, but when he's halfway there he steps into the middle of the hallway. All he's got to lean on is this metal pole, kinda like a cane on wheels, except this one holds a plastic bag hooked into his arm. The nurse says it feeds him sugar water through a tube so he never gets thirsty. The pole looks like it could snap, so I walk up next to him and give him my shoulder. I thought he would only use it to steady himself a little bit, but he wraps his arm around me and I walk with him down to the nurse's station. He keeps his eyes on the ground with every step, not looking at any of us. I can hear how hard it is for him to breathe, how his chest rattles like an old man, and I'm scared that he's going to pass out right there with only me to catch him.

When we get to the end of the hallway he says he wants to rest and he leans against the wall with his free hand. The nurses clap and bring him the lollipop, which he slips into the pocket of his bathrobe.

I start to step away, but his fingers dig into my shoulder like he's falling off a cliff and he says, "Don't go, Cristo. Please."

So I stand right next to him, holding him up, and promise to stay like that as long as he needs me.

◆ ❖ ◆

There's mail waiting for me on the kitchen table when I get home from the hospital. The first letter I ever got. No return address, but I recognize the handwriting as Mami's. Hard to believe she sat still long enough to write anything down. It's funny to see my name on the envelope, like I'm somebody important.

I sit down and open the letter slowly. The only light in the room is coming from the streetlight outside. My stomach flips, like when you open a birthday present you think you're not going to like.

> *Dear Cristo,*
>
> *Hello my sweet boy. This is your mother, in case you don't know my handwriting. I'm writing this letter slow so the ink don't smudge and you can read it clear. In case you want to know, I am good. My hair is long so I usually wear it back in a ponytail, like how you like it. The dye is growing out so half of it's dark now. I look like a skunk. If that ain't bad enough, I'm gaining weight from all the pasta they feed us in here. It's mushy like how Luz cooks it, you remember? But I'm not complaining. At least it's all free, right? I can hear you right now saying, "Mami, that's not funny," and you're right, of*

course. But people make jokes when they need them. So I guess that's my way of telling you I need it.

How are you and your sisters? I know you are taking good care of them so I don't have to ask. You ready for school to start? I hope this was an OK summer. It's been hard I bet, but I know there were good times too. Even in here there are good times, like when they serve chocolate pudding for dessert or when we get to see a baseball game on TV. We live for those moments.

I call you every Sunday, but the phone just rings and rings. I'm guessing Lucho turned it off. I know you can't hear my voice, but try to remember that I am with you always, in the air that we breathe and the sky that floats above us. I am always your mother. And I miss you very much.

When I get home I'm going to tell you the truth. Life is hard for people like me. I made mistakes. But I'm OK now. I'm better. But I'm gonna need your help to stay that way. Can you do that for your mother? Can you help me?

Te quiero mucho, mijo. Siempre.
Your loving Mami

I fold the letter back up and leave it on the table like how I found it. The windows are closed and the room is hot, but I'm starting to feel cold, like I'm sitting in front of the AC. Kinda funny, since we don't even have a fan. All of a sudden I hear the ticking of a clock I don't remember we had. I look around the room and after a while I see it sitting on the wall above the cabinets, a small yellow clock with a picture of a bird on its face. An eagle, I think, with its wings spread wide like a cape. The time is way off so the batteries must almost be dead. Probably something Mami bought at the flea market because it reminded her of Puerto Rico. I wonder what she has on the walls in her jail cell to remind her of us. Not a picture, she needs something with weight. Maybe I should send her the clock, or a frying pan, or that radio she used to listen to for hours. Something she can hold onto or throw against the wall if she needs to. Something that will remind her of the things she left behind.

Hearing her voice in my head makes me miss her all over again. I thought it would be okay for her to be gone this long, since we never really spent that much time together, but it's not. I always knew she was around before. I could find her when I needed to.

I use my chair as a stool and reach for the clock. When I turn it over to check the batteries, I see a wad of bills taped to the backside. I tear off the tape and count the money: sixty-seven dollars in tens, fives, and ones. *The presents are with the birds*, Mami had said. Is this what she meant? I look at the front of the clock. The bird stares back at me. One bird. But then I see it: above the eagle's wing there's another bird, a smaller one flying back to the nest, back to his mother. *The presents are with the birds*. They've been here the whole time.

I tuck the money in my pocket and search the drawers for new batteries. When I can't find any I take one from the smoke alarm in the ceiling and put it in the clock. Then I set the time and clean the front with my T-shirt before putting it back on the wall. I look at the eagles, wishing I could be that little bird right now, flying across the city to see his mother.

◆ ❖ ◆

Scottie shows up early the next Saturday, before we have time to get Trini ready. When he honks Luz is brushing Trini's hair and I'm looking through the dirty clothes for a semi-clean dress for her to wear. We take so long Scottie gets out of the car and walks into the house.

"What the fuck happened here?" He lifts his sunglasses and looks around the room, squinting.

"Nothing," I say, shoving the clothes into a pile with my foot. "We've been busy."

"Yeah, busy turning this place into a pigsty." Scottie steps on a pizza box and almost trips. "What's wrong with that chick, it's like she's letting you guys run the house."

"She works a lot," I say.

"All the time," Luz adds.

"And there's not a lot of time to clean." I put the pile back into the laundry hamper.

Trini runs by in a T-shirt with no underwear, laughing uncontrollably.

"Hey, you think that's funny? Running around like a tramp with no underpants on?" Scottie points toward the bedroom. "Go get dressed. Now."

She listens to him, but walks away with a smile on her face. I nod for Luz to follow her to the room, hoping she can find something decent to put on her.

Scottie sniffs an empty carton of milk that's been sitting out for a few days. His face curls in disgust. He walks into the kitchen and opens the fridge. After a second he shakes his head. "Looks like she's cooking some real gourmet food, huh? I bet you're missing your mom right about now."

"It's not that bad," I tell him, collecting a bunch of the garbage in my arms. I go to throw it out but the trash can is already full. It should have gone out weeks ago, but the can is so big I can't drag it to the curb by myself. I put the garbage on the floor, starting another pile.

"I hope not, kid. 'Cause it looks really bad."

He walks around the apartment, peeking his head into every corner. He goes to Mami's bedroom last. The room is spotless, probably cleaner than when she left it. The bed looks like it never gets slept in.

"You know what I think?" He sits down on the bed. "I think you've been lying to me. I think Lucho never lived here, and that you kids have been living here by yourselves all along."

"No way, Lucho was here. She slept right there." I point to the other side of the bed. The side that used to be his.

"Sure, when your mother was here. I bet she slept here all the time. And it pisses me off, too, don't think it doesn't." He stands up, turning around to fix the blanket where he was sitting. "But when Arcelia left, she left. There was nothing else to keep her here."

"That's not how it happened, Scottie."

"But it happened didn't it? She left you guys alone."

I don't say anymore. We stand there in silence, staring at each other. After a while Luz walks into the room holding

Trini's hand.

"Okay, she's all set." She hands Scottie a pink bag with a picture of Barbie painted on the outside. "I put in some dolls and books and an extra change of clothes, just in case."

"You know what," Scottie says, "we're gonna need a lot more than that."

He picks Trini up and carries her back into our bedroom, asking her to point to her favorite things. Trini says the window is her favorite thing. He stuffs the bag with as many clothes as he can and tucks a few stuffed animals in his armpit. He grabs her blanket from the crib but Luz tears it away from him.

"What are you doing?" Luz asks. "Cristo, what's he doing?"

I look at her but don't say anything.

"Well, do something, don't just stand there. Stop him." Luz throws herself at Scottie and starts pulling the stuffed animals from his arms. He shoves her away and she falls to the ground, knocking her head on the bed frame. It sounds like a watermelon hitting the ground.

"Don't touch her." I get in Scottie's face. "Don't you dare touch my sister." I help Luz get up and we stand together, blocking his way out of the room.

"Move, Cristo." I can tell by the tone of his voice he's getting angry. "Don't make me do something we'll both regret."

I look up at Scottie, who towers over me like a building. "I can't make you do anything."

"You're right," he says. Then he walks straight through us like we're not even there. I grab onto his belt buckle, but he knocks me off with a backhand. His fist feels like a boot in my chest. He covers my face with his hand and pushes me to the ground. "Stay down, kid. Don't make me fight you."

"Fuck off."

When I stand up I come face to face with his fist, which is as hard as a doorknob. I feel needles coming from my nose and suddenly I can't breathe. The right side of my face goes numb. Blood spills into my mouth and I bend over to spit it onto the carpet. One of my silver teeth, smooth and pointed like a bullet, sits in the middle of the pool of blood.

Scottie rubs his hand. "Damn you got a hard head." Then

he grabs Trini and walks out of the room.

More blood pours from my nose as I stand up. I wipe it on the back of my hand. Luz picks up my tooth but I can't see what she does with it. She runs to the door after him. "Why are you doing this? Why are you taking her?"

Trini is crying and yelling, "No, no, no" over and over again. Scottie tries to keep her quiet by covering her mouth with his hand. She flops in his arms like a huge fish.

"She's my daughter," he says, struggling to keep hold of her. "I'm just trying to protect her."

"And what about us?" Luz follows him down the stairs, her face filled with fury. "Why don't you want to protect us?"

Scottie stops next to his car, which is parked sideways in the driveway like a blind person was driving. "I'm calling the social worker when I get home. You guys shouldn't be living here, not alone like this. It ain't right." He shoves Trini into the car and buckles her into the backseat, ignoring the car seat that waits in the driveway like a well-trained dog.

"This ain't right, Scottie," I say. "You taking Trini like this ain't right." I spit a chunk of bloody snot onto the sidewalk. The hole where my tooth used to be starts to ache, but I ignore it. Trini is still crying as she waves good-bye with two hands, one for each of us. I force myself to wave back.

Luz looks at me. "Cristo. Please."

I turn away. "What do you want me to do? He's her father."

"I don't care," Luz says. "That doesn't mean anything."

Scottie looks back at us. He stands next to the car, his hand on the opened door.

"What do you guys want from me?" He shakes his head, as if he can't believe what we're doing to him. "You know I can't take all three of you. You aren't even my kids for Christ sake."

"Fuck you, Scottie," I say. "Fuck you and fuck the social worker and fuck Lucho. We don't need any of you." I give him the finger as he hops into the car and drives away.

"Come on, Luz, come inside." I poke her in the arm. "We don't need the whole neighborhood knowing our business." I walk back to the porch, hoping she'll follow.

She turns her head to me without moving the rest of her

body. Her face has no expression, but her eyes are filled with tears. I don't remember the last time I saw her cry.

"I can't believe this," she says. She blinks to keep the tears from falling. "I can't believe he would do that."

"Why not? He's always been an asshole. Some things don't change."

"He took her like she was a piece of furniture. Like he owns her." She slowly climbs up the stairs, coming to stand next to me on the porch. "We have to get her back, Cristo. I don't know how, but we have to do something."

"I know." I don't say it out loud, but all I can think is it would kill Mami if she knew what Scottie just did. It would make her want to kill.

"He's right about one thing," I tell her. "We aren't his. We don't belong with him."

Luz looks down at her feet. "Sometimes I used to wish he was our real father, when he and Mami were together and he used to do nice things for us. But now I'm happy he's not." She picks up a sock that's lying on the porch and tucks it into her pocket. "I just wish he wasn't Trini's either. Then he would forget about her just like he's forgotten about us."

I nod, even though I don't agree with her, because I know she needs me to. Now that it's just the two of us, I'm gonna have to do a lot of things I don't want to do, like spend extra time with her like when we were little and I couldn't get her to stop following me around.

We walk inside and clean up the best we can. If Scottie really does call the social worker, I figure we only got a day or two in this place, until some lady from DCYF shows up asking lots of questions about where our guardian went. I don't say anything to Luz, but in my mind I'm packing up the house already, taking only the small things we can carry on our backs. Fuck if I know where to go, but if Scottie calls the state we can't stay here. Lots of kids from school end up in foster homes and from what they say it never works out. They think kids can't take care of themselves, but we've done okay so far. Nobody died and we didn't burn the house down, and before Scottie flipped out all three of us were still together. Adults always think they know what's best, but all I ever see is them making everything worse.

The fridge is empty so I make oatmeal for dinner, with nondairy creamer and Sweet'n Low I grabbed from Dunkin' Donuts. My mouth still hurts from where Scottie popped me, so I ask Luz to check it out after we eat. We find a piece of tinfoil to use as a mirror and stand under the brightest light in the kitchen.

"It looks okay," she says, poking around in my mouth with a chopstick. "The bleeding stopped."

I feel the fleshy gum with my tongue. "It feels like a piece of the tooth is still in there."

"I don't see anything." She pokes it again, which makes me cry out. A hot pain shoots into my skull, worse than an ice cream headache.

"Jesus Christ, Luz."

"Sorry."

I grab the tinfoil away from her and look for myself. It looks better than how it feels in my mouth so I decide to forget about it.

"At least it's on the bottom," Luz says. "Nobody will be able to see it unless you smile real big."

I ignore her lame joke and ask her what she did with the tooth.

"I put it in Mami's jewelry box, with Trini's baby teeth. In case she wants to see it."

I laugh. "She don't want my busted tooth."

"You never know," Luz says. "She's kept stranger things." We both look at the clock with the eagles on it and I'm about to tell her about the money when she hands me a bottle of baby aspirin.

"Here, I found these in the medicine cabinet. For the pain," she says.

I grab a few and chew them up into a sweet cherry paste, which I jam into the toothless gum with the tip of my tongue. It burns a little, but then goes numb.

We play a few games of dominoes before bed. I let Luz beat me so she'll go to bed happy. When she asks for a bedtime snack I think about using some of the money from Mami's clock to buy a couple of pizzas, but I figure if I spend it on food it will disappear by the end of the weekend. Instead, I empty packets of soy sauce into a bowl and we dip stale crackers into it. I thought we gave Trini the last of the powdered milk, but Luz finds some in a box under the sink. She offers to share it with me but there's only enough for one cup and I want one of us to feel full. She drinks it fast like she doesn't want me to feel bad and then fills the cup with water and drinks that, too.

After she goes to sleep my stomach is still growling so I pour ketchup into some water and pretend I'm drinking tomato juice. I thought I could handle being hungry all the time, but lately it's been hard. Some nights I can't sleep because my stomach aches so bad, and later when I do sleep I always have crazy dreams about eating tons of food. Then I'm sad when I wake up in the morning and that feeling of being full disappears.

When I'm lying in bed at the end of the night, I'm still thinking about Trini. I wonder how much she understands and if she knows she's not coming back here. She's the same age I was when Mami left me in Puerto Rico and all I knew was that Mami was gone and she didn't take me with her. We moved in with Abuela in the house where Papi grew up, and I slept on a cot in his old bedroom. All I had was a bear she left me and my baby blanket, and I remember looking at the ceiling for hours, crying while I tried to fall asleep. One night I cried so hard my nose started to bleed and when I woke up Papi, he told me to use my shirt to wipe it up. In the morning there was blood all over my pajamas and when Abuela came in she fell to her knees at the side of my bed and started screaming. When I sat up she closed her eyes and crossed herself and said *Gracias por Dios* again and again until she lost her voice.

Tonight Trini will go to sleep in a room by herself for the first time in her life. When she loses her blanket in the middle of the night, nobody will be there to cover her back up. She won't know what's wrong or why she's cold, but a part of her will know that something's missing.

In three months our family's been cut in half. If that happens again, I'll be the only one left.

Miss Valentín

The best thing about not being pregnant is that I can have a drink whenever I want. The worst thing: I'm still alone. I give myself the first week of summer to mourn the baby I never had. I sit around in my pajamas and watch tapes of *General Hospital* and eat entire packages of Entenmanns's coffee cake. I listen to gospel music and stare at a journal I bought years ago but have never written in. Then, on the eighth day, I make myself get over it. I shower and get dressed and thank God for sparing me the phone conversation with my parents, the morning sickness, the midwife checkups on my own, and the hours of drug-free labor I would have guilted myself into enduring. I tell myself I'm okay, maybe actually happy, with not being pregnant. But there's a part of me, the smallest, quietest, most frightened part, that still wants a baby.

That's when I decide to research adoption. I look into the options in Rhode Island and internationally, and then I contact the state about how to get started. They tell me there are classes I'd need to take and home studies to be done, but that if I wanted a child in my house, if I wasn't picky about race, sex, or ability, then foster care would be the fastest way. They say that some placements become permanent if the match is right, but others only last a few weeks or months. They ask me if I'm okay with that, or if I'll find it impossible to say good-bye.

"Well," I tell the woman over the phone, "I want to be a mother, not a boardinghouse." There is a long pause before she responds.

"You're looking for TPR kids then, the ones whose parents have already lost their rights. Those are the kids who are free."

Before she hangs up she asks if I have any other concerns. I can't help but laugh.

"Lady, I bet I have as many concerns as you've got kids in the system."

She doesn't laugh. "I doubt that."

It takes me several minutes to list all my worries. She tells me I've cut into her lunch hour so she has to go, but I should bring my concerns to the orientation meeting. "Write them down so you don't forget them," she suggests, her voice lighter now that she knows we're almost done.

When we hang up, I'm alone with my anxiety once again. I worry about all the standard problems: behavioral, emotional, and psychological. I worry about the child not attaching to me. I worry about wanting to send him back. I stay up many nights wondering if I'm brave enough to really do this, if I'm dumb enough, rich enough, smart enough, loving enough, desperate enough, hopeful enough to take a stranger into my home and love him like he came out of me. Some nights I don't have an answer.

What saves me is thinking about my class, all my kids, and how I love each one of them. Even the troublemakers, the whiners, the perfectionists, and the merely average. And I think about Cristo. If that kid can still show love after the life he's seen, imagine what you can do with a baby, or a three-year-old. You can practically start over. You can give them the life they deserve.

When César gets shot it makes me more certain—even the children who have homes aren't always safe. I take Cristo to the hospital as often as I can, but I also go on my own, in the off-hours when César's alone in the room and seems to be suffocating under all those tubes. I bring him the books we read in class last year, even the ones he hated (which was most of them) and read to him under the fluorescent lights of the stale hospital room. When he regains consciousness I bring him comic books, and even though he can't read yet he holds them tight by their glossy covers and won't let go. That's when I know he's going to be okay.

I'm not there the day he starts speaking, but two days later, when I show up with lollipops for him and doughnuts for the nurses, the first thing he says to me is, "Damn, Teacher, you just missed Jerry Springer," smiling with the remote control in his hand.

As the summer goes on César continues to get stronger. After they take him off the ventilation tube, he starts to walk and feed himself. The seizures decrease and his headaches, while frequent, are generally less intense. His eyesight in the left eye comes back and he starts playing video games on the Game Boy the nurses got him for his birthday. Sure, he's stuck in the hospital for the whole summer, but at least he's alive—and at least his personality is back. That's a blessing in itself.

In all the times I visit, I only see his grandmother once. It's during the first week, when he's still unconscious and we're all nervous and speaking in hushed voices, not sure which way it will go. She comes into the room while I'm reading to him and places a bouquet of white flowers in the plastic pitcher by his bed. The room fills with the scent of magnolia. I smile at her and she drops her head in response. She hums a song I know from my childhood, from visits to my *abuela*'s apartment on Sunday mornings when I thought every beautiful song in the world was recorded on one of the albums she stacked like books on her shelf. His grandmother leaves before I can ask her the name of the song.

When I walk out I see her sitting in a chair by the elevators, knitting what looks like a baby blanket. I try to make eye contact but she won't look up. She keeps her eyes on her work, tying the knots so quickly her fingers blur together as if her hands were as soft and pliable as yarn, as if she were weaving pieces of herself into the pattern.

◆ ❖ ◆

I get back from Puerto Rico the Friday before Labor Day, tanned and rested and excited about the new school year. I decide to go grocery shopping, the perfect activity for an overweight girl on a Friday night, and my plan is to spend a quiet evening watching the Yankees destroy the Twins. I soon find out God had other plans.

It's after eight when I get back from the store and the game has already started. I carry the bags from my car to the back door in one trip, setting them down in the dark. I'd forgotten to leave the porch light on, still not used to the night coming on so quickly, and I see an odd shape in the corner, something that looks like a body. I'm so startled I bang into the screen door and almost fall right off the porch. At first it looks like only one person, a man, I think, homeless or maybe just drunk and lost, but when I see it move, see it break apart like a magic trick into two smaller bodies, two children's bodies, only then do I recognize them. Cristo and Luz, huddled together like seals on the beach, attempting to sleep under a canvas tarp meant to cover firewood.

"Sorry, Teacher, we didn't mean to scare you." Cristo stands up quickly, struggling to fold the tarp into a neat square.

"Jesus Christ." I lean against the house to catch my breath.

My groceries have spilled all over the porch, cans of beans and olive jars rolling along the dusty wood floor. Luz starts to repack. She picks up several bags of chips.

"You having a party, Miss Valentín?"

"They were on sale," I tell her, which is a lie. It tumbles out of my mouth before I even know I'm forming it. As a child I often lied to my parents about food, but since college I've lived alone, so I'm not used to answering questions about my eating.

"Here, we'll help you carry everything inside." Cristo grabs the remainder of the bags and leads the way up the back staircase. He knows my kitchen like he lives here, even though he's only visited twice, and he puts everything away without my help. When Luz asks to use the bathroom I take her there myself, showing her where the light switch is hidden and how to jiggle the handle on the toilet so the water stops running. Back in the kitchen, I ask Cristo an obvious question.

"What's going on?"

He shrugs and looks out the window into the dark. "Nothing."

"You just happened to be in the neighborhood?"

He smiles that half-crooked smile. "Yeah." He nibbles on the chips I set out, pretending he's not hungry.

"Have you eaten?"

"Today? Sure."

"I meant dinner." I look at the clock on my microwave, which reads 8:42.

"Oh. Not really."

"I've got some rice and beans and leftover chicken from lunch. I'll heat it up for you."

"No, you don't have to go to any trouble," he says. "Unless you were already going to do it for yourself."

I put my hand on his perfectly round head, the buzz cut now grown out, and turn his face to look at me. "Are you hungry or not?"

"Yes." He blinks as if to punctuate it.

I put the leftovers in the oven to heat up and get some plates from the cabinet. He watches me while I set the table.

"How was your trip?" he asks.

"Nice. A little long, but it was good."

"How are your parents?"

I look over at him, gesturing with a handful of silverware. "Can we stop talking about me for a minute? How are you, how is *your* parent?"

He looks down and shrugs. "Not so good, I guess." He picks up his soda, takes a small sip, and puts it back down. "I'm in trouble, Teacher."

"Why? What happened?" I try to keep my voice calm.

"It's a long story."

I pull out a chair so I can sit down next to him. He talks quickly, looking at his hands the entire time.

"Lucho left and Scottie took Trini and we can't stay in the house anymore because he called DCYF and this lady is looking for me and we don't have anything or anywhere to go."

"Okay, okay, hang on a minute. Back up and start from the beginning. Lucho left?"

He nods.

"When?"

"A few weeks ago. Maybe a month."

"Why didn't you tell me?"

"I thought she'd come back. Every other time she came back. But this time, I guess not."

"Where have you been staying?"

"At home."

I cover my face with my hands. "Please don't tell me by yourself."

"It's okay, Teacher. We were fine until Scottie found out and took Trini and called the social worker."

"He did the right thing calling them. I would have too if you had told me."

He plays with the salt and pepper shakers on the table. "So I was right not to tell you."

"Maybe you were."

He leans back in his chair, the front legs off the floor, just like he used to do in class. We listen to the clicks of the oven as it warms, saying nothing. Finally, he brings the chair back down, dropping it onto its front legs without making a sound.

"Well it doesn't matter anyway because we left and now I don't know where to go."

"What about your mom's cousin, can't you stay with him?"

"Chino and Kim are in New York for the weekend. Their place is locked, I already checked. And Scottie doesn't want us, and our neighbors have their grandkids in town and there's nobody else."

"Cristo." I touch his hand. "If you're worried about where you're going to sleep for the weekend, don't. You can stay here, you know that. But once school starts... You need a real solution."

"I'm not going to a foster home, Teacher. They'll split us up." He pulls his hand away from mine. "They always split up older kids."

"Relax, we won't let that happen."

He shakes his head. "I promise you, I'm not going."

"I'll talk to Chino and Kim. We'll work it out."

"Why can't we stay here, Teacher? You've got room. And it would only be for a few months."

"It's not that simple." I stand up to check on the food. "I

can't just keep you like a bird I'd watch for a friend. There's paperwork to fill out and laws we have to follow—"

"Do you want money?" He pulls some crumpled bills from his pocket. "How much do you need?"

"*Dios mío*, put your money away. I don't want your money." I inhale deeply and look up at the ceiling. "We have to do what your mother would want. And what the social worker thinks is best."

"Mami wanted us at home, with Lucho. That's why she made her our guardian. She wanted us to stay together."

Luz walks in and stands in the corner against the wall. She sucks on the end of her braid like it's made of honey.

"Come on, time to eat." I open the oven door, shocked by the rush of dry heat. I close my eyes quickly, before they start to water, and blindly pull out the dish.

I serve them on TV trays and we sit in the living room watching the Yankees beat the Twins, seven to four. When Jeter hits a home run we cheer like we're at Yankee Stadium, sharing a three-way hug. After the game I make up the guest bed and tuck them in, leaving them together in the dark.

A long while later, when I'm certain they're asleep, I go back into the kitchen and serve myself the bowl of ice cream I would have eaten for dinner if they hadn't shown up. I eat it quickly, standing against the kitchen sink, and then I wash all the dishes, making sure to dry the ice cream scoop and hide it in the back in the utensil drawer so nobody sees it. I feel stuffed and guilty now, so I decide to go to bed, hoping to fall asleep before I start listening to the voice in my head that tells me how weak I am, right before it tells me to go eat some more.

I check on Cristo and Luz just once during the night, peeking my head into the room to make sure they're still there. They sleep in two straight lines, not touching each other, with the covers folded down at their waists, as if they don't want to mess up the bed or take full advantage of the heat that the blankets have to offer.

◆ ❖ ◆

The weekend is surprisingly warm, so I decide to take them to the beach. Not to Narragansett, where lots of city employees go, but all the way down to Galilee, where we're less likely to run into anyone we know. I don't let myself think about it, but I'm breaking the law by keeping them; I'm harboring runaways. On the other hand, it seems absurd that there could be anything wrong with what I'm doing, which feels like the most simple and correct thing I've done all summer. I don't think of myself as a risk-taker, but on a scale of one to ten I'd say I'm right at thirteen—my lucky number.

As is my tradition, we eat clam cakes and chowder from Iggy's and watch the ferries come in from Block Island. Luz stands on the breakers and waves at each passing boat for so long her arm must be sore afterwards. We got here late so the beach is mostly empty. Cristo stays in the water all afternoon, but he runs up to me occasionally, dripping cold salt water from his goose-pimpled body, and asks me if I saw him ride to the shore on a big wave, do a handstand in the shallow water, or hold that dead fish by the tail and toss it out to sea. I say, "Yes, of course," even if I missed the entire thing, and he beams with pride, like he has created every wonder in the ocean all by himself.

When he gets out to warm up we talk about everything but school. He asks questions about my childhood, my parents, and why I have no siblings. He wants to know how many countries I've been to, and why the Puerto Rican flag and the Cuban flag look so much alike. He wants to know about my favorite musician, the best meal I've ever had, who I dated in college, the name of my first pet, when I was the most scared in my life, how I knew I wanted to be a grammar school teacher, my birth date, my middle name, and how come I don't wear any jewelry. He also wants to know who I love most in the world.

I do my best to be honest, but many of the answers are things I don't want to admit to myself, let alone to one of my students. I turn the questions around and he tells me he's never had a pet, has only been to Puerto Rico and the States, loves hip-hop, wants to be a DJ when he grows up, and gets scared anytime it's too quiet.

When I ask him about starting school on Tuesday and going

into the fifth grade, his face falls and his mood changes dramatically.

"I don't want to go back, Teacher."

"Come on, it's not that bad. That's how everyone feels in September."

He sits down next to me, soaking the edge of my towel. "Why do I have to change teachers every year?"

"Because you get smarter every year and you need more challenges. You wouldn't want to be fourteen and in the fourth grade would you?"

He runs his hand over the sand, smoothing out the peaks and valleys.

"But why does changing grades have to mean a new teacher? Why can't you move with us?"

"My job is to teach the fourth grade. If I moved up to fifth, what would Mrs. Reed do?"

"You could switch with her."

I adjust myself on the towel, bumping into his body. His skin still holds the temperature of the ocean, which cools my leg like an ice pack.

"And what about when you get to junior high, would you want me to change schools?"

He shrugs. "You could." He smiles. "You're smart, they'd hire you over there, too."

"You're crazy, little boy." I push him gently. When his body separates from my leg I feel the loss instantly.

"I just like your class, Teacher."

"You'll like other classes, too. You just have to get used to it. Remember how you hated my class last fall, how you wanted to go back to third grade with Mr. Clauser?"

He digs into the sand with his foot. "Yeah."

"Just give it time."

"But it's going to be different this year. With Marco in Regular Ed and César..."

"You'll still see Marco, his classroom is right next door to yours. And César will be back, as soon as the doctors say he's ready."

The hole he digs is big enough for both his feet, and he

buries them together in the sand.

"What if he's never ready? If his headaches never go away and his eyes stay messed up and he has to wear that stupid helmet for the rest of his life? Then what?"

"He's a tough kid. He survived a gunshot to the head—don't you think he can handle fifth grade?"

He places a chunk of driftwood in the sand above his feet like a gravestone. "They're going to tease him. When he wears that helmet to school."

"Not if you explain it to them."

He looks up. "He's got a bullet in his head, it's not that hard to get."

I put my arm around him and pull him to me, breaking his body out of the burial ground. His bony shoulders are warm from the sun. An older lady walks by and smiles at us. I smile back, knowing that she thinks I'm with my son.

"He'll be okay, Cristo. You'll both be okay."

He goes back in the water after that, and when Luz joins him later they play catch with a tennis ball. As I watch them I let myself imagine that they are mine, that I will bring them here again and again over the years, watching their bodies grow into teenagers, then adults. I know right now that I want to take him, and I would take Luz, too, but what he needs is a temporary solution, a temporary mother, and I'm looking for something real. Something permanent. All they need is someone to help for a few more months, until his mother gets out of prison, and that person can't be me. I know that for certain. If I get any more involved, I'm going to get my heart broken.

After a while they call my name and wave for me to come into the water. I shake my head and yell that I'm too tired, but when they threaten to come get me I finally give in. I finish the doughboy I'm eating and wipe my sugary fingers on the towel, scanning the near-empty beach. An old man watching birds, a family napping under an umbrella, teenagers holding hands. It is safe, I decide; no one will notice me. Then I undress down to my swimsuit, fighting the desire to keep my T-shirt on. The sun feels good on my skin and for a second I don't think about my body. I walk into the water slowly, wincing at the shock of cold, and wait to go numb.

They are splashing in the surf and laughing like the waves are telling jokes, and even though I'm smiling at them I suddenly start to cry. The tears feel cold on my suntanned cheeks. I lean over the water and splash my face as the tears fall, trying to wash them away. I walk blindly into the surf and when I'm covered up to my thighs, I dive in and swim out to meet them. I keep my face in the water and repeat the same phrase over and over again as I pull my body through the choppy waves. Something I first heard in graduate school, and what the principal tells us every year in the opening assembly. What my mother says when I tell her too many stories about my class.

These are not your children.

Luz

During César's first week back at school, Cristo gets into three fights. Each one starts when someone teases César about the plastic helmet he has to wear. Each one ends with Cristo being pulled off the kid and dragged down to the principal's office. After the third incident, he gets an in-school suspension for two weeks and has his lunch periods taken away. While the rest of the fifth grade has lunch in the cafeteria, he has to sit on a bench outside the principal's office, eating breakfast leftovers with the secretary. Rumors around school say they wanted to kick him out but a teacher fought for him to stay. No mystery who that could be.

On the last day of his suspension I see him in the principal's office with Mrs. Reed. Since I'm the president of my class I have to deliver the attendance sheets from my teacher to the office every Friday. I usually give it to the secretary but last year she taught me how to copy the sheets myself and file them in the class folder in case she was ever gone. Today she's out on a D'Angelo's run when I get there, so I walk around her desk without needing permission and start to make the copies. I can tell something's going on in the principal's office, since the door is mostly shut and the voices inside sound low and serious. When I peek around the corner, I see a slice of the principal's desk, the edge of Mrs. Reed's red skirt, and Cristo's legs hanging down from his seat, his big old sneakers swaying in sync with the flash of the copy machine.

The principal, Dr. Hoover, comes out from behind the

desk to talk to Cristo. He's wearing a dark gray suit that makes him look like the mayor.

"We're only three weeks into school, Mr. Perez. If this is what you're doing now I can't imagine what we have to look forward to as the semester unfolds."

"I don't think it's that bad," Mrs. Reed cuts in. "Not yet. I'm expecting things to settle down as he gets more comfortable in my class. This has been a hard transition for him. Understandably so…"

"All our students come from…challenging homes. I don't think we can use that as an excuse." Dr. Hoover sits on the edge of his desk.

"I'm not saying it's an excuse. I think it's an explanation."

"And last year, when his mother *was* home, what was the explanation then?"

Mrs. Reed fixes the hem on her skirt. She doesn't have an answer. Nobody talks for a while and even though I'm finished, I stand at the copier and pretend to collect my sheets. I watch Dr. Hoover pull out the attendance log for Mrs. Reed's class.

"According to these sheets you've been late to school every day. What's the problem here?"

"He just moved," Mrs. Reed cuts in. "He and his sister, they have a new guardian. Your uncle, right?"

"Cousin," Cristo says. "My cousin Chino."

"So they're no longer on the bus route—"

"How do you get to school?" Dr. Hoover asks.

"I walk," Cristo says.

"From where?"

"Mount Pleasant."

"That's a pretty far walk."

Cristo shrugs. "It's cool." He plays with his sneakers, slipping the heels on and off. They look big enough to fit a man.

"Well, I can overlook the tardiness for a while. But the behavior issues will not be tolerated." Dr. Hoover points at Cristo with a ruler. "The bottom line is this: you follow the rules at this school or you'll be asked to leave. Is that understood?"

I see Cristo cross his feet at the ankles. "Yeah."

Dr. Hoover leans forward. "I'm sorry, did you say

something?"

Cristo clears his throat. "Yes."

"Yes, what?"

"Yes, I understand."

"Good." Dr. Hoover stands. "Now, if you'll excuse us, I need to speak with Mrs. Reed alone for a few minutes."

Cristo leaves the room, closing the door behind him. He keeps his head down and goes right back to his spot on the bench. For a few seconds I stare at him without him seeing me, but he seems so sad I end up looking away.

"You spying on me now?" His voice shoots like an arrow across the room.

"No. I had to copy the attendance sheets for my teacher." I lift up the folder to show him. "Besides, I didn't hear anything."

He makes a face at me. "Whatever." He can always tell when I'm lying.

"You all right?" I hesitate before eventually walking toward him. "You get in more trouble?"

He shrugs. "They can't do anything to me."

"They can expel you."

"So what? There's always another school." He leans back, tapping his head softly against the wall.

"Not one with Bilingual. Not one with Miss Valentín." I push his lunch tray over to make room for myself on the bench. He picks up a piece of leftover waffle, inspecting it.

"They think this is punishment, eating up here all alone. Who cares?" Cristo pops the waffle into his mouth. "Shit, it's the only quiet part of my day."

"I'm pretty sure the food is better up here," I tell him. "We had meatloaf."

He takes another bite and talks with his mouth full. "They think it's bad because it's cold and dry, but they don't know bad." He drops the fork, which falls loudly onto his tray. "Try no food."

I want to say something funny, but what I come up with makes no sense.

"I think it's better to eat breakfast in the middle of the day," I finally say. "Then it stays with you longer."

He laughs and shakes his head. "Seriously, Luz, where do you get this stuff?"

"Books, mostly." I feel my cheeks get hot so I try to hide my face behind the folder. Isn't that where everybody learns things?

"Course you'd say that."

The bell rings and I stand up automatically, heading for the door. Cristo doesn't move.

"Aren't you coming?"

"I gotta wait." He points toward the closed door.

"Why didn't you tell them about César? How you were sticking up for him and not just starting fights for no reason?"

"They don't care about the truth, Luz. It only matters what they see."

"But that's stupid. They can't see everything."

He looks at me but doesn't say anything else. The room starts to fill up with people—teachers checking their boxes, kids turning in permission slips—and soon I can't see him clearly anymore. Within seconds he's lost in the chaos of the crowd.

◆ ❖ ◆

I don't care what anybody says, this place isn't my home. I wake up here, I eat dinner here, I watch TV here, I read books here—I even shower here—but I don't live here. Chino does, and Kim, and Sammy, and their parrot, Lucas, but not me. Not Cristo. We're here because we don't have anyplace else to go.

I wanted to stay with Miss Valentín, but turns out she didn't want us. We were there for a weekend, but by the time school started she had us packed up and shipped over here like we had never set foot in her house. It was fun over there, too, watching baseball games and doing 1,000-piece jigsaw puzzles, eating popcorn out of the bowl with no hands. Leaving her place was a lot harder than leaving our house on Sophia Street. I asked my mother once what the difference was between a house and a home and she said you can move in and out of a house, but once you have a home you never leave it.

We're supposed to feel at home here, since Chino's our

family and we've known Kim and Sammy since Trini was born, but I still feel weird hanging around in my pajamas or walking in the front door without knocking. I don't even open the fridge without asking first. And forget about the TV—I won't even turn it on by myself, or hold onto the clicker for more than a couple of seconds. Especially if Sammy's around. It's hard to believe he's an only child since that kid fights for things like he's competing for an Olympic medal. He's supposed to be sharing his bedroom with Cristo but he won't even give him a drawer for his clothes or a pillow to sleep on, even though he's got three big ones that are taller than me. Every night Cristo pretends to go to bed in there, but after Kim goes into her room he sneaks out to the living room where I'm sleeping on the pull-out couch and climbs in with me. Then, since Chino gets up early to open the garage, he sneaks back into Sammy's bedroom before the sun rises and gets dressed in the dark.

Their house is bigger than our old apartment, but it feels cheap, like you could easily put your hand right through the wall just by touching it. The same dull yellow carpet runs through every room, patchy and grayed in spots like an old stray dog, and the curtains are always closed, even on a sunny day. Their fridge is huge—the kind you see in a cafeteria—and it takes over most of the kitchen. The funny thing is, it's usually half empty. Kim never cooks, she either brings home takeout from the Chinese place next to the salon she works at, or just orders from the sub shop down the street. The TV is half the size of the fridge; if I stand in front of the middle of it and try to stretch out my hands to touch either side, I can't reach. Seriously, I don't know how they got it in the front door. I guess it's like a crib, how you buy it in a million pieces and have to build it inside the room. But nobody around here looks like they could build anything.

They live in Mount Pleasant, which is close enough to Olneyville that we can walk back to our old bus stop and catch the school bus in the mornings, but usually we're late and we have to walk the whole way. Which makes us even later. But in other ways it seems real far away. Like for one thing, the streets are completely empty at night. Which I think is kind of spooky, but the old people say it's safer that way. I think it feels lonely, like going to the park on a holiday. People here have grass in their backyards and short fences around their front-yards, with flowerpots and miniature plastic animals stuck into the ground. Most of the people are Italian, like Kim, and I never hear anyone speaking Spanish on the streets. The worst part is, we can't speak it inside either because Kim says it's rude to say things that she and Sammy can't understand. Then she asks how would we like to be left out of conversations and made to feel stupid all the time. I don't bother saying that's how every kid in America feels, and every Puerto Rican who's ever moved to the United States. You'd think a grownup would have figured that out. At the beginning we kept slipping, but now Cristo never speaks to me in Spanish, even when Kim's not around. Next thing you know he'll stop eating rice and beans, and he'll record over all his salsa tapes and be just like any other American kid, eating pizza and Pop-Tarts and listening to rap music. In the future you might be able to be Puerto Rican and American at the same time, but I don't think it's happening anytime soon.

Kim has a bunch of other rules, too, like we have to stay inside after dinner and always tell her where we're going, even if it's just to the backyard. And she makes us do all the dishes, wash our own clothes, and take out the trash every day so the kitchen doesn't start to smell like a Chinese restaurant. I don't know why, but she runs this place like a detention center instead of a house. I try to follow her rules, not because I want to, but because it's easier to shut up and blend into the wallpaper. Cristo hates dealing with any adult who isn't his teacher or his boss, so he doesn't say anything when Kim tells him what to do, but when the time comes he just sneaks out and does what he wants anyway.

I always finish my homework right after school, while Cristo and Sammy play video games, so by the time dinner's over and we've done our chores there's not much to do. Sometimes we watch *Law & Order* reruns or old sitcoms from the '80s, but mostly I read books I find at the Laundromat or the flea market. While the rest of them watch wrestling or action movies, I sit on the floor with my back to them, trying to shut out the sound of cars crashing and angry rich people having sex.

I miss having Trini around. Even though it was a lot of work to look after her, she was also fun to play with, and to hold and rock to sleep if she was scared. When I think of her now I see her wearing mismatched socks pulled up high to her knees like a soccer player, laughing at some stupid joke I'm telling her and feeding popcorn to the cat. We never had our own cat, but she used to do it to the neighbor's cat Gus all the time.

It's been a month since Scottie took her and we've only seen her one time. He promised we could see her whenever we wanted, but every time we try to meet them at the park he says she's not feeling too good and he needs to keep her home. We call her before bed some nights and she cries about missing us and her blankie and the way Cristo used to rock her crib in the night with his foot. "I want to come home," she always says before hanging up, and then we have to tell her we don't have a home anymore.

Cristo never says he misses her but I know he does. He just doesn't like to talk about things he can't fix. I guess that's why we don't talk about our mother either. But it's different with her because part of her leaving was her own fault. Not when they took her out in handcuffs, but before, when she did all the bad things that got her into trouble. Maybe if she had thought about us more she wouldn't have done them in the first place and now we'd all be together in our old apartment watching old movies and eating *pasteles* and *mofongo*, wondering what to name our new cat.

One night before going to bed, Cristo tells me he thinks Kim agreed to take us so they can get money from the state.

"She's going to file for temporary custody and collect checks like César's grandmother did when she agreed to take him in."

He pulls the cushions off the couch and starts making up the bed.

"But she's not even related to us. Chino is."

"Exactly, dummy, that's why it'll work. She'll get money because she's taking in kids she doesn't have any ties to. So she ends up looking like this nice lady who's just trying to help."

I put down my book to get our pillows from the closet. "I thought she *was* trying to help us."

He shakes his head. "You know, for a straight-A student you're not always that smart."

"Well, she is letting us stay here."

"Yeah, right," he says, making a face. "And she's letting us do all the dishes and take out the trash and eat cold chicken wings instead of giving them to the stray dogs to finish off. Sure, she's going out of her way to help us. A real fucking saint."

He spreads the comforter over the mattress and tucks it in at the bottom. Then he climbs into bed with his English Reader textbook and opens it to Chapter One, even though we're three weeks into the school year and my class is already on Chapter Five. I sit down next to him, pulling my backpack onto my lap. I take out my math book and slowly peel off the recycled paper cover the teachers always ask us to put over our books. I pull out a thick white envelope from the inside of the cover, where I hid it back in June, right after they took her away. It has my mother's name written in block letters across the top, right under the printed words that say: *Women, Infants, and Children.*

"Here." I hand Cristo the envelope.

"Where'd you get this?" he asks, turning it over to examine both sides.

"From the jar in the kitchen, where she used to keep it."

"Hang on," he says, sliding his finger inside the envelope to count the remaining checks. "I looked for these in the summer, when she first went away. I thought we were all out."

His eyes narrow and for the first time since taking them, I worry that he might be mad.

"I didn't want anything to happen to them," I tell him. "I was trying to help."

"And you didn't think we needed them, after Lucho left?"

"Look at the dates. They weren't good back then." I point to the place on each check where it lists the dates you can use them. "See, they're only good now. Two hundred each, for September, October, and November."

He studies the checks like he doesn't believe me. "Does

Kim know you have these?"

I shake my head. "I didn't tell anyone. I knew you wouldn't want me to."

"Good." He tucks the checks back into the envelope. "You did good, Luz." He smiles at me, and then tugs on one of my braids. I reach out and tug on a piece of his hair to get him back. Usually his hair is so short I can't grab anything, but now it's so long it's starting to curl.

"Wow, you need a haircut," I tell him, hoping he doesn't take it as an insult.

"Yeah, I was thinking about asking Kim, but..." He runs his hand over the top of his head like he's checking a carpet for wet spots.

"What, you don't want her touching your head?"

"Nah, it's not that." He shrugs. "I just don't want to owe her anything. Anything more."

I guess he's talking about how she's letting us stay here and everything, but I'm not thinking about what we owe her or anybody else. We're the ones who lost our home and our mother and our baby sister. Why doesn't anyone think about who owes us?

I already finished my homework, so I put away my math book and pull out a novel by some guy named John Irving I found sitting on the roof of an abandoned car. I like reading about a family crazier than mine. For a long time we sit like that, reading together on the pull-out couch. If somebody passed by and looked in the window I bet we'd look like a normal family spending time together on a Tuesday night. Occasionally, when Cristo doesn't know a word, he leans over and points to it, and I say it out loud and he repeats it and then we go back to the quiet.

A little bit later his pager goes off, startling us both. He checks it without saying a word, then exhales and closes his book. He gets out of the bed and pulls on his sneakers and a sweatshirt.

"I thought you stopped working for Snowman."

"I never said that."

"But when we left Sophia Street, I just figured...you didn't need to do it anymore."

"Well you figured wrong."

I hold my finger in the book to keep my place. "Is he paying you yet?"

"I'm keeping track of it."

"What's that supposed to mean?"

"It means I'm saving up, so we can look for a new place when Mami comes home. Something even nicer than before."

Somehow I doubt that an eleven-year-old can make enough money running errands to land us a better apartment than Mami's welfare checks and Section 8 could, but I don't say anything. We all have our dreams.

"Cover for me, okay? If anybody asks where I am." He shoves his backpack under the covers, trying to make it look like a sleeping body. "Tell them I fell asleep here so you covered me up."

I cross my arms. "And what will you bring me if I do?"

He exhales. "What do you want?"

"A KitKat bar. Or maybe M&Ms." I pause to think. "No, no, Skittles. Two bags."

"I'll see what there is," he says, and before I can thank him he slips out the door like a ghost.

It's late now, and I know I should just turn out the lights and go to sleep, but I've never had to sleep alone. I'm just not used to it. I pick up Cristo's notebook and check over his homework. Most of what he's done is right, but almost all of the worksheets are empty. I go through them and fill in all the answers, copying his handwriting the best I can. I even mess up a few to make it look like he did it. When I finish spelling, I move on to math, then life science and history. It takes me almost an hour to finish what was probably every one of his assignments since the beginning of the year.

I flip to the back of his notebook and start doodling on the empty pages, writing my name in all different styles. Then I write all our names: *Cristoval. Trinidad. Lucila.* When I write my mother's name, *Arcelia*, it looks like a foreign word, something beautiful that I wouldn't know how to pronounce. I stare at it for a while and then without meaning to I start to write down the first words that come into my head.

Mother.

Skinny.

Sick.

Gone.

I stare at the list for what feels like hours. Then I start a new list, of things I remember from when I was Trini's age. Good things.

Pretty smile.

Wet hair.

Painted fingernails.

The smell of lavender.

The sound of her laughing, like pennies dropping.

I close my eyes. I can see her so clearly it's like I'm looking straight into a photograph. When I open my eyes I compare the two lists. I stare at the words for a long time. On a new page I write: *Why don't you do those things anymore? Why don't you laugh?*

Next thing I know I'm writing a letter to my mother, asking her everything I've wanted to ask since I can remember. I wrote her lots of letters over the summer, but none were longer than a paragraph, and none asked her anything directly. The questions come so fast my hand can hardly keep up with them.

Why did you leave Puerto Rico for America?

Why did you take me with you?

Why did you leave Cristo behind?

Why did you stop cooking Spanish food?

Why did you stop eating?

Why can't you get a real job so we can live in our own house?

Are we homeless?

Why did you tell me not to tell Cristo they wanted me to skip a grade?

Why doesn't Scottie take us out anymore?

Do you still love him?

Do you love my father?

Do you love Lucho like you love a man?

Why did Lucho leave us?

Why did you leave us?

Is Papi still your husband, even though you left him behind?
Does he miss me?
Do you miss me?
Are my grandparents still alive?
Do I have any cousins?
Why do some people understand Spanish and others can't?
Do you think I'm pretty, even though I look like my father?
Do you have any pictures of him?
Do you have any pictures of me?
Why can't we come visit you?
Are you ever coming home again?
Can we still be a family, even though we don't live together?
If you die, will you still be my mother?

I read over the page, thinking about how to put those questions into a letter that I could actually send her. I read it one more time. Then, on a fresh sheet of paper I start a new letter.

Dear Mami,
How are you? We are fine. We are living with Chino and Kim because Lucho left. It is nice here. Their TV is huge and it gets over 100 stations. School is good. I am the class president again. I like my teacher and I like the fifth grade. My locker is near the library so I get all the best books.
I hope you come home soon.
Love, Luz

This is the letter I send.

SHE SEES the girl standing in the shower. The girl is older now, almost thirteen. Almost a woman. She touches the tiles on the wall, white with pink flowers. They are cool like metal. She is not alone. Her cousin is with her. He stands against her, his front to her backside. She can feel his penis against the small of her back. He is taller than her now, almost as tall as a man. She holds her breath as he enters her. She prays to leave her body. She stares at the tiles and imagines that she is in that field of pink flowers. When he is done, he cleans her body with a washcloth. The soap burns between her legs as he washes himself out of her. She doesn't even flinch. She is used to pain. She begins to cry, but he doesn't notice. She puts her face in the water to hide her tears. The water is hot. It burns her skin.

Arcelia

Once my numbers are up and I'm feeling better, the doctors start coming clean about how sick I really was. They say I had walking pneumonia and a low T-cell count and in a few more weeks I coulda died. I guess getting arrested saved my life. Maybe I should write those cops a thank-you letter.

Yeah, right.

But seriously, I am thankful for some things. Not to be in here—but to be alive. To be clean. To be more than a hundred pounds. Those are two of the things I put on my gratitude list, this stupid thing the counselor has us do in our group sessions. She says it's an important part of our recovery, 'cause every addict needs to find something to be grateful for when they're sober or else they're gonna go back to using. We're supposed to go to those twelve-step meetings too, but I can only handle so much God-talk in one week. I'm a good Catholic—I believe in God and all that shit—but I'm pretty sure He's got bigger things to worry about than keeping me clean.

Our counselor is this blond-haired white girl who says she's twenty-five but looks fifteen and is in college getting a degree in social work. First off, I don't get why someone would want to go to school just to study poor people. Can't you just hang out at the local Dunkin' Donuts and learn it all for free? And second, why is it that the people with the real problems—addicts, mothers on welfare, guys in prison—always get the student interns, but the wealthy folks on the east side who worry about their cats being depressed get the doctors with licenses and a shitload of experience?

But, whatever, she's a decent kid. She don't preach, and she don't talk down to us. A few times we met alone and I felt like she listened to me—at least better than sober people usually do—and she didn't say anything dumb about how it was all gonna be okay. We didn't really do much besides talk but I felt better when I left and maybe for a few hours after. Usually nothing can make me feel good for too long, except drugs or eating a bunch of food that feels like home. The problem is when I start thinking about having three months left and being sick and missing my kids so bad I end up drawing pictures of them in my notebook when I run out of words. Then I feel pretty lousy all over again.

One of the things they're always saying in here is, "One day at a time." Easy for them to say. They're not looking at one or two hundred of those days laid out end to end, knowing each one is gonna look exactly like the one before it. They don't have to count those days by marking the wall with lipstick or chewing gum 'cause someone stole your calendar while you were waiting in line for your meds. They also say, "We can't keep it unless we give it away." What the fuck does that mean? If I give it away then I don't have it anymore, so how can I keep it? Sometimes I think I'm the only sober one in the group. At least I'm over here trying to tell the truth.

When a new girl joins the group—clean only four days—she sits in the corner and picks her nails the whole time. I tell her after how I did the same thing to get through my first meeting and she needs to stick it out 'cause even though she feels like shit right now it does get better. Not easier really, but somehow okay. Then I tell her all you have to do to survive is to make it out alive. She thinks it's cute—how I make it rhyme like that— and tells me she's gonna say it to herself over and over again to get through the night. I see her in the cafeteria the next day and we been talking ever since.

Her name is Candy and she's twenty-one and grew up in South Providence. She says she's only ever left RI twice, both times to buy drugs outside Boston. Pills were her thing—and coke when she could get it—but she don't drink nothing but

Diet Dr Pepper. She had a really good job dancing at the Pink Lady until she got jumped by a client and quit when the manager said it was her fault. She doesn't have any kids and she doesn't want any. She says it's hard enough looking after herself and her younger sister, who's still in high school and has to get by with a part-time job at Burger King and their grandmother's Social Security checks.

Candy's real pretty and she keeps touching my hand when we talk, in that girl way that means she wants to kiss me. Straight girls always like me—something about not feeling threatened—but nothing happens till a few nights later, when I bite into a peach pit in the cobbler and crack my tooth. By nighttime it hurts so bad I can't sleep, so I call to the guard and beg for some aspirin. She says I have to wait until morning to see the nurse so I bury my head in the pillow so nobody can hear me cry. One of the ladies in my room gives me a soda can to use as an ice pack but after twenty minutes it's not cold anymore and I end up drinking it instead, pouring it straight down my throat so it won't touch my tooth.

I guess I finally fall asleep 'cause I feel someone shaking my arm later and when I turn over there's Candy, sitting on the side of my bed holding out a bunch of pills.

"Here, I cheeked them during my detox," she whispers. "They'll make everything go away."

I swallow two dry and put the rest in my bra for later. I can't make out her face in the dark room but her hair is all puffed out and lit up from behind. It spirals away from her head like a child's drawing of the sun.

"How'd you get out of your room?" I ask her. "I thought you were in the locked wing."

"I did a few favors for the guard. Now she's paying me back."

I sit up to give her more room on the bed.

"No, lay down," she says, pushing me against the bed. She keeps her hand on my chest. "You should rest." After a few seconds she touches my face with her fingertips. "Which side hurts?"

"Right there," I say. "On the top."

She starts rubbing my cheek in small circles, real soft so I can barely feel her touching me.

"It should feel better in a few minutes," she says. "Once it gets into your bloodstream."

"I don't have a good sense of time," I tell her. My eyes are used to the dark by now and I can see a little smile on her face.

"I'll know," she says, still rubbing my cheek.

I don't remember who makes the first move, but next thing I know Candy is laying on top of me and we're kissing and taking off our clothes and trying not to make any noise. The pain in my tooth goes away and soon I can't feel anything except Candy's lips on my skin and the weight of her body pressed against me, pinning me to the bed. I forgot how much I like the feeling of another person's body against mine—the heat of her thighs; her strong, surprising tongue; the weight of her tits against my belly—it all feels like magic, like I never been touched before.

I don't sleep at all that night, but when I get out of bed in the morning—an hour after Candy sneaks back to her own room—I feel good inside, like I slept for twenty-four hours straight. And I feel full, as if all those magazine pictures on my wall became real food and we had stayed up eating all night long and now I just got to wait for my body to fill up and realize I been fed.

◆ ❖ ◆

It's October and I haven't had a visitor in over a month. It's like they all forgot about me. But I still get letters from Luz every week, bless her heart, lying to me about how great everything is. Or maybe she's telling the truth—which is even more fucked up. I don't want my kids to struggle, but if they have it too easy, they won't need me to come back. She says they want to come visit but there's no way I'm gonna let that happen. Knowing I'm in here is bad enough—they don't need to see it, too. Drowning in this ugly jumpsuit with my dye-job grown out and my bangs too long, my skin yellow under these fluorescent lights—who wants to remember that? If I let them come, this is how they're gonna remember me—even when I'm free they'll still see me behind bars.

I finally get word that Lucho left. I can't say I'm surprised, but I wanted to believe she changed—or at least tried to. But I guess people don't change unless they got no other choice. No different than me really. Would I be clean if I wasn't locked up? No. Would I be talking to a counselor? No. Would I be eating three meals a day? No. People change when life makes them change. Simple as that.

I still don't like writing letters, but the counselor has me doing it every week. I feel stupid holding a pen and trying to come up with something to say. She keeps telling me to open up to my kids about my past. Tell them how I was hurt and try to fix the things I did to hurt them. If I do it now when I'm locked up, then I don't got to look them in the face when I tell them. Guess I'm a coward for needing to hide behind a letter, but other times I think I got balls just to put it all down. Either way, I'm telling them things they could probably figure out on their own. Kids don't miss shit. They were there for lots of fights between me and Scottie, and they got to remember something from the time with their father. They saw more than I wanted them to see and I know I can never make up for that.

When I find out my kids are living with Chino and Kim it makes me want to get out of here even faster. Once somebody saves your kids you pretty much owe them the world. I don't want to owe anybody that much. All Kim's talk about not being able to take all three—I knew that was bullshit. I guess it just took Chino a while to talk her into it.

I still don't sleep much, but when I do I dream about Puerto Rico. The scent of magnolia blossoms so strong I wake up still smelling them. I picture the sky at night and the feeling of the breeze, the sound of guitar music coming from somebody's open window. I remember the smell of fields burning to clear the old crops, and the sound the coqui frogs make when they're mating, loud like sirens. I don't think I had a lot of dreams before getting locked up—or maybe I just forgot them—but they're so real in here I wake up thinking I'm still at home. That I'm a little girl again, sleeping at the foot of my mother's bed after another nightmare, the warmth of her body still held in the sheets.

Mostly I'm alone in my dreams, walking through the old parts of town, but other times I'm with my mother, picking mangos from the tree in our backyard. Once I dream I'm with my own children, showing them parts of the island they never got to see or were too young to remember. I wish those dreams made me feel better, but they don't really. Probably because I spend too much time trying to figure out if they're from the past or the future.

I know it's dangerous to even think this way, but some days I do have hope. Hope that I'll make it back to my kids so we can start a new life together. Hope that I can give them a home. Hope that one day I'll think back to these days—being locked up in here and even the time I lived in Providence—and they'll feel so distant and strange that I'll wonder if this, too, was all just a dream.

◆ ❖ ◆

Without the drugs to block it out, my memory starts to slowly come back. I still have flashes, but they're longer now, like scenes from a movie I don't remember making, my childhood a story someone told me that I tried to forget. I tell the counselor what I see in the flashes. She asks where I am, who the man is, and why I'm not afraid of the boy, even though he ends up doing the same things to my body that the man does.

I tell her the man is our neighbor, a farmer with large, dark hands and a mustache he rolls into points with candle wax. He is also my father's boss, and later hires three of my brothers to build a fence around his property so the goats don't escape. He smells sweet like hay and always has fresh-picked carrots in his pocket, their bushy green stems like a bouquet of wildflowers, which he lets me feed to his horses one at a time. He tells me there are no words for what he does to me, so we can never talk about it. My voice is the second thing he takes from me—my memory, the last.

I tell her the boy is my cousin, the son of my mother's only brother, and that he lives in the mountains but comes down to our village every summer to stay with us. He is a few years older than me and I love how he tells stories that make everybody laugh. He can make animal sounds so real my mother thinks there's a goat trapped in the closet. He is different from the man because he is just a boy when it starts, and he is part of my family. And he tells me he loves me. But it is still wrong. I know that. I feel it in the sickness in my belly every time he leaves my room. But I don't do anything to stop it. I don't want to fight him. I don't want to fight him and lose.

During siestas, while everybody sleeps, he comes into my room and pushes the dresser in front of the door. He says I will get in trouble if I tell—that it's my fault for being pretty and wearing flowers in my hair and thin cotton dresses—and I believe him. The first time he just jerks off in front of me, but then he makes me touch it—first with my hand and later with my mouth—and when he comes he leaves a stain on the quilt I can still see even weeks after I wash it out. I don't think I ever really stop seeing it, even after I get married and leave everything in that house behind.

When the counselor asks about my husband, I tell her about our wedding night, how we sleep together for the first time in the bed he grew up in, with only a thin wall separating us from his parents. It feels good because he takes his time and waits for me to be ready, and he keeps whispering my name over and over again like a lullaby. I'm so in love with him I can feel the ache all the way down to my toes. I want him so badly I can't look into his eyes. I try to block out the flashes, but as soon as Javier is inside me, I think of the first time with my cousin, of a shower so hot it burns my skin, of running as fast as I can even though I'm standing still. I feel other hands touching me, other people taking things that were only mine to give.

We met when we were fourteen and I told him I was a virgin, but when I don't bleed on our wedding night I know he thinks I'm a liar. He says it doesn't matter but he's quiet afterwards. He rolls off me and pulls the sheet up around his naked body like he's cold, even though it's hot in that room, with only one small window to catch the breeze. Years later, during a fight when I'm pregnant with Luz—our second child together—he tells me he knows I wasn't a virgin on our wedding night and that he never trusted me after that. Sometimes he wonders if these kids are even his.

"How did that make you feel?" the counselor asks me. "When he said that your kids might not be his."

"I didn't feel anything."

She stares at me till I look away. "I don't know," I finally say, sitting up in my chair. "I felt like there were too many feelings and they blocked each other out."

"Did you tell him that?"

"No. I didn't tell him anything."

She folds her hands together. "Why not?"

"'Cause then I'd have to remember it myself."

"And that's dangerous, isn't it?"

I don't say anything, just stare out the window behind her desk. The wind is blowing and I watch dark red leaves fall from branches as black as dirt.

"We had a garden," I tell her. "At our first house. We used to put Cristo and Luz to sleep in the swing and water the plants together at night. It was the only time we had alone, just the two of us."

She nods. I can see she wants me to say more.

"We used to eat tomatoes straight off the vine, like apples. They were sweeter than any fruit you can find in this country."

I don't tell her about the bad times. How he got so drunk he used to throw baseballs at me. How he yelled at the kids when they couldn't dress themselves. How he disappeared for days in a row. I don't tell her how I started to separate myself, testing to see what life would be like without him even before he was gone. Just like when my mother got sick and I used to hide in my bedroom for days, pretending she was already gone—ignoring her coughing fits, the clumps of her hair in the sink, her bloodstained towels hanging over the tub—just to see if I could survive without her. I did the same thing with my husband, creating a world where I didn't need him so I wouldn't miss him when he left.

But he got so comfortable with the distance he never had

to leave. He used to threaten to go away forever, but he always came back a few days later, without a word, like he had just been at the market buying meat. So I knew it was gonna have to be me. At first I thought a different house would be enough, then a different city, but I really didn't feel like he was gone until I put an ocean between us—and even on the streets of New York City I used to look for him in the crowds. I still look for his face and I always find it—every time I look at Luz.

"Are you in love with him?"

She's not even looking at me when she asks the question, so I look away when I answer.

"I love him. I think I always will."

"And you're comfortable with that?"

"Lady, I'm not comfortable with anything." I cross my legs and then uncross them.

She smiles. "You know what I mean."

"It was hard when I first left him. Like I was trying to breathe under water."

"Like getting clean?" she says.

I nod. "But I'm okay now. I survived."

She drinks from a tall bottle of water. "Are you surviving now?"

I shrug. "Some days better than others."

"You never answered my question, about being in love with him."

I cross my legs again, trying to keep myself in the chair. "I don't know. Maybe."

She leans back in her chair, waiting for me to say more.

"Maybe I didn't get over him, but I got on without him. That's what matters."

"Have you ever fallen in love again? With someone else?"

"Sure, I slept with lots of other people."

"I'm talking about love, Arcelia."

Fuck love, is what I want to say to her. But instead, I tell her the truth. "I thought I did once, with my baby's father. But it wasn't really love. Not like with Javier. I guess I was faithful to my husband in that way." I untie my shoelaces just so I can re-tie them tighter. "You think that means I'm still in love with him?"

She finishes the water in her bottle. "Only you can answer that."

"It's been a long time. Five years since I last saw him."

She smiles. "In the grand scheme of life, five years isn't a long time."

I wrap the shoelace around my finger, cutting off the blood. "I got close with Lucho but it's not the same. I don't love her like I loved my husband. I love her like I loved getting high." I watch my fingertip turn purple. "At first I thought it was because she's a woman, but now I think it was just my heart."

"What about your heart?"

I unwrap my finger and bend it to make sure it still works. "I won't let myself love like that again. It took too much from me, to love that hard."

"What about your children? You love them."

"That's different. It doesn't take anything away from you to love your kids. It makes you bigger."

The counselor smiles to herself as she writes something in my chart. Then she puts the pencil down and sits back in her chair.

"You've had a lot of pain in your life, Arcelia. A lot of bad things have happened to you. It makes sense that you want to numb yourself. That you've tried to run away from everything."

My feet start tapping the linoleum floor. I want to run right now, but there is nowhere to go.

"Leaving Puerto Rico helped, leaving your husband, and, of course, getting high. That was a good escape. But you can't run forever. You know that, don't you? And you can't run away from yourself."

"I can try."

"You're right. You can. And how do you think that's working out so far?"

I turn away from her, feeling my face get hot. My feet are still tapping. I steady my knees with my hands, trying to be as still as the tree outside her window. The leaves keep falling, the branches bend, but the tree itself don't ever move.

◆ ❖ ◆

With Candy I don't have to worry about things like love. We talk about old TV shows and stupid movies and all of our best highs, but we don't talk about ourselves really. There's no place for that in here. We're just friends—friends with benefits the white ladies call it—and even when we have sex, we don't really share anything. After we're done we lie together in the dark for a few minutes, catching our breath and staring up at the dirty mattress on the top bunk, rubbing our legs together, sharing a flimsy pillow, sometimes falling asleep. That's when I feel closest to her.

I finally go to the infirmary and end up having that cracked tooth pulled. The doctor says I can get a root canal and have a fake tooth put in after a long, painful surgery that will cost the state plenty in insurance premiums, or I can be sensible and just have them pull it out. He offers to give me twice the pain meds I'd get for the fake tooth, and promises that my sacrifice will earn me plenty of brownie points with the staff—which could pay off in extra dessert, longer visiting hours, and the guards looking the other way if I have any nighttime visitors. I know I might regret it later, when I'm back in the real world with a nasty gap in my smile, but I take the pain meds and the brownie points and never think about that tooth again.

I give the meds to Candy that night after they pull my tooth, as a thank-you for her kindness, and she shows her appreciation two times in a row. After, when we're lying in bed like two lazy cats, she asks me about the magazine clippings on my wall.

"You a gourmet cook or something?"

"Nah. I just like looking at pretty things." I stare at her, hoping to make her blush, but her skin is a shade of brown that makes it hard to see.

"Well don't look at me then." "What are you talking about," I whisper. "You're pretty."

"Yeah, when I was eight. I look old now."

"You're twenty-one."

"You know how we age...the drugs, the late nights." She rolls over and buries her face in the pillow.

"Quit messing. You look like a teenager." I tickle her until she lifts her head.

"And you look like your little boy." She kisses me on the nose. "Show me the pictures again."

I reach under the bed for my notebook, pulling out the pictures that teacher sent. Candy nods when she looks at Cristo.

"Yep, just like you." She stares at the picture of Luz. "Your daughter's pretty. A little angry maybe, but pretty." She's right—Luz is staring into the camera like it's a rifle.

"She doesn't look like you," Candy says.

"She looks like her father."

Candy plays with my hair, wrapping it around her finger like a ring. "Where's he at?"

"Puerto Rico."

"You ever see him?"

I shake my head.

"The kids ever see him?"

"Not since we left."

We're both quiet for a while. Candy picks broken hairs off the pillow and sprinkles them onto the floor.

"Was that his idea or yours?"

I don't know how to answer that so I don't say anything.

"Does he know you're in here?"

I shrug. "I didn't tell him."

"All those letters you write and none for him? Seems kinda unfair."

"Why? I don't owe him anything."

"I mean for your kids. Maybe if he knew you were in here he'd want to help out, come visit or something."

"I doubt it." I turn over and pull the covers up, shrinking into the bed for warmth.

"Only one way to find out though." She presses her body against mine from behind, warming every spot she touches.

She leaves around 5:30 and instead of falling back asleep I get dressed and sit at the desk. I open my notebook to a clean page. The room is still dark so I use the light from an alarm clock as a lamp. I hold the pen above the paper, waiting for the words to come. Finally, when the sun is almost up and there's enough light in the room to see that my roommates are still asleep, I write *Querido Javier*, and begin the letter I been needing to write for months.

Cristo

After working for almost three months I get my first pay-check from Snowman. It's not a check, really, but that's what he says when he hands me the cash.

"Here, kid, your first paycheck."

The bills are so new they stick together. They feel fake, like Monopoly money. I have to lick my fingers just to count the twenties—five of them—which is more money than I've ever had. I keep thanking him over and over again.

"Don't thank me, you earned it." He squeezes my shoulder. "Hey, don't you have a wallet or something? You can't just walk around holding it in your hand like a concert ticket."

I fold the cash in half and tuck it into my front pocket. Then I run my fingers over the bulge on the outside of my jeans, making sure it doesn't disappear. I keep doing that during the day, until I get back to Kim and Chino's place and hide it in a couch cushion so I can sit on top of it all night long.

I guess I should call it Kim's place now, since Chino moved out last week. But who knows—it's probably not even Kim's. All I know is Chino's gone and the rest of us are still here, acting like nothing changed. I keep waiting for Kim to come out of her room and ask us to leave since he was our only connection to her, but nothing's happened yet. Mostly she just nods like a mute if one of us asks her something. She spends all her time in her bedroom with the door locked and the stereo on, playing Michael Bolton songs on repeat. She stopped buying food and usually forgets to bring home dinner, so we've been getting by with the WIC checks I forged and anything else I can get for free. I guess I could buy us some food now, but it seems easier just to keep on stealing it so I can save the money for an apartment when Mami gets out. A hundred dollars might seem like a lot, but when you got rent and food and clothes to buy it runs out pretty quick. Fuck if I know how anybody gets by without stealing or asking the government for help.

I stopped cutting my hair back in August and now it's long and curly like boys I used to see at the beaches in Puerto Rico. Before it was so short I didn't even know I had curly hair. Now I want it to grow out into a big Afro like Snoop Dogg or Kobe Bryant. Sometimes I wish I was black. Not black-skinned, but black on the inside, just like Snowman. I want everybody to think I'm black. It wouldn't be hard really, I could just stop speaking Spanish on the street and only eat rice and beans when I'm inside. I could say my father lives in Brooklyn, nah, maybe Harlem sounds better, and Mami is from one of those southern states like Alabama where she couldn't go to school with white people. And if they asked I could say my grandmother still lives down there, on this huge farm with pigs and dandelions and no cotton. I could have people from both the city and the country be my family, and they'd all be some shade of black, and they'd all be American.

Mami says Puerto Ricans aren't real Americans, we're like people who live together without being a family. Even though we got the same blood as black people, it's different 'cause they been in this country for hundreds of years. That's what gives them the right to be American. I want to know how long I gotta be here before I can say that. Sometimes I think even if I spend my whole life here it still won't be enough, and I'll never feel like I really belong.

◆ ❖ ◆

When the first-quarter grades get handed out in October, I find out I'm failing fifth grade. Mrs. Reed says I don't turn in enough of the homework on time and I got to do better on quizzes and class participation. And then she says that even though my reading and writing has improved, my math and geography are as weak as the kids who just got here from Guatemala or Peru. I tell her that Teacher would never fail me and she says it doesn't matter because Teacher's not my teacher anymore. She sends me back to my desk and calls another student up, talking to each one alone until she makes it through the entire class. With everybody else she smiles at least once, and with César she holds his shoulder the entire time and looks like she's trying not to cry.

"No worse than last year," César says as he shows me his report card, a line of Ds marching straight down the page. He laughs as he puts the paper away, but it's a quick laugh, not like the one he gave last year when he asked Teacher if her typewriter key had gotten jammed. He tries to act the same as before the accident, but it never works. It's like he's trying too hard to be himself. He wears his helmet tilted back on his head like a baseball cap, and all I can see is the bullet still inside his skull, messing up the insides and covering up the part of his brain that made him who he was. He's having another operation to remove the bullet next week and I keep hoping that when it's gone, my friend will finally come back.

There's a new girl in our class named Graciela and on her first day she smiled through every lesson and never said a word. She's got a pretty smile. She just moved here from Colombia and she's the darkest girl in our class. And just like Luz, she's always reading. Even in the middle of class she has a book open on her lap. And she always has that smile on her face, even when she's not looking at anyone. Last year I woulda probably asked her out, or at least sat next to her at lunch or on the bus, but now I don't have time for that type of kid stuff.

Besides, I usually try to save a seat for Marco during lunch, even though he has new friends from Regular Ed and he usually eats with them. Sometimes he asks me to sit with them, but none of those kids speak Spanish and they all bring their lunch from home and make fun of anyone who eats the cafeteria food. Like we have a choice. I try not to blame Marco 'cause I know it's not his fault he's smart and had to move into Regular Ed, but lately I feel like everybody else is moving forward and

I'm the only one standing still.

After she gives us our report cards Mrs. Reed tells us about a new assignment we're spending the rest of the year working on. She tells us we're each gonna make a book of our favorite poems, with a cover and page numbers so they look like real books. Then she says we're gonna have to work on it outside of school, too, at the public library or whatever, since our school library is only open a few times a week and doesn't let us check out any books. When the bell goes off I try to sneak out of the classroom, but she calls me over to her desk. She stares at me over her glasses like I got something she wants.

"So?" Mrs. Reed leans forward.

"So what?"

"What do you think about the assignment? The poetry book?"

I shrug.

"I was hoping for more enthusiasm than that. If you do well on this it can really turn your grades around."

"Okay."

She takes off her glasses. "You do want to pass the fifth grade, don't you?"

"Yeah."

"Then you should be thanking me. I came up with this assignment for you, Cristo. I thought it would be something you could work on in your own time."

Fuck if I know what she means by that. I don't really own anything.

"I expect a lot from you with this project. I hope you don't let me down."

Thanks. No pressure.

After class I see Graciela in front of her locker and when I say hi I guess I startle her because she drops all her books onto the ground. I kneel down to help her pick them up and when I hand them to her she pushes one at me. "You should keep that one, I already read it like ten times."

"No, thanks. I'm good."

"But you haven't even looked at the title."

I look down and pretend I'm reading the title. "No, I've

read this already."

"Really? I didn't think any boy would read it."

"I don't want your damn book." I shove it into her arms.

"Fine, you don't have to yell." She walks away from me, holding her books with both arms like how Trini holds her teddy bear.

I run to catch up to her. "Look, I'm sorry. I just don't like reading books. In Spanish I'm okay, but in English...I'm not that good."

My heart is pounding like I just ran five blocks.

"I could help you, if you wanted. I taught my brother how to read and he's only five."

"I know how to read. I just don't have time...to practice or whatever. To read a whole book, you know?"

Her eyes are wide when she looks at me.

"How do you expect to get better if you don't practice?"

I jam my hands into my pockets. "I read other things."

"Like what?"

"Signs, movie posters, ads on the sides of buses. Candy wrappers." I look at my feet, realizing how crazy this must sound.

"How about menus?" she asks.

I look up to see if she's just messing with me. Nope, she's serious.

"Sure," I say. "But not at Chinese restaurants."

She laughs and I can feel my face get hot.

"I can see why you drive the teacher crazy."

"Yeah, well...it's a tough job, but somebody's gotta do it."

"I think the teacher's got the toughest job," Graciela says. "She has to stand alone in front of a room full of kids every day and try to sound smart. And stay calm. I could never do that."

I never thought of it that way before, that teachers have to try to do something. I just thought it was something they are.

"Don't you think it's easy for some of them? Like getting up to dance."

"Even dancing is work," she says. "It takes time to learn all those steps. And practice."

"Okay, okay, I get it." I can't stop myself from smiling. "It's all about practice."

She hides her smile in the top of her books. "If you say so," she says, finally turning to leave.

The stairwell is empty by now and I watch her climb the steps two at a time. When a book drops from the stack in her arms, she doesn't stop or bend down to pick it up. She looks at me near the top of the staircase, making sure I saw it, and then disappears around the bend.

I walk over and pick up the book. *The House on Mango Street*. I tuck it under my arm, like I dropped it myself, and head back to my locker. It's the first book I ever wanted to bring home.

◆ ❖ ◆

César calls me at Kim's house the night before he's scheduled to go into the hospital for surgery. His voice is so low I can hardly hear him.

"You busy?" he whispers into the phone.

I put down the book from Graciela I was trying to read. "Just watching TV." No point having him laugh at me too.

"Can you come out?"

"Now? It's ten o'clock."

Luz lifts her eyes from her book to look at me.

"I thought you don't have a curfew," César says.

"I don't."

"So what's the problem?"

"Nothing. I'll meet you at Anthony's in five."

I hang up the phone and grab my sweatshirt off the floor. Luz doesn't say anything. Then she picks up the remote and turns up the volume on the TV, covering up the sound of the door closing as I sneak out the front. It's cold for the end of October and there's already a bunch of leaves on the ground. I zip up my sweatshirt and tuck my hands into the sleeves, wishing I had a winter coat.

When I get to Anthony's, César is waiting for me in the parking lot, sucking on a lollipop. He's wearing a fleece pullover and a blue ski hat with the New England Patriots logo on it, but he still looks cold. He pulls another lollipop out of his pocket and hands it to me.

"Here. They only had grape."

"Grape's good." I tear off the wrapper and shove the lollipop in my mouth. It takes me a while to taste the flavor, my mouth warming up slow like tap water.

"So what's up?"

He shrugs. "Nothing." He pulls at his hat, stretching the folded rim to cover the awkward shape of his helmet. I'm actually surprised to see him wearing it.

"You wanna walk around the block?"

I figure maybe I'll warm up if we keep moving. César shrugs, then follows me down Manton. Sections of the sidewalk are torn up so we walk down the middle of the street like we're part of the traffic. Like we can stand up against a two-ton car.

"You worried about tomorrow?"

"Nah. I'll sleep through most of the bad parts."

"Plus you get to miss school. That alone should make it worth it."

"Yeah." César tries to smile.

A car speeding up the hill has to slam on the brakes when it finally sees us. We step to the side slowly, as the driver blasts the horn and waves her arms from behind the wheel. I drop my head and give her the finger as she drives away.

Once we're walking again César says, "They said I could lose the eye, though. Or I could keep the eye but lose my eyesight completely. I could be blind."

"Or you could get it all back. Get rid of those damn headaches and stupid seizures and stop having to take all them pills. You gotta look on the bright side, kid."

After pissing off another car, we end up cutting down a side street, one of the few that has working streetlights. The bulbs are almost burned out and they cast a spooky glow over the empty street.

In the half-dark I hear him say, "I don't want to die, Cristo."

I knock him in the arm. "What the fuck are you talking about? You're not gonna die."

"But I could. The doctors said there's like a twenty-percent chance. I heard them tell my grandmother last week." He stops walking and turns to me.

"Fuck twenty percent. It's not gonna happen."

"But it could." He sounds like he's about to cry. "Last time it almost did."

I grab him by the shoulders. "Listen. You're not going to die. You're a little kid, you got your whole life ahead of you." I loosen my grip but keep my hands on him, holding him up. "If that bullet wanted your life it would have taken it back in June. You beat it then and you're going to beat it now, okay? You gotta believe that."

He looks at me for a long time.

"Promise me," he says.

I drop my head. "Come on, César."

"Promise me."

"I'm not God." I look him in the good eye. "I'm not even your doctor."

He looks at me, both eyes steady and unblinking, and doesn't say a word.

"I promise," I finally say.

He closes his eyes and takes a deep breath. I let go of him, and he falls back into the telephone pole, letting it catch him. Tears fall down his cheeks and he wipes them away without opening his eyes.

Neither one of us talks during the walk back to Anthony's. I tell César to wait outside while I run into the store for a minute, wishing I had time to go to a real store in the mall instead of this broke-down drugstore in Olneyville. I find the sunglasses rack near the checkout counter and try a bunch on, looking at myself in the plastic mirror that's no bigger than a deck of cards. I see the pair I want out of the corner of my eye, gold rims with big, round lenses dark enough to cover a flashlight, but I don't try them on. Instead, I look at the cheap plastic ones, pretending that I'm deciding on the color. I slip the gold pair into the sleeve of my sweatshirt with my left hand, and pick up a bright pink pair with my right and put them on.

"Hey, what do you think?" I ask the lady at the counter.

"I don't think that's your color," she says. "Kinda girlie."

"Yeah, you're right. I guess you don't have what I'm looking for." And then I take the pink ones off in front of her and put them neatly back on the rack. I say good night and walk out of the store.

Once I'm on the sidewalk, I reach into my sleeve and pull out the gold sunglasses. I rip off the tag and hand the glasses to César. "Here, a good luck present. Either way you're going to have a big old bandage and one hell of a black eye."

"*Gracias*," he says, slipping the glasses onto his small face. They cover his eyes completely, from his eyebrows to the tops of his cheeks, and make him look even younger than he is. He takes them off and puts them in his pocket. "Thanks," he says again, punching me softly in the shoulder.

"*De nada.*"

"Hey kid, come here a minute."

A loud, rough voice calls out from the street. A white guy with a scruffy beard and a long, blond ponytail waves me over from the passenger side of a parked car. I look around, but the only other person on the street is an old lady folding newspaper from a broken recycling bin.

"What, you don't remember me?" He drops his sunglasses so I can see him better. "You brought me a package last week, on Atwells. You were right on time, too, as reliable as the fucking post office."

"Sure, I remember now." A late-night delivery for Snowman. I walk a few steps toward the car, a two-door Pontiac that looks older than I am. The color is a faded black, like it was spray-painted on. "How's it going?"

"Well that depends on you, and on your answer to my next question. You working tonight?"

"No." I nod toward César. "I'm with a friend."

"I'd make it worth your while." He rubs his fingertips together, yellow from smoke.

I step up to the window. "What you need?"

He lifts a pizza box from his lap. "Take this to the address on this card." He hands me a business card. "Memorize the address and then burn the card. When you go inside, ask for a guy named Pincher. You think you can do that?"

"You want me to deliver a pizza?"

He laughs. "The pizza's gone. But you can buy another one with the twenty bucks I'll give you."

"Twenty bucks to deliver an empty pizza box?"

He winks. "I never said it was empty."

"Oh." I look back at César, who's still messing with his hat. "Well…"

"You interested or not?" the guy says, pulling a crumpled twenty out of his front pocket. "We don't have time to wait around."

"Forget about it," the driver says, starting the car. "We shouldn't give this shit to a kid, Charley."

"What are you talking about, that's the beauty of it," Charley says, like I'm not even standing there. "They don't mess with kids."

A passing bus lights up the inside of the car. The driver squints. "So why should we?" He bites his fingernails, spitting them onto the floor of the car. Something about him looks familiar.

"Come on, Jimmy," Charley shrugs. "Snowman trusts him."

"Oh, Christ." Jimmy slaps the steering wheel. "You treat that guy like he's the fucking Dalai Lama."

"Okay, I'll do it," I say quickly, hoping to stop their argument before it becomes a fight.

Charley smiles, first at me, and then at Jimmy. He's missing one of his front teeth, and the rest look like they could fall out if he sneezed too hard. Jimmy pulls the hood of his sweatshirt over his buzzed head and goes back to biting his nails. Charley turns back to me, his smile fading. He tucks the twenty into the front pocket of my jeans and pulls me against the car in one motion.

"I'm calling over there in forty-five minutes, and if they don't have it by then I'm coming back here to find you. It shouldn't be too hard to find a green-eyed Spanish kid with an Afro, now should it. But I hope it doesn't come to that."

He pulls me closer for a quick second, and then pushes

me away from the car. I stumble, but I don't let myself fall. My heart is beating so fast I can hear it in my ears, but I try to stay calm. He hands me the pizza box, which is so heavy on one side I almost drop it.

"Use two hands," he says. "And don't open it. I'll know if you do." Charley drops low in his seat to light a cigarette. "One more thing: don't say anything to Snowman about this, okay? No point making him jealous." He laughs hard, the cigarette hanging out of his mouth like a walrus tooth.

They drive away, leaving me standing there like I just had a pizza delivered to the sidewalk. I hold the box still, trying not to tempt myself by shaking it. I'm kinda curious, but then I remember rule #1: Don't ask questions. That way you won't have to lie if you ever get busted. One of the first things Snowman ever taught me.

César walks up to me, shaking his helmeted head. "Man, I don't know how you do it. You're always in the right place at the right time."

"It's not what you think," I say. "I've got to bring this home."

"Come on, just give me one slice." César reaches for the box.

"No, I'm serious. I gotta go." I back away from him. "I'll see you later, okay?"

César zips up his fleece, covering his freckled face. "You're coming, right?" he calls after me. "To the hospital?"

"Of course," I say. "I'll be the first face you see."

"You better." César pulls down his hat to cover the helmet. Then he takes off in the other direction. He runs quickly down the street, like he's memorized every bump and curve on Manton Avenue, every pothole, every piece of garbage, and has no fear of taking the wrong step, no fear of falling.

He runs like a boy who can see in the dark.

Miss Valentín

If every woman who wanted to get pregnant had to go through foster care classes first, the human race would come to an end. Not because the classes are hard, or boring, or even especially time-consuming—the problem is that they are thorough: incredibly, horrifyingly, overwhelmingly thorough. When I realize what it means to really parent someone, how all encompassing it will be, how much kids need (and how many things can go wrong), it's enough to make me want to give up right there. And maybe that's their plan. Like law schools, they're actually trying to get a third of us to quit in the first semester.

But I'm no quitter, even when it might be the smart thing to do. So I stick it out in the five-week course, fill out the proper papers, have all the interviews, list my principal and old professors as references, and begin to wait. Wait for the call that will change my life. Wait for my future to begin.

The first call I get is for an emergency placement. A three-year-old who was found in the backyard after a house fire killed his parents and two older sisters. He stays with me for three nights, until they can locate a second cousin in Connecticut, and he never speaks a word. He cries most of the first night, sobbing in my arms as I rock him for eight hours straight, cotton jammed into my ears to mute the sound. He sleeps the entire second day, and I finally have to wake him at dinnertime to give him milk and mashed potatoes, which he eats sitting up on the edge of the bed before falling back asleep at my side. The third day, as we wait for the social worker to pick him up, he stares at me from the couch and eats Halloween candy straight from the bag. He won't talk or play with any of the toys I've bought; he won't even watch TV.

When the doorbell rings, he runs back to the guest bedroom and jumps onto the bed. He buries his head in the comforter and kicks the social worker in the face as she tries to pull him off. It surprises me that he doesn't want to leave, but she says it's a normal reaction. It's not that he's grown attached to me personally, he's just used to the environment; he doesn't want to have to adjust again.

After they leave, the apartment is quiet. Not any quieter than when he was here, but it still feels different. Now I know how the boy felt: I don't want to adjust again either. I don't really want *him* back, although I'm sure with time he would have warmed up, I just want the situation back. I want my life to be constant, the players to remain the same. I call up my caseworker and ask her to take me off of the "emergency" list. She says I might not get called for a while if I do that and I say that's fine. It's hard, but I know I'm making the right decision for my own sanity, and I'm following my instincts. The rest—who, if, and when I get a child—is out of my hands, and it feels good to finally give up any pretense of control.

◆ ❖ ◆

When I get to school the following Monday I can tell something is wrong. The playground is deserted, which is rare even in the winter, and the hallways are eerily quiet. The kids I do see stand together in small packs, whispering to each other with their hands over their mouths. I go to the teacher's lounge looking for answers, and run into Mrs. Reed, Cristo's teacher. She walks over to me quickly, shaking her head.

"It's so sad," she says.

"What is? What happened?"

"César," she whispers his name. "The surgery failed. He lost the eye."

I cover my mouth, as if to quiet a scream, but no sound comes out.

"I thought you might have been there, at the hospital."

I shake my head. "Cristo didn't call me."

"Well, here, sign this card we got for him. I'll bring it by his grandmother's house after school."

"He's home already?"

"Today, I heard." She hands me a pen, already uncapped.

I lean over the card, reading it again and again to make sense of the words. *Hey Kid, Get Well Soon! School Is Not the Same Without You!* There is a dog on the cover, who wears a baseball cap and stands up on his hind legs like he's human. His smile shows a row of perfect teeth. The inside of the card is mostly bare, except for a few signatures from the secretaries and the janitorial staff floating around the edges of the card. I want to say more than just my name but I can't think of something that sounds sincere. I want to apologize—for the accident, the surgery, even this pathetic card. Why a card, anyway, when he'll hardly be able to read it?

I quickly sign *Love, Miss Valentín*, and hand the card back to Mrs. Reed.

"So the left eye is okay?"

"The same. Thirty percent last I heard."

"Thirty percent," I repeat, nodding as if I know what that means. Does he see everything with just thirty percent of the brightness, or does he only see thirty percent of all things? Or maybe he sees everything perfectly, but only thirty percent of the time?

"I know it's horrible to say, but I wonder if this is it for him now." She stops herself and looks around the empty room. The coffee pot gurgles in the corner, but otherwise it's silent. She lowers her voice. "I don't want to give up on him, but you know how he is. How will he ever catch up?"

I shake my head. "I don't know."

"It seems so unfair, to cripple a kid who's barely making it to begin with."

"Barely making it?"

"You know what I mean."

"Yes, I do. And I also know that this school is barely making it. His grandmother is barely making it." I can't hide my anger as my voice begins to rise. "The projects, this city, our country is barely making it. He's just following suit."

She backs up, as if afraid of me. "I'm not blaming him, Vanessa, if that's what you think. I know what these kids are up against, all of them. Even the ones with parents. I've taught here longer than you, remember."

"I know, I know." I lower my voice and touch her shoulder as a peace offering. "I'm sorry, I'm just upset."

She puts her arm around me and squeezes softly. "We'll get through this." And I know she means a career spent teaching, not just César losing his eye.

"I keep thinking about Cristo," she finally says. "This is going to devastate him." She looks at me over her glasses. "Have you seen him lately?"

"Not enough. I've tried, but...I think he's avoiding me."

"He avoids me all the time, and I'm his actual teacher." She tries to keep the resentment out of her voice but it doesn't work. She softens her tone. "He's not doing well, Vanessa."

I lean against the filing cabinet, which shakes under my weight.

"Tell me," I say.

"His grades are in the toilet."

"How bad?"

"Cs and Ds mostly, Fs if I didn't like him so much. He falls asleep in class and never turns in homework. He used to give me all these crazy excuses why he didn't have it, but now he just shrugs and says he forgot."

"*Dios mio*, I don't know what to do with that boy." I cross my arms over my chest, suddenly feeling cold. "Have you talked to Chino or Kim?"

"Chino's a sweet guy, but he's not living there anymore. And if I call the social worker...well, you know what happens after that."

"Wait a minute, so they're living with Kim? Their mother's cousin's ex-girlfriend?" A feeling of dread sets in, as I realize I should have checked in sooner.

"It could be worse. At least she hasn't kicked them out. And she has a job."

"And her own kid to watch after," I add, suddenly feeling sick to my stomach. I shouldn't have backed so far away, trusting everyone else to handle it.

"Will you talk to him, Vanessa? See if you can get through to him..."

"I try all the time, when I see him in the hallway—"

"No, not here, not in passing," she says. "I think he'd take it more seriously if it was outside of school, on his own turf. His own terms." She taps César's card against her clipboard. "He just tunes out here, like this is some practice life, while his real life is taking place outside these doors. Find him in that world and talk to him there."

I don't know what to say, so I simply nod my head, accepting the responsibility that's once again been handed to me. What else can I do?

"Good. I'm glad we talked." She sounds relieved, as if we have already solved the problem. She's halfway to the door when she turns back to me. "You may be the only thing that boy has left, the only thing that can keep him from becoming another statistic. Another César."

I listen to the click of her heels as she walks out of the room, leaving me alone in the teacher's lounge, wondering if I'm qualified for any of the jobs I actually perform.

◆ ❖ ◆

I find Cristo easily enough, standing on the corner outside Anthony's Drugs. It's the same spot where six months before I had seen his mother sell Ecstasy to a carful of students from Providence College. She used to sit on top of the covered garbage cans so she could see the cars coming in every direction. If she made eye contact and someone was interested, she'd hop down quickly and approach the car window, taking only a few seconds to decide whether to slide in or head back to her post.

Her son stands with his back to the street, leaning against a telephone pole. There are two older guys next to him, late teens, maybe early twenties, and they look like they just stepped out of a rap video. The darker one wears a gold chain with a huge #1 around his neck, which jumps from his chest as he gesticulates; he is telling a story that has Cristo and the other guy bent over laughing. I park my car and walk over to them slowly, the same way I used to walk up to stray cats I wanted to bring home as a child.

Cristo stops laughing as soon as he sees me, but the other two keep going, oblivious to my presence. The lighter man has a tattoo of a girl's face on his neck; her hands are clasped together like she's praying, right underneath the man's earlobe.

"*Hola*," I call out, testing the waters. "*¿Como estás?*"

"Hi," he says in English.

"Can we talk?"

"Sure." He crosses his arms. "What's up?"

"Alone."

He looks at each of the men and then back to me. "Later," he says to no one in particular.

"You want us to wait?" The lighter man scratches at his neck as if the tattoo still itches.

"Nah, she's cool." Cristo steps away from the telephone pole, strolling in my direction. He can't contain his smile. "She's just my teacher."

"Cool," I hear the man say as we walk away. "A teacher who makes house calls."

We walk across the parking lot, stopping next to a small vacant lot. The grass hasn't been cut in months, and it grows in wild, dry patches.

"Nice tattoo," I say, once we're out of earshot.

Cristo shrugs. "He's all right."

"A prince, I'm sure."

He stops short. "You come here to bust up my friends?"

"You think those guys are your friends? Those men?"

"Why not?"

"Those thugs are twice your age, Cristo. What about Marco and César? I thought they were your friends."

He shrugs. "I never see Marco anymore. Not since you switched him to Regular Ed."

"I didn't switch him, Cristo, he was ready to move."

"Whatever."

"And César?"

"He don't need me." He picks up a bottle cap and throws it into the overgrown grass.

"Doesn't need you," I correct.

He glares at me but I ignore it.

"How can you say that? Of course he needs you."

"He needed a good doctor. And a fucking miracle. But he didn't get either one." He blinks quickly, and I can tell he's holding back tears.

"Please don't swear in front of me."

"Swear? Come on, Teacher. My friend just lost his eye but you want me to watch my mouth?"

"You have every right to be upset. To be angry and to yell and to scream, to want to break things. Nobody's going to blame you for any of that."

He turns away from me. "Then what will they blame me for?" he asks, his voice starting to break.

"What do you mean, blame you?"

He walks into the field, his legs swallowed up by the tall grass. I hear the sound of twigs snapping.

"None of this is your fault, Cristo. You know that."

"I promised him, Teacher. I promised him that everything would be all right. And he believed me. That little shit believed me, but I was wrong." He's crying now, tears streaming down his cheeks.

"You had faith, Cristo. There's nothing wrong with that."

I take him into my arms and hug him as tightly as I can. At first he holds back, as stiff as a dead bird, but when I don't loosen my hold or abandon the hug, he gives in, sinking further into me. He buries his face in my coat and sobs into the wool, the sound of his ragged breath muffled by the dense fabric. His body goes limp in my arms and I know that I'm the only thing keeping him off the ground.

We stand like that for several minutes, rocking together in the chilly November afternoon. The temperature is dropping along with the sun, and the wind kicks up gravel and bits of garbage, but I'm not about to let go of him. I'll stand here all night, in the bitter darkness of Manton Avenue, if it will make this boy feel better.

Finally, he peels himself off me and takes a few steps back, squinting as his eyes adjust to the light. He wipes his face on the sleeve of his sweatshirt and sniffs loudly, then spits several times into the grass before looking at me.

"Sorry, Teacher," he says.

I smile but don't say anything.

He crosses his arms. "So, what'd you want to talk about?"

"I just wanted to see you, to find out how you're doing."

He sniffs again. "I guess you got your answer."

"Part of it, maybe. But not everything. How's Trini?"

"I saw her last week, for Halloween. She was a stray cat."

"That's pretty ironic," I say.

"What's that mean?"

"It means it's fitting. You know, because she doesn't have a home."

"Scottie thinks she does," he says. "With him."

"And what do you think?"

He looks at his hands. "I think I miss my sister."

I want to hug him again, but I don't. "And how's Luz?"

"Good. You hear she got class president again?"

"Yes, I heard."

He shakes his head. "Sometimes I can't believe we come from the same family."

"You're just as smart as she is, you know that. You just don't work for it."

"I work, Teacher." He looks across the lot toward the street.

"But you don't study. That should be your only job."

"Sure, Teacher, whatever you say." He starts to walk away from me.

"Any word from your mother?"

I feel bad for mentioning her, but I do it because I know it will make him stop. He turns to face me.

"She's supposed to get out next month. An early Christmas present, I guess."

"For her or for you?"

He shrugs. "I'll let you know."

"And you're okay until then, staying with Kim?"

"What choice do I got?" He's looking at me, but also somewhere over my head. "Where else can I go?"

As he walks away, I get a sick feeling in the pit of my stomach, like I'm sending a kitten into a pack of wolves.

"*Adios*, Cristo."

"*Adios*," he calls out without turning back around.

He walks back to the corner and takes up his position on the telephone pole. The wind blows harder and he steadies himself against the pole, as if he's afraid he could blow away. Soon there are several men standing with him, creating a barrier against the cold. They are smoking shared cigarettes and passing a forty-ounce bottle of beer back and forth. One man holds a pizza box under his arm like a magazine. Cristo doesn't take the cigarettes or the beer, but he still looks like one of them. Like he belongs. An eleven-year-old boy hanging out on the corner like it's his job. And I guess maybe it is.

As I walk away I hear someone ask him if he speaks Spanish. I turn around to see him wearing a look of disgust, as if they had asked if he ate dog shit.

"Hell no," he says, looking straight through me.

◆ ❖ ◆

I spend the next few weeks trying to figure out how I can help Cristo without hurting myself or compromising my career. Some nights I can't sleep, so I make chocolate chip cookie dough and eat half the batter before I even bake one cookie. I watch old movies and write long letters to my parents that I know I'll never send. I count time like I'm in prison, which makes me wonder what Arcelia does to pass her days, and if she, too, is up at night worrying about the fate of her son.

A few days before Thanksgiving vacation, while spending my lunch break in the library to replace the librarian laid off during cutbacks, I watch as Mrs. Reed brings her fifth-grade class into the large, empty room. She had warned me that they would be coming, to work on a class project about poetry, and I had tried to prepare by bringing all the tables into the center of the room. She goes to the meager poetry section and pulls every book off the shelf, randomly handing them to the kids. For those who read only in Spanish, she takes some books from the LIBROS EN ESPAÑOL section, which comprises a single aisle in the stacks, even though the Spanish-speaking population in our school is about sixty percent.

A few of the girls I had last year come over to me, begging me to read the poems out loud, and asking which one is my favorite. I read them everything from Shel Silverstein to Robert Frost and they seem to love every word, especially the ones they don't understand. I see Cristo look over at us from time to time, and then look away, pretending not to listen. After the girls have chosen their favorites and are carefully copying the words into their spiral notebooks, I walk over to the small table where Cristo is sitting by himself. There is a small book of poems in front of him, but he has not picked it up. Instead, he's reading a comic book that he tries to hide under the table as I approach.

"Read something to me," I say, pushing the book toward him.

He flips through it quickly, and seems to stop on a random page.

"*Noche, fabricadora de embelecos, loca, imaginativa, quimerista, que muestras al que en ti su bien conquista los montes llanos y los mares secos; Que vele o duerma, media vida es tuya: si velo, te lo pago con el día, y si duermo, no siento lo que vivo.*" He puts the book down, giving up after the first stanza.

"Now in English." I push the book back to him.

He sighs, but picks up the book, reading the poem in English. He goes slow and stutters a few times, but it sounds much better than I thought it would.

"*Night, you fabricator of deceptions, insane, fantastic, and chimerical, who show those who derive delight from you the mountains flattened and the seas gone dry; Whether I sleep or wake, half my life is yours: if I'm awake, I pay you the next day, and if I sleep, I sense not what I live.*"

"That's pretty good."

"It's all right." He shrugs. "I like other stuff better."

"I was talking about how you read."

"Oh." He sits up in his seat. "I've been practicing."

"By reading Lope de Vega? I'm impressed."

"You told us to practice. Last year, at the end of school. Remember?"

"I didn't know anyone was listening."

He nods, as if he understands the frustrations of teaching children. The door to the library opens with a squeak and Marco slides inside, closing the door gently behind him. I instantly see Cristo's expression change as his mood lightens. He raises his hand to wave and Marco waves back, a big smile on his pale face. But instead of coming to our table, he looks around the room until he sees Mrs. Reed, who waves him over to a small table where she sits with a new girl I don't recognize.

"Who's that?" I ask Cristo.

"Graciela," he whispers. "She's Colombian. She's reads all the time, just like Luz."

After pointing out a few pages to Marco, Mrs. Reed leaves them alone. Graciela reads out loud while Marco listens, making corrections to her pronunciation when necessary.

"That's nice of Marco, to help her catch up."

"Sure," Cristo says. "With Marco's help I'll bet she moves into Regular Ed by Christmas." I can hear the resentment in his voice.

"I'm sure he would help you, too. If you asked."

"What makes you think I want his help? I don't want to be in Regular Ed. I like it where I am just fine." He closes the book and pushes it away.

"Really?" I move closer to him and try to keep my voice down. "Because I heard you weren't doing so well. I heard you were barely passing in fact."

"I'm passing, Teacher, don't overreact."

"Ds don't count as passing. Not in my class."

"Well I'm not in your class anymore, am I? So it doesn't matter what you think."

I stare at him for a long time, letting the words sink it. "Is that really what you believe?"

He looks away, blinking to keep his eyes from filling with tears. I don't want to see him cry, but a part of me feels happy that my words can still affect him. I reach out to cover his hand with mine. At first he doesn't react, but after a few seconds he squeezes my hand.

"I didn't think so."

"Don't worry," he says after a while. "This new project, it's going to give me a chance to catch up. I'll do a good job, you'll see."

I want to believe him but I just don't know how that will ever happen. He squeezes my hand again and I wrap my other arm around him, giving him a quick hug.

"I know you will," I say, trying to sound encouraging, but even I'm not sure it's possible.

I look around the tiny library, knowing that what he needs to really catch up isn't here in this mildewed room that's only open during lunchtime and has no circulating books. He needs a different space, with more light, more books, and more people. He needs a real library.

"What are you doing after school today?"

"I'm working."

"Okay, how about tomorrow?"

"It's Thanksgiving."

"Oh. How about after that?" I open my planner. Another weekend void of plans.

"Don't know," he says. "Nothing, I guess."

"Well, now you've got plans with me. We're going out."

"Where are you taking me, Teacher?"

I shake my head. "It's a surprise."

He gives me a crooked grin. "A good surprise?"

"Have I ever given you a bad one?"

When he shrugs, I pretend to punch him in the arm, which makes him smile. For the first time in months, I leave him feeling a real sense of hope.

Snowman

I was fifteen the first time I walked into the downtown branch of the Providence Public Library. It was during a snowstorm and I was walking home from school. My momma had just died. The snow was coming down so hard it stuck in my eyelashes. My plan was to stop in for a minute or two, to escape from the burning wind and wait until I could feel my ears again. My sneakers made wet, gritty tracks on the hardwood floors as I squeaked across the lobby, but nobody said anything. The inside walls were covered with sheets of polished wood and in the main lobby there was a painting of angels on the ceiling. It was neat and quiet like my Uncle Dayton's funeral home, and I liked it right away. Something about it was comforting, like the darkness of a movie theater.

I walked around slowly that first time, looking at magazines laid out in clean plastic covers and flipping through a dictionary so big it needed its own table. I walked through the stacks, which were no taller than I was, and cocked my head to scan the titles of books I would never read, many in languages I couldn't make out. I heard classical music coming from a closed door and stumbled upon a kid playing the piano in a room that was barely bigger than his upright. Through a small Plexiglas window I could see the kid jamming away, pounding the keys so hard I thought he was going to break his fingers. I sat down on a plastic chair in the hallway and listened to that kid play for at least five minutes. When he stopped and left the room after his time was up, I still sat there listening to nothing.

I stayed until eight o'clock, when the lady came from behind the counter to say she was closing early because of the storm. I watched her pull the blinds down one by one and turn off every light in that room, more than a dozen, with just one switch. I helped her dig out the front door, which was propped open by packed snow, and watched her lock it with a key no bigger than the ones in my pocket. The next day I went back and checked out my first book: *The Autobiography of Malcolm X*. I've gone there almost every day since.

The first time I see Cristo at the library, it surprises me. I'm not prepared to see anyone I know in this building, let alone a kid from my neighborhood. He stands alone in the periodicals room, balancing a pile of books between his hands and his chin. He looks even smaller in such a big room. There's a huge wooden table behind him, as big as two pool tables, and he leans against it without putting down the books. A lady comes up to him carrying a bunch of papers, a librarian I assume. She's got a pretty face, even though she could stand to lose a few pounds, and she looks like she takes everything way too seriously.

When I approach him he finally sits down, as if the sight of me makes him weak. He gestures toward the woman and says, "This is Teacher," but doesn't tell me her name.

She looks at me, her face beginning to harden. "And you are?"

I hesitate, trying to think of what to say.

"My boss," Cristo says before I can speak.

She gives me her hand so I shake it. It feels strange to hold a woman's hand, and I wonder if I'm doing it wrong. It's warm, like she just took off her gloves, and her fingernails, painted a shade I never saw before, are long enough to scratch the palm of my hand. She surprises me by saying she's heard all about me. I can't remember him ever talking about her or school or anything else having to do with his life outside of me. Take that back, he has talked about his sisters a few times. And he told me a story about his father taking him fishing in Puerto Rico, the only thing he claims to remember about the island, or his old man.

"I guess you got a term paper or something?" I motion toward the books.

Cristo nods. "I need to do well on this. For extra credit."

"He's putting together a book of poems," his teacher says, restacking the books. "We're trying to find a wide variety."

"I can see that."

"Do you want to help?" Cristo asks me.

"I don't read much poetry," I say.

"How about this one?" He pushes a book by Langston Hughes across the table. I recognize the name from high school English. I pick up the book and thumb through it quickly, looking for the one poem of his I remember having to memorize and recite to the class. I don't find it, but I find a short one that talks about New York City.

"Here." I hand the book back, opened to the page I was reading. "You'll like this one."

"Is it about a girl?" Cristo's face brightens.

"No, it's about a city." I don't bother telling him that I think Langston Hughes was gay. "Sometimes cities are better than girls. They're more predictable, and you don't have to take them out to dinner."

He looks at his teacher before dropping his head to laugh. I shrug and look away. She takes a dollar from her purse and tells him to go buy a soda in the lobby and to finish it out there and not spill anything. He runs away without questioning her.

"Listen, I don't know how much you know about him," she drops her voice. "About his home life and his mother—"

"I know enough."

"Well, good. Then we don't have to waste any time on catch-up. The bottom line is that he's not doing well. Not in school and not in life."

I cross my arms. "He seems fine to me."

"He's failing the fifth grade."

"Come on, he's a smart kid."

"Yeah, but he's still a kid." She waves a book at me. "He needs to do his homework, go to bed at a reasonable hour, and sit down at a table to eat his dinner. He doesn't need to be running the streets with you."

"I don't run the streets, lady."

"You know what I mean."

"No, I don't." I put my hands on the back of the chair in front of me, gripping it like a steering wheel. "I don't know what he told you about me—"

"He didn't have to tell me."

"But you think you know me?"

She sits back in her chair. "I know your type."

I laugh and force myself to relax my hands, loosen my grip on the chair. I spread my fingers out wide. "I don't have a type. There is nobody like me."

She drops her eyes and I can see her notice my bleached-white hands, the spotted brown of my knuckles. She starts to rub her own hands.

"Look, I know he needs men in his life. And he obviously latched onto you for a reason. I'm not stupid enough to think that will change. But what you need to ask yourself is this: Who do you want to be for this kid? What influence do you want to have on him? Because we all know you're going to have one. Good or bad. Right or wrong. He's going to get something from all the time he's spending with you. And it's up to you to decide what that is."

"I don't have that much control, lady. Who do you think I am?"

She gets up from the table, her eyes on the copy machine. "I have no idea," she says. "Like you said, only you know who you are."

One of the books she leaves behind catches my eye. It has a crazy cover with all these little faces, and an even crazier title: *Every Shut Eye Ain't Asleep*. According to the cover, a black person wrote every poem in it. It's weird to think there are that many of us writing poetry. Enough to fill up a book, I mean.

I pick it up and flip through it, scanning the pages for something I recognize. Not a poem necessarily, but a word or an image that's familiar. One poem catches my eye because it has a whole bunch of short sections, like little fortunes. Before I know it I've read every one of them. One stanza blows me away and I read it over and over again. I memorize it right then, without even trying to, and I know I'll never forget it. It's the epigraph I want on my grave.

> There is the sorrow of blackmen
> lost in cities. But who can conceive
> of cities lost in a blackman?

♦ ❖ ♦

They call me first. Not the police or the lady he lives with. Not his teacher. They call me and ask me what I want them to do. When I ask about protocol, Tony, the night manager, tells me the pharmacy doesn't have a strict policy on shoplifters.

"Either we call the cops or beat the guy up in the vacant lot."

"Christ, Tony, he's only eleven." I balance the phone on my shoulder as I pull on my boots. I can already tell I'm gonna have to go down there.

"When I was eleven I dropped out of school to work full-time in my father's cigar shop."

"So what, are you proud of that?"

"I'm not ashamed," Tony says.

"And when's the last time you read a book?"

"I don't read books."

"Nuff said."

I hang up the phone after telling him I'm on my way. Before walking out of my place, I put my dinner in the oven to keep it warm and leave several candles burning. I hate coming home to a dark apartment.

I walk up to the pharmacy and find Cristo in the back office, sitting on the floor with his arms tucked around his knees.

"Why's he on the floor, Tony? He's not a dog."

"He didn't want a chair. We asked."

I look down at him but he won't make eye contact.

"You ready?"

He doesn't say anything so I bend down to his level. I lean into him and whisper, "You want to stay here all night or do you want to leave with me?"

After a few seconds he says, "Leave with you," his voice so soft it's like I imagined it. He stands up slowly, unfolding his body along the wall like an inchworm.

"Did you give them back the stuff?"

He nods. I look over at Tony, who is pretending to clean the shelves outside the office.

"Is it all there?" I call to him.

"Sure, Snow, it's all here." He pulls two large bottles of Advil from his pocket and shakes each one, as if that will convince me that every pill is there.

"Did you check?"

"He didn't open them. They're fine."

I pull a fifty-dollar bill from my wallet and hand it to Tony. "Here. For your trouble."

"No, no, we don't need that." Tony puts up his hand, as if taking the money would burn him. "Everything's okay now."

I tuck the bill into his chest pocket. "Thanks for calling me," I say, patting him twice on the shoulder, something I saw in a movie once. Then I walk out through a back door marked EMERGENCY EXIT ONLY. Cristo lags a few steps behind me.

I stop short in the alley, even though it's too cold to stand outside for long. A stray dog at the corner sniffs the ground for food. I count to ten, waiting for my pulse to stop racing. When I turn to face him, Cristo takes a deep breath, as if preparing to go under water.

"Are you trying to embarrass me?" I bend down to look him in the eye. "'Cause that's what it seems like."

"I didn't ask them to call you," he says. "I swear."

"What else are they going to do? They know you work for me."

He takes a step back, hiding his face in the shadow of a Dumpster.

"Do you need a raise?" I ask him.

"What's that mean?"

"Do you need to make more money? Maybe I don't pay you enough?"

"You pay me good," he says. He pulls the hood of his sweatshirt over his head, hiding most of his face from my view.

"Then why steal?"

He shrugs. "It's easier."

"Just because it's easy doesn't make it right."

He tucks his hands into his jeans. The pockets are so deep his hands disappear almost to the elbow.

"Do you always know what's right?" he asks me. When I make a face he says, "I'm serious."

I spit onto the ground before answering. "Sometimes. Usually."

He rocks back and forth on the balls of his feet. His ankles lift out of the heel when he bends forward, reminding me that he's wearing somebody else's shoes. I wonder if he's ever owned anything brand new.

"But do you always do it?" he asks. "The right thing?"

I pull off my hat to scratch my head. "Look, this conversation isn't going exactly as I'd planned."

He looks up at me. The edge of his hood covers his eyes, but I see his mouth, opened in a half smile. The silver caps on his teeth sparkle in the darkness like he's got a mouth full of diamonds.

"Here's the thing: I don't always want you to do what I do. In fact, I usually don't want you to do what I do." I put my hat back on, pulling the brim low to cover my ears. "I'm a businessman, Cristo, and I've got to make hard decisions. Sometimes I don't like my choices, but I have to live with them. That's part of being an adult. But you, you're still a kid. You've got time to make mistakes. And you have to learn from them. I'm hoping that's what's going to happen here."

He nods his head and keeps looking at me. "Am I gonna get in trouble?"

"With who? You know they didn't call the police."

"My teacher. School. You."

"I'm not going to tell anyone else about this. I'll take the fifty I just gave Tony out of your check this week and as far as I'm concerned, we're done on this topic. Is that all right with you?"

He nods again. Then he looks away. "I'm sorry," he says to the ground.

"Sorry you stole or sorry you got caught."

He thinks for a second. "Both."

I want to laugh, but instead I say, "I guess that's fair."

"I won't do it again," he says. "If you don't want me to."

"It's not about what I want. What do *you* want?"

He shrugs. "Don't know."

"Well, figure it out," I say. " 'Cause if it happens again you're on your own."

I walk away, leaving him alone in the alley. My hands hurt from the cold so I blow on them repeatedly. A hollow sound comes out, like some pathetic birdcall, which makes a cat crossing in front of me stop its prowl.

"It wasn't for me," he says, calling after me. "The pills were for my friend César, the one who got shot. He lost his eye."

I stop walking. When I look back he's picking a scab on his hand.

"Why?"

He keeps his head down when he talks, still picking at the scab. "He's got a prescription for painkillers, something real strong, but his grandmother can't afford them. I thought these could help."

I walk back to him slowly, shortening my steps to avoid the chill of my skin touching the inside of my pant legs, wishing I'd grabbed the pair with the fleece lining. When I get to him he's still looking down.

"You gotta stop taking care of everybody else and start taking care of yourself. Otherwise you're gonna end up like your friend."

I reach out and palm his head with my hand. His skull feels so small under all that hair.

"You hear me under all that hair?"

He nods.

"You better watch out, kid. You're about to have a real Afro."

He shrugs and finally looks up. "What's wrong with that?"

"Nothing, I guess. Shit, if I had your hair I'd grow it out, too."

"You still could."

"Please, you ever seen a white Afro? It ain't pretty."

"Is that why you shave your head?"

I nod. "It's just easier to keep it short."

We start walking together, through the alley and back onto Manton. The night is still and dark, and we walk for a while without talking. No cars pass by on the street.

"You heading home?" I ask him.

"Nope," he says, shaking his head harder than he needs to. "I'm going to Kim's."

"Come on, I'll walk you."

"You don't have to do that."

"I know, kid. I don't have to do any of this."

I can feel him look over at me. "Then why do you do it?"

"'Cause you're a good kid," I say. "And I like you." What I don't say out loud is that I like myself when I'm with him.

His ears are bright red, so I zip his sweatshirt all the way up and tighten the drawstring on his hood. "Didn't your momma teach you to cover your head in the cold?"

He tries to pull away from me, but I can see him smile in the dark. "Mami's from Puerto Rico, what's she know about the cold?"

"Good point," I say, stepping off the sidewalk to take a shortcut down Pope. We pass behind a taco stand and the smell of grilled meat fills the air. Cristo inhales the scent like it's oxygen.

"You hungry?" I ask him. "I was just sitting down to eat when Tony called. I got extra."

"Nah, that's cool. I already ate."

"I thought kids could always eat."

"I'm straight. I can find something at Kim's."

I stop walking. "I'm asking you to eat with me."

He looks at me. I can tell he's choosing his words carefully. "I thought that was one of your rules. That nobody knows where you live."

I spit on the ground next to him. "You ain't nobody."

He chews on the string to his hood and smiles. "Is it far?"

I point to the rooftop towers of Atlantic Mills, twin globes that make the skyline look like some Russian ghetto. "Right over there."

"Atlantic Mills?" he says. "I thought that was just a factory."

"Used to be."

Along with the needle exchange, it's home to the loft I bought when I was eighteen, on the same floor where the Providence Jewelry Exchange used to make engagement rings for the Kennedys.

"I didn't know anybody lived there," he says, his feet falling into step with mine.

I look down at him and wink. "Nobody does."

◆ ❖ ◆

We enter through the back, beside the loading dock, since the building has no official front door. There's an elevator for freight, but I never use it. We climb the stairs—six flights—and at the top Cristo pretends he isn't winded. The hallway is cluttered with boxes from the manufacturing company that shares the floor with me. My downstairs neighbors are a wholesale furniture dealer and a gospel music producer. I'm the only one who actually lives here.

Cristo keeps looking around as we walk down the hallway. He notices the stack of pizza boxes by my front door, a tower as high as his waist.

"Damn," he says. "Guess you like yourself some pizza." He starts to count the boxes.

"Not really." I look down at them. I want to tell him that I never eat the stuff, that the boxes are strictly for transport, but I decide against it. The less the kid knows the better.

"Don't worry, I recycle."

The door to my unit is oversized, like a barn door, and it slides on wheels as big as a plate. Cristo holds his breath, tapping his fingers against his jeans as I unlock the door. I can tell he's scared—not of what's out here in the hallway, but of what's inside. I slide the door open slowly, revealing my home inch by inch. His mouth falls open.

"Wow, this place is huge. Like a supermarket."

I laugh. "Come inside. Don't let all the heat out."

He closes the door and stares at all the deadbolts.

"Which do I lock?"

"All of them."

I turn on the lights as he walks into the living room.

"I don't get it," he says. "Where are the walls?"

"It's a loft. There are no walls."

"You like it like that?" He stands in the same spot, slowly spinning around.

I shrug, walking toward the kitchen. "Without walls, I don't have to worry about who's hiding on the other side." I open the fridge. "You thirsty?"

"Sure," he says. "Whatever you got."

"I got rice milk and green tea."

"I'll take water," he says.

"Wow. The kid's got jokes."

Across the room, he's smiling to himself. He walks to the other end of the living room, where there's a pool table next to a long wall of windows. The billiard balls are scattered across the tabletop, but he lines them up along one side, ordering them based on number. He puts the cue ball at the head of the line.

"You got cats?" he calls to me.

"No."

"Good. A cat could get lost up in here."

He walks up to the thirty-gallon glass tank where my python lives. He peeks inside, stepping back when he sees the snake.

"He's sleeping or I'd let you pick him up."

"No thanks. I only like animals with legs."

I shrug. "He's quiet. And he doesn't need a lot of attention."

"You had him a long time?"

"Since high school. I got him after my momma died."

He looks surprised, like he thought I didn't have one.

"You got any other family?"

"No. Not anymore."

He taps the side of the glass, trying to wake Kingston up. "So you're like me then?"

"Nope. You got family. You're just separated right now. They'll come back."

"How you know that?"

"Some people are meant to be alone. You're not one of them."

He looks at me. "Are you?"

I open my mouth to answer, but end up telling him we need to eat soon so I can walk him home.

"Okay, boss. Whatever you say."

We sit in the dining room, at a wide mahogany table that came from my Uncle Dayton's estate. It was the only thing I kept when I sold the house. I like it because it's massive—it sits twenty people with elbow room—but it's made from one solid piece of wood. It took four men to carry it inside. Cristo is the first person to sit down at the table to eat with me.

Dinner is takeout from Thai Patio, where I eat almost every day. Cristo says he's never had Thai food, but he eats a few spring rolls and all the noodles from the pad thai, and says the chicken satay is the best chicken he ever ate. He leaves the coconut soup for me. We eat in silence; him staring at his food, me staring at him. The light from the candle makes him look darker than he really is, and with his hair all curly he looks like any black kid I could have brought home from the South Side, including my own son. The thought of having a son makes me smile. Imagine that—having somebody walking around with my blood, somebody I made.

He looks up and sees me smiling, which makes him look away.

"You want some more?" I hold up a piece of chicken.

"Nah. I'm good." A second later he points to the extra spring rolls. "You gonna eat those?"

"Help yourself," I tell him.

He wraps the rolls in a napkin and puts them in his pocket. "For Luz," he says, looking through the containers for anything else he could bring her.

◆ ❖ ◆

I don't take Cristo with me when I start working on his old apartment on Sophia Street. No need to bring up the past. I leave the front door half open to air out the room while I paint, risking cats and other riffraff sneaking in. I like the smell of paint, even though it gives me a headache. It's the closest I ever get to being intoxicated.

The lady from DCYF shows up unannounced. They usually do. She slips in sideways without touching anything, and waits until she's standing in the middle of the kitchen to call out hello. She startles me, but I pretend I'm not surprised to see her standing there. I get down from the ladder, a paintbrush in my hand.

"Can I help you with something?"

"I certainly hope so. Do you work here?"

"I own the building."

"Well that's even better." She crosses the room to approach me. "My name is Sylvia Sousa and I'm from the Department of Children, Youth, and Their Families." She holds out a business card but I don't take it. "I'm looking for information about a family that used to live here. Mom's name was Arcelia Perez De La Cruz. Obviously you knew her...?" She looks down at her clipboard and back up at me.

"Yeah, she lived here about six months ago. Haven't seen her since."

"Well, no, you wouldn't have. She's currently incarcerated." She clicks the top of her ballpoint pen, making marks on the paper. "What can you tell me about her children?"

I gesture around the empty room. "They're not here."

"Well I can see that." She looks at her paper again. "It says here there are three children. A son, Cristoval Luna Perez, age eleven; daughter, Lucila Luna Perez, age ten; and daughter, Trinidad Collazo, age three, currently residing with her biological father. The older children were placed with one guardian at this address for several months, a Luciana Cuaron, and were recently relocated to a nearby family member."

I turn around to dip the brush into the paint can. "Are you asking me a question, lady?"

She flashes a fake smile, a line of offensively white partials. "I'm simply reviewing the facts I've gathered thus far. I'm newly assigned to the case."

"So what do you want from me?"

"General impressions would be helpful. Of the children and their relationships with their mother, as a start. If there were any signs of neglect or abuse in the children, or if you saw any illegal activity on the part of the guardians, that would be helpful to know. That sort of thing..."

"I really don't get that involved with my tenants," I say, turning to go back to work.

"Of course, yes, I understand. It's just that it's hard to make a determination about whether or not these people are suitable caretakers, without getting a few more impressions from people who actually knew them."

I begin painting the wall in smooth, even strokes. "I wouldn't say I knew them. I saw them around, that's it."

"Recently?" She clicks her pen again.

"I can't say for sure." I keep painting.

"Do you have any reason to believe the children shouldn't be reunited with their mother, assuming she passes random drug tests and finds suitable housing?"

"That's not my call to make. Isn't that your job?"

"Ideally my job wouldn't need to exist. If every parent was a reliable, law-abiding citizen."

"Sorry, lady, but I can't help you." I move around the room, using the ladder to reach the high parts of the wall. She watches me for a while, before losing interest and walking around the apartment to peer into the empty rooms. When she returns, her pen is once again hovering over the clipboard.

"Listen, Mister..." she pauses, wanting me to fill in my name, but I ignore her. "Listen, we're not trying to get anyone in trouble here. We just want to do what's best for the children. And the family."

I rest the paintbrush on the edge of the can and turn around to face her. "And how do you know what that is?" I peel dried paint from my hands and roll the gummy drops into a ball.

"That's a very good question," she says. She bites down on the stem of her eyeglasses. "How do you know the best color for this room? The best price for this apartment?" She puts her glasses back on her face. She looks almost pretty now, or at least smart. "We all struggle to uphold the standards in any line of work."

"I'm dealing with a rental unit, not someone's life," I tell her. "I don't have to worry about the best, I worry about good enough."

"Hmmm," she says, with exaggerated thoughtfulness, "I guess we're not that dissimilar after all." She leans into the doorway to examine the trim, which is covered in layers of old paint. "It must be a lot of work, to cover up all the lead paint in these old houses. But that's what you have to do, isn't it, in order to follow the law?" She touches a loose part with her fingernail and a large chip of paint breaks off.

"That trim's next on my list," I say. "A little more work and this place will look new again."

"I'm sure it will," she says, nodding her head firmly. "Either way, I doubt you'll have trouble renting it. As long as everything's up to code."

I try to read her face but I can't get much from across the room. I wonder if she really has the nerve to threaten me.

"Do you happen to know if she has any other family in town?" she asks, changing her voice to sound like we're talking about a friend we have in common.

"Nope."

"I'm trying to track down her cousin, but all of his contact information seems to have changed. These people move around so much."

I look at her. "*These* people? What kind of people is that?"

She clears her throat. "You know what I mean. All the foreigners, and the Spanish people on state aid. It's hard for them to find steady work and keep up with the rent. You must know that better than anyone."

"There was a time when we were all foreign," I tell her.

"Yes, of course. But that was a long time ago. My family has been here for three generations. All in Fox Point."

"And my family came here in chains—what's your point, lady?"

She puts up her hand, shielding her eyes as if I'm too bright to look at.

"I'm sorry, I've overstayed my welcome. I'll let you get back to your work." She places her business card on the counter, and backs out of the room. "Thank you for your time," she calls out, closing the door behind her. "Please get in touch if you remember anything else."

There's just enough daylight left for me to finish painting the ceiling and the front half of the living room. The paint is a bright white acrylic that dries quickly, and when I walk back into the room it doesn't look like I painted at all. It looks like I just washed the dirt from half the walls. The unpainted part looks so dingy I force myself to quickly finish the room, painting in the half-dark with large, sloppy strokes just to cover it all up. I rinse out my roller in the kitchen, leaving white droplets in the sink that look like spilt milk.

Before I leave, I walk through the darkening rooms, trying to imagine living in this apartment myself. I wonder if I would feel comfortable and safe, if I would think of it as my home. I try to imagine being Cristo, or being any kid really, and coming here after school and eating dinner, doing my homework, and falling asleep. I see myself at eight or ten, standing on the ripped linoleum floor in my bare feet, lying down to watch TV on the matted carpet, counting watermarks on the ceiling instead of saying my prayers. I see Justin. At four, six, eight—ages when I no longer knew him—and wonder, what would be good enough for him?

I remember the home I grew up in, how it smelled like Pine Sol, lilacs, and cornbread all at the same time. How big and clean it was, how silent. I walk into the smaller bedroom, where Cristo and his sisters lived in an eight-by-eight-foot space, and lift up a corner of the carpet to check the hardwood floors. They're old and dirty, but they can be salvaged, I realize, and if I have them sanded and refinished they would look almost new again. I glance around the room. A ceiling fan would help, and a new pane of glass in the front window. I could do that for the next family that moves in here. It doesn't have to be the best, but it can be better than it was. It can be good.

When I move the dresser to tear up more carpet, I come across a wall covered with pencil marks. I look closer and see that it's handwriting: the word *Luz* written over and over again in a flowery script, like an after-school punishment on a chalkboard. My walls were tagged by a ten-year-old. Either this kid is an egomaniac, or she's proving to someone somewhere that she does exist.

Cristo once told me that his sister's name means "light" in Spanish, but that everything about her is dark. He said her hair is black, and her eyes are the color of Coca-Cola. I move the dresser back to its place and return her name to the darkness for one more night.

Luz

When I get back from school on a rainy day after Thanks-giving there's a package waiting for me. A small, flat square with my name written on the outside in black magic marker, a mix of upper and lowercase letters like how a child would write it. It's from my mother, no surprise there, but I'm not sure if it's a very late birthday present or an early Christmas gift. I can instantly tell it's a book, which makes me feel like there's a flower blooming in my chest. But then I read the title: *A Cat's Meow, Sounds and Shapes for Your Toddler*. My flower dies before I can pick it.

Even my own mother doesn't know me.

There's a letter inside, handwritten on a small sheet of lined paper. I go outside to the porch to read it, careful to stay under the roof so I don't get wet. It says she's thinking about me every day, and that she sees me in her dreams. I wonder what she can dream of from a locked cell. She asks about my brother and sister and tells me to give them each a kiss from her. She asks about school and the weather and what we're watching on TV. She asks about Lucho. What she forgets to ask is what we're eating, how we're sleeping, and if our clothes still fit. She also forgets to ask about anyone else, which is good because I don't know how to say that Chino is gone, that Sammy only talks to the Nintendo machine, and that Kim doesn't leave her room for more than ten minutes every night.

If she wanted to know more than that, I'd have to tell her that Sammy's *gordito* now because all he does is sit in front of the

TV eating Pringles by the can, claiming it's a vegetable. None of his clothes fit, which Kim hasn't noticed, so he wears an old pair of sweatpants that Chino left behind, rolled up at the bottom so he doesn't trip. He says he eats a balanced diet—his meat is Slim Jim's, his fruit, cherry-flavored Twizzlers. When he has money from his grandmother he eats a bag a day, otherwise he steals them from the Dumpster behind the movie theater on Academy. His teeth are always a shade of light pink. I tell him they're going to all fall out if he doesn't brush them more, but he tells me to mind my own business. "If you knew as much as you think you do," he says to me one night when we're home by ourselves, "you wouldn't be living on somebody else's couch eating fortune cookies for dinner." I guess he has a point.

If she wanted anything close to the truth, I'd have to tell her that all Kim does is work, sleep, and drink boxes of wine that look like pink lemonade. That's what she said it was when she poured it over ice and drank it with a straw. I believed her until I found a half-empty glass she left in the bathroom and it tasted sour like vinegar. When Cristo tried it he said it's either wine or vodka or maybe both. When she's lying down she's okay, but when she stumbles into the kitchen to freshen her drink she talks funny and her hands shake. Sometimes she forgets our names. Her eyes are always red, so she tries to hide them behind sunglasses. She stopped using the oven on Halloween, when she started a fire by putting two whole frozen pizzas inside, boxes included. That small oversight left half the kitchen looking like a crash site. Now she leaves all food preparation to us.

The last thing my mother writes is a promise: *I promise to tell you the truth when I get home.* Just imagining my mother's version of the truth makes my neck itch. I heard a teacher once say, "Careful what you wish for—you just might get it." Now I understand what she meant. I don't really want to know the truth, especially if it means I have to turn around and tell the truth back to her. Thanks, but no thanks.

I tuck the letter into one of the books I'm reading. I don't use many bookmarks since I finish them so fast, but at least I can look at her handwriting and maybe feel like she's close by.

It's still raining when I go outside to throw the package away. I hate rain, especially when it's freezing out, and I hate being wet. Winters here are the worst. They're cold and gray and we never have enough snow to make it fun. And the schools around here never get cancelled, even when it dumps like a foot of snow overnight. Which it never does, no matter how much they promise it's coming.

The garbage cans live at the top of the driveway, below a rusted-out basketball hoop that's missing the net. When he takes out the garbage, Cristo likes to shoot the small bags into the hoop and watch them fall into the open cans below. He's good at making things fun, so they don't feel like work. Since I'm alone, I throw out the package the easy way. I wonder if I should toss the book as well, since Trini's not here for me to read it to. I've got the book in one hand and the metal lid to the garbage in the other when I notice Kim's car in the driveway. The lights are off but the car's still running. The windows are foggy but I can see her inside, leaning over the passenger seat. She looks like she's picking her nose with her pinkie finger. Then she sniffs and pinches her nose together. She leans back in her seat and rolls her head in my direction. Her eyes are closed.

I stand perfectly still, careful not to make a sound, and wait for two full minutes before I put the lid back on the garbage can and sneak inside. When the boys get home, I don't tell them what I saw. She comes in through the kitchen almost an hour later and gives the room a tight smile. Sammy waves to her and Cristo nods, but I don't look at her. She keeps walking, like she doesn't see any of us. Nobody in this house talks anymore.

After Sammy goes to sleep I tell Cristo what I saw. We wait till Kim's asleep and then sneak into her room. I watch the door while he grabs her purse. We search through it in the bathroom, huddled around a Tweety Bird night-light. In a small pocket meant to hold lipstick, Cristo finds a prescription bottle filled with round green pills that say "OC" on one side and "80" on the other. The label says it's OxyContin, which means nothing to me, but the name on the bottle does: Scottie Collazo.

"What the hell is Kim doing with Scottie's pills?" Cristo asks, but I know he doesn't expect me to answer.

I grab the bottle, looking for clues. "What's it for anyway?"

"I bet they're pain meds. Remember how Scottie hurt his back last year?"

"Yeah, but look at the date. These pills are new." I turn the bottle around and point out the date. It was filled last week. "Maybe she got hurt," I say.

Cristo looks at me funny.

"Nobody snorts medicine," he finally says.

I remember walking into the bathroom last year and finding a man with a straw in his nose, sniffing a light-brown powder off a picture frame. He was sitting on the edge of the bathtub. When he looked up at me, he smiled and said, "I know you." Then he tilted the picture frame in my direction, flashing a photograph of Cristo and me standing in front of the airport the day he arrived in New York. We were holding hands in the picture, but I remember not wanting to touch a stranger. My mother grabbed my arm, saying, "This is your brother, now hold his hand," so I did. The man held the picture frame up to his face and licked the residue from the glass. Then he made a sound that twisted my stomach, a growl-laugh I could still hear when I closed the door and ran back to my room.

When I look at Cristo now, his face half shadowed in the dim light, I realize he's sometimes still a stranger to me.

"It's bad, huh, what she's doing."

He looks at me like I'm stupid. "All drugs are bad."

I want to ask if he thinks our mother is bad, but I can't make myself say it. I know stories are always showing how good people do bad things, but it's hard to believe when it's your own mother.

"At school they say snorting them is really bad. That's how people lose their jobs and houses and stuff." I wrap my hair around my finger, tight enough to cut off circulation.

Cristo puts the bottle back and zips up her purse. My finger starts to throb.

"If that bad stuff happens to Kim, then where will we go?"

"Don't worry about it," he says. "It's not going to happen."

I want to ask him how he knows but he already seems pissed.

"Did Mami do that?" I finally say. My finger looks bruised like a dark plum.

"I never saw her," he says, his hand on the doorknob. He looks at me for a long time before opening the door.

We both know it's not the same thing as saying no.

◆ ❖ ◆

I find a pizza box under the couch when I'm looking for a lost Hello Kitty mitten a few days later. It says *Allessandro's Pizzeria* along the side, a place I've never heard of. There's no address or phone number on it, just the name and picture of a man tossing a pizza crust as big as a table. I feel the top, to see if it's warm. It's not. The corner of the box has a footprint on it, one from a very large boot. I know there's no pizza inside, since food doesn't last long in this house, but I open it away, hoping for a miracle. What I see doesn't make sense to me.

Tiny boxes the size of matchbooks are stacked on their sides and tied together with rubber bands. There is no writing anywhere on them. I pick up a bundle, surprised that it's heavier than it looks, like a block of cheese. I shake it and hear what sounds like broken pieces of candy inside. Something hard like peanut brittle. I fight the urge to open one, to taste the sharp candied slivers. Something makes me bring it to my nose and sniff. All I can smell is the gummy newness of the rubber bands and a sharp scent like rubbing alcohol.

"Luz, what the fuck? Put that away." Cristo runs into the room and kicks the pizza box closed. I scoot backward on the carpeted floor, dropping the bundle.

"Gimme that," he says, snatching it off the carpet. "I could get my ass kicked if something was missing." He inspects the bundle.

I move closer to him, looking over his shoulder. "What is it anyway?"

"Don't ask stupid questions," he says. From how he's acting, I can tell he doesn't know what it is either. "It ain't your business, that's what it is." He opens the pizza box and neatly places the bundle back inside. He checks the rest of the bundles before closing the box.

"Is it yours?"

"Course not."

He smells his fingers. I want to ask if he recognizes the smell but I don't.

"Then how'd it get here?"

"I brought it here, but it ain't mine. I'm just making a delivery."

"You think it's smart to deliver something if you don't know what it is?"

"I think it's a lot smarter than asking too many questions." He stands up, holding the pizza box out in front of his body like he doesn't want it to touch him.

"Where you going?"

"I just told you. I gotta make a delivery."

"It's almost midnight."

"So?" He puts the pizza box on the couch and sits down to pull on his sneakers.

"Can't you do it in the morning?"

"We got school in the morning."

"That's what I'm saying, you should go to sleep."

He looks at me. "Okay, Mom."

"I'm serious."

He zips another sweatshirt over the one he's already wearing and grabs his hat off the carpet. "It's a job, Luz. The guy needs it tonight. Why do you suddenly care so much?"

"I care when Snowman has you delivering pizza boxes in the middle of the night. You could get mugged by some drunk college kids."

"Ha ha." He pinches me on the cheek. "Good one, *chuleta.* But I never said this was for him."

He smiles, like he's proud of himself for keeping a secret from me.

"How many jobs you got?" I ask.

"A few."

"That's not an answer."

He exhales. "I don't work regular for this guy, just whenever he gets a late-night delivery. His old lady won't let him out after second shift."

"This guy got a name?"

He shrugs. "He's somebody Snowman knows."

"So, what, like Frosty?"

He flashes that smile again. "You got a lotta jokes tonight." He pulls his hat low over his face, almost covering his eyes. "His name's Charley."

"Where you going for this Charley?"

He pulls up his hood, adding an extra layer of protection. "Not sure."

"Don't lie. You know something."

He stands up. "The Laundromat, okay? Jesus."

"Which one?"

"On Manton."

"Who you meeting?"

He bites the edge of his lip and won't look at me. He rubs his eyes. "Christ, Luz."

I try to act casual, but I feel my belly start to bubble from nerves. I would never say it out loud, but I'm suddenly scared for my brother. "Consider it insurance. I won't have to say anything unless you go missing."

"Stop being so dramatic."

"Not a word, I promise." I hold out my little finger. "Pinkie swear." We haven't done one in years, but I figure I might win points for nostalgia.

He grabs my pinkie with his and we shake on it. "Some guy named Jimmy," he finally says, reaching for the pizza box.

"Jimmy," I say it slowly like I don't want to mispronounce it. "Jimmy with the tattoo?"

"How am I supposed to know? I've only seen him a few times."

"You can't miss it. It says CUT HERE, with a line right across his neck." I make the gesture with my finger.

"I've heard about that guy," he says. "That's a pretty sick tattoo."

"Well, he'd have to be sick to make a deal with Scottie."

"Scottie?" Cristo stops short. "What does Scottie have to

do with anything?"

"I saw them talking once, back in the summer. Jimmy stopped by the house looking for Mami. Said she owed him some money."

"They seem like friends?"

"No. Scottie told him to stop coming around us kids."

Cristo holds the pizza box between us. "Guess that's what Snowman meant when he said never turn your back on someone you know."

"Snowman doesn't like Scottie, does he?"

"He don't trust him."

"*Doesn't* trust him," I say, even though I know he hates to be corrected.

"Right, he doesn't trust him," Cristo repeats after me. "Snowman said he could tell right away Scottie has no loyalty. He told me once that an orphan's got enough loyalty to kill or none at all."

If we became orphans, I wonder which one I'd be.

Cristo looks down at the box. I can see all the questions knocking around in his head.

"Maybe you should open one up again, just to see." I reach for the box. "Or I will, and then I can tell you what's inside."

He grabs my hand to stop me. "You probably won't even know what it is."

"Bet you I will."

"Bet what? You don't have anything to give me."

Since that's true, I don't bother saying anything else. The look on my face must make him feel bad because after that he sits down on the couch and waves me over.

"Okay, come here. And turn out the lights."

"How will we see without lights?" I whisper.

He points to the TV. I follow his orders and soon we're kneeling on the carpet surrounded by small piles of multi-colored pills, the dim light from the screen making our faces glow like neon. The pills look like M&Ms or Skittles and I keep wanting to pop a few into my mouth without letting Cristo see. One box has the same green pills that were in the bottle we found in Kim's purse, but most of them I've never seen before.

"It's like a fucking pharmacy," Cristo whispers.

"What does one guy need with all these pills?" I ask. "How sick could he be?"

Cristo doesn't answer. Instead, he carefully drops the pills back into their containers one by one. "Maybe he's not the one who's sick." His lips are moving as he counts silently to himself. "Maybe the sick people come to him."

"Like a doctor?"

Cristo shrugs. I help him re-stack the containers.

"You think Kim went to a guy like that?"

"Maybe. Or she went to Scottie so she didn't have to."

What neither one of us says out loud is, maybe Scottie is the doctor. Cristo looks at me.

"You can't ever tell anyone that you saw this. You understand?"

I nod.

"Not Sammy, not Teacher, not the kids at school. Nobody."

"I won't, Cristo."

"This is just between you and me."

The nerves in my belly are back. "Are we going to get in trouble?"

"Of course not. We didn't do anything wrong." He finishes organizing the bundles and closes the lid to the pizza box. "Especially you. You don't know anything."

"I know what I just saw."

He grabs my shoulders and stares at me like he sees right through my body and all the way out to the street.

"You didn't see anything," he says, like he's trying to convince me it's true. "You're just my little sister, okay?" He tugs on my braid and pinches my cheek like he always does. "You're a kid, Luz. You don't know what you saw."

I know he's just trying to protect me and do what our mother isn't here to do, but it still bothers me. Why does taking care of someone mean you have to make them feel like a baby?

He throws his arm around me, hugging me sideways. This is his way of trying to make me feel better. Of saying he's sorry. "You got it, Lucita?"

I nod to agree with him, but really I'm lying. I don't get

any of this. In her letter, Mami said she would tell us the truth when she got home and now I think I'm ready to hear it. I want to know if Kim is sick and if Scottie is breaking the law and if she ever takes pills like they do and calls it medicine. My head is spinning with questions and I'm afraid I won't get answers to any of them, especially the most important: Are we going to lose all the grownups in our family one at a time, till in the end it's just Cristo and me with nobody left to take care of us? Since I *am* his little sister and I *am* still a kid, I know he'll take care of me no matter what, but then I wonder who will be there to take care of him?

SHE SEES the girl in a white dress. Her hair plaited with ribbons. She is not a girl, she is a woman now. A wife. The church bells rings. There is music, dancing, laughter all around. She dances with her father. He is crying, the first time since her mother died. She dances with her husband. He is smiling as he bows before her. He takes a flower from her hair and places it between his teeth. She is sick with joy, wondering what she's done to deserve such happiness. She kisses her husband while they dance together, dizzy and breathless. She tastes the wine on his tongue, swallows his hunger. He whispers in her ear. She feels him inside her, even before she opens herself to him. She gives him everything he asks for, all of her. Except the truth.

Javier

He hasn't held a bat, or a glove, or even stood on a baseball diamond in more than ten years, but there is something about him that makes him seem like a ball player. His eyes dart around a lot, never staying focused too long, and he has a habit of standing on his toes, as if at any moment he could get the signal to steal second. He drinks too much, but he is still quite lean, though the only exercise he gets is walking to the mailbox at his mother's house—a half-mile down a winding dirt road that she can no longer navigate with her cane and artificial hip—and his shoulders, at one time so strong he could do consecutive dips for more than three minutes, are still coiled with muscles; the tanned skin that covers each deltoid is taut, as if concealing a hard ball.

When he thinks of himself, he sees his body in a baseball uniform: the tight polyester pants that were always too long, their tapered ends tucked into his socks; the loose jersey with stiff block letters across the front and thin, round buttons as smooth as lemon drops; the fitted cap, always a dark color like navy or black, with its brim bent into a perfect C. When he's bored, lonely, or sad, he imagines himself in his windup, slowly dropping back to the mound, or trotting off the field after striking out the cleanup hitter, barely aware of the applause, or even doing something as mundane as putting on his jacket to keep his arm warm between innings, and he instantly feels better, as if the memories are enough. But they aren't. He knows those moments were the best of his life—at eighteen he had reached the apex—and he will never feel that comfortable, that confident, that controlled, again.

When he gets the letter from Arcelia he doesn't know what to do. He can't bring himself to open it, but he doesn't want to let it out of his sight. He carries it in his pocket for three days, rubbing it with his fingertips during breaks from work, his calloused hands barely able to feel the difference between the paper and his blue jeans. When he finally reads it, he is sitting in the empty bleachers of a stadium where for three summers in a row he played baseball for the local farm team. He realizes, with some sadness, that he has never actually sat here before, that he has never watched a game that he didn't play in. But this is where Arcelia always sat, when she came with her cousins to the games on weekend afternoons and spent each inning stomping on the aluminum benches as she cheered for him, calling his name and number until her voice broke.

He has to read the letter several times, particularly the parts written in English, which he never learned to read very well. He can tell that she was crying as she wrote it, partly because she admits to being unhappy in the letter, but mostly because he can feel several puckered spots on the paper where her tears must have dried. He is glad to know that he can still make her cry. She talks in circles in the letter, telling and retelling the story of why she left, how she's survived, and how she ended up having to serve six months in a prison in Rhode Island. Of course she is in a women's facility, but every time he reads the word *prison*, he imagines her locked up with hundreds of men, and a rage builds in his chest that makes his pulse quicken and his mouth water. He wonders several times if he's going to be sick.

Most of the letter is about their children. She tells him that at eleven Cristo is still small and wiry, like his father, but that he's confident, funny, and quick. She says that he is brave because he isn't afraid to swim in the ocean in March, or walk alone down a dark street, and that he takes care of things around the house like a man. She talks about how smart Luz is, how she's already in the Regular classes and reads books by famous American authors, how she can sit for hours in the same spot on the sofa, sometimes reading an entire novel in one day. She tells him how beautiful she is, how she still has his brown skin and dark eyes, and how her hair is thick and black like molasses. She tells him about Trini, her baby, who she had with an American man, describing how sharp her dimples are and how she laughs all the time, even though she hasn't seen much in this world worth smiling about. She says that she wishes Trini were his child, too, and that she used to watch her sleep for hours as a baby, wishing she had never left Puerto Rico.

The biggest surprise of the letter comes at the end, when she tells him that she has forgiven him. For the fights and the name-calling; for all the nights he didn't come home; for the two times he hit her, once while she was pregnant and yelled at him about gambling away his paycheck, and once when he accused her of cheating on him with the butcher's son; for not standing up to her father when she wanted to borrow money to buy a house; for giving up on baseball after his knee injury; and for not following her to the States, even though she never invited him and, in fact, threatened to disappear forever if he followed her. And, of course, she wants to be forgiven, too.

Most of it he thinks he can do. He can forgive her for not being a virgin on their wedding night; for drinking too much and not keeping the house clean; for convincing him to move out of his mother's house before they had saved enough money; for letting him give up on his dream of pitching in the Major Leagues; for being young and foolish and turning to drugs and easy money in order to survive in the States. But forgive her for taking his children away? For having another one with another man? For not talking to him for more than five years?

He's not so sure he will ever be able to forgive her for that.

◆ ❖ ◆

The last time he saw his son was at the airport in San Juan. Cristo was five years old and was just learning how to read. He wanted to read every sign along the way: the street signs on the newly paved highway, the flight information at the check-in gate, the magazine covers at every newsstand. He held his ticket in both hands and tried to read every word printed on it, even the minuscule terms of agreement at the bottom of the paper. Javier had borrowed a friend's car to drive to the airport, and as they walked to the gate he kept looking at his watch; the friend had to be at work in an hour.

The flight was delayed due to thunderstorms in Miami, and for several minutes he thought about leaving Cristo with an older lady flying home to New York. Eventually, he decided he should wait. He knew it would be a long time before he saw his son again.

His mother had packed food for the boy, enough for several meals even though the flight was only four hours, but when Cristo asked for a basket of *tostones*, Javier couldn't say no. He bought the largest size and asked the lady for the crispiest pieces, and he and Cristo sat together on a wooden bench in front of the window and ate the entire basket while watching other planes take off and land. Javier licked the salt off his fingers one by one, and pretended not to notice later when Cristo did the same thing.

When they finally announced his flight over the loud-speaker, Javier handed Cristo the backpack he had been carrying. Inside was the food, Cristo's teddy bear Chachi, several children's books, and a set of dominoes in a walnut case that Arcelia had asked his mother to pack, a wedding present from her grandmother and the only valuable thing the two of them owned. Cristo put the backpack on, tightening both shoulder straps, and tried not to bend under the weight. When they got near the front of the line, Javier slipped off his jean jacket. He tucked a twenty-dollar bill into the pocket before handing it to his son.

"I know it's too big, but it will be cold up there," he said. "Like you've never felt."

"*Sí*, Papi." Cristo held the jacket against his chest, as if already bracing for the cold.

After the attendant collected his ticket, Javier knelt down in front of his son. He gave him a long, hard hug and a quick kiss on the cheek. Cristo smiled up at his father, who turned away at the last minute so his son wouldn't see his eyes well up with tears. He reached out, lightly cupping his hand over Cristo's head, and felt his soft, curly hair for the last time.

"*Adios, mijo*," Javier called after him, as Cristo walked down the jetway. He lifted his arm to wave but Cristo never turned back around. The last time he saw his son, he was walking away from him.

Javier waited at the gate so he could watch the plane depart, even though he knew he would be late to return his friend's car and would have to buy him a pitcher of beer at the bar later that night. He stood alone in the window, apart from the others, so that if Cristo had a window seat, and was looking out of the plane trying to find him, he would be easier to see.

He left the airport a few minutes later and has never had a reason to go back.

◆ ❖ ◆

The sun has set now, and the lights in the stadium are already turned on, huge fluorescent spotlights that can be seen from the next town. The whole park was recently remodeled, after a hurricane leveled much of the town. The stands have filled up slowly, with families coming out to watch a high school championship game, but Javier hasn't moved; when the players take the field he is still sitting in the bleachers, the letter from Arcelia tucked into his back pocket.

He watches the home team warm up; the first baseman throws ground balls to the infield while Javier wonders how he should respond to his wife. Should he take his time before writing back, at least a month or two, or should he hop on a plane and fly to Providence right away, to see her at the prison during visiting hours? Should he pick up the phone and call her? Can she even get calls? And if he did get through, if he heard her voice on the phone, what then? What could he possibly say?

The pitcher is tall and skinny, and has a funny way of tucking his hand into his glove during the windup that seems to be throwing off the batters. He strikes out the first two and then ducks as the third one hits a line drive straight into the second baseman's glove. Javier watches the pitcher jog off the field and disappear into the dugout, a huge smile on his carefree face. He wants to leave, to go to his mother's house for dinner or catch an American football game with his friends at the bar, but he can't bring himself to walk out in the middle of the game. He remembers what it was like to play in front of a crowd, to feel important, and he doesn't want to rob these boys of their evening of glory. It's only a few more hours, he tells himself, certainly not a lot in the span of his life. He can spare that for these kids, his hometown team, even if he doesn't know any of them personally.

A man sitting next to him buys ice cream cones for his three children, who sit in the row below. He passes the cones down to them one by one. Javier wonders if his children eat a lot of ice cream, and what their favorite flavors are, and if it is too late for him to learn such insignificant things. The little girl sitting in front of him drops her cone, crying out as it hits the grass below. Her brother tries to comfort her, but she doesn't stop crying until her father has given her the remainder of his own cone. Javier smiles at the father when he catches him staring. The father shrugs and throws his head back with a laugh, smiling up at the night sky.

Javier turns away and has to bite the insides of his cheeks to keep from crying.

THIS SIDE OF PROVIDENCE

Arcelia

They finally agree to let me out of this dump, just in time for Christmas. First I gotta go to an appointment with discharge planning, where a lady who looks like she don't know how to laugh gives me a bunch of papers with names and addresses of agencies I know I won't visit. The first name on the list is AIDS Care Ocean State, some place that helps people with AIDS get housing, free food, and clothes. I ask her if I qualify, even though I only have HIV.

"Yes, of course," the lady says without looking up.

"And they can get me an apartment?"

"They'll put you on the list right away. Depending on what you need it could be a month or several months before they find you something. Do you have anywhere to stay in the meantime?"

"I can stay with my cousin for a while. He's been watching my kids."

She nods and writes something down in my file. "Sounds good," she says after being quiet for a really long time.

The lady gives me the name of a doctor I'll be seeing at RI Hospital, a different one from the guy I'm seeing in here. She tells me he's used to the same population—IV drug users—as if that means we'll understand each other. The card she gives me has his name and address printed on the front, and the date and time of the appointment written out neatly on the other side. It looks like she tried to write it out as clear as possible, so she won't get in trouble if I don't show up.

She hands me three small bottles of pills, a one-week supply, and tells me that I have to fill my prescription as soon as I get out.

"They warned you about med adherence, right?"

"Yeah. But what's that mean again?"

"That means you have to keep taking your meds, even though you feel fine, because if you stop and then try to get back on, they could stop working for your body."

"It's medicine. I thought it either works or it don't."

"It's not that simple, Arcelia." She checks the clock on the wall. "You can ask the doctor about it if you have more questions. Our time here is almost over." She looks through the rest of my file. "What are you planning as far as work?"

I shrug. "I don't know yet."

"Do you have any job experience?"

"I got lots of experience, lady. But maybe not in the right kind of jobs."

She stares at me like she hates her job. "Okay," she finally says, putting her hands flat on the desk. "What did you do before you came here? Aside from what you got arrested for."

"I was raising my kids. I've got three of them. That's triple the experience, right?"

She bites her pencil. "Child care is probably not going to work. They want your record to be crystal clean. But what about food services, have you ever been a waitress?"

"I used to work at a 7-Eleven."

"Okay. Are you still in touch with them? Anyone that could give you a reference?"

"I got fired. Plus, it was like five years ago. In New York."

She shuffles some papers on her desk. "I think they've got some space in a janitorial training site in Cranston. Cranston or Warwick, I can't remember which. Do you have a means of transportation?"

"A what?"

"A way to get there?"

"All I got is my legs."

"Well, your case manager at AIDS Care should be able to get you a bus pass. I'll jot down a note about it in your file. You might want to mention it yourself, though, just in case. Sometimes the files get held up."

She writes something down on a Post-it note and sticks it in the file. I know right now if it ever gets lost, I won't say anything.

"Okay, that pretty much wraps it up for us. Do you have any other questions?"

She looks at me, while questions go off in my head like gunfire.

How am I going to feed my children?
How will I stay clean on the outside?
How sick am I?
How much time do I have?
What do I do if I miss the life I had in here?

But I don't ask any of them out loud. I shake my head and walk out of her office, jamming the papers into my back pocket like a dirty rag.

The night before I leave, I pack my things into a small duffel bag Kim and Chino brought me the first time they visited. It's weird that I can pack up all my crap in three minutes, even though I lived here more than six months.

Candy comes by earlier than usual, right after lights out, and slips into bed with me for the last time. We fool around a little, but halfway through she stops and hides her face in the pillow and starts to cry. I don't know what to do, since Candy isn't the type of girl who usually cries, so I ignore it at first, hoping she'll stop on her own. When she don't stop, I put my arm around her and hold her as tight as I can and tell her that everything is gonna be fine and that soon she can go home like me.

A while later, with her back against me and her knees curled into the cement wall, she finally speaks.

"Why didn't you ever tell me you were positive?"

I was gonna tell her a few weeks earlier, when she saw me standing in the med line, but I never thought of a good way to bring it up.

"Is that why you're crying?"

"Yes," she says, wiping her nose on the sheet. "Not because

you have it. Because you didn't trust me enough to tell me."

"Sorry," I tell her. "I thought it was too much."

She hugs her knees, rocking like a baby. I wonder if Trini still rocks like that.

"Everything is too much in here," she says. "It's not like one thing is going to make a big difference."

"But it's a big thing."

"Why? Because you're sick?" She finally turns over to look at me. "We're all sick. And we're all going to die eventually. What's the difference if it's next week or next year? Nobody's going to outrun death. Especially us."

I close my eyes and bury my head in her chest. I breathe her in—a mix of hair oil, vanilla, and cigarettes that's become as familiar as her face in the dark. She rubs the back of my neck with her fingertips. I pull up her skirt and kiss her naked belly. Goose bumps spread over her skin as I touch it. She pulls my head to her breast, guiding my mouth to the stiffness of her nipple. It softens against my tongue as she raises her chest to me. As soon as I hear her moan I know I been forgiven. If only it was this easy to wipe away all my sins.

Later, when she's almost asleep, I ask her a question I been thinking about since we met.

"Why Candy?" I whisper into her ear.

"What you mean?" She pulls away from me to look at my eyes.

"Why not Caramel or Cocoa or Cinnamon?"

She laughs, coming back to kiss me. "Candy's not a stage name. It's short for Candace."

"Candace," I repeat it slowly, like a foreign word. "I never heard that name before."

I hear her yawn. "Well, it's mine."

Something changes after that. Knowing her name makes everything we're doing suddenly real, and it scares the hell out of me. I don't want to be real to her. Most days I think the people we are in here don't really exist, we just make up a person we think can survive this. Once I get out, I figure I can make up a brand-new person, some lady who's totally different from who I been. And who knows, maybe it will be the person I really am.

The bus they put me on is supposed to take me straight to Kim and Chino's place, but I get off on Pocasset Avenue so I can stop at the CVS, instead of using Anthony's in my old neighborhood where everybody knows me. I drop off my prescriptions with a lady in a white lab coat who looks like a teenager, and while she's filling it I look around the store for Christmas presents. They gave me fifty bucks to spend, which seemed like a lot at the time, but I know I have to be careful with it if I want to get something for everybody, even Kim. They sell some T-shirts, but nothing as nice as the stuff at the flea market in Atlantic Mills, so I decide to pick up a snack for now and get the real presents later.

I buy a package of Skittles for Luz, red licorice for Cristo, SweeTARTS for Trini, a king-sized chocolate bar for Chino, and Cracker Jacks for Kim and her son. I buy a box of Sugar Babies for myself and suck on them as I wait in line, hoping all my teeth won't fall out. My tongue finds the gap where my cracked tooth used to be and gently tests the gum. I wince from the pressure. It's been two months but it still hurts to chew on it. The Sugar Babies get stuck in my teeth and I need help getting them out. They don't have any toothpicks, but the lady at the checkout counter gives me a book of wooden matches to use. I feel kinda dumb, but I figure it's worth it. After six months inside, it tasted like sunshine on my tongue.

When I walk back to the pharmacy it's suddenly crowded. A pregnant lady with a baby on her hip is talking to the pharmacist, asking why her insurance won't cover her baby's medicine, and a man with yellow skin coughs into the sleeve of his canvas jacket. Two teenage boys joke in front of a rack of condoms. When one of them sees me looking at him, he raises his eyes and I look away. The clock behind the counter says 4:15—I still have ten minutes before the lady said it would be ready. I been waiting six months to see my children, what's another ten minutes?

I sit in the pickup area to wait, but when it's not ready in thirty minutes, I get antsy and end up walking out of that CVS with only my duffel bag, ten dollars' worth of candy, and a promise that I'll come back later in the week. Now that I'm free, I figure I got plenty of time.

I walk all the way to Kim and Chino's instead of taking another bus because I want to feel my legs move. It's cold outside, and it's almost dark, but I walk as slow as I can. The pavement feels good under my feet. I smile at the wind, even when it almost knocks me into a parked car and makes my eyes fill with tears. I take the long way, walking through the heart of Olneyville—past the Rent-A-Center, the D'Angelo's, and the car wash—instead of up Manton Avenue and over to Mount Pleasant, even though it adds almost twenty minutes to the walk. I don't want to see my old neighborhood just yet. My corner. My Dunkin' Donuts. My Laundromat. In fact, I wonder if I'll ever be ready to see those places again.

When I get to their street my heart starts to pound and all of a sudden I have to go to the bathroom. I walk up to the porch and stand there for several seconds, trying to catch my breath. Finally, I ring the doorbell. I see my reflection in the living room window and for a second I don't recognize myself. My hair is longer now—past my shoulders—and all the dye is gone. I haven't had brown hair since Trini was born. I'm probably ten pounds heavier than when I left, and my skin has cleared up. And I'm clean. For the first time since I started to use, I'm clean.

Kim opens the door and hugs me like I just got back from war. It feels weird to be held like that, especially by her. Luz stands as stiff as a pencil when I hug her, and I'm scared I'm gonna snap her in two. I see her notice the gap where my tooth should be, but she doesn't say anything. Sammy waves at me from the couch and don't get up. When Cristo sees me he freezes. Then he runs straight at me and tackles me in the middle of the room. He wraps his legs around me and we fall onto the carpet together, rolling around and laughing like we're both kids. I don't let go of him until he lets go first, which feels like a pretty long time.

When I ask to see my baby everybody gets real quiet. Kim

tells me to sit down at the kitchen table. Then she brings me coffee and tells me how Scottie came and took Trini when the kids were alone after Lucho left, and that he moved in with his sister so she could help. She tells me that Cristo and Luz see her once a week now—when they go by his sister's house on Sundays—and she's pretty sure that he's fed up with taking care of her.

"Now that you're home I bet he's gonna make things right." She squeezes my arm and gives me another hug.

I nod my head and act like I understand, but inside I feel the anger coming. I want to start yelling, but Cristo and Luz are looking at me and I don't want to lose it in front of them. I just keep nodding my head.

Kim orders pizza and when it comes I offer to pay for it but she won't let me.

"What kind of family would I be if I made you pay for dinner on your first night home?" She pays the delivery guy and sets the box on the table. "That's some wack shit, Arcelia."

"Come on, money must be tight since Chino moved out."

"Course it is. But I'm okay. Plus, he still helps out with rent and my car payment. He's a good guy like that. Even if he did mess around—"

She stops herself, since the kids are right there. We give them a whole pie to split and send them into the living room, since there's only two chairs in the kitchen. I take a slice from the second box and eat all the pepperoni off it before I take a bite of the crust. They had pizza inside, but never any good toppings. The sauce is so hot it burns my mouth but I don't care because it's so good.

"So what happened with you two?" I ask her. "Why'd he move out?"

"Shit. How much time you got?" Kim's smiling but I can tell she's not happy.

"All I got is time," I say. When I finish the first one, I grab another slice.

Kim pours herself another drink. She keeps making me coffee 'cause I say I've quit everything stronger and when we run out she promises to pick some up at the grocery store next time she goes out. We talk about her and Chino, how he cheated on her with some Guatemalan chick who works at the Price Rite and now Kim refuses to go grocery shopping. There's two sides to every story, but I know my cousin's no saint. I figure she's telling the truth about it, otherwise he'd be here with everyone right now to welcome me home.

After we eat I ask my kids to show me their report cards. Luz brings me a paper with straight As on it.

"Wow. Look at you, superstar."

"Actually, it's not straight As. I got an A-minus in gym because I never did a pull-up, but the teacher felt bad ruining my record so he gave me the full A. But technically, I don't deserve it."

Cristo's got a million excuses when he hands his over.

"It's gonna get better next term, Mami. When I get extra credit on this project I'm doing with Teacher."

"What teacher is that?"

"Miss Valentín," he says.

"You know she's the only one he ever talks about," Luz adds. He's too busy making a face at his sister to see me roll my eyes. Luz tries to elbow him, but I reach out in between them, tickling them both. She pulls away, but he lets me catch him, laughing so hard he chokes on his soda.

"What about your teacher this year?"

"Mrs. Reed," Luz says.

"I can answer for myself," he says, still coughing.

"Then why don't you?"

"She's all right," he says, looking at me now, "but she doesn't really like me."

"Not true," Luz tells me. "She'd like you fine if you weren't tardy all the time and turning in your homework so late."

Cristo kicks her in the leg, but she doesn't even wince.

"Here, look at my project so far." Cristo comes and sits on my lap to show me a binder full of loose pages. "See, these are all different poems, about love and nature and stuff. I'm putting them together to make a book, with a real cover and everything."

"A book of poetry? Wow, aren't you a romantic." I pretend

to read the poems. "You understand all this?" I ask him. "Seriously?"

"It's not that hard, Mami. If you slow down and really read it." He takes the binder from me and closes it gently, like it's one of those old books from a museum with pages that dissolve between your fingers. "I know you don't like books, but maybe you can look at it sometime, when it's done."

"Of course, sweetheart. I will love any book you make." Then I kiss him and tell him I like a lot of things I didn't used to like, and I hate a few things I used to love. He says he'll give it to me once it's finished and looks like a real book.

While the kids get ready for bed Kim brings me into her bedroom and gives me a nightgown to wear and some old socks of Chino's that I can use as slippers. I help Luz pull out the couch and the three of us climb into bed together just like we used to when we first got to New York and were staying in Chino's apartment in the Bronx. I'm in the middle with one kid on either side. As soon as they fall asleep, they curl into me, tucked into balls like when they were tiny babies inside me. I lean over and kiss Luz on the top of her head. The smell of her hair makes me want to cry. All those years I was using, I couldn't smell anything, but now that it's back, I can hardly take it.

The living room is dark, but there's enough light coming from the street to see Cristo's face. He's thinner than when I left, and a little more grownup looking, I guess. And he looks even more like me. I reach out to touch his hair. The curls are long again, like when he was a baby. I brush them with my fingers until my arm gets tired and then I rest it on his pillow, still holding onto his head.

"You are always gonna be my baby," I whisper to him in the dark room. "No matter how big you get or how old you are."

I close my eyes and think of Trini, my sweet little girl, and a smile comes across my face. Suddenly I feel my eyes fill up and when I open them, tears run down my cheeks and onto the pillow. I feel her missing from the bed, like how people say you can still feel your leg after it gets cut off. My nose is running and I have to bite into my knuckle to keep myself from sobbing. I take a deep breath and focus on lying still. I think of the night before, how I was lying in a prison bunk with Candy, and how crazy it seems that twenty-four hours later I'm here on a pull-out couch with my children, free to come and go as I please.

But I don't have all my children.

◆ ❖ ◆

The first thing I do in the morning is call Scottie. The number I have for him is old and it just rings and rings. Then I call his sister's house and leave a message on her answering machine. I try to sound real nice, just saying that I'm back and I want to see my daughter. An hour later I call again and leave the same message. When I don't hear from him by lunchtime, I call the boxing gym where he works and tell the manager it's an emergency about his daughter and that he needs to call this number right away. Scottie's real pissed when he calls back and finds out it's just me.

I tell him I want to see Trini and he says she's with his sister but he can bring her to me after work. I make myself say thank you, but when he asks me how I like being free, I hang up the phone.

I don't want to be alone in the house so I go to the flea market at Atlantic Mills to do my last-minute Christmas shopping. I buy sweatshirts and socks for my kids and a suitcase with wheels for Kim. All my money is gone now and I'm happy that I don't have to keep thinking of ways to spend it.

When I'm still in the parking lot I see one of the ladies who works at the needle exchange carrying supplies into the building. She sings a song to herself about outlaws. I remember bringing Trini with me one time last year, when I couldn't get anyone to watch her. At first the lady pissed me off 'cause she said I couldn't bring anyone under eighteen into the room, but then she came out and stood with the stroller so I could go in and exchange my needles. I remember her singing a few Ricky Martin songs to keep Trini distracted. She was the first person who knew I was a junkie and still looked me in the eyes, so I always liked her for that. She looks my way now, like she knows I'm thinking about her, but I turn away before she sees me. I put all my presents into the suitcase and wheel it back to Kim's. I keep my head down when I walk down Manton, praying nobody will recognize me.

Scottie never comes by. I call him and his sister again, but nobody answers. This time, the answering machine don't even pick up. When Kim comes home I borrow her car and go by the house. I can't remember the last time I was alone in a car. I keep forgetting how to shift so the car stalls on all the hills. The driveway's empty so I figure nobody's there. I wait for a while, watching the neighbor walk his Doberman up and down the street. When he lets the dog take a dump in the yard I laugh.

Once it's dark I can see lights on in the house. I get out of the car and knock on the front door. The door's been repainted so many times it barely stays shut. His sister's inside with her boyfriend watching a baseball game on their wide-screen TV. A space heater in the corner makes the room so hot I don't step inside. She says Scottie's working late tonight so I should go by there. As I'm walking back to Kim's car I hear her yell out, "Welcome home," and then I hear the boyfriend laugh like it was the punch line of a real funny joke.

As soon as I get to the gym I see his old Cadillac. Trini's car seat is in the back, next to a basket of dirty laundry and some pizza boxes. Her stuffed elephant is on the floor next to an empty sippy cup. The sign says they're closed, but a bunch of guys are working out inside, all sweaty and shirtless. I recognize most of them, but I don't say hi and neither do they. When I ask for Scottie the manager tells me he's in the back office cleaning up.

I see Trini first, sitting on the floor in the middle of a huge pile of white towels. Only her head is visible. Her hair is darker than I remember it, and it's tied back in two pink ribbons. She's singing a song to herself, but when she sees me she stops. We lock eyes. I am smiling as I bend down to look at her.

"*Hola, mija*," I whisper like I'm telling her a secret. "I been waiting a long time to see you."

She flashes a quick smile before hiding her face in the towels. Scottie is not in the room, which doesn't surprise me. Trini lifts up her head and stares at me.

"You know who I am, don't you?" I touch her arm and

squeeze her chubby hand. She pulls it away from me. "You remember Mami, don't you, baby?"

She blinks and looks down at my hand. I turn it over, showing her both sides. She touches my scar, then pulls her hand away.

"Where's your daddy, Trini? *Dónde está tu papá*?"

She opens her eyes wide and says, "Daddy's working."

I fix one of her ribbons, retying it into a large bow. She stares at my hands again.

"Do you like my ribbon?" she asks me.

"Si, es muy bonita." I move some towels and help her stand up. She takes a few steps away, but keeps her eyes on me the whole time.

"My favorite color is pink," I tell her.

"I know," she says. "I like pink, too."

I am smiling at her but tears are filling my eyes. I don't want to cry, but I can't stop myself.

"Are you sad?" she asks.

"No, I'm very happy." I wipe the tears off my face and smile at her again. When I try to hug my daughter she twists out of my hands. She goes back to stand next to the pile of towels.

"Can you help me find your daddy?" I hold my hand out to her. "Come on, let's go look for him."

She sucks on the end of her hair, just like Luz when she's nervous. When she finally gives me her hand, I hold it gently, like I'm holding something already broken. We walk down a wide hallway and into a storage room in the back.

"There he is," she says, pointing to a wall of boxes.

I see the cigarette smoke first, then his long, skinny body steps into view. "You found me," he says with a bright voice. He is talking to her, but looking at me. He stamps out his cigarette on the concrete floor.

"It's late. I figured it was best to come to you." I'm trying not to sound as pissed off as I feel.

"I know it's late. Things got crazy. My bad."

"She should be in bed."

He laughs. "You hear that, pumpkin? Mami thinks it's bedtime."

Trini looks at me. I can see her trying to fit the pieces together, trying to match the word *Mami* with this lady standing next to her, not quite holding her hand.

"What do you think," Scottie asks her, "do you want to go to bed?"

She shakes her head. He reaches down to tickle her as he passes by.

"I didn't think so."

"It's nine o'clock, Scottie."

He looks at his watch. "She just took a nap."

"Are you kidding me?"

"Relax. She's fine."

We follow him back to the office, no longer holding hands. Trini drags a box filled with plastic horses to a small rug under his desk. She stands them in two lines, facing each other.

"I want to take her home."

"And where exactly is that?" He stands with his back to me, folding the towels into perfect squares.

"To Kim's."

"No way. There's not even a bed for you there."

I step closer to him, ignoring my instincts. "How would you know?"

He shrugs. "I see Kim around, we talk."

"Then you should know it's only temporary. I'm gonna get my own place."

"Let me know when you do and we can work something out."

He won't look at me.

"She's my daughter, Scott."

"I know that," he says. "She's mine, too."

I watch Trini knock over the line of horses like dominoes.

"Fine. But I want her on Christmas."

He snaps the towel to flatten it, which sounds like a whip cracking.

"Okay. I'll bring her over after we open presents with my sister."

"And then she can spend the night."

"I don't think she'll want to."

"Bullshit." I spit the word at him, wetting his arm. "I'm her mother." I look at my daughter again. Her lips are moving, but I can't hear what she's saying. "You should think about her, not you."

"I am thinking about her. If I was thinking about me I'd ask you to pay me back for the money I spotted you."

I look at him like he's crazy. "What money?"

"A guy named Jimmy came by looking for you, back in the summer. Said you owed him a significant amount of money. His word, not mine."

"How much he say?"

"A couple grand."

"He's lying. It was only one."

"Good." Scottie's smile takes up half his face. "'Cause that's all I paid him."

"You didn't have to do that."

He shrugs. "I didn't want him to keep coming around the kids."

"So you're a saint now?"

He looks at Trini, and then back at me. "Gotta protect what's mine."

"We ain't been yours for a long time." I look him in the eye when I say it. He smiles at me.

"Things change." He grabs the zipper on my sweatshirt and slowly zips me up. I stop his hand at my chest.

"That won't."

He drops the zipper and puts his hands in his pockets. "No sweat," he says. "You can figure out another way to pay me back."

As if giving him my baby wasn't payment enough.

◆ ❖ ◆

On Christmas Eve Kim brings home Chinese food and we eat with chopsticks right out of the boxes. The doorbell rings halfway through dinner and Luz runs to the door, convinced it's Santa Claus. That fat white man was the one thing I ever got her to believe in and even at ten, she acts like he's real. Turns out she isn't far off since it's that teacher Cristo loves from school and she has a whole bunch of presents in a shopping bag.

"I'm on my way to the airport," she says, trying to catch her breath, "but I wanted to drop these off." She hands Luz the bag.

"Look, there's even one for you," Luz says, waving a small box at me. She carries the bag into the living room and arranges the packages neatly on the floor.

I walk to the door. "That isn't necessary, you know," I say. "You done enough."

"I just wanted to make sure…" She clears her throat. "I wasn't sure when you were getting home and if you'd have… time to shop."

"Well, here I am. We got everything we need."

"Yes, I can see that." She looks over my shoulder into the apartment. We don't have a Christmas tree, but the kids hung up the paper stockings they made in school as a way of decorating. And now, with her presents, it's starting to look like we're actually celebrating a holiday.

"Do you want to come in?" I ask her.

"Oh, no, I'm running late as it is. Just tell Cristo I said Merry Christmas."

"Tell him yourself," I say, opening the door to let her in. She steps into the hallway carefully, like she thinks she's gonna break something. I call Cristo, who comes running to the door like a puppy.

"Hey, Teacher." He hugs her. *"Feliz Navidad."*

"Feliz Navidad," she says. "I should have just brought them to school, but I didn't want the other kids to feel bad." She looks at me, saying something with her eyes.

"No big deal," I say. "Everybody loves Santa Claus."

"No," she says, "not everyone. Your children are…special to me."

"They're special to me, too."

She smiles down at Cristo. "Okay, I really should be going now." She pinches his cheek. "I'll see you in the new year, Cristoval."

"Feliz Año Nuevo," he says, giving her another hug. "Have a

nice trip, Teacher." He walks out to the porch with her, standing in his socks. "Thanks for the presents."

"You're very welcome." She's talking to him but looking at me.

He watches her get into the car, still waving as she drives down the street. When he comes back inside, I lean out to grab his arm but he's too far away for me to reach.

After dinner I tell the kids they can watch the Charlie Brown special on TV but Kim makes them clean up the kitchen first and by the time they're done the show is almost over. Kim sits with them on the couch and I have to sit on the floor between their legs, which is good because I like to keep touching them. In the movie the kids are teasing Charlie Brown about the Christmas tree he bought.

"Those kids are mean," Luz says. "A tree is a tree."

"And we don't even have that much," Cristo says.

"You guys want a tree?" I say. "I can get you a tree."

"I thought we agreed a tree was too much work," Kim says. "Cleaning up all those needles."

"And they're dangerous. My teacher says they're a fire hazard." Cristo laughs at the TV, his face lit up in the darkness.

"I don't mind cleaning," Luz says, her head in a book even though we all agreed to watch the special together.

Kim tells me I can stay as long as I want, but I already know there's not room for the two of us in this apartment. My children only have one mother and I need them to be clear about that. It was okay for her to help out while I was gone, but now that I'm back they don't really need her.

Before we go to sleep Cristo and Luz beg me to make *pasteles* for Christmas dinner. It's a traditional Puerto Rican dish, made out of meat and root vegetables. It's easy to make, but it takes a long time, so most people don't eat it too often. My mother taught me how to make it before she died, even though she was so weak in the end that she had to sit on the kitchen floor while I peeled the vegetables. She didn't want me to be motherless and not know how to cook like a real *Boricua*. When they were little I used to make it all the time, but I can't even remember the last time I made it. I'm actually surprised they even remember what it is.

After the kids are asleep I decide to surprise them. Kim don't have any of the things I need, so I borrow her car and drive over to the meat market in my old neighborhood. The old man acts like he remembers me from other late-night trips and he gives me a good deal. In the morning I get up real early to start cooking. Everybody else is still asleep. I shred all the vegetables by hand, scraping my knuckles over the peeler just like my mother used to, and then I brown the meat in a small frying pan. I mix the meat and shredded vegetables together, and place a spoonful of the mixture in the center of a banana leaf. I wrap each one up like a Christmas present—just how she taught me—and tie the string in several knots so it won't come apart in the boiling water. I boil them for twenty minutes and then turn it off to cool, watching them bob in the water like dead fish.

When everybody wakes up we open presents and eat day-old doughnuts Chino brings over from the Jewish bakery on Atwells. It feels good to see my cousin and he hugs me for a long time, lifting me off the floor. I call Scottie and he promises to bring Trini over after breakfast, but a few hours later he calls again and says she ate too much and is too sick to come. When I start to curse him out on the phone he hangs up. I call right back but he doesn't answer. I'm so pissed I throw the phone against the wall and break the mouthpiece. Cristo picks it up and tries to fix it. When I say I'm sorry he tells me it's okay.

"We can see her tomorrow, Mami." He puts his arm around me, trying to make me feel better. "Christmas two days in a row, how sweet is that?"

Fighting with Scottie makes me want to take a fucking drink, but then I see what a mess Kim is from drinking half a box of Zinfandel by herself every night and I tell myself I'm gonna be okay without it. I didn't think it would be this hard to live with someone who was still partying all the time, but so far it sucks. All I got left is food and cigarettes, so I spend all day going back and forth between the two. Kim passes out on the couch before dinner's ready, so we eat without her, stuffing ourselves with hot rolls and *pasteles* until we can't eat anymore. We wrap the leftovers in a plastic bag and put them in the freezer for a cold spring day, just like my mother used to do. Then I go outside to smoke a cigarette.

"Next time, will you teach me how to make them?" Cristo reaches for my hand and follows me onto the porch.

"Me, too," Luz says. "Every Puerto Rican girl should know how to make *pasteles*."

"When we have our own apartment," I promise them. "Then we'll make our own traditions."

I know it's gonna take time, but I decide right then to do whatever it takes to get a place of my own. For years we've been living in other people's houses, and I want to give my kids their own home. I don't want to lie to them or make promises I can't keep, so I don't say anything out loud. But in my head I'm working out all the angles, figuring out exactly how much room the four of us will need and how much cash I have to get.

I smoke my cigarette as fast as I can, the wind blowing so hard I think it's gonna go out. My kids huddle around me, and even though it's freezing, I feel warm inside just being able to touch them. I close my eyes and say a prayer for Trini—to have God tell her I love her—and to show me the way back home.

SHE SEES the girl in front of a stove. Her belly is round, full with life. She peels a ripe mango with a knife. Eats the fruit while she waits. The chicken she made goes cold on the stove. Her husband is late again. He comes home in the dark with apologies. He smells like beer and sweat. She doesn't want him to touch her. He blames the bar, and the baseball diamond. He doesn't want to grow up. He doesn't want to lose her. She takes a bath alone. He falls asleep at the kitchen table. When he wakes up, she's feeding his dinner to the animals. He yells at her to stop. She yells at him to be quiet. He smacks her with the back of his hand. She tastes the blood in her mouth.

Cristo

A few weeks before Christmas vacation, César stops coming to school. He doesn't call in sick or send his grandmother by to pick up assignments, he just stops showing up. Mrs. Reed keeps calling his name every day during attendance, but when it's time to pick Secret Santas she takes him off the list. I draw Esteban's name, but I decide to make César a mix-tape instead. I find an old tape of Lucho's and record over it, erasing some Mariah Carey album with all our favorite songs off the radio. I finish it two days before Christmas, and bring it over to his grandmother's place to surprise him. It starts to snow as I'm walking so by the time I get there there's a thin layer covering the ground. The snow is like magic. It makes even the projects look clean.

The door's half open, but I knock anyway. His grandmother lets me in without saying a word. She has crochet needles and a thick chunk of yellow yarn in her hand. She continues to knit as she walks back to the living room. The needles move so fast it looks like she's in a sword fight with herself.

I walk myself to the back bedroom César shares with his uncle Antonio. The same one who shot him. César says they don't really talk no more, even though they sleep in the same room. Antonio feels so bad he won't even look at him. Whenever he tries, it makes César feel worse. All they ever do together now is play cards, since they only have to look at the deck and not each other.

I step into the room and hear a man's voice on the radio

singing in Spanish. César's on the floor, playing video games on a small black-and-white TV. It's afternoon, but he's still in his pajamas. The stubble on his head is growing back in, like a soldier on leave. He's wearing a flesh-colored leather patch over the eye he just lost.

I sit down on the edge of the bed. "Hi."

"Hey," he says, without looking at me.

"Here, I brought you something." I hand him the tape but he doesn't take it.

"Just put it on the bed."

"Don't you want to listen to it?"

He looks at me. "My stereo's broken."

"Maybe it just needs new batteries. Remember the last time you thought it was—"

"It's broken, all right? I'm not an idiot." He walks over to his dresser, opens a drawer, and pulls out a plastic bag filled with pieces of the broken stereo. It looks like he's showing me a bag of Legos.

"Oh. Sorry."

"No biggie," he says as he closes the drawer. He sits down on the bed. "I dropped it from the Route 6 overpass. I watched it break into a hundred pieces."

"Why?"

He shrugs. "I didn't want to be the only thing broken in this house."

I don't know what to say to that, so I don't say anything. I try not to move.

"How's school?" he finally asks.

"We're on vacation. Till next week."

"Oh yeah. It's hard to remember what day it is, since I'm not always writing it down."

"You ever coming back?" I try to sound casual, like I'm asking him what time it is.

"Maybe. They say I don't have to yet, not while I'm on all these pills. They mess up my stomach so bad I'd have to move my desk into the bathroom." He's making a joke, but neither one of us laughs.

Then he grabs a shoe box from his night table, lifting the

lid to show me all the pill bottles inside. They're all the same type—those see-through orange plastic ones with round white lids—but there's a bunch of different sizes, depending on the pills. Some are big and dark like chewable vitamins, but others look just like Tic Tacs, all shiny and white. The small ones look like the pills I saw in Kim's purse, and the ones in the pizza boxes I delivered for Charley. But I don't say that out loud.

"They look like candy," I tell him.

César nods. "But they don't taste like candy." He opens one bottle and pours it into his hand. The pills are long and round, kinda like the licorice they sell at the movie theater, but these are a mix of half white and half red.

"They're for the seizures," he says. "They stop my brain from freezing up. But if I took them all at once, it would kill me."

I must have a weird look on my face because then he says, "Not that I wanna do something crazy like that. But I'm just saying. That's what would happen."

"What *do* you want to do?" I ask him, watching carefully as he pours the pills back in the bottle. Then he puts the bottles back into the shoe box, lining them up straight. I see his name printed on all the labels, over and over again.

He lies back on the bed and looks up at the ceiling. "I want to be able to see," he says. "That's what I want." After a few seconds he turns over to face me. "You wanna check out my eye?"

I guess a part of me is curious, but the bigger part is worried about passing out right onto the carpeting because it looks so gross. But fuck if I know how to say no to him.

"Okay, if you want me to."

He moves to the edge of the bed and sits right next to me. Outside I can hear the beeping of a large truck as it backs up. I feel my pulse beating in my neck. He peels off the patch and carefully slides it onto his forehead. He closes his good eye, and exhales before turning toward me.

I glance over at the missing eye, and then quickly look away. The wound is a deep pink, like raw meat. I'm surprised that there's no blood, even though it's been healing for weeks. I take a deep breath and look back. The scar that holds the eyelid together is smooth and thick, with several thin scars crossing it from top to bottom. His eyelashes are gone. The eyelid skin is so thin and pale I can see the veins running underneath. He reminds me of a newborn baby or a little bird, something that can't take care of itself.

"Pretty gross, huh?" César opens his left eye to look at me. The right one flutters, but doesn't open.

"No, it's not that bad," I say. With his good eye, he sees me look away.

"It still hurts. Deep inside, where I can't get to it." He runs the tip of his finger under his eyebrow, patting it gently. It's the only part of his eye that isn't damaged. The skin is perfect actually, like the outside of a hard-boiled egg. I'm thinking of a way to tell him that when he speaks again.

"They say the pain will go away later, when my nerves forget, but sometimes I think they'll never forget."

I'm still looking at the scar. The eye socket looks deeper than the other one, like some of the bone was scraped away too. I try to imagine what it looks like inside, under the skin. His eyelid flutters again, like it wants to open up. I wonder what they did with his eyeball.

"How long you gotta wear the patch?"

"As long as I want," he says. "Forever, probably." Then he pulls it down from his forehead to cover the scar. It's easier to look at him now, even though I know what's under the patch, like putting a sheet over a dead body.

"*Vamonos, César, es muy tarde ya,*" his grandmother calls from the kitchen. "*Esta tiempo para cocinar, bien?*"

"I gotta go," César says. "Now that I'm home my grandmother expects me to help out more. She's got me cooking almost every night, like I'm a girl or something."

"But you just got home from the hospital."

César shrugs. "Just another mouth to feed."

He walks out, leaving me alone in the bedroom. I realize I'm still holding the tape I made him. It feels strange, like a toy I don't know how to play with. I read through the titles of the songs, but now the words mean nothing to me. I can't even hear any of the music in my head. I decide to leave it for him, even though he doesn't have a way to listen to it. I put it on his pillow, like how Abuela used to put the Bible out to remind herself to read to me before bed.

When I pass through the kitchen I see him bent over the sink, squinting to read the label on a can of black beans. I wave good-bye but he doesn't see me.

There's already an inch of snow on the ground as I make my way home, and the small, steady flakes continue to fall. A few people pass me on the sidewalk, all looking up at the sky. The streets look clean under the fallen snow, making the neighborhood look almost pretty, as if we live on the nice side of town.

I see a girl ahead of me, her head in a book as she walks to the bus stop. She's wearing a pink hat that looks familiar and when I see her brown skin, dark against the background of snow, I figure out I'm looking at Graciela. I want to say hi to her, but when I pass by she's looking down so I don't say anything. Her voice startles me.

"Weren't you even going to say hi?"

I turn back to look at her. "Didn't want to scare you."

"I don't scare that easily."

I tuck my hands into my pockets. "Hi," I say.

She smiles. "Hi yourself."

I want to ask her about the book she's reading, and what she wants for Christmas, and if this is the first time she's ever seen snow. Instead I say, "You waiting for the bus?"

"Yeah. I have a piano lesson." She looks down at her feet.

I want her to tell me something about Colombia, about how she likes the food here compared to back home, and maybe how long it takes her to braid her hair that tight, but the words won't come out. Instead, I ask her where she's going.

"The east side," she says. "The ride's not too bad."

I nod my head. "Good thing you got your book."

"I always have a book. That way I'm never bored."

I watch the snow as it falls on her face and turns into droplets of water.

"Well, have a good lesson." I turn to go.

"You in a hurry?" she asks.

"No, not really."

"You could wait with me, just until the bus comes. It shouldn't be long."

"Okay."

The snow keeps falling as we stand together at the bus stop. My sneakers are wet and I can't feel the tips of my fingers but I hardly notice anything but her smile, as white and clean as the blanket of snow now covering our feet.

◆ ❖ ◆

It's weird living in a house with two different moms in charge. I know Mami doesn't really like it here, because she's always closing her eyes and shaking her head or just walking straight out of the room. Sometimes I hear her talking to herself, repeating things under her breath like she's praying. She and Kim don't fight though. They usually aren't even in the same room together. Mami told me she's on a waiting list with some agency to get a nice apartment in a better part of town, but we just don't have the money right now. She doesn't know about everything I made working for Snowman and I'm not gonna tell her yet. I'm waiting to surprise her when we really need it.

Most days she hangs around the apartment, but sometimes she has to go to meetings, usually with her parole officer and other people who want to help her stay out of trouble. It's funny to have her here when I get home from school or the library, like she's one of those moms on TV now. The kind that figure out the problem before you even tell them what's wrong.

One day in January I come home and she tells me that it's time to pack up because we're moving out. She says she's on her way to a meeting, but that I should get my things together tonight so we'll be ready to go in the morning. Sammy and Kim are away for the weekend, and when Mami leaves it's just Luz and me in the apartment. Just like old times. I make macaroni and cheese for dinner and when we're eating I tell her she needs to start packing.

"I'm not leaving," Luz says. She doesn't even bother to look up from her bowl.

"What do you mean? Mami says it's time to go."

"For her, maybe. For you if you want. But not for me." Luz jabs at the macaroni with her fork, stacking as many pieces as she can onto the pointy tips.

"Don't be crazy, Luz. You're coming."

"I'm serious. I already asked Kim and she said it's okay."

I push my bowl away. "You want to stay with Sammy and Kim but not with us? Kim's drunk all the time and she doesn't even leave her room. She can't take care of her own son, but you want her to take care of you?"

Luz nibbles on the macaroni at the end of her fork. "I'm just sick of moving around."

"We have to stay together. That's what we promised." I try not to sound like I'm begging.

"I just want to stay in one place for a while, to be somewhere familiar. Why is that too much to ask?" Luz looks like she's going to cry.

"Mami's more familiar than this place."

She looks down at the table. "Sure. But for how long?"

I shake my head. "Don't say that, Luz. Don't even think that." I might have the same thought, in the way way back of my head, but I'd never say it out loud.

"She hasn't even been home a month," Luz says, "and here she is, already leaving. Is that supposed to be encouraging?"

"Listen, she's trying to make us a family again." I grab onto the table, needing to hold something solid.

"Why can't we do that here?"

"Why can't you give her a chance?"

Luz drops her fork into the bowl. The macaroni splatters onto the table, a few pieces hitting my arm. "Give her a chance? How many chances should one person get?"

"This is our mother we're talking about. Not some lady in the street."

Luz opens her mouth to say something, but stops herself. She puts her dish in the sink and walks out of the room without saying another word. I sit at the table alone, counting the pieces of spilled macaroni. I pick them up with my fork, eating every cold, greasy piece like it was medicine. Like I have to take it.

I don't remember anything from the day Mami left me in

Puerto Rico. I don't remember saying good-bye to her or driving to the airport to watch her plane take off. I don't remember driving home alone with my father. But I do remember other things, things from after she was gone. I remember sleeping by myself on an air mattress in the corner of my father's bedroom. I remember counting the cracks in the ceiling, how I never got past twenty-one. I remember waking up early and eating breakfast alone in a dark room. I remember eating dinner with my *abuela*, sitting together on the couch as we listened to the announcer's voice on the radio, calling a local baseball game. I remember being scared whenever the phone rang, breaking the silence of that empty house. Mostly, I remember missing my mother.

I finish the macaroni and drop my fork into the bowl. I get why Luz is upset, but she acts like there weren't any good times. Did she forget all the birthday parties and holidays and trips to the store for new clothes, how Mami would buy us things even when she was wearing the same coat she first had in the Bronx? Or what about eating *pasteles* at Christmas and watching late-night TV shows with the sound turned down, how Mami used to laugh like we were in the studio audience? Or last year on Mami's birthday, when we woke her up with frozen waffles for breakfast and iced coffee and then sang this song Trini made up, and how Mami laughed so hard she spit her coffee through her nose, and then later she let Luz do her hair and makeup. Does none of that mean anything?

I get up from the table and start washing all the dishes by myself. I could go into the living room and drag Luz back in here to help, but I figure it's better to give her some time to cool off. The way she's acting you'd think Luz was the one Mami left behind when she moved here from Puerto Rico. That she flew by herself all the way to New York when she was five. That she was the one traveling alone on the plane, landing in a strange smelling airport with her belly twisted up from the grease, perfume, and cigarettes, her head pounding from the noise. But it wasn't Luz, it was me. So why can I forgive her?

When I got off the plane I didn't recognize anything. All the signs were in English and I couldn't read them. At home

I was learning how to read, but in New York, I was suddenly stupid. No one ever said that, but I knew. Why else would I just stop understanding? I knew there was something wrong with me. First my mother leaves, and now this. After I walked through the gate, they told me to wait behind some ropes in this special area and my mother would come find me. I didn't believe them, but I had nowhere else to go. And then I saw her, this lady with dyed blonde hair running up the walkway and calling my name. She looked so happy. She was supposed to wait until they checked her ID, but she just slipped under the ropes and grabbed me, picking me up and kissing me all over my face. I didn't even recognize her really, this skinny pale woman who hugged me so tight I thought I was gonna pass out, but she smelled familiar. She was smiling as tears fell down her face, and suddenly I recognized her as clearly as if I was looking into the mirror.

This lady is your mother, I thought to myself. You came out of her just like your hand grows out of your arm. If you lose her, you lose everything that tells you who you are.

◆ ❖ ◆

Luz is already asleep when Mami gets home later that night. I turn off the TV, which makes the whole room suddenly dark, and wait for her in the kitchen. I hear her stumble around in the hallway until I turn on a light. She freezes like a cat, like I caught her doing something wrong. I blink against the brightness, and it takes me a few seconds to recognize her.

"*Gracias, mijo*," she says, unzipping her coat. She leaves the scarf around her neck and hands me a small coffee cup from Dunkin' Donuts. Her hands are freezing.

"Here, it's hot cocoa."

The cocoa is lukewarm and thick like pudding. It's too sweet so I add some milk and heat it back up in the microwave.

"You don't have to drink it if it's no good."

"No, it's good. Thanks."

"Bring it out to the porch. I want to talk to you."

She walks to the back porch, lighting a cigarette as she goes.

Another one of Kim's rules she ignores: no smoking in the house. I bring the cocoa outside, my hands wrapped around the cup for warmth. The back porch is enclosed, but the heat doesn't work, so it's probably about forty degrees out here. I can see my breath, thick like the smoke from her cigarette.

"Did you talk to Luz?"

I nod. "She doesn't want to go." I lean against the door frame, wishing I had thought to grab a sweatshirt or at least pulled on my sneakers. Goose bumps break out across my arms like a rash. "She wants to stay here."

Mami exhales. "Why's she think she got a choice?"

I shrug. "Kim said she can."

"That what you want?" She takes a drag off her cigarette.

"It's for Luz to decide."

"I mean for you. Do you want to stay here, too?"

I shake my head. "This isn't my home." I peel a chip of paint off the windowsill and flick it into the darkness. "I want to stay with you."

Mami sits down on the edge of an old recliner.

"I want to tell you something first, before you decide if you want to come with me. Two things, really." She holds two fingers out, like a peace sign. "First off, we need to find a place to live. Rent is expensive and since I'm not working yet that part isn't going to be easy. We might need to stay at a shelter for a few nights, just until we find something more permanent. Is that okay with you?"

I nod. "What's the other thing?"

I can feel the floorboards through my socks, warped and cracked from years of neglect, and suddenly I'm afraid to move. I picture myself falling through the porch and landing helpless on the sidewalk, like a baby bird knocked from its nest.

She clears her throat. "I'm sick, Cristo." She looks at me, as if that's all she's going to say. As if that is the whole story. I open my mouth but she holds up her hand to keep me quiet.

"They found a virus in my blood, when I was inside, and now I take all these pills every day just to keep me healthy. It's a pain in the ass and I wish I didn't have to do it, but if I want to feel better and stick around for you and your sisters, it's got to be part of the plan. Just like how I got to go to all those meetings and not drink anymore, it's just something I have to do now."

I'm suddenly not cold anymore. I can't even feel the part of my arm that's leaning against the door frame or the splinters that are digging into my socks. "Did you get it from someone in there?"

"No, sweetie." She reaches out to touch my hand. "I had it when I got inside."

"Who gave it to you?"

She takes her hand away and coughs into her sleeve. "There's no way to know."

"What is it, pneumonia? They told us about that in health class. Teacher said it goes away if you take the right pills."

She looks down at her hands. "It's called HIV. Have they told you about that in health class?"

I shake my head.

"Well, that's probably a good thing. It's not something people like to talk about. It's a private thing, you know?"

"So I shouldn't tell anyone that you have it?"

"No, not now. Let's just keep it between us, okay?"

"What about Luz?"

She shakes her head. "Just you and me, okay?"

I nod. It's like the old days, when Mami and me had secrets from the world.

"How long will it take for you to get better?"

"They say I'm better already. A lot better than when I got there." She puts out the cigarette and flicks the butt onto the ground. "But nobody knows for sure how you get better from something like this. You just keep taking your pills, every day without forgetting, and you hope for the best."

She stands up and we're looking eye to eye, almost the exact same height. The door frame gives me a few inches, but I'm still catching up to her. Weird how I didn't even feel myself growing.

"Maybe I can help," I say. "I could put them in one of those pill boxes that César's grandmother has and help remind you to take them. I could make up a chart on the calendar."

"That's a great idea," Mami says. "I would love that." She

wraps her arms around me, pulling me into a tight hug. I can feel her fists against my back, hard like onions. She doesn't seem sick.

"I think your father was right," she whispers into my ear. "I should have named you Angel." She bends down and kisses me on the side of my head, hard enough that I can still feel her lips when she takes them away.

"*Tu eres un angel,*" she says softly. Her voice cracks and I hear her take a deep breath. She looks like she's going to cry, but no tears fall. She is strong like Luz, and I wonder why all the girls in my family are tough like men. They act like they don't need to cry. I could cry every day if I let myself.

She leans into me and gives me another hug. I have to brace myself against the door frame just to hold the two of us up.

Arcelia

Nothing changes in the ghetto. A street don't change. Flowers don't grow from broken glass. Trash don't bloom. They talk about how Providence is better now—how it's been revitalized or some shit—but they don't mean this neighborhood. They don't mean my street. Everything's exactly the same as when I left—same dogs, same corners, same men—so every time I go outside I remember what it was like. What I was like. The counselors tell you to avoid your old hangouts and any spots where you used to score, but if I do that there won't be a street in Olneyville I can walk down. And half of South Providence would be off-limits, too. It was okay for the first few days, but by New Year's I know it was too much to come back here. But what choice do I got? There's nowhere else to go.

Truth is I'm not tough enough for the street. Not anymore. On the inside, every day was in order—meetings, counseling, dinner, bed—so you always knew what was coming next. It's like being a kid and having your mother tell you what to do. But the streets—that's like being an orphan. Nobody cares how much TV you watch, where you stand, what you eat, who you see. Nobody checks to make sure you're still there.

In January we move out of Kim's and into the shelter. Just Cristo and me. Luz don't change her mind about coming and I don't force her. Seems to me ten is old enough to decide something like that. It's just for a few weeks anyway, till I get settled in a new place. By then I know she's gonna want to come too, especially when I get her sister back. The shelter's got house rules, a curfew, and bag check every time I come in or out. I figure it's like a stepmom—one step off the street. Most nights we go to Oxford House for dinner, or St. Patrick's if we're on the other side of town. That's the only way to get a hot, home-cooked meal. It's not great, but it's better than anything Kim ever made.

I meet with Cece, my case manager at AIDS Care, and she gives me some clothes and toiletries and cans of Ensure for when I don't feel like eating real food. Sometimes the pills take my hunger away and if nobody reminds me, I won't eat for days. I don't have my own room at the shelter so I carry the Ensure cans around in my duffel bag. I feel like a kid going to school every day, packing my lunch in the morning. Cece thinks I'm crazy for moving out of Kim's place, but I tell her I don't have no regrets. Back there I was too close to the old neighborhood, and too far away from being myself.

"How long do you think you can last at the shelter?" Cece asks at my last appointment. She taps her manicured fingernails on the desk.

"Long as I have to."

"And your kids?"

"They're okay," I say, trying to sound like I believe it.

"I just talked to the housing guy," she says. She picks up a file and reads over her notes. "We've got a one-bedroom in Pawtucket that's available in February, or you can wait for a two-bedroom in the West End. The schools are better in Pawtucket, but it's a small place and we can only secure a month-to-month lease. It's your choice."

"We need a two-bed," I tell her. "I got three kids. And we need to stay in the West End, near their school. They been through enough changes."

She nods. "Okay, I'll let him know to keep you on the list." She stands up. "Anything else?"

"What about my daughter, the one who's staying with her father. Can you help me get her back?"

She sits back down. "That's not really my department, Arcelia. But with your history, it's not going to be easy." She tilts her chair back, lifting off the ground. "On the other hand, the state likes to see children with their mothers. Which is part of the reason you have your son. They're on your side."

"Let me tell you who's not on my side. My ex. The bastard only lets me see her two times a week." I point two fingers at her, a peace sign, even though all I can think about is war. "Two times. Not even overnight. This is my daughter I'm talking about. My baby." I sit back in my chair and lower my voice. "She came out of my body, you know. My body, not his. That ain't right."

"I understand that it's difficult, but all you can do is take care of the things you control. Keep going to meetings, check in with your parole officer, and most important of all: stay healthy. If you get run-down you're not going to be able to handle any of this." She closes her file. "Next week let's focus on getting you a job and a nice place to live, okay? You have to show them how much you've changed. After that, it's all going to fall into place."

"Okay," I say. "I can do that." But in my head I'm thinking, *How can I show them I've changed on the inside?*

She walks to the office door. "How are you feeling, aside from that?"

"Shit, I don't know. It changes minute to minute."

"That's normal," she says, making herself smile, "for you to feel confused and overwhelmed. You have a whole new reality to get used to. Sometimes it takes a while." She puts her hand on the doorknob. "Why don't we talk about that when you come in next week, okay?"

She gives me her card with my appointment time written on the back. Then she puts her hand on my shoulder and escorts me to the front desk. She's trying to be nice, but all I can feel is her nails through my shirt, the tips filed like claws.

"I'll see you then," she says, smiling at me.

I say okay but I'm already thinking it's gonna take a miracle to get me back here on that exact day and at the right time. I never been good with dates or numbers aside from money. A week seems like a lifetime now that I'm back on the outside. And who knows how many lifetimes I'm gonna get.

I keep forgetting to go back to the pharmacy to pick up my meds, so I end up missing a lot of doses. As soon as I get the pills I'm back on track, but I liked those days when I didn't have to take them. I felt like a normal person again. Inside I used to tell my counselor how much I hated taking all them pills. How it was hard to think of myself as different. Sick. On the outside I don't know who to talk to like that. I have a case manager and a doctor and an advocate at the shelter, but I don't have any friends. Or a lover. Everybody else is getting paid to listen to my problems, and knowing that makes it hard to open up.

Cristo asks me questions but I don't know how much to tell him. He already does more than he should. Every time I bring home my meds, he counts them out and organizes them in the fancy pillbox I get from the doctor. He watches me while I take them—one by one with milk so I won't gag—and then he puts a big red check on the daily planner he got from his teacher. He carries that thing in his backpack like it's keeping him alive.

One time when I'm at the CVS, I run into Snowman on my way out. He's buying an ice cream bar at the checkout counter, even though it's twenty-five degrees outside. The cashier keeps asking him if he's serious. Snowman takes off his gloves and pays for it with exact change. He spots me in line and stops. I can see him look twice at me. Like he can't believe it's me.

"Hey." He nods at me. "How's it going?"

He approaches me slowly, like I'm an ex-girlfriend he thinks might make a scene.

I shrug. "It's going." I tuck the bag with my meds under my arm.

"I guess that's better than it not going," he says.

"You're right about that," I say.

He looks me up and down. "You look good." From anyone else it would seem like flirting, but he's just making an observation.

"Thanks."

He looks exactly the same. Pale and cold, like that statue in

Prospect Park of the man who settled Rhode Island.

"So how's business?" I ask him.

He unwraps the ice cream bar slowly, not answering me.

"I mean, with the houses and shit," I say. "The rentals."

"Business is good. It's a good time to own." He takes a bite of the chocolate shell, which cracks like a piece of ice. "Hey, I fixed up your old place. Redid the floors and painted everything. Got a new fridge. It looks real nice inside."

"Oh yeah?" I make myself smile, even though I feel sad just thinking about it. "I guess that means you rented it."

"Yeah, they're moving in next month," he says. "A young couple with little kids. I could have doubled the rent after fixing it up, but I decided to give them a break, you know? Since they're just starting out."

"I'm starting out, too," I tell him. He looks at me real hard, like he's trying to see something that isn't there. "Starting again."

"Yeah, I heard—" he cuts himself off. "Well. Cristo says you're doing better."

"You talked to my son?"

He shrugs, taking another bite of the chocolate shell. It's dark against his white skin. "I see him around sometimes, in the neighborhood. He's a good kid." I wonder if it bothers him, to be so pale.

"Course he is," I say. "All my kids are good." It's the truth, even if it's hard to believe some days. Even if I don't have much to do with it.

"Yeah. Well. I don't see the girls that much."

"They like to stay close by," I tell him. "But Cristo...he's like a bird."

Snowman moves to leave, but I step in front of him. I lose my place in line but I don't care.

"So listen, you got anything else open? Any other apartments?"

He thinks for a long second. "Not right now, Arcelia. Not in this neighborhood."

"I could live somewhere else. They keep saying that's better for me anyway. The counselors and everybody."

"Can you afford to pay more?" He finishes the ice cream bar and sucks on the wooden stick like a toothpick.

"A little more," I say. "I've got a case manager now, they can pay some of the rent. She called it a sub-city, or something like that."

"A subsidy?"

"Yeah, that's it."

"I can't always take that grant money," he says, making a face like he really cares. "Where's she work at?"

This is it—the moment when I have to tell him the truth. If I want his help.

Finally I say, "ACOS," using the initials instead of saying the whole name.

"What's that?" he asks.

There's no taking it back once I say it, like telling someone they have to move out, or that you don't love them anymore.

"AIDS Care Ocean State." I say it real fast, like it's one word.

"AIDS," he repeats, "like the disease?" He bites on the stick, which breaks in half in his mouth. I nod. "I didn't know," he says.

"Neither did I."

He spits the smaller piece out of his mouth, but keeps the bigger one, biting on it again. "You okay?" His eyes narrow, like he's actually worried about me.

"Sure, yeah. For now."

He bites on this one until it breaks too. "I'll see what I can do," he finally says.

"Thanks," I tell him. "Appreciate it."

The door opens behind him as a couple walks in, bringing the cold with them. I smell winter in the air as they pass by us. He turns to leave, but I reach out and touch his hand. It surprises me, how warm it is.

"Hey, Snowman, one more thing." He looks down at where I'm holding onto him, then looks back up at my face. "If I ever come to you later and want something else. Not help with an apartment but..." I squeeze his hand. "Just don't give me anything, okay? No matter what I say."

He keeps looking at me, his eyes clear like water. It's the first time I've ever really looked at him, and what I see is a surprise. He is a decent man.

"Okay," he says. "Consider it done."

He squeezes my hand back, almost like we're shaking on it, and then puts on his headphones and walks out of the store. From the street outside, I catch him looking back at me.

I got nothing to do for the rest of the day, so after I pay for my meds I go back outside. It's cold out, but the sun is shining. I stand in front of a Mexican restaurant for twenty minutes, imagining what I would order if I had the money to eat out. The sun warms the back of my head and it feels good to stand there and not have to move. If I was still inside and writing those gratitude lists I'd add this moment—Snowman, the sun, the smell of winter.

The sidewalks are empty. I keep my head down as I walk, wondering how my feet can look so small when my boots—Kim's boots—are two sizes too big. I step over a pink carnation with a broken stalk, lying in the middle of the sidewalk. I can't remember the last time I saw a flower. In Puerto Rico they're everywhere, growing like weeds at the side of the road. People always have them in small vases on the dining room table and you can smell them as soon as you walk in. But in the States I never see them, and the few times I did—before I got locked up—I never stopped to look at them. I knew it was a waste, since the drugs took away my sense of smell.

I turn around and walk back to the broken carnation to pick it up, wiping off the gritty slush from the street. I bring it to my nose. The fragrance is subtle, more like a flower shop than the flower itself. But it's nice to be able to smell it. I straighten out the stalk, trying to make it whole again. The weight of the bulb's head makes it bend slightly, like the breeze is trying to knock it over. I hold it together for the entire walk back to the shelter, my hand closed tight to hide the break.

◆ ❖ ◆

Later I pass the flea market and see a Chinese man selling

encyclopedias. He gets my attention by saying he has something that will guarantee my kids will go to college.

"What's funny?" he says when I laugh. "You don't want your children to get an education?"

"If I had all those books, I'd live in a library."

"Ninety-nine bucks for the whole set. Twenty-six volumes, that's less than five dollars a book. For your children, no? To invest in their future?"

"I only got one kid who reads."

"Okay, okay. She like stories?" He pulls out a box from under the table. "I've got just the thing." He hands me a book with a shiny white cover. "This has stories from all over the world."

"How much?"

"Five dollars."

"I only got two."

"Take it," he says, waving me away. "Give me the rest later."

"I don't like to owe people."

"Don't like to owe?" He has a wide smile on his face. "Who isn't in debt? To someone, for something?" He hands me the book. I see my face in the cover, my eyes so small I can't even see them. "Without debt, you have no life."

I give him the two dollars and he bows to me. "Money passes between people just like knowledge. There is nothing to count, it just is."

"*Gracias.*"

"Thank you for your time," he says, kissing the dollar bills in his hand.

I zip the book into my jacket—Kim's jacket—and walk with my head down into the wind. I hear church bells ringing up the street and when I pass the church the clock says it's two o'clock. If I go now I can make it to school in time to catch my kids before they get on the bus. I can even meet their teachers and see their classrooms. One visit can't make up for all the time I been gone, but maybe it'll do something. At least show them that I care.

I take the shortcut over the highway and get there early, before the bell rings. The crossing guard watches me like she thinks I'm gonna do something wrong. When I cross the street to get closer to the school she doesn't walk with me. She stands against the stop sign chewing bubble gum and talking on her walkie-talkie. The bell rings and the older kids come out first. They run like they're trying to escape. I wait for them to pass me, then I walk up the steps and stand by the front door. The doors look heavy. I see a teacher I recognize from when Cristo was younger and they called me into the school 'cause he pushed a kid down the stairs. I hide behind the open door, hoping she won't see me.

"You going inside?" A red-faced kid holds the door open.

I shake my head and walk down the stairs, crossing the street with the crowd. When I'm safe on the other side I look back. I stand behind the chain-link fence and scan the crowd for my kids. I see Luz walking alone with her head in a book. She doesn't stumble or slow down, even when she crosses the street to line up for the bus. When I call her name she stops and looks up. She doesn't see me. I say her name again and when her eyes find mine she looks confused, like she doesn't know who I am. I wave her over to me. She looks around first, like she's making sure it's okay.

"What are you doing here?" She looks worried. "Is something wrong?"

"I just wanted to see you. To see your school."

"Oh. Well, school's over," she says.

"I see that. But I still wanted to come by."

Luz looks back to the bus line. "Cristo left early. He said he had to work."

"Work?" I wonder what kind of work an eleven-year-old does.

"I think he had to help a teacher or something. I don't know." She twists her braid around her finger and chews on the end. Like I'm making her nervous.

"Here, I got this for you." I hand her the book, still warm from being inside my jacket.

"What's this for?" She takes it, but won't open it. "It's not my birthday or anything."

"I know. But I thought you would like it. Stories from

around the world." I cough into my sleeve. "You like stories, right?"

She turns it over and flips through the pages, like she's checking to make sure it's real. "Thanks." She's looking down when she says it so I can't tell if she really means it.

"I'm sorry about the last book I got you," I tell her. "The one I sent from inside. They didn't have a lot of choices."

"That's okay," she says. She tries to smile but she still looks upset.

The wind whips my hair into my eyes, making them burn.

"Well, I should go," Luz says, "so I don't miss the bus." She takes a step away from me.

"*Espera. Por favor.*" I reach out and tuck a loose piece of hair behind her ear. It's just an excuse to touch her. "I know you're mad at me. 'Cause I left you with Lucho, and then she left. Or maybe you're mad from way before that." She looks at me but don't say nothing. "But you know what? I'm kinda pissed off, too. Here I am waiting all these months to get back to my kids, and now two of them aren't even with me. That sucks." I try not to look at the other kids as they walk by us. "But I keep telling myself that it's okay because it's not gonna be like this forever. It's just a temporary thing, okay?"

"I know." She looks away like she's bored.

"You're ten years old, and you think you know a lot of things. But I'm your mother, Luz. I could make you come with me. I could force you if I wanted. But I don't want to do that to my daughter. I want you to want to be with me."

"Okay," she says, leaning against the fence. "Can I go now?" She wrinkles up her face, looking just like Javier when he used to get mad if I stopped him on the way to the ballpark. My beautiful, angry little girl.

"I want you to know I forgive you," I tell her.

"You forgive me?" Her face tightens up like she's confused.

"I was younger than you when my mother died and I missed her so much it made my belly sick. I threw up all the time. But before that, when she was alive and dying, I got so mad I used to sit outside her bedroom door and refuse to answer when she called me. I loved her so much, but I couldn't see her in pain.

I couldn't watch her die."

Luz jams the toe of her sneaker into the fence, like she's gonna climb away from me. I put my hand on her shoulder. "It's okay to be pissed. I get it. But I'm telling you right now, it's gonna be different. I'll make things right and then you'll see. All of you are gonna see who I am."

Luz tries to walk away but I won't let her. I squeeze my arms around her till she finally softens into me, like chocolate melting. She puts her face against my chest and I swear I feel my heart swell. I kiss her head and breathe in the smell of her shampoo.

"I like your shampoo," I say into her ear. "You smell like a big juicy grapefruit."

She laughs and tries to push me away. "You're silly, Mami." Then she puts her head back down.

I hug her even tighter. *Mami.* A short, easy word. One she hasn't said in almost a year.

◆ ❖ ◆

Back in June, when I was inside, I went to my first twelve-step meeting at the ACI. Surprise, surprise—I hated it. The meetings on the outside are pretty much the same, and I don't like them either. They tell me to go to both meetings—NA and AA— but I like the snacks at the NA meetings better. And the people are just as fucked up as I am. I try going to one in Spanish but it's filled with a bunch of old men who hit on me during the fellowship break and offer to drive me home in cars that smell like their wives. The English meetings are better since they always follow the script. When a part comes I don't under- stand, I let my mind wander like it did when I was a little girl in church. Maybe that's the point—to get you thinking about something other than yourself.

The worst part is when they talk about God and how we need to follow His will and not our own. I gave up following God a long time ago, and He don't seem to have any real prob- lem with it. They say if I don't want to use God I can choose anything else to be my higher power—a table, a chair, or some other person—but I don't want to give myself over to any of those things either. I don't want to surrender. To me, that's like giving up. I'm tired as hell, but I still don't want to do that. I don't want to quit. Quitting means dying, as far as I can tell, and after all I went through I'm not gonna let that happen. It seems weak to admit you got no power over the addiction, and I don't want to be weaker than anything.

I keep going to different meetings so everybody will think I'm still a newcomer. That way I can always ask questions, and I don't have to remember anything about anyone else's story. I go to one meeting at St. Joe's and realize halfway through that I been there before, two years earlier for a six-day detox. During the break some lady comes up to me and tells me to just *keep coming back*, even if it doesn't make sense to me. I tell her I'll try, but really I just want her to leave me alone. She smiles and hugs me like we been best friends for years. I can't remember if her name is Karen or Kathy, but as she holds onto me in the middle of the room, I feel okay. Then she lets go and suddenly I feel light-headed. The bright fluorescent lights are shining down on me and I think I might faint.

"Are you okay?" she asks, holding onto me with both her hands.

"No," I say, shaking my head. "I can't do this."

She squeezes my hands as she holds them. "You don't have to do it by yourself, sweetheart. Remember that." She hands me a copy of the big book of Alcoholics Anonymous. "Here, take this. I have another one at home. Just remember to keep coming back, okay? Even when you think it doesn't make sense."

"That's what everybody keeps saying."

She nods and rubs my shoulder. It's hard to let strangers touch me when I'm not fucked up, but I don't push her away. I know she's just trying to help.

"It's the truth," she says, smiling at me, like she knows some secret I don't.

I walk out before it's over because I don't want to stand in the circle and hold hands with everybody and act like I think I'm gonna be okay. I know it's early—I only got out a month ago—but I don't know how long I can go on like this without getting outside of myself. They tell me to do that by giving my will to God but I only know how to escape into the highs and lows of a good fix.

I walk down the hallway quickly, trying to outrun the sound of their prayers. I try to quiet the noise in my head, but it just keeps getting louder. I look at every person I see along Broad Street, hoping to recognize someone or something familiar. I watch a line of cars pull into D.L.'s Funeral Home. My mother's funeral is the only one I ever went to. After that, I promised myself the next one I'd be at was gonna be my own.

Within seconds, the sidewalk is packed with mourners, men in dark suits escorting women with their heads down, sunglasses covering eyes that cried all night. I walk to the bus stop wondering why it's easier to celebrate the dead than the living.

SHE SEES the girl in the backseat of an old Buick. Waiting to go to the hospital. The interior is all white, the leather as soft as the inside of a shell. Her legs are spread. Her skirt is lifted up, high above her waist. The leather is hot on the backs of her legs. She doesn't want to give birth here, but the baby is coming. Her second one in two years. Her insides begin to ache. She's afraid of the pain. The car door opens. A burst of sunshine blinds the girl. Someone calls her name. "Mami." A voice she recognizes. The girl squints. Her son comes into focus. He climbs into the car to sit beside her. Her eyes adjust. She looks at him. He wants to meet his baby sister. He tells her it's okay. She waits for her husband to arrive. Her son never lets go of her hand.

Miss Valentín

Cristo surprises me with a present on Valentine's Day. Other kids make cards, or bring bouquets of pink and white carnations, which they drop on my desk like late assignments, but Cristo gives me a solid chocolate heart the size of a plate. I need to get a knife from the teacher's lounge just to break off a piece.

"You shouldn't have gotten something so big, it's too much."

"I know how you like chocolate, Teacher. Don't act like you won't eat it."

I blush, embarrassed by how well he knows me. "I just mean that you shouldn't have spent so much money," I tell him when we're talking after school.

"I have a job, you know." He sits on the edge of my desk. "Speaking of jobs, since this holiday's named after your family, I think you should get the day off."

"Oh really? I didn't think you knew my last name."

"I know your name, Teacher. I just don't like to use it."

I cut into the heart and hand him a waxy sliver. "So, how's school going?"

"It's going good," he says.

"How does Mrs. Reed think you're doing?"

"She thinks I'm doing good."

"Good, or just better than before?"

He bites on his fingernail to stall. "Better than before, I guess. But there's still time for me to do good."

"How's it been with your mother back?"

He shrugs, looking down at the floor.

"I heard you're forgetting assignments again, turning pages in half-done. Is that true?"

"It'll be better once we have our own place. I can't keep track of my things there."

"Kim didn't give you a desk? Or a bookshelf?"

He shifts against the desk. "There's not a lot of extra room. I try not to complain."

I cut off another piece of chocolate. I don't want to eat this much in front of him, but I can't help myself. Why does this always happen, with even the smallest taste in my mouth? "How's your mom doing? It's got to be hard for her, to come back and have everything turned upside down."

"She's okay."

My mouth is full so I gesture for him to say more. He clears his throat.

"I mean she's good. She's going to a bunch of meetings and she has some job training class she's gonna take. She's really trying."

I force myself to put the chocolate away in my desk drawer, though I continue to think about it during the rest of our conversation. I am beginning to think I am no different from her, or from any addict. The only difference is that my drug is legal.

"How are things at home?" I ask him, sensing there's something he's not telling me.

"All right."

"It's got to be hard for her, moving in with another family like that." He makes a face, but I decide to keep pushing. "How are she and Kim getting along?"

He stands up quickly and grabs his backpack off the floor. There's something he's not telling me.

"She's going to be all right, Teacher. I'm helping her, okay? Don't worry."

"And who's helping you?"

He shrugs.

"Don't say you don't need help."

"You're helping me." He adjusts a stack of books on my

desk, neatening the row.

I pick up my bag. "You want a ride home?"

"No, thanks. I'm going to walk."

"Come on, it's freezing outside. They say it might snow."

"I'm going to the library first."

"Well, I can drop you there if you want."

He shakes his head. "Nah, I'll be okay."

"You sure?"

He heads for the door. "See you later, okay?"

I follow him out, locking the classroom door behind me. When I call his name from the hallway, he's already gone. I know he's lying to me, that much is clear, but what I can't figure out is why.

◆ ❖ ◆

The phone rings after ten, waking me from a dream. A half-eaten bag of potato chips falls from my lap as I reach for the handset. A rerun of *Law & Order* plays on the TV.

"Hi, I'm looking for Miss Valentine, a teacher at Hartford Avenue School. Do I have the right number?"

"Yes, this is Vanessa Valentín. Is there something wrong?" I put the TV on mute. I can hear the woman sniff and clear her throat.

"My name is Kim Douglas and I'm Cristo and Luz—"

"I know who you are. The kids have mentioned you several times."

"Okay, good." She sounds nervous, like a drunk person trying really hard to act sober. "Well, I guess you know that I've been taking care of the two of them for a while now. Well actually just Luz for the last month..." She sniffs again.

"What do you mean just Luz? Cristo told me he lived with you."

"He did, until a few weeks ago. Him and his mother moved out."

They moved, that's why he wouldn't let me drive him home. "I see. I didn't know they had found a place."

"They haven't yet." She starts speaking slowly. "They're in

that shelter on Pine Street, the one that takes kids."

"They're in a shelter?"

"Listen, that's not really why I'm calling. I've got a problem with Luz—"

"What kind of problem?" I sit up on the couch.

"Somebody called DCYF on me and now Luz is in the system. They took Sammy, too, my son, but he's back already. Luz isn't coming back."

I try to stay calm. "What happened?"

"It's not a big deal. I'm a single parent, you know? And I work for a living. I can't always be around to keep them out of trouble. I'm not Wonder Woman, Miss Valentine." By now I'm convinced her sniff is a nervous habit.

"So what do you want me to do?"

"I want you to take her."

"Take her? From where?"

"They didn't tell me. I've got the name and number of her caseworker. You can ask them all these questions." She sniffs again.

I wrap the phone cord around my hand. "Why are you calling me? I'm just a teacher. I can't fix anything."

I'm lying, of course, always my first instinct. I don't mention that I just got D-Rate status with the state, which means that in addition to regular kids I'm cleared to take ones with behavioral issues as well. Apparently my certification got pushed through because I'm a teacher. (Finally someone values this job.) So to request a child like Luz would be easy. But just because I look good on paper, doesn't mean I'll do a good job. And Luz is someone I already know and care about. It would break my heart to be another person who fails her.

"The kids are quite attached to you. They talk about you all the time." I hear Kim exhale. Then sniff. "I just thought you'd want to know. I thought maybe you could help."

I unwrap my hand and watch it fill back up with blood. Is she trying to make me feel guilty?

"But I'm not their family," I say.

"The foster home she's staying at isn't her family either."

I imagine Luz going to bed in a strange house and reading

under a lamp until she falls asleep. I picture Cristo living in a shelter, having to keep his backpack on so nothing gets stolen, and it makes me ill. I can see it all clearly, but it hardly seems real.

"There's one more thing, Miss Valentine. It's about their mother. She's sick, you know, with that liver disease that junkies get."

"Hepatitis?"

"Yeah, that's it. I guess she's had it for a while, but she had never really treated it before. Now she's taking all these pills, AZT and Crixivan, things I've never heard of. I just found the bottles when she moved out."

"AZT? Are you sure?" I recognize the name as an HIV drug.

"Yep, that one I know for certain. I'm looking at the bottle right now."

Damn. If Kim has no idea what it means I'm not going to be the one to tell her.

"All I'm saying is...she needs help, you know? This is a tough time for her. I thought that if she knew that Luz was with you...instead of a stranger...that it might make it easier for her to accept. She's already lost the baby, you know."

"I know." I stand up to get a pen. "Give me the number. I'll make a few calls."

She makes a joke about selling the pills if she can't get in touch with Arcelia, but I don't laugh. I tell her it's illegal to sell the pills from someone else's prescription. She claims she was only joking.

When I get off the phone with Kim I place the call to DCYF. No one answers, so I leave all my information on the caseworker's voice mail. I hang up and sit there for a while, letting it all sink in.

I watch the muted TV, men in fancy suits standing in wood-paneled rooms deciding a poor person's fate. I feel like the defendant as they wait for the verdict to be read, sick with fear and anticipation. It's hard to admit that I'm not in charge of my fate, and that the only thing I know for certain is that everything is about to change.

THIS SIDE OF PROVIDENCE

Luz

It's always warm in Miss Valentín's apartment. All the heaters work and the sun shines straight into my room in the morning. Plus, she can afford to pay the gas bill. Every room is painted a different color—peach, yellow, and many of shades of blue—and all the appliances work. The floors are all a shiny, caramel-colored wood, even in the kitchen, and I like to run on them in my socks and slide halfway across the room. Miss Valentín says I might get a sliver in my foot but she lets me do it anyway. Sometimes I wonder how long I'm going to stay here, but most of the time I pretend that it's going to be forever. I could ask Miss Valentín but usually I don't want to know the answer.

The night she came to get me from the foster home seems like a hundred years ago. She showed up after dinner with a short white lady who wore a badge on her lapel like she was a detective. Nobody told me she was coming. When I saw her I stood up from the table and didn't even finish my bowl of ramen noodles. I gave her a hug with both arms and she picked me up off the floor. I thought she was just coming to visit me, but when she said I was going home to live with her I started to cry. And I don't cry easily like some girls.

I didn't have to pack my bag because I had never unpacked it, even though I stayed there for almost a week. I said thank you and good-bye to the lady who ran the house, and she waved at me from the recliner she spent most evenings stuck in. None of the other kids came out to say good-bye and I didn't want to walk into the back of the house to see them. I've already forgotten their names and pretty soon I'll forget their faces, too.

The first time Cristo comes to visit me here I show him my new bedroom, the same room where he and I slept that weekend back in September when we ran away from home. I know he's jealous because we painted the walls and put up new curtains that Miss Valentín let me pick out.

"Why'd she paint the room yellow?" he asks.

"She said the old color made it look small."

"Small? This is a huge room, you could fit three beds in here." He hops onto my bed and puts his feet up.

"I could share, if you want to come back."

"And what about Mami?" He glares at me. "I can't just leave her."

"We could ask Miss Valentín if she could come, too."

"Mami didn't want to live with Kim, why would she want to live with Teacher?"

"Look around. It's nice here," I can't help but say it with a huge smile on my face.

He shrugs. "The shelter's not so bad."

"You said they stole your books and your Yankees hat."

"That was my fault," he says, using two pillows to prop himself up. "I shouldn't have left anything out. Now I know to leave my books at school."

"But how can you do your homework if you have to leave your books at school?"

He stares at me like I'm an idiot. "We only have a few more weeks to wait anyway, before Mami's case manager finds us a new apartment. Then we'll get Trini back and you can come live with us and we can all be a family again." He sounds just like Mami when he talks like that, but I don't believe him anymore than I believe her. I decide it's best to change the conversation.

"That Colombian girl asked about you the other day. Graciela."

"Who?" He pretends for a second to not know who I'm talking about. "What'd she say?"

"She wanted to know if you were my brother."

"What'd you say?"

"I told her the truth, dummy."

"Did she say anything else?"

I shake my head. "She didn't have to."

"What's that mean?"

"It means she likes you." I lower my voice. "You should ask her out."

"Why, so I can bring her back to the shelter?"

I can't think of a response so I just stare at him. After a while there's a knock on the door. I've never lived with anyone who knocks on doors.

"Come in," Cristo says, as if he lives here. He kicks off his sneakers and slips his socked feet under my comforter.

Miss Valentín peeks her head in the door. "I'm making *pernil* and *arroz con gandules*. Are you staying for dinner?" She looks at Cristo and smiles. "Well don't you look comfy?"

"No, I should go back. I have to meet Mami."

"Why don't you wait until it's done, so I can send you home with some. For you and your mother."

"Okay." Cristo looks around the room. "By the way, I like the paint job, Teacher."

"Thank you. Luz helped around the baseboards." She points toward the floor as if we don't know where they are. "You're welcome to stay over any night. You know that, right?"

"I'm going to help Mami get back on her feet and then neither one of us will have to stay here."

Miss Valentín nods, and makes herself smile. She tries to cover the hurt on her face but I can still see it. She closes the door behind her, her head bowed like she's in church. Cristo leans against the wall behind him. I try to look into his eyes but he keeps them focused on the ceiling. He stares into the light as if he's trying to make himself go blind.

"Have you seen César lately?" I ask him.

"Sure, I seen him around."

"You talk to him?"

He turns to face me. "Just spit it out, Luz. What are you asking me?"

"I heard he dropped out."

"He's ten. He can't drop out."

"Well, he's on medical leave or something. And he's so far behind that even if he does come back, he's going to have to repeat the fifth grade."

"Who told you that?"

"I can't reveal my source," I say, using a cliché I've heard a bunch of times on TV. Besides, what am I going to say, that I was eavesdropping outside the principal's office?

"Well I think I'd know if my best friend was dropping out of school." Cristo stands up to put his sneakers back on. "Don't go spreading any rumors, okay? And don't believe everything you hear in the office."

He walks out before I can say anything else, just like he's always done. Part of me wants to go after him and part of me wants to stay here by myself and enjoy the silence of an empty room. I roll into the space where he just was, smelling his head in the pillow, and close my eyes. Just like that, I'm home.

◆ ❖ ◆

Today my baby sister Trini turns four years old. I still call her that, but she's not my baby anymore. Cristo picks me up at Miss Valentín's and we bike together to Scottie's sister's house for the party. Miss Valentín bought my bike at a yard sale, a girl's Huffy with knobby pink tires. Cristo rides a ten-speed that he's holding for a guy from the shelter who went to Pittsburgh to bury his mother. It's way too big for him, and it surprises me each time when he can actually reach the pedals. With an umbrella, it could be part of a circus act.

The house is packed with people when we get there. It's hot inside and there's enough food on the dining room table to feed the whole block. Scottie waves at us from a chair in the corner and tells us to get drinks from the cooler in the hallway. He doesn't introduce us to anyone. We find Trini in the kitchen, eating spaghetti out of the serving bowl with her fingers. She looks so grownup today, like her face knows it is an entire year older. Her round cheeks are mostly gone and Scottie has let her hair grow long, tying it in a braid down the middle of her back.

Cristo tackles her in a bear hug, and when they get up off the floor I kiss her dimpled cheek and rub her head like my mother used to do. She asks where Mami is and we tell her she's coming by later, after her doctor's appointment. Trini wants to know what her present is but Cristo holds the bag above her head and won't let her see inside.

After we fill our plates, Trini entertains the party by dancing all alone in the middle of the living room. She's wearing a long pink dress and she keeps picking up the bottom to twirl it around. She laughs and falls onto the carpeted floor. It makes me happy to see that she is still laughing. The music they're playing is that old Motown stuff that only adults and little kids like to dance to. Scottie dances with her standing on his feet. She marches like a soldier, stamping his boots like she's trying to break them. He lifts her onto his shoulder and spins around and around, almost knocking down the light fixture. He stops suddenly. His eyes are closed and he has a goofy smile on his face. He drops Trini onto the couch by her leg. Then he collapses into the coat rack, too dizzy to stand. Several coats drop to the ground, as heavy as falling bodies.

Cristo sits next to me on a folding chair, balancing a plate of meatballs on his lap. He eats them in single bites like doughnut holes. We both stare at our sister and at her father.

"Do you think she's doing okay here?" I ask him. I don't want to admit that this stranger's house, this strange family, could be better than our own.

He shrugs. "She seems fine."

I twirl the spaghetti onto my fork. "They look like they have a lot of fun."

"This is a party," he says. "You know every day isn't like this."

"But it's better than the shelter, don't you think?"

Cristo gives a mean laugh. "The only thing the shelter's better than is the street."

He sounds older when he talks like that, like the teenagers who hang out on street corners with their pants falling off. He pops another meatball into his mouth and shakes his head like the whole world is ridiculous. Scottie stumbles out of the room with a drunken smile on his face. My eyes follow him to the hallway, where he takes another beer from the cooler.

"She's lucky to have a father." I don't know why I say that out loud.

Cristo looks at me. "We have one, too, you know."

"Ours doesn't count. He doesn't live with us." I take a bite of the coleslaw on my plate. "And he doesn't think about us."

Cristo wipes his mouth with a napkin. "Do you think about him?"

"Sometimes." I sit back in my chair, trying to remember the last time.

"Well I bet he thinks about you, too."

After we eat, Cristo goes into the kitchen to throw away our plates. Later, I find him taking the empty beer cans out of the garbage and lining them up on the countertop in a straight line. He does that with a lot of things—cigarette cartons, juice boxes, sugar packets—like he's trying to organize the world. When I pass through on my way to the bathroom, I count twenty-two cans. There are several other people drinking beer, like the girl with too much makeup who hangs on Scottie like a wet sweater and the men that he works with, but Scottie drinks the most, and it shows. He trips over a stool and spills a bowl of rice and beans, then yells at his sister for leaving it so close to the edge of the table. I spend the next ten minutes on my knees, helping his sister pick rice kernels out of the thick yellow carpet.

When we sing "Happy Birthday," Scottie shouts at the top of his lungs and keeps singing even when the song is over. Trini reads the letters on her birthday cake while the candles continue to burn. She touches each letter of her name, collecting bright red frosting on her fingertips. When she licks it off she says, "Umm," purring like a cat. She closes her eyes to blow out the candles, squeezing them so tight she looks furious. I know it's her birthday, but I make a wish, too. For her to come back to us. After three tries she blows out all the candles. The whole room claps together. The room vibrates with the sound of applause.

Trini looks at me. "Your hands were like balloons," she says. I'm not sure what she means but it makes me smile. She reaches for my hand, looking inside it.

"What makes that sound?" she asks. "You holding something?"

"Only the air," I say.

I watch Scottie stare at Trini from across the room. He can't stop looking at her, his angel, his sweet little girl. There's something sad about how he looks at her, like he can't quite believe she's his. It's the same way he used to look at my mother. I don't like to think about it, but I wonder what's going to happen when she gets older and loses some of that sweetness. Will he yell at her like he did us? Will he hit her? I guess it's different because she's his real daughter and doesn't need to get punished for not being his. I make another wish right then, while I'm watching him, and while I can still watch over her: that he loves her in a way he never loved us.

My mother shows up when we're cutting the cake. She takes a small piece and stands alone in a corner, trying to blend into the wallpaper. She doesn't talk to anyone. Cristo brings her a soda and stands by her side like a bodyguard. She puts her hand on his shoulder to steady herself. Trini pushes a plastic lawn mower into the room. When she sees our mother she jumps up and down and claps. She spends the next twenty minutes mowing the carpet in front of her, over and over again. I should go over there, too, but I don't. Nobody needs two bodyguards. Nobody needs two daughters.

Scottie stands on the back porch with the other men and watches a football game on their portable TV. I watch him pour liquor into a cup of coffee that his sister brought him to help sober him up. Why are adults so stupid? The men roll their own cigarettes and smoke them quickly by taking long, deep drags. The smell is sweet like summer grass. They pass them around and joke about burning their fingertips. My mother watches them quietly. She smokes her own cigarettes, from a red and white carton she carries in her chest pocket. She looks like she's thinking about a faraway place, not someplace she's been, but someplace she'll never get to see.

I see my mother and Scottie in the same room only once during the party. They look at each other for a long time, over the heads of other people, but don't say anything. When he walks up to her she's holding an empty plate. He takes it from her and says something I can't hear. She shakes her head. He smiles. She says something while Scottie lights two cigarettes. He offers one to her, but she hesitates before taking it, as if she doesn't trust what it could be. She places it gently between her lips, like even the filter could burn her. He holds up a baggie filled with small green pills, just like the ones we found in Kim's purse, and rubs it between his fingers. My mother shakes her head. He's looking at her, but she's looking at the bag.

I lean over to tell Cristo but he's already watching the whole thing go down. "Don't worry," he says to me. "Mami can take care of herself." I want to believe him but I'm not convinced. We both watch her as she backs away from us and out of the room, her eyes locked on Scottie.

When it's time to say good-bye Trini doesn't want us to leave. She wraps her legs tight around Mami's waist and buries her head in her neck. She cries as Scottie pulls her off, taking her out the back door like an animal that's misbehaving. The screen door slams and I can hear her wails from the driveway. Mami wipes her eyes on the sleeve of her shirt and walks out the front door without saying a word. I thank Scottie's sister before we leave, and wrap up a big piece of birthday cake to bring home for Miss Valentín.

The sun is setting when we leave the party. Mami walks on the sidewalk while Cristo and I bike along a row of parked cars in the street. Cristo sings a song by Lauryn Hill, something about how you might win some but you just lost one. Mami and I don't speak. I want to say something to comfort her but I don't know what that would be. We stop at the CVS on Hartford Avenue and Mami goes inside to fill a prescription she just got from her doctor. Once she's inside I ask Cristo why she still takes the medicine if she's not sick anymore.

"What do you mean?" he asks. "She's still sick."

"But she looks better now. She seems all right."

"That's just the outside. On the inside she's still fighting. That's why she's got to keep taking the medicine, even when she feels okay." He taps the handlebars on his bike. "The sickness she got is the kind you can't see."

I put my feet on the ground to balance my bike. "You mean like spilling juice on a dark carpet? You can't see it but the stain is still there."

"Yeah. Kinda like that."

The sun falls behind the hills and the street gets darker. "Why'd she get sick?"

"Fuck if I know," Cristo says.

"Is it because of the drugs?"

He looks at me. "Which drugs?"

"The ones she used to take when we lived on Sophia Street. The kind you buy on the corner instead of in the pharmacy."

He's quiet for a few seconds. "I think so. Maybe. But she stopped doing them a while ago. I don't think it matters anymore."

"Maybe getting sick is her punishment."

He spits on the ground. "Going to jail was her punishment. Being sick is extra."

I roll forward on my bike, making checkerboard tracks in the mud. "Is that why she's mad all the time?"

"She's mad because they keep taking her kids away. We're all she's got but she can't even get us under one roof. How would it make you feel if we were your kids?"

I don't want to have kids. To be a mother. To love something so much but not be able to control it.

"Do you think Trini's ever coming back to live with us?" I ask him.

"Of course she is. What are you talking about?"

"I don't know...sometimes I think maybe she won't."

Cristo grabs the handlebars on my bike, stopping me in my tracks. "Don't ever say that again, okay? And don't ever let Mami hear you say that. Trini belongs with us, Luz. Period. She's our sister for God's sake. *Tu hermana.* No one can take that away."

He lets go of the handlebars and pushes me backward. The bike wobbles and I have to stand to keep it from crashing to the ground. One foot lands in a puddle, splashing mud across the bottom of my pants. When Mami comes out she yells at me for getting dirty and I don't bother to defend myself. My pants stay wet for the whole ride home, which seems like punishment for my lack of faith.

We split up at the Elmhurst cemetery. Cristo and Mami head down Broad Street while I stay on Elmwood to go home to Miss Valentín's. I feel guilty as I bike away, knowing that I'm going back to a nice apartment while they're going to a loud and crowded shelter, but I don't know what to do about it. I know staying together is supposed to be the most important thing, but I don't think it's worth any cost. But I'd never tell Cristo that. Maybe he's a better person than I am, since he's willing to sacrifice his own comfort to stay with Mami. Maybe he's a better son to her than I am a daughter.

◆ ❖ ◆

When I bring Miss Valentín the piece of birthday cake her eyes get big and she tells me German chocolate cake is her favorite. She says she's gonna put it in the freezer to save, but after dinner I see her in the pantry, eating it right off the plate with no fork. She eats the whole thing in a few bites, like she's racing to be the first to finish. When she's done, she wipes the crumbs off her face and buries the plate at the bottom of the garbage so nobody sees it.

I hide behind the door when she comes out so she doesn't think I'm spying on her. But I am. I like to watch her when she doesn't know I'm looking. I noticed a long time ago she's weird with food, but seeing her every day makes it obvious. Adults think they're so sneaky, but everything they do is so predictable. She eats the way my mother smokes cigarettes and Kim drank that pink wine. Like they can't see anything else, even if it's right in front of their face.

After I finish all my homework I lie in bed and write on the wall. The part next to the window so the curtain hides it. Every night since I've been here I've written my name at least once. When Miss Valentín comes in to say good night I stop writing. I hide the pencil under the covers like she hides her food.

"Luz. I want to talk to you about something." She comes

into my room after I brush my teeth and sits on the bed. Her nightgown rises up, exposing the pale skin of her legs. They look like they've never seen the sun. "You know how you write your name on your papers at school, so the teachers know it's yours?"

I nod. Maybe I'm not so good at being sneaky either.

"Or how you write your name in your coat, or on your lunch box? You do that so it doesn't get lost or so someone else can't claim it as theirs. But with bigger things, you don't have to do that. When you have something that everyone knows is yours, when it really belongs to you, you don't have to mark it like that."

I try not to look at the wall, but my eyes keep going straight there.

"Slave owners used to mark their slaves," I tell her, "because they were their property. They owned them. I read that in a book once."

"You're right," she says. "But they were wrong to do that. You can't own another person, not like you'd own a car or a house or a book."

I feel the pencil under the blankets, hard like bone.

"But when you love someone, don't you belong to them?" It doesn't make a lot of sense to me, but I've heard about it in love songs.

"Sure," she says. "But in a different way. When you really belong to someone they don't have to mark you, not in a literal way. The branding is on the inside."

I don't know what to say so I look away. I still feel her staring at me.

"Everything you have here is yours. Everything in this room. No one's going to take it away from you."

I let go of the pencil, afraid I'll snap it in two. I look back at her. Her eyes are big like a cat's and she's holding her hands together as if she's about to pray.

"You say that now, but what if I don't get to stay? What if they move me again?"

My voice starts to crack so I stop talking. I hate the fact that I'm sometimes soft like a little kid, that I want to cry. Miss

Valentín turns to me, her elbows digging large red grooves into her thighs. "I'm not going to lie to you, Luz. I don't know what's going to happen. But I can promise you this much: you will always have a place in my home. The door will always be open."

She says good night and leaves me alone in the room. My room. I grab the book of stories from my mother and climb back in bed, scooting my body deep under the blankets. When I usually start a new book, the first thing I do is write my name inside the front cover. This time, I leave it blank. I don't even look for the pencil, lost somewhere in the warm darkness of my bed. I don't need to own the book, just the story inside. Because once I read it, nobody can ever take it away from me.

Cristo

When we get to the shelter, the first thing they give us is a list of where to eat. The soup kitchens are the best, since the food is hot and free, and, luckily, they serve more than soup. The closest one is Oxford House, right off Broad just a few blocks from the shelter, and the food's actually pretty good. Much better than the cafeteria at school, and way better than everything we used to make at Chino and Kim's. The trick is to get there early and get a good seat. I like sitting at the end of the table, that way I don't get squashed between two old dudes who never shower. I usually sit near the kitchen, so I can get up for more bread and refill Mami's coffee cup with milk when she takes her pills. There's a room in back with a few dozen beds, but only men can stay overnight. Most times I'm the only kid in here and Mami's the only lady. Once I saw a lady eating with three little kids, but the men stared so much she left before dessert and never came back. Can't blame her, after what I heard them say in the bathroom.

The people here are supposed to be all nice and thankful since they're poor and usually homeless, but a lot of what I see is people hanging out in small groups making fun of each other. It's pretty much divided by color, with the black people on one side and all the whites on the other. The Puerto Ricans and the Dominicans are split up, too, neither getting too close to the whites or the blacks. And the women, if they show up, usually hang by themselves within those groups. Sometimes I'll see an old couple together, cutting up their meat into baby-sized bites, and it makes me sad to think they don't have anywhere else to go.

There's a backyard behind the building, a fenced-in square lot covered with picnic tables, but it's been too cold to eat outside. After dinner most people stand by the door, smoking and talking shit about the food. One night when Mami and I are standing there this guy in a hooded parka comes up behind her, throws his arm around her neck and says, "Stop or I'll shoot." I'm about to kick the guy in the balls when Mami turns around and hugs him and says, "Hey asshole, what rock have you been hiding under?"

When he unzips the parka and drops his hood, I'm shocked to see Charley staring at me. He looks equally surprised, though he hides it well.

"Hey, I want you to meet my kid," Mami says, pushing me in front of her. I shake Charley's hand and we both pretend this is the first time we laid eyes on each other.

They laugh for a while, talking about places and people I never heard of. Mami lowers her voice every time she says something she don't want me to hear so I can't quite follow the entire conversation. Bottom line, they broke a lot of laws together. It's weird to think of Mami having her own life, completely separate from mine. And I can only imagine how pissed she'd be if she found out about the life I been living without her. I already know I can never tell her about the months I worked for Snowman, and now I know I have to add this to the list.

Mami sends me inside to get dessert, and I come back with three pieces of cherry pie. They don't see me in the doorway because I'm stuck behind a real fat guy who needs two people to help him walk. That's when I hear Charley asking Mami about being in the joint.

"It almost killed me," she says. "But you wanna know what's more fucked up? I miss it sometimes."

Charley laughs. "Try doing six months in the men's unit," he says, lighting another cigarette. "So, you still clean?"

"So far," she says. "What's that shit they say, *One day at a time*? That's where I'm at."

"I wouldn't know anything about that," Charley says. He pulls on his beard and laughs. "So how's that working out for you?"

Mami blinks when a cloud of smoke covers her face. "Got no choice."

He shrugs. "Shit. You always got a choice."

Right then I come out from behind the fat guy and hand them each their pie.

"We should go now," I say to Mami. "Your meeting starts at seven, right?"

"My little assistant," she says to Charley.

"Everybody needs one," Charley says, staring right at me. He puts his cigarette out against the brick wall and gives Mami a kiss on the cheek. Then he pats me on the shoulder. "Hope to see you around, kid."

"Not if I can help it," Mami says, forcing herself to smile.

Charley throws the plastic fork I brought him into the garbage. "Well, sometimes you can't." Then he bites into the pie like it's a slice of pizza.

"Let's go, Mami. I don't want you to be late."

"Slow down, boy," she says, as I pull her inside. "Who do you think you are, my mother?"

I grab her hand and we walk through the crowded dining room together. A bunch of the men lift their heads to watch her pass them by. It's been that way since I was a little kid, everyone staring at Mami like she's famous. I know she's pretty, but there's gotta be something else that makes people stare like that. Even women can't look away.

She walks me back to the shelter and then heads off by herself to catch a bus to her meeting. I sneak down to the corner and hide behind a minivan to watch her as she waits at the bus stop. Just to make sure. A bus comes and goes, without her getting on it. She rubs her arms and hugs herself to keep warm. The air outside feels cold like a refrigerator and I wish both of us had on heavier coats. She walks in a circle looking at her feet, something Trini used to do all the time. From this far away Mami looks like a teenager, taking the bus home after basketball practice, or going to the mall to meet her girlfriends.

She looks like she don't have a problem in the world.

Another bus comes by and this one she gets on. I wait for it to drive past me, so I can read the sign that says where it's going. "Plainfield Ave—Johnston," it reads, the opposite direction of her meeting. First thing I wonder is where she's going. The second, when she stopped telling me the truth. Later, when I'm lying in bed at the shelter, on a mattress no thicker than card-board and probably not as comfortable, I think maybe she's not going anywhere at all. Maybe she spends her nights riding around on that bus, staring out at the dark city just beyond her reach and watching everything in the world pass her by.

◆ ❖ ◆

Snowman once told me there's only one hour of the day when he can't be interrupted: from II a.m. to noon weekday morn-ings, when he swims laps at the downtown YMCA. I know I should wait until school's over, but sometimes he's hard to find later on, so I sneak out of school early and take the bus to the Y. There's a guard at the door who wants to see my pass, but when I tell him I'm lost and that my father's inside, he lets me in.

The pool is in the basement, in a room with a low ceiling and brightly colored flags hanging from the overhead beams. Even in the water he is easy to spot. His body's long and thin like a dolphin bleached white from hours in the sun, and he's the only person in the pool who swims without stopping. During one lap he crosses the entire length of the pool in one breath, which impresses the lifeguard so much he claps when Snowman lifts his head out of the water to finally breathe.

When he gets out, he dries himself off with a stiff towel the size of a washcloth, and then wraps a beach towel around his waist. He's halfway to the locker room when I call his name. The echo is loud and everyone in the room looks at me. He stops, but doesn't turn around. He waits for me to catch up with him.

"What time is it?" he asks me, looking down at the tiled floor and not at my face.

"II:45."

"Do you know what that means?"

I do, but I don't want to admit it. "I waited until you got out of the pool."

"Is that your answer?"

I feel my face get hot. "No. It means that it's still your time."

"When does my time end?"

"Noon."

"Can you wait until then?"

I look at the clock on the wall. The second hand doesn't move, as if time is stopped. I nod.

"Wait here," he says, still not looking at me.

He disappears into the locker room, his flip-flops smacking against the wet floor. I sit on the bleachers while I wait for him, watching a few people swim laps. The sound of laughter echoes throughout the room, but I can't tell where it's coming from. At noon he's back, sitting beside me on the aluminum bench. It smells like he used half a jar of cocoa butter to cover up the smell of the chlorine, but it didn't work.

"What's up?"

"We need a place to live, another apartment."

"Who's we?"

"Mami and me, and my sisters. A two-bedroom at least, maybe three."

He looks up at the ceiling. "Three bedrooms ain't cheap. And they ain't plentiful."

"Okay, two's fine."

"How soon?"

"Now."

He looks at me.

"We're staying at a shelter," I tell him.

He looks confused. "Since when?"

"A few weeks."

"Why didn't you tell me sooner?"

"I didn't want you to think I was using you."

"And now?"

I shrug. "Now I'm desperate."

"Why? What happened?"

"I don't know. Maybe nothing." I rub my hands over my face.

"You wouldn't be here if it was nothing."

"It's Mami," I finally tell him, feeling my heart start to race. "We're too close to everything bad at the shelter. Everything she needs to stay away from."

He nods, scratching his all-white goatee. "Did she slip?"

"Slip where?"

"Never mind."

He looks hot suddenly, and his head starts to shine. He uses a small towel from his bag to wipe up the sweat.

"I might have something open in the Armory," he says. "Should be ready by March 1st. A nice two-bed near the park. How's that sound?"

"Good," I say. "That sounds good. How much you want for it?"

"Right now it goes for seven hundred." He wipes his head again. "I could do it for five if you're willing to shovel out the driveway and clip the trees or whatever."

"Yeah, I can do that. How much you need for a deposit?"

"Five will do. Tell your mother she can bring it by the Laundromat next week."

I pull an old, worn envelope from the back pocket of my jeans and hand it to him. "There's six hundred forty-two dollars in there. Consider it the deposit and some of the first month's rent."

He looks down at the envelope but doesn't take it. "I don't want your money, Cristo."

"It's your money now," I say, offering it to him again.

"Come on, kid. Put that away before the lifeguard sees it."

"Fine." I tuck it back into my pocket. "I'll give it to you outside."

His hands are still holding the towel, damp with sweat. I watch him squeeze it out, until the white part of his knuckles turns red. "You worked hard to save all that. It shouldn't just go all at once."

"But this is what I was saving it for."

He spreads the towel onto the bench and relaxes his hands. In a few seconds the normal color returns, brown and white splotches like the marble cake I've seen Teacher eat in her classroom once all the other kids have gone home. I wonder how he feels looking so different from everybody else.

"Listen," he says, putting his hand on my shoulder. "That's not your job anymore. Paying rent, saving money, buying food. It's your mother's job. She's the grownup." He shakes his head and exhales. "I know she's getting help from the state, and from that agency, so she should have enough to cover things for now." He looks at me. "It needs to come from her, okay? Not from you."

A whistle blows and I hear the slap of bare skin against water. I try to imagine how the pool would look without any water, like the one in my old neighborhood.

"You understand, kid?"

"Yeah. I get it."

"If she needs time to get on her feet with a job or whatever, it's okay. I can give her that."

He stands up and pulls on a hooded sweatshirt, then zips himself into a black down jacket, doubling his size. I grab onto his puffy sleeve and watch my hand sink into the dark fabric. Under the soft feathers, I can feel the strength of his arm.

"Thanks, Snowman."

"No problem," he says, throwing his bag over his shoulder, "but next time you show up here, you're doing laps." I know he means it like a threat, but to me it sounds like a promise.

When we pass the front desk, the guard calls out to us. "I guess you found your dad, huh?"

"Yeah, thanks," I say, careful not to make eye contact with either one of them.

Snowman shakes his head and laughs softly, holding the door open for me to pass through. The cold air shocks me like a slap in the face. I zip up my sweatshirt and pull the hood down over my eyes. Snowman steps in front of me, shielding me from the brutal wind. We walk several blocks like that, until he puts me on a bus and sends me back to school.

◆ ❖ ◆

When Valentine's Day comes I use some of the money I saved

from working to buy presents for the special females in my life. I get a huge chocolate heart for Teacher, a box of Sweethearts candy for Luz, a white teddy bear with a necklace that says "Forever" for Trini, and a dozen red roses for Mami, because since she's been back she's always talking about how much she missed flowers when she was gone. And I know she doesn't have anyone else to give her any. I want to get Graciela something, too, but I can't find a store around here that sells the kind of books she reads, so I end up sending her a card with a handwritten poem inside. I write it out in English, just to show her how my writing got better, but I don't sign it because I figure the poem says enough and if she really cares she'll figure it out.

For a while I was doing better in school but lately I haven't been turning in my homework and sometimes I fall asleep on the bus and miss my stop and don't even get to school until second period. Mrs. Reed always asks me to stay after class to catch up but most days I sneak out the door before she can stop me. Sometimes I go to the library to pick up books for Snowman but sometimes I have to meet Mami at the Free Clinic to help her carry all those cans of Ensure back to the shelter. I don't mind staying there, but it's hard to sleep because the TV's always on and everybody's coughing and talking and getting up to go to the bathroom in the middle of the night. It's like trying to take a nap in a hospital waiting room.

When Mami sticks around it's okay, but when she's gone I get bored and end up playing dominoes or checkers by myself with only half the pieces. I try to stay awake so I can say good night to her when she comes back, just to make sure she looks okay, but most nights I end up falling asleep in the rec room. When I wake up I'm on the cot in my room with my sneakers still on, and I never know if one of the staff people carried me there or if Mami did. When I get up to go to school, she's still asleep, looking so peaceful I don't want to bother her. Sometimes days go by before we actually see each other and it makes me remember old times.

When I turn in the first draft of that book of poems I'm making for school, Mrs. Reed is shocked.

"Wow, Cristo," she says, flipping through it. "I'm impressed.

You have a great breadth of experience represented here."

I look at her. "What's that mean?"

She laughs. "It means you're doing a good job."

"Oh. Nice."

She points to the calendar. "The next project we have is a book report for Black History Month and a personal essay reflecting on cultural diversity. If this is any indication of what you're capable of, you should do quite well."

I ask her what she means by cultural diversity.

"You know, how people act, what they eat, how they dress. A lot of it has to do with where they're from and how they grew up."

"And diversity means different, right?"

She nods. "Some people refer to America as a melting pot, because it's made up of people from all over the world. Sometimes we blend together like in a soup and it makes a new flavor, and sometimes we stay separate, distinct, each with our own taste. I want you to write an essay about why you think that is."

I tell her I think it sounds hard but then she says there's really no right or wrong answer, so that makes me feel better. I look back at the calendar. "So wait, why do black people get a whole month, when we only get a week in April?"

She looks confused. "Well, Puerto Rico is a small island, Cristo, whereas Africa is an entire continent."

"A friend of mine says they're trying to make up for slavery. And for the fact that so many black people are in prison, in the ghetto, or dead." I know *friend* isn't the right word for Snowman, but I can't think of anything else to call him.

"Interesting theory," Mrs. Reed says. "You know, you could celebrate Black History Month as well, if you want to. I'm sure a lot of your ancestors are from Africa."

She moves on to the next student, but I'm still thinking about what that means when the bell rings and it's time to go home.

I meet up with Teacher after school and she brings me to the library where they have a huge table covered with black history books. I read a story about a lady named Rosa Parks who starts some bus boycott in Alabama when she won't give up her seat to a white person. I guess I learn some history by reading that book, but most of what I know about discrimination I learn in real life. In America, it's all about skin color: the darker you are, the faster people cross the street. That's why Snowman trips people out. His skin's white like rice but his nose and mouth look just like some African dude, and even though he reads a lot he sounds like he's never once left the corners of South Providence. People don't know where to put him and that makes them nervous because without a group they can't figure out how good they should treat him. I don't really care about race since everybody I know has the same thing in common: being poor. No matter what color your skin is, being broke don't look good on nobody.

When Teacher asks me what I'm gonna write my essay on I start telling her a story about being in Kennedy Plaza when I first moved to Providence and watching a white couple fight in the street. The guy pulled the lady onto the sidewalk by her hair and started slapping her hard across her face and the back of her neck. Instead of protecting herself, she flung her arms out and started wailing on him in the ribs. He kicked at her like she was a crazy dog and then she dove into him and held him around the waist. She looked like she was hugging him but I could tell she was just trying to keep herself from falling onto the ground.

A group of teenagers, I tell her, all of them black, got off the bus from Hope High School and when they saw what was happening they ran over to the couple and started yelling at the guy and eventually pulled him off. The way they acted I thought they knew him, or maybe even knew her, but after a while it was clear they were strangers. Pretty soon the guy calmed down and left, but the teenagers stayed with the lady and asked her if she wanted them to call the cops or an ambulance or something. She fixed her ponytail and said, "No, thanks," and spit a bloody chunk of snot onto the street, right next to the bus I was waiting for. I watched her pass a few white teenagers as she limped over to the bus and they all kept their eyes on the ground.

When I'm done with the story Teacher asks me what I think it means. I tell her I don't know, but she doesn't like that type of answer so she keeps staring at me till I say more. I finally tell her all I can figure is that white people think it's good to mind their own business, whereas black people figure if something shady's going down then it is their business.

"What about Latinos?" Teacher asks, her eyes twinkling a little bit as she smiles. "Do you think we're more like the whites or the blacks?"

I know the answer is neither because we're our own thing, but then I think maybe it should be both since we're all mixed up thanks to slavery. Before I can answer her she leans forward real close to me and whispers, "What about you, Señor?"

I don't want to laugh in her face, but I can't help it.

"Come on, Teacher. You know I'm not trying to be white, don't you?"

"You trying to be black?"

Is this lady for real? I shake my head and make a face at her until we're both laughing. She looks real pretty when she smiles, like she's happy just being with me. I wonder if I look the same way.

"You know what?" I say. "I'm trying to be. Just *be*."

She nods and I know I don't have to say anymore. When it comes time to write that essay I end up telling the same story about what I saw in Kennedy Plaza instead of writing about Rosa Parks like all the other kids, and at the top of the paper I write my full name, Cristoval Luna Perez, which seems pretty damn culturally diverse to me.

SHE SEES the girl running. Racing through the field as if she were on fire. Her mouth open wide to breathe. To scream. A scream so loud it makes her run. The hot, dry dirt burns her bare feet. She cuts down a path where jasmine blooms in soft bunches like cotton. The smell is so sweet it makes her feel light-headed. There are hills in the distance, covered with kapok trees taller than the houses that surround them. She just wants to make it to the trees. The sun has set; the coqui begin to sing. In the darkness, a hand reaches out to grab her. Instead he catches her skirt, tearing it off. He tells her to come home. He's sorry. He won't do it again. She refuses to stop or turn around when he calls her name. She has to move. As she passes a neighbor's house, she sees her naked reflection in the window. She is the one who is screaming.

Arcelia

Moving into the apartment off Parade is the easiest move of my life. I bring my duffel bag, two boxes of Ensure, and myself. And Cristo, of course. These days he hardly leaves my side.

Snowman did good by me—the place is nice. It's bigger than our old spot on Sophia Street and it's clean like a bank. The crazy part is that everything works—all the burners on the stove, the window locks, and the outlets—and there's a closet in every room. Some mornings it's hard to sleep 'cause it gets so bright in my room. I tried hanging towels in the windows to block out the sun, but they keep falling down. It's good though, 'cause it gets me up and out of bed by the time Cristo goes off to school. Sometimes we even have breakfast together. He heats tortillas on the stove and we eat them with butter and honey, or other days he makes Cream of Wheat in ceramic mugs we got from the flea market that say "Believe in Providence." They're all chipped and some of the handles are broken off, but the words are written in fancy gold letters that feel good against my fingertips.

The neighborhood is loud as hell, but it don't bother me. There's a park around the corner and you can hear children yelling on most afternoons, even though it's the middle of winter. Dogs bark at all hours of the night. There are so many cars on the main street it looks like they're having a parade. I guess that's how they named it. Motorcycles speed between stoplights like they're in a race, and going by the number of fire trucks I see every day, I'm thinking there are more fires in this part of town than anywhere else in the city. It's strange how the sound of a siren can actually become familiar enough to be a comfort, like the voice of somebody you love.

But inside the apartment it's quiet. I didn't know just how silent a place could be with only two people living there, since I've always lived in a full house. Even when he's here Cristo barely makes a sound. Most nights he watches TV with the volume off and pretends to do homework. Or he lies in bed and listens to the Walkman his teacher gave him for Christmas until the batteries run out. Then he collects all the used batteries and lines them up in rows along the windowsill like he's building a miniature army to protect us. When he leaves for school in the morning, I usually go back to bed. I don't fall asleep—for some reason I can't sleep anymore—but I feel better lying down. It's easier for me to breathe.

I don't like being alone. There's too much time to think about all the mistakes I made. Every day I feel like crying but the tears won't come. I'm all dried up inside. I keep thinking it's gonna get better soon, but the next day I feel the same way. Mornings are usually the worst. Right after I wake up, I don't want to move or open my eyes. With my eyes closed, I only see what I want to see. Sometimes I think I can hear the blood rushing through my veins. It makes my belly hurt, but also reminds me I'm alive. And that don't always make me feel better. Just knowing I still have to live.

A week after we move in I get a surprise visitor. I hear a round of knocking on the front door, loud like gunfire. It's almost noon but I'm still in bed. Every time it stops I think they went away, but then it starts again. I finally hear the noise move from the door to the window just off the porch. Scratches almost, like a cat. That's when I get up.

I open the door and the porch is empty. There's a man in a nylon warm-up jacket walking down the steps with his back to me. The sound of the door opening makes him turn around. It's not a man. It's Lucho. She stares at me, her lips slightly parted. Her gold tooth shines in the sunlight. Her body looks the same, still pale and hard, but her face looks softer.

"The doorbell works," I say, gesturing toward it. Her eyes, which usually jump around like a trapped housefly, stay fixed on mine.

"Oh." She shuffles her foot and almost slips off the step. She steadies herself, trying to look like it was on purpose. I'm glad that seeing me can still put her off balance.

"Sorry," she says. "I just assumed it didn't."

"It's the first one I ever had that works."

She nods, like I'm saying something really interesting.

"I heard you just got out."

"For real? It was almost three months ago."

She shrugs. "You moved. Took me a while to find you."

"Must not be looking too hard."

She grabs onto the porch railing, which is covered with peeling red paint. The chips crumble in her hand like dried blood.

"Found you, didn't I?" She wipes her hands on her jeans. "So how you been?"

"Fine."

She steps onto the porch, close enough for me to smell her aftershave. I don't remember it smelling so strong.

"You look good," she says.

I cross my arms over my chest, since I'm not wearing a bra. "Thank you."

"I like your hair. It's different, right?"

"Yep." If I was keeping score I would give her two points for that one. Usually she's just like a man—don't even notice the seasons change.

She steps closer to me. "It's been a long time, Celie. Too long."

"That's more your fault than mine."

She nods. "I tried to—"

"Forget about it, Lucho. I don't want to hear it now."

She puts both hands in the air. "Okay, okay. I won't apologize."

"That's not what I said. What I don't want are your excuses. Apologies are something else."

She motions toward the door. "Can I come inside?"

"No."

"Well, can you come outside?"

I wait a few seconds before I step onto the porch. I close the door behind me and lean against it. The wind is cold so I zip up my sweatshirt.

"I made a mistake, Celie. I shouldn't have left like that. I'm sorry. You needed me and I let you down and I won't blame you if you never forgive me for that. I really won't." She looks up, her eyes full of sadness I never noticed before. "I was messed up back then and I missed you so much. I just got scared that I couldn't do it, you know? I knew that I couldn't be you and me, so I just panicked and—" She runs her fingers through her hair, still short and stiff with gel. She inhales deep and slow, like taking a hit from a joint. "I fucked up, okay? I'm a fuck up."

"Don't say that." I reach for her out of habit, and then stop myself. My arm hangs awkwardly in the air.

"Why not, we both know it's true."

"So what does that make me?" I ask her. "I'm the one who left my kids in the first place."

"You didn't leave."

"Fine. I got taken away. Same difference."

She taps the floorboards on the porch with the toe of her work boot. "We're quite a pair, the two of us." She keeps her eyes down.

"A pair?"

"You know, like a couple?" she says. "Two people together."

"I know what *pair* means. But I don't think it fits with us."

"You used to. You used to say that's all you really wanted."

I tuck my hair behind my ears. "Things change."

She looks up at me, squinting in the sunlight. "Has that?"

I can't help but smile, even if I'm still angry. "You got a lot of fucking nerve."

She smiles back at me, all confidence. "Isn't that what you always loved about me?"

I make her wait before answering. "Not really," I finally say.

Her face falls. "What, you saying you didn't love me?"

I stare at her, my head tilted to the side. She needs something from me, but what I need is to tell her the truth. "What I loved was your passion."

We're both silent for a while. The wind blows a plastic bag onto the porch and it dances in the air like a balloon.

"You eat lunch yet?" Lucho asks.

When I shake my head she says, "Let me buy you a burger, okay? I got a car now, one that runs. Let's drive up to the A&W like we used to, walk around that pond with all the geese."

"It's March, they're not even open yet."

She shrugs. "We'll find something else then. Come on, get your coat."

"I got a job interview at three. I have to be back."

"No problem." She looks at her watch. "How long does it take you to eat a burger?"

I don't answer her right away. I lean against the door frame, letting it hold me up. There was a time, before I went to the ACI, when being with Lucho was all I wanted. I'm not sure why, but she used to make me feel safe—not just from the outside world, but from myself. I lost myself when I was with her. I didn't have to be anybody: not a wife, not a mother, not a failure. I could be whatever I wanted to be. I could be whoever she needed me to be.

I'm standing on the porch looking at her, but what I'm thinking about is how free I felt back then. To be nothing. That was the real high. I can pretend I don't miss it, but that's not the truth. I can pretend I don't need it, but that's not true either. I need to feel that freedom again, even if it's only for a few hours.

I think of my children, my case manager, and my doctor— in that order—and imagine what they'd say if they were standing here right now.

Don't go, Mami.

This is a mistake, Arcelia.

Take care of yourself first.

I hear their voices clearly, but it don't stop me from grabbing my coat and getting into Lucho's car. In the silence of the car I hear my own voice as well.

Trust yourself. Show them how you changed. See how far you can go without getting lost.

I never make it to the job interview. We end up driving down to Iggy's and getting clam cakes and chowder and watching the sunset from Oakland Beach. We sit on the hood of her car to eat, even though it's not even forty degrees outside. The steam from the chowder feels good on my face. For dessert we finish off a box of doughboys, each one as big as my fist. I'm so stuffed I think I'm gonna puke, but I still lick the sugar off my fingertips. It feels good to be full of something.

Once it gets too dark to see each other, we move inside the car. Lucho acts real sweet and says all the right things, like she's been taking lessons in how to be perfect. She lets me pick the radio station. She looks me in the eye when she talks. She doesn't even try to touch me. At first I think I'm not gonna let it get physical—not right away at least—but after being with her for a minute, all my old feelings come back. I want to touch her, and to feel her touching me, so without saying anything I wrap her arm around my shoulder. I let her hold me in the frontseat of her car, just like she used to. I'm so comfortable I almost fall asleep, but when I turn toward her I see the curve of her lip and suddenly I want to taste her. I want her in my mouth like I wanted all that food.

I kiss her hard the first time, like I'm angry, but as we get used to each other again I soften my hold and nibble on her lips like a kitten testing the strength of its own jaw. I trace her mouth with my tongue and taste the oily sweetness of the doughboys on her lips. I grab her head with my hands and bring her to me. The hard spikes of her hair prick my skin like thorns. She lies down on top of me. The weight of her body takes the air out of mine. I lose myself in the dark of the car, in the scent of the leather seats. It feels good to be lost.

I tell her we have to keep all our clothes on. She don't argue. I won't let her hands inside my shirt so she leaves oily fingerprints all over my coat, like she's marking her territory. I give her a hickey like a frustrated teenager, wanting to leave proof that I was there. The taste of her aftershave on my lips makes me sad 'cause all of a sudden it feels like I went back in time, and things are just like they used to be. I guess that means I really didn't change. Time passes, but nothing changes.

When she drops me off it's late—way past dinnertime. The lights are on in every room of the apartment. Cristo's home. I tell her I can't let her come inside.

"I don't want Cristo getting the wrong idea."

"Of course, I understand." She puts the car in park and lets it run. "So, can I see you again?"

I laugh. "What, you wanna go on a date?"

"Sure," she says. "Whatever you want."

I zip up my coat. "I don't know what I want."

"Okay."

She taps the steering wheel. Her fingernails are bitten short, the cuticles dry and rough like a man's. I used to cut them myself, while she watched football on Sunday afternoons, and then I rubbed them with cocoa butter and laughed when the beer bottle slipped out of her greasy hands. I bet she started biting them as soon as I left.

"No, that's not true," I say, shoving my hands into my pockets. "I want time. And I want you to know something." I stare at her till she looks me in the eyes. "I'm clean now. For nine months. I stopped everything—except for cigarettes and coffee—and I don't want to start again. You understand?"

"Of course. That's good, that's real good, Celie." She squeezes my knee gently, leaving her hand there to trace circles on my jeans. "I'm proud of you."

"It's the hardest shit I ever did. Harder than giving birth or leaving Puerto Rico. Harder than surviving all these years by myself."

She nods. "I get it," she says softly. "I wish that could be me."

I look at her pale skin, see the circles under her eyes. I know the answer, but I ask anyway. "You still partying?"

"Just a few drinks here and there. And some weed to help me sleep—nothing hard."

"No dope?"

She shakes her head. "Your boy cut me off last summer

when I fell behind with rent. Don't have a contact."

"Forced to go straight, huh? Not much better than me." I mean it as a joke but her face is real serious.

"Not half as good as you, Celie." Her hand taps the steering wheel, real soft like she's playing the piano. "I could never do what you did."

"Shit, if I can do it any sucker with a pulse can get clean." I squeeze her hand. "The hard part is wanting to." I try to let go but she keeps holding me.

"I'm sorry, Celie."

I want to tell her it's okay, to say I forgive her, but I can't yet. I don't. Instead, I bring her hand to my mouth and kiss her dry, pale knuckles one by one. My lipstick leaves a smudge, which I wipe off with my thumb before I slip out of the car.

"Can I call you?" She leans across the frontseat to look at me, almost falling over.

I stare at her twisted face, her upside-down smile. "I don't have a phone."

"I'll come by then, when your kids aren't around."

I close the car door without answering. *My kids.* How do I tell her I only have one kid left?

I walk to the house as quick as I can, the cold air burning my skin like fire. I climb the porch steps two at a time, but when I get to the door I stop, waiting for the sound of her car to disappear after she drives away. I don't let myself turn around to watch her leave.

"You forget your key?"

The voice comes from the street. It startles me but for some reason I'm not scared. When I turn around Cristo's old teacher is standing by the curb looking up at me with a fake smile. She hides her body in a coat too warm for the weather. Bright red, a color no *gordita* should wear.

"Nope. Just taking my time. It's a nice night."

"Nice, huh? You must love it when it snows." She walks to me real slow, like someone trying to catch a stray cat. "You just getting home from work?" she asks.

"An interview. If I get the job I start next week." Don't know why I lie.

"Good for you." She climbs the stairs like an old person, one hand on the railing, one on her purse. "What's the job?"

"It's at a store. A restaurant." I look down at my hands. "Washing dishes."

"Oh."

She comes closer, so I back up against the door. She seems like a giant standing next to me. A giant in high heel shoes.

"Or I could be a waitress and make the same money in half the time." The lies keep coming out of my mouth. "Then I can be here for the kids."

"Can't argue with that." Her breathing is heavy but she tries to hide it.

"You got any kids?" I say, for no real reason.

She shakes her head. "You asked me that last year."

"Well, sometimes things change."

We are both quiet for too long.

"How's my girl?" I hate having to ask her about my daughter. I wish the state would give her back to me, but I got to prove I have stable housing and a job before I can start the paperwork.

"She's fine." Her purse keeps falling off the shoulder of her thick coat. "And Cristo?" She smiles at me, like we're friends.

"How you expect him to be? He misses his sister. She should be home with us."

She nods. "You're right," she says.

I try to read the look behind her eyes. I wonder if I can trust her.

"If you want you could go get her right now."

"It's not my call," she says, her arms up in the air like she's turning herself in. "The state placed her with me. I have to follow their rules."

"I don't give a damn about their rules." I'm pissed so quick I don't know where it comes from. "You're not her mother."

"I know that." She starts to stutter. "I'm not trying to be." For the first time she steps away from me.

"Just making it clear so you don't get me wrong."

She looks down at the porch. "It's real clear."

"Cool." I unlock the door and open it a crack. "Well. Thanks for stopping by." I stand there, waiting for her to get the hint but she don't.

She coughs into the sleeve of her jacket. "I actually came to see Cristo." She steps toward the door now, like just saying his name gives her confidence. I stop her with my hand on the doorknob.

"It's late, you know. He's got school in the morning."

"Yes, I'm well aware of that. Don't worry, I won't be long. I just want to check in with him."

"Check in? Like for a flight?" I'm trying to make a joke but she looks real serious. Something about her face makes me bust out laughing, even though I'm still pissed and want to slam the door in her face.

I let go of the doorknob and she walks in front of me like we're in her home and she's the one nice enough to let me in. I call Cristo's name and he yells that he's in his room so I point to the hallway and turn on the light for her.

"Thank you," she says. I can feel her staring at me, wanting me to say something else but I don't have nothing to say to her.

When she comes out later I'm watching TV. I don't know how long she was in there, but *Jeopardy!*'s over already and now I'm thinking about how time never passes on TV. The host looks the same as he did when I first got to New York and used to practice my English by watching game shows every night. She says good-bye to me but I just wave at her, pretending to look at something real interesting on the screen when really I'm just watching my own reflection.

Cristo comes in from the kitchen a few minutes later, eating microwave popcorn straight out of the bag. He asks me if I'm hungry and I say no so he eats the whole bag by himself. He thinks I'm late 'cause I was at a meeting and I don't tell him different. When he asks how it went I say it was actually pretty good. That makes him smile. He sits down next to me so we can watch the TV together but I don't pay attention. My eyes wander around the empty room, looking for something to focus on. The bare walls are a blinding white that makes my eyes hurt. I pull open the blinds and stare out the window but all I see is my own face looking back at me.

"You look different," Cristo says later, when he's going to

bed. "Like you finally heard something you been waiting a long time to hear. Like it finally makes sense or something."

I put my arms around him and give him a kiss on the top of his soft, curly head. I don't say anything. No more lies tonight. After he goes to his room, I get out my notebook and start writing a bunch of letters. It's the first time I held a pen since getting out. It feels good to hold something heavy in my hand.

I write to my father and my brothers in Puerto Rico; to Chino, who moved up to Woonsocket looking for work; and to my baby girl, Trini, even though she can't read a word of it. I write to Candy, who should be out by now, and is probably living in her grandmother's house just a few blocks away; and I write to my doctor, telling him how much I hate taking all those pills. I write to my case manager, thanking her for the subsidy so I can live in this apartment, and then I tell her I got real sick today so I had to miss the interview she spent three weeks setting up. I tell her how sorry I am I keep wasting everybody's time. I write letters to all those people, but really I write them for myself 'cause I'm already thinking I won't ever send them.

I never been a person to write things down but I like getting to tell my own truth. There's no yelling in a letter, no fights over who said what, no reason to lie so you don't get punched, and no checking for exits to find the quickest way out. You don't have to soften your words by looking at somebody a certain way or reaching out to touch them, and you don't have to worry about what's gonna happen when it's over, wondering if they're gonna hold you or hit you, or if you'll need to go hide somewhere. The most important thing is that you have a record of what was said—you have proof—and you can reread it as many times as you want and it'll always be the same. A letter is more dependable than most things in my life. That's why I like writing them. That's why I'm never gonna stop, even when I run out of anything good to say.

Miss Valentín

There are no streetlights on their end of the block, so I get out of my car cautiously, holding onto the roof to steady myself. I'm wearing high heels (not a super-functional choice) and I move around the car slowly, careful not to trip over anything. I see broken bottles and a mismatched pair of tennis shoes lying in the gutter like the answer to a question no one dares to ask. I should have changed my shoes before coming here, but I made the decision so quickly I didn't have time to think about my outfit. When my students ask why I wear such high heels I tell them I need the extra three inches, so even as they grow they will still have to look up to me.

It's been dark for almost an hour, though it's not late—just past seven o'clock. The park across the street is empty, except for the few lone dog walkers, shadows moving between the maple trees. I look to the horizon to get my bearings. There, above the skyscrapers, I see the first hint of stars twinkling in the night sky, like kernels of corn about to pop in the oily blackness. Something about the silence makes it feel later than it is and I check my watch again, just to make sure.

When I look up, I see her. She's getting out of a green Honda Civic, the passenger side, of course. I've never seen her behind the wheel. She probably doesn't even drive. I recognize her right away because she's so skinny I can see right between her legs. I was expecting to see her outside like this (on the streets, just like in the old neighborhood), but it still makes me sad. I feel sorry for her, and for Cristo—for the whole family, really—and for a system that thinks you can drop someone into shark-infested water with a bloody foot and expect them to get out alive.

She's not dressed for the weather, which is cold enough to make my hands ache like I've got arthritis, but at least she doesn't look sick. She has a healthy flush to her cheeks, which makes her look a decade younger than last year. If I didn't know, I would never imagine she was HIV positive, or a recovering heroin addict for that matter. Or even an ex-con. If I didn't know her, I would walk by and think she was a teenager home from a date, her voice light and sugary as she flirts with the driver.

"I don't even have a phone," she says with an innocent smile I didn't think she was capable of. But it's not just her voice, her body seems light too, and she almost skips down the sidewalk as she makes her way to the apartment she shares with her son. Like the last one, this one is on the first floor, but the street is nicer. It's also in one of Snowman's houses, a brick-red Victorian almost a hundred years older than the one on Sophia Street, and solid enough to outlast us all.

I pass the car slowly, cutting my eyes to catch a glimpse of Arcelia's suitor. I can't say I'm surprised by the face I see: Lucho, her black eyes staring through me as she scans the street like a sniper tracking her prey. She must be fearless, reckless, or stupid (or some combination of all three) to show up in Arcelia's life right now. To come back after such a long absence. Perhaps the real addiction they have is to each other, not even their drug of choice. Perhaps their relationship is the drug.

I call to her when she's on the porch, standing frozen in front of the door as if she's not sure it's her home. I must startle her because she drops the keys. I try to be nice so I ask her about her job interview but I can tell by how she answers that she doesn't want to talk about it. Or maybe she just doesn't want to talk to me. She's still angry about Luz coming to live with me, and I can't say I blame her. But come on, it's not like I'm the one that took her daughter away. I wasn't expecting an actual thank-you, but maybe a little gratitude would be nice. Instead she's acting like I snatched her lunch out of her hand while she was still eating it.

When she opens the door she doesn't invite me in. I have to say, "I'm here to see Cristo," for her to actually let me into the house. She can't even be bothered to take me to his room. She points down the hall and lets me find it for myself. The first two doors are closed, but I see light coming from the bottom of the last door before the bathroom. I knock twice, soft at first, but then harder.

"What you need, Mami?" Cristo says as he walks toward the door. He stops when he sees me, a small smile creeping across his face. "Hey, Teacher. What are you doing here?" His smile quickly fades. "Is Luz okay?"

"She's fine. I'm actually here to check on you."

He taps his pencil against his leg. "I'm cool."

I look around the room. It is bare except for a mattress on the floor and a hard-shelled suitcase he's using as a desk. His shoes are neatly placed at the side of the bed, like how my grandfather used to leave his bedtime slippers.

"I like your room."

He looks around, like he's never seen it before. "It's kinda empty," he apologizes. "I'm not used to having a room to myself."

"You just need a female touch, that's all. Let me take you down to the flea market on Saturday and we can get you some things. Maybe a rug and a dresser?"

"No, thanks. I can wait till Mami's next check." He sits down on his bed. "You wanna sit?" He moves over to make room for me.

"Umm," I look around, hoping I just overlooked the chair. I'm five years too old and fifty pounds too heavy to sit on a twin-sized mattress on the floor.

"Or you can sit here," he says, turning the suitcase on its side. I stare at it skeptically, wondering if it's strong enough to hold me. "Come on, Mami sits here all the time," he tells me.

Yes, but she's half my size, I want to say. Instead, I hover over the suitcase like it's a dirty toilet seat, my legs holding the bulk of my weight. I'm not sure how long I can keep this up.

"How's she doing, your mother?" I ask him.

"She's good," he says. "Real good." He taps his leg with the pencil again.

"Yeah?"

He nods, looking at the closed door as if he can see straight through it and is staring right at her. "I mean it. She's different than she was before. She's better now."

"That's good." I rest more weight on the suitcase, hoping it holds me up. "Does she talk about her health with you?"

"Sometimes. But she don't—doesn't—have to say much. I can see in her eyes how she's feeling."

"And she's feeling good now?"

"Yeah. She's good. She's not sick like she was."

This surprises me, that he knows she was sick. "She told you? That she was sick?"

"Yeah, when she first got back. She told me she was real sick before, pneumonia and some other stuff. But she's good now, so long as she takes her medicine."

"And if she doesn't?"

He shakes his head. "She has to. That's why it's my job to remind her."

"That's a big job."

He shrugs. "Who else is going to do it?"

I rearrange myself on the suitcase. "Doesn't she have doctors?"

"It's cool. I like to help." He gets up to close the shades. His shadow looms on the wall as tall as a man's.

"I hope she appreciates how you take care of her."

"We take care of each other," he says with his back to me.

"You're a good boy, Cristo."

"And Mami, she's a good mother." He turns around to face me. "You guys all think she's not a good mother, but she is. A person can change, you know. They can decide to be different and clean up their act or whatever, and they can have a better life. She's doing that, Mami is doing that, and I just wish everybody would see that and leave her alone."

"I'm glad she's doing well. That's all I want for her, and for you."

He comes back over to the bed, but doesn't sit back down.

I stand up, too, grateful to be on my own feet.

"Have you seen Lucho?"

"Lucho?" He says her name like it's a bitter taste he's trying to spit off his tongue. "She's not coming around no more. She's smart enough to stay away."

"I thought maybe she was helping your mom, taking her to meetings or something."

"Lucho? Going to meetings? No way. That's a fucking joke." He stares at me, shaking his head. "Sorry, Teacher, but that's just crazy."

"Have you asked her?" I keep prodding, wanting him to connect the dots.

"'I don't need to."

"But maybe if you—"

"I already told you. She doesn't come around here." He bites the pencil. "And God help her if she did."

I hesitate, weighing my options carefully. "Cristo, I want to tell you something about your mother."

"I don't think I wanna hear it."

"Maybe not. But I think you should."

He cuts me off, his voice sharp. "Okay. But first let me tell you something." I look down, waiting for him to speak. "I know you want to help me. And you think that coming over here and asking me how things are going helps me. But it doesn't."

"Listen, Cristo—"

"And even if it did," he says, cutting me off, "well, I don't need your help anymore. Mami is here now and she's going to take care of things."

"I'm glad. That's how it should be."

"No, you're not. Stop saying you're happy about anything she does." He raises his voice and I can see the anger in his eyes. "I know you don't like her. I know you wanted her to get out of prison and fall on her face so you could sweep in like the big hero and save all of us—"

"That's not true—"

"—and I hate to disappoint you, Teacher, but Mami's doing good now and we're gonna get my sisters back home. Maybe then you'll figure out we don't need you anymore."

I feel the breath leak out of me, slow and thick like blood from an animal carcass.

"I don't need you anymore," he says, his voice softer now, which somehow makes it worse. That he could say something so hurtful without even a trace of anger. He crosses his arms, rubbing them for warmth.

"That's all," he says. "Now it's your turn."

I look at him like he's speaking another language. What could I possibly say to all that? I reach for the doorknob, shaking my head. "It's fine. I've already said enough."

I walk out of his bedroom and down the dark hallway alone. Arcelia is watching TV when I pass her in the living room. I force myself to say good-bye to her, even though what I really want to do is confront her about Lucho and the job interview and the meetings she's lying to her son about going to. She waves good-bye, too engrossed in the show to even lift her eyes off the screen.

"Good luck," I whisper under my breath. As if luck has anything to do with it.

Lucho

In Spanish, the word *luchar* means *to fight*. *Lucho* means *I fight*. My name is who I am.

My name is Lucho. I fight.

They named me Luciana but I took Lucho when I was eight 'cause it sounded hard and I wanted people to think I was a boy. I still do. Boys got it easier on all sides. They make more money, get the best girls, and only bleed when they get cut. Best of all, they can disappear. And later, when they're men, they can hide in plain sight.

My name is Lucho. I hide.

Been hiding all my life. Run and hide, stay and fight. Only two choices. What they call that? That thing animals do? Fight or flight? Yeah, that's right. That's who I am. But now I can't fight anymore. Don't want to. Not if I'm gonna win Celie back. So what's that make me now? Who am I, if I don't know my own name?

My name is Lucho. I'm lost.

A flyer at the supermarket tells me there are answers. Hope. For those willing to find it. People like me, who run out of places to hide. The guy at the door tells me these meetings are anonymous, but I recognize half the faces in here. From the needle exchange and the strip clubs on Eddy Street, but also from the park, the bus station, and the corner store on Manton. Junkies are everywhere. And now they got us meeting in the basement of a church. How fucked up is that? Gotta get the sinners inside somehow.

My name is Lucho. I'm here.

They sit in a broken circle, on metal folding chairs that look fifty years old. Most of them are white, half are men. They pass around a book as thick as the Bible. The leader reads a few pages. People nod their heads. People laugh. Somebody asks if there are any newcomers. Everybody looks at me so I raise my hand. I never raised my hand in school, even when I knew the answer. I didn't want to hear the sound of my own voice. Soft and weak like a girl. I still don't talk that much. Don't got a lot to say.

My name is Lucho. I'm silent.

Somebody asks my name. I look down. "Lucho," I hear myself say. My voice sounds steady. Even. Unfamiliar. The whole room claps, as loud as fireworks. Nobody's ever clapped for me before. I feel my face get hot and my palms start to sweat, like I'm jonesing again. "Welcome," they say all together, like how people say amen at the end of a prayer. They look at me with smiles on their faces. Like they want to know who I am. Or like they already know me.

My name is Lucho. I'm learning.

An old man with eyebrows as thick as cigars passes me a matchbook. His face is covered with lines that look like scars. He wrote his number inside the flap. "Call me anytime," he says. "I don't sleep anymore." His name is Louis. He pats my leg with a wrinkled hand thick like a glove. He is not afraid to touch me. A lady on my other side offers me a box of chocolate chip cookies. "Sugar's the only high I get anymore," she whispers, like it's a secret.

My name is Lucho. I'm sorry.

I don't know when I started to hurt people. Seems like something I always did. Find their weak spot. Pounce. Devour. Never look back. Where'd I learn that? Who taught me? Everybody has two sides. Sometimes good and bad. Sometimes bad and worse. That's why I don't like people. I like animals. Dogs, cats, horses. Anything I can put my arms around. Dogs are simple. You know if a dog is your friend. How many people can you say that about? A dog only has one side: yours. Loyalty like that can't be bred.

My name is Lucho. I listen.

Louis stands up. He leans against his cane for support. The room is so quiet I can hear somebody's pager vibrate. Louis coughs. His lungs sound wet. He wipes his mouth on a folded bandana and thanks us for being here. A few people bow their heads. He calls this room his home. He calls us his family. Everybody claps when he says he's been sober for eight years. He says today is the only day that matters. He promises to be clean for today. No booze, no coke, no weed, no needles, no sex, no gambling, no lies. He smiles when he runs out of breath. He's missing a few teeth. I have a good life, he says. I'm one of the lucky ones. He coughs again. Sounds like he only has a few months to live.

My name is Lucho. I remember.

I got a good memory, just don't like to use it. I remember everything. Like where I learned how to hurt people. And who taught me. But who wants to think about that? Some things I'm scared to remember. My childhood. My past. Don't want to feel that lonely again. But with Arcelia it's different. She makes me feel everything—good and bad. With her, I'm not afraid to remember. When she was locked up, all I had was the memories. The hole she left. Tried to fill it but I couldn't. Tried to forget but I couldn't. All I could do was wait. Dream. Plan. Hope. Pray for a second chance. Hard to believe it's finally here. Can't blow it this time.

My name is Lucho. I feel.

I didn't mean to abandon those kids. Truth is, I thought they were better off without me. When I'm messed up, I got nothing but poison to give. They deserve better. Course I want them to forgive me. But none of this is about what I want. Maybe I don't deserve their forgiveness. Maybe I don't deserve anything. The people here tell me I have to give in. Surrender. That's Step One. That's where I'm at. No more hiding. No more fighting. So what's that leave? Who am I now? I know my name, but I don't know what it means.

My name is Lucho. I talk.

When it's my turn to share, I stay in my seat. I look at the floor to find the words. Not sure anything I say makes sense, but they don't seem to care. I talk and they listen. I close my eyes to the sound of my own voice. For the first time, I feel safe with my eyes closed. My chest opens up. My shoulders relax. I feel the tears fall onto my face. A hot, salty burn that makes my eyes open. They are looking at me. They see me. See my pain. But they don't look away.

My name is Lucho. I cry.

Before Arcelia, I didn't cry. Even as a kid. I thought it meant I was soft. I still don't cry much, especially in front of other people. But I'll do it if it makes me better. If it brings her back to me. I'm done crying for today. Now I have to sit with it. This is the worst part. My skin feels hot and tight. Like the itch after a haircut. The hairs that cover your neck and shoulders. The ones you want to scratch off but can't.

My name is Lucho. I love.

Arcelia's gonna be my wife. I'm gonna marry her. Put a ring on her finger. But I won't tell her yet. Don't want to seem soft. Don't want to scare her away. So I'll wait. See how it all plays out. She knows I love her. Told her a bunch of times. But she always says, Show me. Words are for pussies. Love is action.

My name is Lucho. I'm clean.

Been clean for six hours now, ever since I saw her. Clean for real. How's that for action? I told her before I wasn't using, but the truth is I'm always using whatever's close by. If not dope then pills or liquor, whatever's cheap and easy to get. But all that's about to change. It's gonna be different this time. I swear. Seeing her clean, that's all the inspiration I need. And when she comes back to me, I won't need the drugs anymore. I know I can do it. With her by my side, I can do anything.

My name is Lucho. I live.

Arcelia

It only takes Lucho a few days to come back. She waits till the weekend is over, but on Monday morning—right after Cristo leaves for school—I find her standing on my front porch, holding a box of doughnut holes. She comes by a bunch of times that first week, and every time she brings food with her—Mexican one day, pizza the next, and then fried chicken when she really wants to tempt me. She tries to come in the house but I won't let her. I tell her it's too soon, that I'm still mad at her, and she laughs and says okay and we stand on the porch and eat the food straight out of the box.

She drops by again on Saturday when it's just me and the baby. She must have been watching the house 'cause she rings the doorbell a few minutes after Scottie leaves. Cristo and Luz are at the library with that teacher so we have the place to ourselves.

"Here, you can come in," I tell her, opening the door. "It's too cold to stand outside."

"No, I'm cool. I just wanted to bring you this." She hands me food from the Chinese place around the corner. "I got enough for the kids."

"Thank you. That was nice."

Trini runs up behind me and hides behind my legs.

"Wow, she's huge," Lucho says. "She's gotta be four by now, huh?"

"Yeah. Last month. Even my baby's not a baby no more."

Lucho bends down to look Trini in the eyes. *"Hola, bonita.* *"¿Como estás?"*

Trini laughs and twists around in a circle, still holding onto my jeans. "What's your name?"

Lucho smiles at her, but doesn't answer. Instead she says, "I'm sorry I missed your birthday."

"I had a party," Trini says, looking over at me. "And we sang songs and danced and ate cake." She looks up at Lucho. "You didn't eat cake."

"You're right. I'm sorry I missed the cake."

"That's okay. We ate your piece."

Lucho laughs. She runs her fingers through Trini's hair. "How'd you get such pretty hair?"

"From Mami, silly. I was inside her belly but now I'm out."

Lucho tucks a loose strand of hair behind Trini's ear and then tugs on her ear, pretending to pull something from it. A tiny doll appears in her hand. "Oh snap, how'd you get this?" Lucho asks, her eyes wide and bright.

Trini's mouth falls open and she looks at both of us with amazement.

"If it came out of your ear then it must be yours," Lucho says, handing it to her.

"*¿Es verdad, Mami?*"

"*Sí, mija.* You can keep it."

Trini claps her hands together and runs back into the apartment with the doll held tight in her fist like a prize.

"You didn't have to do that."

"I wanted to."

"But you shouldn't have. Now she'll keep asking about you."

"Is that so bad?"

I take a second to pick my words. "It depends how long you're staying."

"Well, I'm on my lunch break. I gotta get back soon."

I laugh. "I don't mean right now. Just in general."

Lucho looks down at her feet. "I'll stay as long as you let me."

"Don't do that." My voice is softer than it should be.

She looks up at me. "Do what?"

"Don't try to sweet-talk me."

Lucho smiles and I punch her lightly in the chest. "I mean it."

She grabs my fist and closes her hand around it. "Okay," she says, whispering into the space between my knuckles.

◆ ❖ ◆

At first she's always sober when she visits—I can tell by how nervous she is, hesitating before she puts her hands on anything—but soon I smell the beer on her breath, even though she tries to hide it with coffee and Tic Tacs. I always liked the smell of alcohol on someone's breath—even as a child I remember liking to kiss my father goodnight on holidays or after an evening at the local bar—and I find myself trying to smell it under all those flavors.

But when she tries to kiss me I back away. I know better than to try to taste it. I offer her my cheek instead. She rests her forehead on my temple and puts her lips against my jaw and kisses me. She kisses me so softly I can't even tell if she's touching me. I feel like I'm gonna faint so I tell her to stop. She laughs. Her laughter gives me chills that make my nipples ache. I feel myself slipping. I grab for the wall but it's a few feet behind me, too far to reach. After she's gone I'm still not sure where I'm standing.

◆ ❖ ◆

The next time she comes over she brings a six-pack with the food and takes sips on the sly when she's eating. I let her think she's fooling me. I give her that power 'cause it makes me feel powerful. To give something I can easily take away. But later it's not so easy.

She swallows before kissing me but I can still taste the beer on her tongue. That first taste is all I need to bring it all rushing back. It's like walking through a door and being right back in the past—my old self, my old space, my old friend. The smell was the first crack in the armor, but the taste is the real break. It reminds me of who I used to be and who we used to be together. And then next thing I know time starts to change. First it slows, then it speeds up, then it stops altogether.

After that first taste, I can't keep the memories from coming. They pop into my head like the flashes from my childhood. But these don't scare me. They make me feel safe. They relax me. But then the craving hits, just like it used to, and soon all I want is to hold the liquid in my mouth. I want to feel it bubble against my tongue and slide down my throat. I want to wait for the heat to spread through my chest and warm me like only another body can. I can't control how much I want it. I can't control anything.

◆ ❖ ◆

But I keep fighting. I fight the cravings like I fight everything—the pain over losing Trini, the sadness of Luz staying behind, my anger toward Scottie, my fear of everybody else. I can fight the feelings and I can fight the people, but the one thing I can't fight is myself. My own head is my biggest enemy. So I wait for the day it turns on me.

I don't have to wait too long.

I'm alone when it happens, so I can hide it from Lucho and keep lying to myself about what I'm doing. I start sneaking sips from her bottle while she's in the bathroom, but later she starts opening two at a time and leaving one out on the table. It sits there like the answer to a question I'm too afraid to ask. At first I drink only a little. I savor the beer like it's a rare and exotic drink. I nurse one bottle for several hours—proving how different I am, how much I've changed. That's my first mistake—to think I'm normal again. To think I'm in control. It only takes a few days to see how wrong that is.

I tell myself I don't have to be afraid. I don't need those twelve-step meetings. I don't need to be completely sober. I'm just drinking, right? It's not like I'm shooting up. All I need is to relax. Take it easy. Chill. All I need is moderation. But what does an addict know about moderation? That is the question I never ask myself. I don't care if we're talking about food, alcohol, drugs, or sex—I don't understand what limits are. I've never found my bottom, but I still have a crazy need to keep looking.

Lucho is no different; that's why we make sense together.

I'm drawn to her—just like how I'm drawn to using. The only difference is that with dope, I feel like I'm in control, and with Lucho, I give up control.

Once I'm drinking, we start having sex again. There's no good reason to say no. The first few days it's like being a teenager again, all wet with desire and frustration. We fumble and roll across the living room like kittens getting used to a new home. We do it sitting in the windowsill, standing up against doorways, bent over the stove, and on top of the kitchen table. We grace every room in the apartment like newlyweds. Every room except my bedroom. That's the one place I tell her is off-limits. It's the only place that's just mine, and the one place where I'm always clean. I gotta keep something for myself.

◆ ❖ ◆

One night Lucho calls me from a bar downtown and asks me to come meet her for two-dollar beers that are dyed some crazy green color for St. Patrick's Day. Cristo is already asleep so all I have to do is sneak out the back door and walk a few blocks down Westminster. If it was colder I wouldn't go, but we're having one of those March thaws and the air feels almost tropical as I walk down to meet her. When I close my eyes I pretend I'm walking through old San Juan.

I don't count my drinks but I never see any change from the twenty I bring. I don't remember the walk home or letting Lucho into my bedroom. But I do remember the sex. She makes it impossible for me to forget that.

She undresses me in the dark and pulls my naked body on top of her. She keeps her boxer shorts on and a tight white tank top that blends into her pale skin. We kiss. We kiss so hard and deep I think I'm under water. I struggle to breathe. She runs her hands up and down my body, giving me goose bumps. She waits until my nipples ache from hardness, then pulls and twists them until I moan and push them into her mouth. She sucks on them for what feels like hours. I hold her hand between my legs, desperate for her to peel me open, but she won't slip her fingers inside me. She holds her hand in a fist and I ride it until my body feels bruised. I'm so turned on I can hear the sound of my own wetness. Lucho groans and bites into my neck. When I let out a small scream she covers my mouth with hers. She holds my head in one hand, then pulls her fingers through my hair and tugs it gently. I open my eyes and stare at the ceiling, trying to trace a line of cracks in the dark.

Next thing I know Lucho is on her knees on the floor. She grabs my hips and pulls them toward her, stopping when my ass is at the edge of the bed. My knees fall open as I offer myself to her. She brings her mouth down on top of me, splits me open with her lips and slides her tongue into me with a rush of wet heat. I can hear myself moan, but it sounds distant, like it's coming from outside. I come in a quick burst, rocking my hips against her mouth. Pleasure seeps through my skin and I have to bite my arm to keep from yelling. I try to sit up, but Lucho isn't done tasting me. She runs her tongue up and down the edge for several minutes, avoiding the sensitive spot until I'm ready for her. Then she's back to work, licking me with strong, steady strokes, until I come again. As I fall asleep, I feel her tracing small circles onto my hips with her fingertips, drawing pictures I'll never be able to see.

I get her up before sunrise, so she can sneak out before Cristo wakes up. She dresses quickly, without complaint, and comes back over to the edge of the bed. She pulls the blankets up around my face.

"Thank you," she says softly. She leans down to kiss me and I taste myself on her lips.

"Don't start," I whisper.

Lucho smiles and grabs my hand, weaving her fingers through mine. "I still love you, Celie. I never stopped. I just wanted you to know that."

I look away from her. I don't want to talk about love. Love is action.

"You don't have to say it back," she says. "Not if you don't feel it yet. I can wait."

She runs her fingers up my wrist, stopping on an old burn scar. I watch her touch it softly, but I can't feel anything. I lost sensation a long time ago.

"I missed this spot, when you were away."

"You missed my scar?"

Lucho nods. "It's so smooth." She kisses the inside of my arm. "I used to touch it while you were sleeping. Like a rabbit's foot, I'd rub it for good luck."

"Did it bring you any?"

"Of course. It brought me you." She kisses my open hand. "One day I'll have to thank your brother for dropping that iron on you."

Lucho looks at me. Her big, black eyes are oily like licorice. Suddenly, I need her to know the truth.

"I lied about how I got that burn," I tell her. "It didn't come from a childhood accident." She squints her eyes at me. "I used to have a tattoo there, of my husband's name. Javier. We got them together back in high school. Scottie never liked it. It used to drive him crazy—having to read another man's name whenever he held my hand. He hated to be second place. So one night we were fighting and he got all crazy and told me I had to get rid of that tattoo or he would take it off himself. I thought he was full of shit so I ignored him and went to sleep, but when I woke up my arm was on fire. He burned it right off of me."

Lucho picks up my arm and stares at the scar, like she's looking for his fingerprints.

"Jesus Christ," she whispers. "I knew he was crazy, but… Shit, that's unbelievable."

"You're the only person I ever told. At the hospital they thought it was a drug burn and we told the kids it was from the stove. Everybody got a different story."

She covers the scar with her hand. "I'm glad you trust me," she says, squeezing my arm softly. "Enough to tell me the truth."

She's wrong—I don't trust her. But I don't trust anybody, including myself. If I trusted her, I would tell her about the flashes I get from my childhood, how I wake up in the night crying but no tears come out. I would tell her how I blame myself for letting the neighbor touch me all those years when I was a little girl, how I wish I told my father or my brothers so I wouldn't be the only one who has to remember what he took from me. I would tell her I still love my husband, even though I know I'll never see him again, because sometimes your heart knows things you don't even understand. I would tell her that sometimes I'm afraid I don't love my children enough, because if I did, wouldn't I be able to stay clean for longer than a baseball season? I want to share these things—my dreams and nightmares—just to get them out of my head, but I don't know how to do that. I don't know how to be someone I never been.

Lucho looks at me. "You're a survivor, Celie. I always knew that about you. Promise me you'll never forget."

I smile at her as my head sinks deeper into the pillow. She's right—I have survived—but I don't think surviving is good enough. There has to be something better.

After she leaves I can't fall back asleep, even though it's dark in my room and feels like the middle of the night. I curl onto my side and look into the blackness. All I see are the roses Cristo got me for Valentine's Day, drying in a glass pitcher on top of my dresser. They shrunk a little, but even in the dark they look beautiful. I grab the pitcher and bring it back to bed with me, holding it between my legs. I pull each rose out, one at a time, and bring it to my nose. I want to smell something sweet while I still can.

Some are too strong. They smell fake like soap or lotion. Others have no scent at all. The prettiest, most perfect one has a sharp, almost sour smell. The one that's dried up the most— the ugliest one—smells the best, bright like fresh laundry. I want to put the whole bulb into my mouth, so my own breath can smell that clean.

I collect all the roses together, holding the dried-out bouquet in my hand. I'm careful not to prick my skin on the thorns. It's strange to watch a flower die. The petals dry out, thin and weak like tissue paper, but the stem gets hard like a knife. How can one thing die in two different ways?

I put my face over the flowers and breathe in as much of the scent as I can, holding it until my lungs give out. I know I'll never smell anything this deeply again.

SHE SEES the girl washing laundry in the sink. She scrubs an old rug until her knuckles ache. No, it is not a rug. It is her dress. Passed down from her mother. She holds it under the running water, rinsing out a stain as wide as her chest. The water turns pink with her blood. Her nose begins to run. She wipes it on a towel. Now the towel is stained too. There is blood everywhere. He doesn't mean to hit her. He doesn't mean to get angry. She packs her bag when she is alone in the house. The baby's bag, too. Her son is sleeping when she leaves. She holds her hand over his heart. Counts the beats. Kisses him good-bye. She carries her daughter in her bruised arms. She can't leave her behind. Not like she was left. The only girl in a house of men.

Luz

Everything in Miss Valentín's bathroom is white. The floor, the walls, the ceiling, the tub, and the sink. All of it. I don't usually pay attention to things like that, but in books they're always using colors to talk about something the author wants you to know without coming straight out and telling you. My teacher calls this symbolism, and she says it's a sign that the author's a very smart person. And the reader is, too, if she picks up on it. In the dictionary, *white* means a lot of good things like pure, innocent, and harmless. I guess that's why Caucasians started using it for themselves. Another definition is fortunate, which is what I keep thinking about every time I walk in here and see all this endless white, like they covered the whole room in powdered sugar. I figure it's got to mean something good's about to happen for Miss Valentín, but maybe for me too since it's right next to my bedroom and she basically said it was mine.

Every Saturday I help Miss Valentín do chores. One of my jobs is to clean the bathtub, even though neither one of us ever uses it. It's so shiny it looks like a polished rock. Miss Valentín says it's made out of porcelain, which means it's old and hard like a tooth. She tells me she loves baths, that she used to sit for hours when she was a kid, trying to watch the hair on her legs grow. She used to sleep in the bathtub, too, she says, and dream, and hide. When I ask her why she doesn't take baths anymore she laughs and says she doesn't have the time, but sometimes I catch her staring at the tub like it's a person she hasn't seen for a while but still mentions every night in her prayers.

Me, I don't like taking baths. It's too boring to sit down for all that time, and too babyish. Instead, I shower twice a week in the small, stand-alone shower in the other bathroom. Or whenever she makes me. The showerhead is so tall, and I'm so short, it's like the heavens themselves are raining down on me. Sometimes I imagine I'm drowning, but other times I act like a fish and pretend to breathe under water. I don't really like either one, but at least in the shower I can stand up. I always keep my eyes open, no matter what, and I always lock the door. I trust Miss Valentín as much as I trust anyone, but I trust a locked door even more than that.

One Saturday while we're doing chores, I find Miss Valentín kneeling in front of the bathtub. Her eyes are closed and she's holding onto the side like it's the only thing keeping her from being laid out on the tiled floor. She's moving her lips and I hear her say something about God. I try to be completely silent, but I end up making the door creak. Her eyes flip open.

"Sorry." I back out of the room, trying to disappear.

"No," she says, "it's okay. I was just praying."

I stand in the doorway, a plastic bucket hanging from the bend in my arm. I'm holding a sponge as thick as a book in my hand, wet from cleaning the kitchen floor.

"Come here." She motions for me to enter, but I only take a small step toward her. "I used to pray all the time when I was a kid. My parents expected it. But I never knew what to say." She struggles to stand up, her knees covered with marks from the bath mat. She pulls her skirt down to cover them. "Now I can't figure out when to stop."

"Mami used to say prayers are just a list of what you want."

Miss Valentín smiles. "I'm praying to God, not Santa Claus." She folds a towel that was hanging around her neck like a scarf. "God gives you what you need, Luz, which is not always the same as what you want."

I look down at the sponge in my hand. Water drips from it, leaving gray drops as round as quarters on the floor. I bend down to wipe them up, but I only make it worse, turning the spots into large dirty swirls.

"How do you know the difference," I ask her, "between

a want and a need?" She doesn't answer right away, she just stands there cracking her knuckles. They pop like gunfire. When I'm done wiping up the swirls, I stand back up.

"By looking at what you have in your life," she finally says. "You only get the things you need."

I rinse the sponge in the sink, using both my hands to squeeze it dry.

"Did you need me?" I ask, keeping my back to her. "When I came here to stay with you?" I watch the dirty water run down the drain, leaving a trail of sand and grit in the sink. When I turn the faucet on, the water washes all traces of the dirt away.

"Yes," she says. "But I wanted you, too. Maybe not under these circumstances, but I wanted you regardless."

"We wanted to be here," I tell her. "Back in September. We thought you didn't want us." I run my fingertips over the sink, just to feel the squeak of something clean.

"I always wanted you. You and your brother. But back then I thought you needed something else. I don't know, maybe I was wrong."

When I turn around Miss Valentín's shaking her head. She looked worried before, when she was praying, but now she just seems sad.

"It must be hard being a parent. They're always telling kids it's okay to make mistakes. But you're not supposed to be wrong."

"I wouldn't know," she says, "not yet." She tries to smile. "But you're right. They say parenting is one of the hardest things to do well."

"It's hard for my mother." I feel bad saying it, but we both know it's true. Miss Valentín looks at me for a long time before speaking. "It's hard for everyone," she finally says. "For all of us."

I turn back to the sink, catching my reflection in the mirror. I can see her, too, high in the corner like she's floating above me, and from this angle we look like we could be mother and daughter. She looks small in the mirror, and young, like how she must have looked as a child, and I look strangely big, my features distorted from standing so close. In this moment, she is me and I am her, which somehow makes me think that we belong together. That it makes sense for me to be here, to be with her, when my own mother is just a few miles away.

"Does it work?" I ask her.

"Does what work?"

"Praying. Does it make you feel better?"

She starts to laugh but then realizes I'm not joking.

"Well, that depends on the day. But yes, usually it does."

"Good," I say. "Maybe I'll try it."

She smiles at me on her way out, closing the door behind her. I stand completely still, staring at the spot in the mirror where she just was. I hear my heart beating in my ears. It's strange, how people can disappear even when you're looking right at them.

I turn around and stare at the bathtub. It's long and skinny like a casket. Without thinking, I drop to the ground in front of it. The tiles are cold and hard against my knees. I press my palms together like I've seen people do on TV and close my eyes. I try to stay like that but my eyes won't stay shut. They keep popping open, every time I think there's someone in here looking at me.

I stand up and turn around, looking from the tub to the toilet and back again. I can either sit on the toilet or lie down in the tub. Those are my two choices. Christ, who knew it was so much work to pray. Even with my prejudice against baths, I end up choosing the tub. I climb into it and sit down with my legs stretched all the way out. It's empty, cold, and hard, but it's still more comfortable than kneeling on the floor. The bottom is smooth against my bare feet. I lean back and rest my head on the curved lip. It smells like Ajax, which comforts me enough that I close my eyes and take a deep breath. God, I like when things are clean. My eyes pop open. Does that count as my first prayer? Probably not, since I forgot to put my hands together. And I'm lying in an empty bathtub with all my clothes on.

I close my eyes again and the first thing I see is my mother. She's standing over Trini's crib, laughing. Her hair falls onto her face, covering her eyes and mouth. She disappears. I open my eyes. Check the door. Check my body. Nothing has changed.

I close them again and this time my mother is grating yucca at the kitchen table, working so hard she doesn't see me. I touch her shoulder and she turns to me, says my name like it's a question. I sit in the chair next to her, but it is not a chair, it is her lap and she holds me like a baby, stroking my hair as I melt into her. *God, I miss my mother.*

I suddenly remember that the bathroom door is unlocked. My eyes pop open. *It's okay*, a voice tells me. *You're safe here.* I close them again and see myself as a child, a little girl in a bubble bath. Someone is washing my hair. I feel the warm water run down my back, chilling me with how good it feels. Cristo is laughing, shooting me with water from a plastic pig. I hear my mother's voice telling him to stop, protecting me. She wipes the hair from my eyes, kisses my head, smiles at me. I feel her presence, her love, stronger than I ever have. *God, I want to feel that again.* I wonder if it's possible, even when I'm not with her. Can I carry her love anywhere I go? Anywhere she goes?

I open my eyes. The bathroom door is still closed. I am still safe. I lean forward and turn the water on full blast. It comes out bubbling, like soda from a shaken can. I imagine it's cold like the ocean, but the faucet is so far away I can't feel it yet. By the time the water creeps up to where my feet rest, it's hot, and after a few seconds I have to turn on the cold so I won't get burned.

I'm wearing a pair of tan shorts with a pink butterfly sewn on the pocket. I would hate to be that butterfly, to have both my wings pinned down. When the water touches my shorts they turn a darker brown, almost the color of my legs. As the water rises, it covers my T-shirt as well, which clings to my belly like tight skin. I slip down into the tub as it continues to fill, floating in the warm, clear light of the water. I am completely covered now, and I swim like a baby in her mother's belly. My clothes feel heavy, unnecessary, and I slip from them to let my body be free. They sink to the bottom and hover over the drain, abandoned like snakeskin.

I pull the shower curtain closed. A map of the world spreads out above me, painted on the plastic curtain. Every continent is a different color, the names printed in bold, black letters. I run my hand over the map, touching places I've only read about. With a glance, I can go anywhere. Providence is so small it's not even a dot on the map. And yet here I am. We are all here, even when we can't be seen. I dip my finger in the water and write my name on every country I see, again and again and again. I place myself all over the world.

Snowman

For years I had the same dream, over and over again. A nightmare, really, about Justin drowning. We were swimming in a waveless ocean, somewhere warm and bright where the sun is always shining. Everything was white: the buildings, the clouds, the sand, and me. Only Momma and Justin were dark, like penguins against the snow.

At first we were all swimming together, but then Momma got out to lie in the sun. I was holding Justin, teaching him how to kick and blow bubbles and paddle his hands like a dog. A wave came from behind me, crashing over us. The salt water burned so I closed my eyes and just as I did I felt Justin slip out of my hands. I opened my eyes to look for him. I scanned the water, but the surface was completely still. He was gone. I dove under the water but it was too dark to see. I couldn't even see my own hand in front of my face.

I yelled for Momma to come quick, that Justin had gone under the water. She stood in the sand, towering like an ancient tree, one that would not grow on the beach and yet somehow did, learning to adapt to the constant wind, the salt, the sea-thick air, and told me to find her son.

"Bring me my boy," she yelled from the water's edge. "I don't care what you have to do. Bring my boy back to me."

I dove under the water again and this time I saw him right away. He was frozen in motion, his eyes wide open like a doll. I picked him up; his body was stiff and cold. His lips were slightly parted like he was talking or about to smile. I stepped from the water to a chill I'd never known. I held him in my arms and walked out of the sea, his body limp and breathless. The sand was cold against my feet, packed hard like snow. I tried to revive him, to bring him back to life, but nothing I did worked.

By the time I looked up to face Momma, she was gone. She and Justin were both gone, and I knew I was going to spend the rest of my life alone.

◆ ❖ ◆

I realize I'm probably making a huge mistake by renting Arcelia the apartment, but I did it for the kid and his sisters. And for her. So that's how I justify it. She's sick and I took pity on her. How am I going to say no to a lady that's dying?

To convince myself, I try to believe she's changed. That she can really stay clean. But I've seen enough of my neighbors try to straighten out to know it's close to impossible. Heroin fucks with your brain chemistry, not just your body, and that shit never heals no matter how long you're clean. It's like cutting out the piece of your brain that makes you feel good, and then hoping you're going to be okay without it. When you got a hole like that, you spend all day filling it; by nightfall, if you're lucky, you're back up even with the ground. The hardcore junkies don't even get a high, they're just using to maintain. Because if they didn't the hole would grow to the size of the Grand Canyon and they'd feel so sick by the end they would rather just be dead.

The first few weeks go pretty smoothly. She gets the subsidy and pays first month's rent and the security deposit, and every time I stop by everything seems okay. She's by herself most of the time, usually washing dishes or cooking, sometimes writing in this fat spiral notebook she leaves on the kitchen table. She looks more comfortable with a knife than a pen. She seems calm, or actually more like somber, and I take that as a good sign. It must mean she's still clean.

When I see Cristo he looks happy. The smile on that kid's face when I show him his bedroom—when he slides across the clean wood floors in his socks, when he opens the brand-new refrigerator and shows me the ice maker—that makes it all worth it. Even if I regret it later it's worth those few seconds of joy. For him and me.

He comes to see me at the pool one day and brings a pair of cutoff jeans to swim in. There's problem number one: the kid needs a real bathing suit. He says he's ready to do laps with me, but after a few seconds in the water I can tell he can't really swim. He keeps himself afloat, but he doesn't know any strokes except the doggy paddle. Problem number two. I tell him to come back next weekend after my workout and I'll show him a few things.

In the meantime, I buy him a pair of goggles and a spandex cap to keep his hair out of his face. And a Speedo so he isn't dragging all that unnecessary weight through the water. When he's all suited up I teach him how to move his arms for the crawl and how to breathe on alternating sides. I show him the flutter kick, and I hold his hands in the water as he practices.

I used to imagine bringing Justin to this pool when he got bigger, to swim laps with me and do backflips off the diving board. After he got adopted, I wouldn't let myself think about him too much—not while I ate his favorite chicken potpie dinners or walked to the corner store to buy ice pops and orange soda, his favorite combo during a heat wave. But I did keep seeing him whenever I was in the water. I heard his laugh echoing across the crowded pool. I could see his smile on the faces of all the little boys in the preschool swim class. For years I would come here every day and swim laps for over an hour, just so I could have that time with my brother. So I could see his face and remember how much I missed him. So I could cry without any trace of tears.

Cristo's a natural and by the end of the first lesson he can swim a few laps without resting. As he gets more confident, his strokes get stronger until next thing I know he's slipping into the fast lane, trying to catch me.

When we walk out of the locker room I ask him if he wants me to put him on my membership. "That way, you don't have to keep sneaking in."

He looks at me, water still dripping from his hair. "You'd

let me do that?"

"Of course. It's no big deal."

I stop at the counter and tell the lady I want to update my card so I can add him on. She scans the card in the computer.

"You have an individual membership, Mr. Lewis. The only way to add him is if you change to a family one."

"Okay."

"Is he part of your family?"

"Yes."

She looks at me.

"He's my son." I don't even hesitate. I don't even think about the lie.

She opens her mouth to speak. She's wondering how she could see me almost every day for years and never have seen him before. She thought she knew me.

I smile at her, which makes her close her mouth. "Okay," she says.

They take his picture and make him his own card so he can get in anytime, even when I'm not there. Cristo holds the card like it's a driver's license or a credit card, something that makes him a grownup. He stares at the photograph as if he doesn't recognize himself.

"What's up? You don't like it?"

"No. It's not that. It's just the first photograph I seen of myself since the class picture last year." He raises his eyebrows. "I didn't know I looked so old."

Maybe it's putting him on my card, with the name Cristoval Lewis printed next to his picture, or maybe it's the form I have to sign about being the responsible party if he gets hurt on their property, but something changes for me right then and I realize I have to take care of this kid no matter what. I have to watch out for him. And I have to trust that nobody's going to take him away from me—not his teacher, not his mother, not the state.

After Justin I used to swear I'd never get attached to anyone again, and I kept that promise for more than fifteen years, till this skinny Puerto Rican kid with an Afro and an attitude as big as Rhode Island made me break it.

◆ ❖ ◆

I know it's a bad sign when I hear she's looking for me. First in the Laundromat, then from Lorenzo, my corner man, and finally from the ladies at Dunkin' Donuts.

"Arcelia's looking for you," they say when I stop by for a bran muffin after my swim. "She acted like she was going to die if she didn't find you right then."

"When was that?"

"Last night sometime."

I nod like it's no big deal but inside my stomach twists and when I walk out the door I throw the muffin away without even taking a bite. I have work to do on a house in the Armory but instead of going straight there I head over to her apartment first. I wait for almost half an hour but nobody's home. I go around to the back and peek in the kitchen window. There's no sign of anything wrong so I decide not to let myself in. No reason to panic.

I'm walking down Westminster when I notice a car driving slow behind me. I sneak a look at the driver and recognize Lucho's sullen expression instantly. She turns her head away, as if not looking at me means that I can't see her. She pulls into a driveway, figuring I'll walk away I guess, but instead I walk straight up to the car. All the windows are down and she's blasting some Spanish dance music.

"You looking for someone?" I bend down to scan the inside of her car, making sure it's empty.

"No." She turns the music down.

"Why you driving so slow then?"

She puts up her hands like I'm a cop. "I'm just driving around the neighborhood."

"I thought you might be looking for me, since you owe me some rent on the last place. You're not looking to pay up, are you?"

"My name wasn't on that lease," she says.

"Oh, so now you pay attention to the law, huh?"

She looks away. "How much does she owe?"

"You just said it wasn't your business, didn't you?"

"Fine." She puts the car in reverse. "Don't say I didn't offer."

"You're about six months too late, champ. Somebody else paid your debts."

She shrugs. "Anything I owe Arcelia is between her and me."

"I wasn't talking about Arcelia."

She stares at me with a confused look.

"The kid covered your ass," I tell her. "Cristo. He's the one you owe."

"Cristo?" She says his name like she doesn't know who I'm talking about.

"Arcelia's son."

"I know who he is."

"You don't act like it."

She taps on the steering wheel, which is covered in fake leather. The car, a Honda that can't be more than a few years old, is a great improvement over the last junker I saw her in. I stand back and admire it, the silvery green paint shimmering in the sunlight.

"Nice car."

"Thanks."

"You pay it off yet?"

"Almost. Not everybody has the cash flow you got, Snowman."

"Shit, I don't even own a car."

That makes her laugh, which takes several years off her face. "That's 'cause you're cheap, not poor."

I shrug. "Walking clears my head. Just like the Indians. I figure if I can't walk there, I probably don't need to go that far."

"If my people followed that rule they never would've left Puerto Rico."

"And would that have been such a bad thing?"

She lights a cigarette. "Do the math, man. If all the Spanish people left this city tomorrow, half your houses would be empty. And let's not even count your other business." She offers me the pack but I decline. The only chemical I allow into my body is the chlorine from the swimming pool.

"You're right," I say. "But it wouldn't take long for another group to show up and fill them back up. If you've got a good product there's always someone willing to buy."

She exhales a long stream of smoke. "And you always had the best, didn't you?"

I cross my arms. "I guess the customer's always right."

She flicks the cigarette onto the sidewalk. "Listen, I know after last summer you said it was over for me and you, but the guy I been using just got popped and I'm kind of in a jam." She tucks her hands into her armpits. "I'm not talking a lot, just something to help me out until I find somebody else. A couple of dime bags and some weed. Whatever you got laying around."

I look up and down the street before answering. "I can't do it, Lucho. It's not the right time."

"What's that mean? I got the money."

I look toward Arcelia's apartment, a thin red house on the other side of the park. I wonder if Lucho knows how close we are to her ex. I look back at her.

"Have you seen her, since she got out?"

"No." Lucho answers, too quickly. "But I heard she was doing good. And that she was still clean." She cracks her knuckles, which sounds like her fingers breaking.

I nod. "I just want to keep it that way."

"What's that got to do with me?"

I tap my fingers on the roof of her car. "Can you promise that you'll stay away from her?"

She drops her head. "Give me a fucking break, Snowman."

"Exactly." I say, nodding my head as I back away from the car. "That's exactly why I can't help you."

"You don't make any sense, man. I thought you were a businessman."

"Some things are more important than business. Some people."

I walk back through the park so I don't have to worry about her following me. I wish I could get lost in this city. I want to find a neighborhood so foreign it feels like I'm walking through the woods at night with only the stars to guide me. But I know every alley and back road in Providence and even when I try to disorient myself, I always know exactly where I am.

◆ ❖ ◆

Arcelia finds me at the flea market. I see her first, picking through piles of tube socks, and a part of me wants to hide, but I know I have to face her sooner or later. No point putting it off any longer.

When she sees me she waves, like we're old friends, and something about the gesture makes me feel sorry for her. She walks over to me with a crooked smile, trying to hide the fact that she's missing a tooth, and suddenly she looks exactly like her son. That makes me smile. She's a pretty lady, no doubt, but she looks older than she is, and her body seems burdened by all she's been through.

"Hey," she says.

"Hey. I heard you were looking for me."

She nods. "Yeah. I need a favor."

"I thought I just did you a favor." I've never had a girl-friend, but I can imagine conversations like this one being part of the territory.

"You did. And I'm grateful." She rubs my arm just above the elbow. "But now I need something else."

I stare down at her, trying to ignore the feeling of her hand on my arm. It's hard to focus when she's this close to me, hard to keep the distance we both need. Her eyes dart around and she shifts her weight from one foot to the other. She's jonesing.

"I need to buy some stuff from you."

I knew this moment would come, but it still surprises me. Saddens me, really.

"It wasn't that long ago you asked me not to sell to you," I remind her.

"It's not for me, it's for a friend. Really." She lets go of my arm.

I take a step back, so I can see her more clearly. "A friend?"

She nods. "His dealer got arrested. He's got a small stash, but he's gonna get sick real soon if he runs out. You know the deal."

"He? So your friend is a man?"

She bites her fingernail. "Is that a problem?"

I shake my head. "Go on." I want to see how many lies she'll tell.

"That's it. That's the story." She spits a piece of her fingernail onto the ground between us.

"Sorry, Arcelia." I shrug. "I made a promise."

"But it was with me," she says, her voice pleading. "And I don't care if you break it. Honestly." She grabs my sleeve again. "I want you to. Need you to."

I look down at her hand. Her skin is dry and the polish on her nails is chipped. "That's not the promise I'm talking about."

She drops her head and softens the tone of her voice. "Do I have to beg?"

"Please don't do that." I look around to see if anyone is watching. The streets are empty except for the occasional car rolling down Manton.

When she speaks again she sounds almost angry. "So what are you saying, you want me to go to somebody else?"

I shrug. "I can't control what you do."

"Come on, you know how fucked up most of the shit out there is. Half of it's cut with baby formula, brick dust, or gasoline. You want my friend to end up in the ER?"

"Of course not. Don't be stupid." I glance toward the ENCORE van, which is parked by the front door to Atlantic Mills. "At least go to the needle exchange. Find someone who knows what they're getting."

"They only give you the works," she says, "they're not handing out dime bags."

"I know that. I meant someone who goes there, someone you used to score with maybe." I can't believe I'm suggesting this, but what else can I do?

"I spent the last nine months trying to forget all those motherfuckers. Now I'm supposed to walk back in there and beg for a connection? You must be crazy."

"You're supposed to walk away," I tell her, leaning in close so I don't have to raise my voice. "If you really want to take care of yourself. If you want to help your family. You have to leave it all behind."

"Pretty easy for you to say."

"Actually, no, it isn't easy. Giving in would be a lot easier."

She spits onto the muddy ground. "I thought you were one of the good guys."

"Guess you were wrong."

I walk away before I change my mind. Saying no to her shouldn't be this hard. I try to ignore it, but the sound of her voice fills my head, her desperation like a drum beating against my skull. I don't want to think about how much power I have over someone else's life. Someone I don't even love. Or can't.

The sun is warm on my neck and I smell barbecue in the air, floating across the parking lot from Wes's Rib Shack. I think of Cristo, of taking him out for pulled pork after our last swim lesson, and picturing his face makes me turn around and go back for her. Maybe I do love her, through her son. Or maybe I love him through her.

When I get back to the flea market, she's gone. The spot where I left her just a few minutes before is empty. But I still call out her name, like a lost child calling for his mother. I walk up and down Manton Avenue looking for her, but she's not in any of the usual places. She just vanished. Like a passing car picked her up off the street.

Nobody can run that fast.

Cristo

When Mrs. Reed passes our essays back, it turns out I got my first A. Crazy, huh? Especially since I wrote the whole thing in English and didn't even make any mistakes. I gotta give some credit to Graciela because I got her to read it before I turned it in and she made a lot of changes. But still. It was all my own ideas and had my name across the top.

To celebrate, I ask Mami when I get home if we can go out for Chinese food. She says she's got a meeting later and besides we don't have the money.

"I can pay for it." I pull a wad of cash from my pocket, but she waves my money away.

"Thanks, *mijo*, but I got to stay home anyway. In case my case manager comes by."

I stand in front of her, holding my essay like a shield against my chest. "You wanna read it?"

"Of course I do. But maybe later, okay?" She lies down on the couch. "I can't focus on words right now."

"You sick, Mami?"

"No, *cariño*. I'm okay. Just got a little headache."

"You need me to make you something?"

She curls under a blanket, even though it's warm in the apartment and outside it's almost seventy degrees.

She shakes her head. "*No tengo hambre.*"

"But you didn't eat anything. For breakfast or lunch."

"Nothing sounds good right now. Nothing we got anyway."

She covers her face with the blanket, trying to block out the sunlight. I leave her alone for a while, but then I go back and tell her what I really want is for her to teach me how to make *pasteles*.

"Come on, Mami. I'll go to the market and get everything, you won't even have to move."

When I pull back the blanket she opens her eyes halfway.

"I'll even wash all the vegetables myself."

"Are you serious?" She blinks and I can see the veins in her eyelids. "That's a lot of work. Just order a pizza, okay?"

"We eat pizza all the time. That's not special." I wave the essay in her face. "Mami. It's my first A. Ever."

She finally gives in. "Go to the market on Broad Street, even though it's far, 'cause the prices are better and his banana leaves are nice and oily." She points to the kitchen. "Go get my purse."

"That's okay, I got it." I kiss her on the cheek. "Thanks, Mami. I'll be right back. So quick you won't have time to miss me."

She closes her eyes again. "I always miss you," she says, which is something we started saying to each other after she left me in Puerto Rico.

"I always miss you, too." Then I run out of the apartment before she changes her mind.

On the way to the market I see a guy getting into a green Honda parked in front of the liquor store. Something about him seems familiar so I look back again. He pulls up his hood and drives away before I can see his face. Nobody I know drives a nice car, except some of the teachers at my school, so I figure I must be wrong about knowing him. He rolls through a stop sign at the next block and drives around a school bus with blinking red lights, almost hitting two kids as they cross the street.

When I get to the market it takes me a while to collect all the vegetables because I know Mami's picky about getting the best ones. I ask the lady at the register to help, and without saying anything she comes around from behind the counter and grabs the calabaza from my basket, testing the weight of each squash in her hand. Then she knocks on the shells before handing me the ones to keep. She exchanges my ripe plantains for green ones, gives me two more pounds of malanga, and throws an extra head of garlic into the bag. Her husband uses a butcher's knife to cut twenty-five plantain leaf squares, which he ties together with a long piece of twine, like a binding for some primitive book. He asks if I have more twine at home, to tie around each *pastel* after we wrap them, and when I say no he gives me the rest of the roll for free.

My bags are too heavy to carry all the way home so I decide to take the bus. I run into Graciela at the bus stop, coming back from her piano lesson. At first she's just looking at the ground, but when she recognizes me, she finally smiles.

"I thought you only like junk food?" she says, noticing the food spilling from my bags and onto the sidewalk.

"No, I like real food, too." I bend down to pick up the onions that slipped out, each one hard like a baseball. "I just don't like to cook it."

"So who's going to cook all that?" She reaches for the twine before it rolls into the gutter.

"Mami. Who else?"

"She's back?" Graciela's kneeling next to me now, helping me repack the bags. I feel my face starting to get hot, but I try to keep my voice calm.

"What do you mean 'back'?"

"Nothing. I just heard she was away for a while."

I look over at her. I can tell by the look on her face she's not trying to be mean.

"My uncle went away once," she says. "For a long time. And when he came back my cousins didn't even recognize him."

"Well, Mami wasn't gone that long."

"That's good." She stands up and brushes off her knees. Then she holds out her hand to help me up. I don't want her help, but I take her hand anyway, just to touch her.

"You wanna come over and meet her? You can eat dinner with us."

I want to keep holding her hand, but she pulls it away to pick up her backpack, putting both shoulder straps on like she's about to go hiking.

"You sure it's okay?"

"Course it is. It's my home, too."

I don't really want her to meet Mami yet, but I do want to show her that I live in a real apartment with heat and electricity and a TV that works. When some other kids from school found out I was living in the shelter they teased me about being homeless until Mrs. Reed threatened to send them outside to pick up garbage. Graciela wasn't part of the group that messed with me, but I still saw pity in her eyes when she looked at me that day during recess and I want her to know she can save that for someone who really needs it.

She offers to help me carry something, so I give her the smallest bag, with green bananas, a half gallon of milk, and the pork shoulder, and we decide to ditch the bus and walk to my house together. It's dark by now and there aren't a lot of people on the street. An old lady passes us and smiles, probably thinking we're brother and sister, or maybe the youngest married couple in America. The thought of marrying Graciela, of being old enough to marry anyone, gives me butterflies. I smile at her but she's looking for a break in the traffic and doesn't see it. When we step into the street, she puts her arm in front of me, to make sure I don't step out too far, like a mother would. Normally, someone trying to take care of me like that would piss me off, but I like when she does it. It's only her jacket that's touching me but it still feels good.

"You never told me if you liked the valentine," I say, when we're a few blocks from the house.

She stops to look at me. "Wait, that was from you?"

I nod, watching her face change as she pretends to get mad. She swats me on the arm. "Why didn't you tell me? Or at least sign your name?" She hits me again, softer this time, and we both start to laugh.

"I thought you could figure it out."

"Well, yeah, I kind of thought it was from you. But I didn't want to embarrass myself by saying anything. I thought it might be a joke, from one of the other boys."

"It wasn't a joke," I say, shifting the weight of the bags in my hands.

"Good," she says. "It was beautiful. I still have it, in my locker at school. But I already memorized it."

Damn. I copied it over a bunch of times, and even I don't know it by heart.

She starts walking again. "I didn't know you liked poetry."

"I don't, not really. But it just made sense to me. Even in English."

"Your English is good now, you're just too close to hear for yourself. I bet you could take the test for Regular Ed and pass just fine."

I shake my head. "I'm not taking that test. Ever."

"That's too bad," she says, slowing down to let me catch up. "They're switching me next fall. They said I could go now but I wanted to stay with Mrs. Reed, just to finish out the year in one place."

"I guess everybody moves up eventually."

"Isn't that the point? We *are* in America now."

"You say that like this place isn't filled with immigrants."

"Of course it is," she says, laughing. "It was founded by immigrants."

"Right. And sometimes I think if enough of us keep speaking Spanish then maybe we won't have to get rid of it completely. We can somehow keep both."

"I don't think they want us to keep both. My father says the government thinks we're disloyal if we don't speak their language. He could get fired if they ever hear him speaking Spanish at work."

"If they did that in this neighborhood nobody would have a job."

When we come around the corner I see the green Honda from the liquor store parked in front of our house. No sign of the guy who was driving. I walk up the steps quickly, forgetting to let Graciela go in front of me. I unlock the door and walk into the living room. The apartment looks empty. My heart is beating so fast I think I'm going to faint. All the lights are off except for the ones in the kitchen. A six-pack of beer sits on the table, missing two bottles. Corona Light, just like Lucho used to buy. Lucho. Of course. Anger floods my body and I feel like

I'm gonna faint. She must be doing good if she got a new car.

I check Mami's bedroom from the hallway, see the door closed. I don't call her name, my plan is to just open the door, but at the last second I get scared and decide to knock.

"Oh, fuck," somebody says, and I hear the sound of glass clinking and bodies shuffling around.

"Mami?"

"Just a sec, Cristo."

I try to open the door but it's locked.

"Mami, open the door. Who's in there with you?" I pound on the door. "Is Lucho in there?" I kick the door a few times, leaving gray smudges on the paint. My toes start to hurt but I don't stop kicking.

When the door opens I see Lucho first. She's standing next to the bed, trying to look relaxed. She has an empty beer bottle in her hand. The other one, half full, is on the nightstand.

"Hey kid, how's it going?"

I ignore Lucho, figuring that's better than what I want to say to her. Mami's leaning against the wall behind the door. She's wearing pajama bottoms and a shirt that's only buttoned halfway. Her eyes are small and her face looks flat, like she was just slapped.

"What time is it?" She pushes her hair out of her face several times. "You must be starved." There's something small tucked into her shirt pocket, and she touches it a few times to make sure it's still there.

She walks by me, picking up a glass of water from the dresser before leaving the room. The air is filled with a sour heat, and I can smell cheap incense burning. There's something horribly familiar about this moment.

"What the hell is Lucho doing here?" I ask, following Mami down the hall. "When did she get back?"

She stops short in the dining room. "Who's this?" She points at Graciela, standing in the middle of the dark room, still holding the bag of groceries. I forgot she was here.

I take the shopping bag out of her hand and put it on the floor. "Thanks." I grab her sleeve and walk her to the front door. "You should go now, okay?"

"Is everything all right?"

"Sure, of course. I just forgot we had plans. I'm sorry I wasted your time."

"It's not a problem—"

"Okay, good. See you later." I close the door on her face.

When I get back to the kitchen Mami is unpacking the food. She keeps putting the same items in and out of the bag.

"I don't see any meat," she says. "I thought I told you to get meat."

"It must be in the other bag."

"Can you bring it to me?" Her voice is sharp. "It might be nice to get a little help around here."

I'm so shocked I can't even say anything. I get the other bag from the floor and carry it into the kitchen. When I come back in, Lucho has her foot on a chair and she's bending over to tie her shoe. Just seeing her do something that casual, as if she lives here, makes me furious. My voice comes back suddenly, spraying out of me like vomit.

"You want this bag? Here, take it. Take it all." I dump it onto the kitchen floor, watching the pork roll over the bananas, splitting their green skins, as milk spills from the dented carton.

"Cristo, what the hell are you doing?" Mami stands there, an onion in each hand, and for a second I think she's going to throw them at me.

"What am I doing? I'm doing your errands, that's what I'm doing." I pick up the six-pack, waving it in front of her face. "What the hell are *you* doing, Mami?"

Lucho drops her foot onto the ground. "Hey, watch your mouth."

I step toward her. "Are you kidding me? You can't tell me what to do. You don't live here."

Mami looks at Lucho and shakes her head. "Leave him alone," she says.

She walks over to the spilled food, her flip-flops making tracks in the milk. When she bends down, two bottle caps fall out of her pocket and roll under the oven. She hurries to pick them up, tucking them back into her pocket without even wiping off the dust.

"Get out of our house," I yell, walking toward Lucho. "You don't belong here." I shove the six-pack into her hands.

She takes a few steps back. "Come on, Cristo, you just need to calm down. Can't we talk about this?"

"You wanna talk? Okay. Let's start with why you left us. Let's talk about that."

Lucho looks at Mami, who is still kneeling on the ground, now counting the green bananas.

"Don't look at me," she says to Lucho. "This is between the two of you."

Lucho turns back to me. She clears her throat before speaking. "I'm sorry, kid. I wish it hadn't turned out like that. I really do."

"Save it for someone who cares."

Lucho shrugs. "Listen, if I could go back and change things I would. I hope you believe that."

"Are you kidding me? I don't believe a word you say."

Lucho stands there for a minute, then picks up her sweat-shirt and walks out of the room. Mami follows her to the front door, carrying the bananas in her shirt like she used to do when I was little and we'd pick our dinner from the vegetable garden. I can't hear what they're saying, but I see Mami put her hand on Lucho's chest as she says good-bye. That's the only time I see them touch.

After Lucho leaves, Mami locks the dead bolt and pulls the chain lock through a deep groove carved into the wood, a homemade security system. She rests her head against the door, tapping it repeatedly, a little harder every time.

"Knock it off, Mami. You trying to give yourself a concussion?"

"I'm just trying to wake up," she says.

I pull her away from the door. "You're awake," I say.

Her eyes fill with tears and she looks away from me.

"Don't do that," I say. "You don't get to cry yet."

She closes her eyes and sniffs loudly, trying to pull herself together. I soften my voice, so I don't sound like I'm yelling at her, but it doesn't work. The anger can't seem to find another way out of my body.

"When did it start?"

She shakes her head.

"When?" I ask again, my voice suddenly louder.

She looks down, like she's reading the answers off the floor.

"It's only been a few weeks," she says.

"The drinking?"

She nods.

"And the rest?"

She closes her eyes.

"Don't make me check your room." I sound like I'm her father, which would make me laugh if I wasn't so pissed off.

She looks at me and then looks away. "It's just a slip, Cristo. It's not going to happen again."

"Why'd you stop going to those meetings? I thought they made it better."

She takes a deep breath, refusing to look at me. "Sometimes they did. But sometimes just being there made me want to kill myself."

"Don't say that, Mami."

"It's just an expression. You know what I mean."

But I don't know what she means. She sits down on the couch, leaving room on either side of her. I want to sit down, but something tells me I have to stand to make it through this conversation.

"Are you still taking your medication?"

She nods. "Most days."

"I thought it was bad, to mix drugs together."

She exhales. "I'm sure it is."

I see my reflection in the windowpane and for a second I think it's someone else. Someone I recognize but haven't seen in a long time.

"What about probation? Couldn't they send you back if they found something?"

"They're not going to find anything. This is it, it's over."

I shake my head. "I don't believe you."

She looks at me, her eyes filled with tears again. "I don't want to be like this. You have to believe that, Cristo."

I look at her feet, which are so small she's wearing a pair of

Luz's shoes. "I do," I tell her. "I believe you. But it's not enough anymore."

"Don't say that, Cristo."

I stare at my reflection again, trying so hard to recognize myself. "I thought being here would make it different, better somehow, but it's still the same."

"No, it's not." She shakes her head again and again like she's in a trance. "I'm not the same." She looks down at her hands, like they can prove what she's saying is true. The skin is dry and wrinkled like an old lady's. "I promise I'm not," she says softly.

I can feel myself wanting to cry, so I bite the insides of my cheeks. I'm still mad, but her voice is starting to break me.

"I know you tried, Mami. I can see that."

"I did it for almost nine months. I was clean for nine whole months." She locks her fingers together, cupping her hands around her knees like she's giving herself a hug. I wish I could comfort myself like that. "I can do it again, Cristo. I can get back there."

"But I can't, Mami. I can't go back there."

"I don't understand what you're saying." She leans onto her knees. Her elbows are so bony it's got to hurt.

"Do you know what I did every day, when I was waiting for you to come back home? I don't mean school or taking care of Luz and Trini, I'm talking about what I did in my head?" She looks at me like I'm speaking in another language. "I tried to forget."

"Forget what?"

I take a deep breath but no words come to me. Instead, I see old clips running through my head: the loud, angry fights Mami and Scottie used to have, and later, the long, drawn-out silences with Lucho; the empty fridge when there was no money or all-night binges when there was too much; strangers stopping by in the middle of the night, asking to borrow things they would never return; the sound of television turned up too loud; flowers rotting on the kitchen table; the smell of cheap cigarettes and liquor, of men with dirt or blood under their fingernails and women with too much perfume, covering not just body odor, but sickness and the dried-out smell of a hunger that will never go away; the constant sight of Mami in pajamas, not able to shower, dress, or leave her room for days, chewing on her fingernails, on ice, on one of Trini's old pacifiers—anything to keep her mouth busy, to keep her from having to explain it all to us.

"It's not fair," I finally say. "None of this is fair."

She shakes her head. "You're right, *mijo.*"

Not fair to ask me to forget, but also, to ask her to change.

"I don't think I can stay here anymore. Not when you're like this." I'm surprised that the words come out of me, and that my voice sounds so calm.

She drops her head into her arms. "*Dios mio,*" she says softly.

"I'm sorry, Mami."

She keeps her head down. "Where you gonna go?"

"I don't know yet. But I can't stay here. I can't watch you do this anymore."

"You were the one I trusted. To stay with me. To never leave."

And now I want to take it all back. I want to hug her and say it's okay, that I will stay, that I'll never leave, but something won't let me do it. I have to blink to keep myself from crying.

"Just until you get clean, okay? When you're ready, we'll all come back. Trini, Luz, all of us."

She lets out a small laugh, but her face isn't smiling. "Okay," she says. "I guess you know what you want."

"I want you to get better," I tell her. "So you gotta promise me one thing, okay? That you'll keep taking your medicine. No matter what."

She nods. A passing car catches her eye and she squints against the headlights. She stands up and pulls the shades down. With her back to me she says, "Will you put all the pills into that box you got me, with the different days? It helps me remember."

"Sure, I can do that."

When she's done pulling the shades she turns around to face me. Her eyes are glassy but she doesn't allow herself to cry.

"You know what's messed up? Using hurts just as much as

not using did."

It's one of the only things she's said all day that I believe.

"So why do you do it?"

She tucks her hands into her armpits, twisting back and forth like a little girl.

"I can't control it. It's an addiction, you know, like when you want something really bad and you have to have it, even if it's not good for you."

"Like too much candy on Halloween?"

"Exactly like that. It controls you. It takes over your mind and makes you think you can't live without it." She scratches her arms, leaving long red streaks on her pale skin. After she rubs them away, she starts the scratching all over again.

"But I thought you were okay before, when you got out. You seemed fine. I thought you didn't need it anymore."

"It's like a virus. It came back."

"Why didn't you fight harder?"

She opens her mouth but nothing comes out. She shakes her head. "I did," she finally says. "I thought I did."

We're eye level now, and we stare at each other for a long time. It's hard to look at her this close up, but harder to look away.

"Do you have to start all over again now, with those twelve steps?"

"Yeah," she says. "I'm back at one."

Her eyes are all puffy and red, and her face looks baggy, like when all the air leaks out of a balloon. She looks like she needs to sleep for a very long time.

"You know what they never tell us at school, when they say all that stuff about not doing drugs? They never say why anyone does it in the first place. If it's so bad for you, why did you ever start?"

She takes a step back, sitting down on the edge of the couch. "I hope you never know the answer to that question." She re-ties her hair in a ponytail, stalling for time. "I guess the truth is that sometimes bad things feel good. Like having sex without a rubber. But if you never do it, you won't know what you're missing." When I look away she says, "I'm serious.

Maybe you're too young to hear that, but I'm not gonna lie to you about something this important." She leans closer to me and locks her eyes with mine. "Most kids whose parents tell them not to do drugs, they're talking out their ass 'cause they've never done anything stronger than Tylenol. But I'm telling you now: don't do it. It's out there and it's going to tempt you, but if you don't mess with it, you'll never know what you're missing."

Fifteen minutes later my backpack is filled with clothes and I'm ready to go. I tell her I'll be back later for the rest of my things. She's still on the couch, lying down now, and still in her pajama bottoms. My hand is on the doorknob, smooth and cold as ice.

"You can come back anytime," she says, her voice low and sleepy. "It's your home, too. You know that. You're always welcome here."

I nod, trying not to think or feel too hard, just knowing I need to go. I'm about to leave without giving her a kiss or a hug but something makes me walk over and kiss her good-bye. She sits up and leans into the kiss, pushing her hollow cheek into my lips. Then she grabs my free arm and pulls herself up. Next thing I know she's hugging me, both arms crossed behind my back. She's holding me as tight as she can, but it still feels like I could slip from her grasp.

When she finally lets go she holds my face in both of her hands. She plants a hard kiss on my forehead. When I look up, she's smiling at me.

"My handsome boy," she says. "You're going to break a lot of hearts, kid. I know that as well as I know my name."

I pull away from her, feeling hot now, needing fresh air. "I'll see you later, Mami."

"Wait." She licks her thumb and rubs it across my forehead. "Lipstick," she says.

"Thanks."

She nods, tears streaming down her face. She brushes them aside, but new ones keep falling. When I close the door she's waving at me, her hand as pale and thin as a tortilla. I look back into the apartment from the porch, watching her through the window. You wouldn't know to look at her, or this house, that anything bad has ever happened inside. She stands in the middle of the room, both arms wrapped around her thin shoulders, hugging herself.

I reach for the door, suddenly wanting to go back in, to touch her one more time, but it locks behind me. When I look back through the window, she's gone.

◆ ❖ ◆

It takes ten minutes of steady knocking to get Snowman to open the door. Lines of shaving cream streak his face like war paint and a towel hangs around his neck. He's holding a razor in his hand, not the cheap disposable ones Scottie used to use, but a long shiny one that looks like a switchblade.

"Yell next time," he says, slapping the huge metal door. "There's no peephole."

I nod, hoping that means there's gonna be a next time.

"You coming in?" He slides the door open and I can see the flicker of candlelight behind him. It smells like one of those stores at the mall, where Teacher took us last year to get school clothes, and for a second I wonder if he's got a lady here.

"Sure. If it's okay."

There must be fifty candles spread throughout the living room. Most are in tin cups, sitting on the floor like lights lining the aisle of a movie theater. It looks like church during Christmas Mass, not that I've been since Abuela took me back in Puerto Rico. But I'm pretty sure this is how it looked.

"You got company?"

"Just my own." He wipes his face with the towel, then uses it to clean the blade before tucking the razor into his pocket. "I don't like artificial lights," he says, like he's apologizing. He stares at me for a few seconds before asking me what's wrong.

"How do you know something's wrong?"

"Come on, kid. We don't have time for this." He crosses his arms. "Spill it."

"Lucho's back, with Mami. I found them together at home."

His lips tighten. "Is she all right, your mom?"

I shake my head. "They were both messed up."

He pulls out a chair for me, so I sit down without taking off my backpack. I put my hands on the table, then remember it's rude and put them in my lap. He sits across from me, a huge candle between us. It's got three wicks, all of them lit, but it barely seems to give off any light.

"She said it was a slip."

"So she's using again?" He pinches the top of his nose, between his eyes, like he suddenly has a headache.

"She promised to stop."

"How long's it been?"

"I don't know."

He scratches his goatee, which seems to glow in the candlelight. "That's a shame. I'm sorry you had to see that." He rubs his hand over his chin, smoothing the hair down, over and over again. All I do is sit there, staring at all those candles. "You hungry?" he asks, his eyes so small they look closed.

I shrug. "A little," I say, when really I'm starving and can't remember the last thing I swallowed except my own spit.

Snowman disappears into the kitchen, which is really just a sink and a line of cupboards along the wall. A few seconds later he comes back with his arms full of Chinese take-out boxes, which he lays on the table in front of me like presents. He tells me there's beef with broccoli, pork egg foo yung, Hunan shrimp, steamed dumplings, and chicken with snow peas. I don't recognize most of it, but it's salty and warm and I don't really care.

"Fork or chopsticks?"

"Chopsticks." I'm no good with them, but I know he thinks it's the right thing to do. I hold them like he shows me, but it feels weird, like writing with my left hand, and I can't even get one dumpling out of the box. I finally stab into it with the end of the chopstick, but it slips off before I get it to my mouth and falls onto the floor. After that he brings me a cloth napkin and lays it over my lap like rich people do on TV.

"Shit, my baby brother could work those better than you." He's laughing as he says it, his eyes looking straight into mine. Then the kettle whistles and he walks away, asking if I want green tea or jasmine. I lean over and pick up the dumpling with my hand, slipping it into my mouth in one bite, not even bothering to wipe it off. It burns my tongue but it's worth it. When he comes back he's carrying a pot of tea to the table, pouring a cup for each of us.

"You got a brother?"

He sits on the edge of the table. "Used to."

I can tell by the look on his face that it's another secret he's gonna keep, so I don't ask him anymore about it.

"Anything else wrong?" He keeps picking up the boxes and putting more food onto my plate, filling it up every time I finish something.

"I need a place to stay."

"You walked out?"

I nod. My heart starts beating faster and I think maybe I shouldn't say anymore. Maybe I should just finish eating and leave. But then I hear myself say, "I want to stay with you."

"Excuse me?"

"Here." I swallow and clear my throat, drink some of the tea he poured me. It's bitter and tastes like old flowers, but at least it's hot. "I want to stay here with you."

Snowman stands up, dropping the empty cartons on the table. "That's a bad idea, Cristo."

"I'd stay out of your way. And I wouldn't ask any questions. I promise."

He walks into the kitchen and turns on the sink. I can see him bent over, splashing water onto his face. "This world is no good for you. My world. I'm sorry."

"But I've been in your world for months."

"As a visitor maybe, but you didn't live here." He comes back with water running down his face like sweat. "You *shouldn't* live here."

"I can handle it."

"No, you can't. And you better never be able to. I was wrong to get you involved." He dries his face with the towel. "This isn't your home."

I'm full now, but I keep on eating. Who knows when I'll eat like this again.

"Listen. I'm sorry." He puts his hand on my shoulder.

"When you're older you'll understand."

I finally put down the chopsticks, laying them across the plate like I've seen him do a bunch of times. I wipe my hands with the napkin and then my mouth. "I don't have anywhere else to go."

"Come on now, what about your teacher? You know she'd take you in."

I shake my head, blinking quickly to keep tears that I didn't know I had from falling. "I told her I didn't need her. I said that Mami and I were gonna get a nice apartment and then bring Luz and Trini back home. I can't go to her like this."

"Yes, you can. You have to." He rubs his chin again. "You belong there, with your sister."

"I want to be with you."

He grabs the back of a chair, slamming it into the table.

"Don't you get it? This isn't about what you want. It's about what you need. You need to be with family. You need to be protected." He stares down at the floor, like he's talking to all those candles.

"You can protect me."

"Damn it, Cristo—you need to be protected from people like me."

"That's not true. There's nothing wrong with you."

"You don't know the first thing about me," he says, his face still looking down. "You don't know what I've done."

"I know you've helped people. In the neighborhood, like that park you rebuilt—"

"And what about your mother?" he shouts, cutting me off. "What about you?"

Snowman looks up at me now and I stare back at him, not sure what to do. Without saying anything else he walks into the dark kitchen and stands with his back to me. He covers his face with the towel and mumbles something under his breath. Then he tucks the towel into his back pocket and comes back into the room, sitting down across from me.

"I need to tell you something. And you better pay attention 'cause I'm only going to say this once. I don't like confessions." He rests one hand on the table, flat and white like a napkin, while the other is jammed into his front pocket. "I used to fill orders for your mother, before she got locked up. Whatever she and Lucho wanted, if they could pay, I got it for them. That was one of my jobs." He clears his throat. "Your mother, she was one of my customers."

I can see his lips moving, and I can still hear the words, but they sound far away, like I'm underwater.

"You see now?" Snowman says. "You get that I'm not what you need?"

"I don't understand."

"And you don't have to. You're a kid. You're not supposed to understand why people do the things they do."

"I thought you were my friend."

He closes his eyes. "You were wrong," he says. "Friends don't pass money between them. It was a job, you got paid. It was never more than that."

I try to swallow but my throat won't let me. "I don't believe you."

He stares at me for a long time. "Believe what you want."

I push my plate away, knocking over empty food boxes and spilling the now cold tea from our cups. "You're a liar," I tell him.

He's looking at the floor, watching the chopsticks roll under the table. He opens his mouth to say something, but then closes it, standing up to clear the table in silence. He looks like a waiter, piling dishes in one hand and using the towel from his back pocket to wipe up the mess.

"I know you're angry. You should be. You love your mother and you want to protect her. Your loyalty is in the right place."

"I don't want to be loyal to her," I say, feeling far away and not quite like myself. "She lied to me, too."

"Everybody lies," Snowman says from the sink, his voice rising over the sound of running water. "She just tried to protect you. From who she was and is. But that's not your job to worry about. She's your mother, that's all you need to know."

I stand up, feeling the weight of my backpack trying to drag me under. I lean against the table for balance. "A mother is supposed to take care of her children."

"You're right," he says, his voice coming again from the dark. "But they're human, too. They're weak, they make mistakes, they die." He walks toward me, a ghost appearing from the night. "But a son can never abandon his mother, no matter what she does. Don't waste your time questioning your loyalty, okay? Don't ever let a friendship or girlfriends or work or any other bullshit separate you from your family. Do you understand me?" He bends down to make sure I'm looking at him. "Family is the only thing that connects you to the world. Without that, you'd be flying around like a balloon some kid forgot to hold onto. Then you'd be no better off than me."

Tears fall onto the table and I wipe them up with my sleeve. I don't even know why I'm crying. Snowman uses the corner of the towel to wipe the tears off my face.

"Don't worry," he says. "It's clean."

"*Nada es limpio*," I say. "Not anymore."

He looks at me as he holds the towel, wrapping it around his arm like a bandage. It's dark brown, probably the color he wishes he was.

"You're allowed to love someone who disappoints you," he says. "That's the nature of real love. To allow someone to devastate you, and to keep loving them. Then you know it's real."

I feel like I don't know anything right now. None of this seems real.

"Go to your teacher's house. Go be with your sister. The two of you need each other." He walks me to the door. "Trust me, you're going to be fine."

I reach into my pocket to get the pager. It seems like I've had it for years, even though he just gave it to me last summer. He looks surprised when I hand it to him.

"You quitting now?"

"I thought maybe you fired me."

He tucks it back into my pocket. "Keep it. That way I'll always be able to find you."

When I turn to leave he puts his hand on my shoulder and squeezes it once. Then he lets go.

◆ ❖ ◆

Teacher's wearing her bathrobe when she answers the door. Her mouth falls open but she doesn't say anything. I guess the look on my face tells her everything she needs to know. She takes my bag and follows me up the stairs. We stand together in the darkness of the kitchen, waiting. The clock on the oven says 10:45 p.m. She waits for me to speak. I wait for the words to come.

I sit at the table while she heats up a plate of chicken and rice. She never even asked if I was hungry. I'm not, but I figure it's smart to eat every time I have the chance. She doesn't turn on the light until after she serves me. I eat with my eyes half closed. When I finish it she serves me another plate.

"At home we never have leftovers," I say, just to break the silence.

She sets down the pot, which makes the table shake. "Well, that's because you come from a big family," she says. "It's hard to make enough for all those kids."

I stare at my reflection in the pot's rounded lid.

"Is Luz asleep?"

She nods. "You should probably wake her up when you go in there, just so you don't give her a heart attack."

"Luz sleeps like she's already dead."

She eats rice straight out of the pot. "Still, you should try."

"Okay, Teacher."

After two pieces of banana bread and a glass of milk, she tells me it's bedtime. She brings me into the bathroom and hands me a stack of clean towels and the toothbrush she bought me back in September. I grab her hand before she leaves.

"I'm sorry, Teacher. I was wrong when I said I didn't need you anymore."

She squeezes my hand. "It's okay. I understand." She kisses the top of my head. When she walks out she reminds me to put the toilet seat down after I'm done.

"Don't worry. I've lived with girls my whole life, Teacher."

When I walk into Luz's bedroom I don't bother to turn on the light. I can picture the room perfectly. Luz is so neat that I know everything is put away, tucked neatly into its proper place. The window is cracked, and the breeze blows the curtains against the windowsill. The room is cold like a porch and it smells like fresh laundry.

"Luz," I whisper. "Luz, wake up." She doesn't respond so I shake her. "Come on, Luz, don't make me sit on you."

"Cristo?" Her voice is scratchy.

"Yeah."

Her head pops off the pillow. "What's wrong?"

"Nothing. We'll talk in the morning." I push her shoulder lightly. "Just make some room, okay?"

She slides into the corner. "Here, take the outside. I know you don't like the window."

By the time I get into bed she's asleep. She curls into me like a baby, pushing against my side. I don't realize I'm cold until I feel her warm body against me. I wrap my arm around her and put my face in her hair, something I would never do when she was awake. The smell of her head is the only familiar thing in the bed. I hope it's enough to put me to sleep.

She's wrong about me not liking the window. What I like is being on the side that's closest to the door, just in case I need a way out.

SHE SEES the girl crying. On an airplane, flying over the ocean. She has never seen the water from so high. It looks dark and cold. Like the surface of another planet. She is afraid of falling out of the sky. She holds her daughter in her lap. She is not alone. She is a mother now. She will never be alone again. They eat the airplane food, like flavored cardboard. They sing songs. They sleep. The airplane lands in a foreign city. They are far from home. She feels lost, but knows exactly where she is. She gets her bags. Holds her baby. She has everything that belongs to her. She walks along the busy streets. People stare at her. Cars honk at her. The city screams at her. She stops. She looks at the buildings that surround her. Nothing is familiar. And none of it is hers. Outside she looks calm, but inside she is running again. She runs until she cannot breathe. She fears she will never stop running.

Arcelia

I can't stand the silence of living alone. Not sure I can survive it. It was bad enough before, when Cristo was at school all day, but since he ain't coming back what's there to look forward to? My days are endless, broken only by the sunrise or night falling. I leave the TV on all day and usually the radio in the kitchen, too, just to keep me company.

Lucho disappears for two days right after Cristo leaves, and I seriously think it might be over between us. The first day is hard—just like breaking any habit—but after that I'm okay and I make an appointment to see my case manager and go to an NA meeting. But then Lucho comes back and she ends up staying with me for the entire weekend. We never really leave my bedroom, even though it's warm outside and there's a spring festival going on in the park. I can hear bells and the sound of children laughing, but I keep forgetting to look out the window.

We lose ourselves in the constant search for a better high— food, alcohol, drugs, sex—everything we can use, we do. Use or abuse, what's the difference? I don't remember deciding to binge, but here I am just doing it. Almost like an instinct. Opening a beer bottle, rolling a joint, packing my caps, bleaching my needle—it's all part of the same routine, as normal as getting dressed after taking a shower. I don't have to ask anyone for help. I don't have to wait on some list. I don't have to pretend to be better than I am—or worse, be something I'm not. I'm in my own skin again, in my own world, and it feels like coming home.

Every time I sober up, even if it's only for an hour or two, I regret using. I think about Cristo, about what I promised him, and I tell myself that I'm gonna stop. Each time is my last time. I vow to start taking my meds again, and to reschedule all the doctor's appointments I missed. I want to stop—I swear to God I do—but I don't know what it feels like to be done, to be full. What does it even mean to be satisfied? Most nights I'm afraid I'll never find the bottom.

What I do know during those brief moments of being straight is that I hate being addicted. The feeling when it bubbles up inside of me—that gnawing hunger—I want to have it cut out of my body like a disease. I try to ignore it first, but that's like trying to ignore a gunshot to the head. So instead I try to quiet it, to give it just a little something to tide it over. But no matter what I do, it's never enough. The need gets so big I can't control it. Eventually I have to give in. And when I do, it only gets bigger. I just don't understand why it has to get so big.

Getting clean the first time almost killed me, and I know it only worked 'cause I was locked up. I didn't have a choice. But on the outside things are different. Nobody is forcing me to do it. Nobody cares one way or the other. One day I have what my old counselor used to call a moment of clarity, where you see your future, and I see that going back in is the only way I'll ever be able to quit again. But I also know I won't survive being locked up a second time. Not sure I have the will to survive anything.

I must have a crazy expression on my face 'cause Lucho rolls over and asks me what's wrong and if I want her to give me another fix.

"No, I'm good," I say, and she falls back into the wall and closes her eyes. I think she's nodding off but then she says, "This shit's all right but not as good as what we used to get from Snowman."

"Nothing's as good as what I used to get in New York," I tell her.

She shakes her head slowly. "Nah, you're just saying that because you were young then. It's always the best when you're just starting out. You don't have to work so hard to fool your body." Her eyes are still closed but she has a silly grin. "There's nothing like those first times, you know?"

I nod. "But we still keep trying to get back there, to that place you can never go again. It's kinda sad."

She looks at me. "Do you feel sad right now?"

"I don't feel anything."

She stretches out on the bed. "Sounds good to me."

I watch her chest rise and fall as she breathes. I look down at my own chest but I don't see nothing move under my bulky sweater. I reach my hand under my shirt to feel my belly. The skin is warm and soft like a baby's. I think of Trini, how I used to tuck my hands inside her pajamas when they were cold. It always surprised me when I made her laugh. I fall asleep sitting up, the sound of my daughter's laugh echoing in my ears.

◆ ❖ ◆

By the end of the weekend we run out of food and drugs, so Lucho goes back to work. We're back in the cycle. The first thing I do when I'm alone is shower. The water is hot and the force of it hurts my skin, but I want to feel something—even pain. I think about going to AIDS Care to get my Ensure and some food vouchers but I'm too tired to leave after drying myself off and getting dressed.

I smoke a few cigarettes to settle my stomach and drink cold, three-day-old coffee to try to wake up. My feet feel like they're made of stone and my left arm tingles from my elbow to my wrist. I sit down at the kitchen table at 10:30 and when I look at the clock again it's noon. I watch a few soaps and fall asleep on the couch and when I wake up Oprah is on. I open a window as wide as I can and sit in front of it. I watch people walk their dogs and their children to the park. I watch birds fly from one branch of a tree to another for no reason I can see.

As I sit, I try to remember what Providence was like when I first saw it. It's a small, peaceful city, and I remember thinking it was much prettier than New York. With big hills and trees and old cobblestoned streets that remind me of San Juan. The trees are what I love the most—how they line the streets just like the telephone poles and are so tall you have to tip your head all the way back just to see their tops. My favorites are the big oaks that look like huge heads of broccoli, and the Christmas pines that make the whole street smell clean. There's a tree in the park so high I can see it from the window. I imagine lying under it and looking up at its dark branches, a tangled mass that blocks out the entire sky. I want to be that tall and strong—that old. I wonder how many kids have climbed its branches. How many teenagers with pocketknives have cut their initials into the bark. How many seasons it's seen. When I think of my own life compared to that tree, I realize how little I know. How little I've seen. I want to see all that tree sees, but I know it's impossible. Still, it don't keep me from dreaming.

I get out my notebook and start writing. Just putting words on paper makes me feel better. When I fill that notebook I go to Cristo's room to see if he has another one. I find an old one he left behind and flip through it, looking for clean pages. There's a page with names written on it in Luz's handwriting. *Cristoval. Lucila. Trini. Arcelia.* Below there are more words. *Mother. Skinny. Sick. Gone.* I find another list, filled with more questions than I've seen in my entire life. Questions my little girl was too afraid to ask me. She wants to know who I am, why I left Puerto Rico and left her father, and why I had to go away last year and leave her and Cristo behind. I owe her so much more than I can put into words—even if the letter was fifty pages long—but I have to try. I sit down on Cristo's bed and write a letter back to her, answering each of her questions. Even the ones I'm scared of.

After Luz, I write to everybody I can think of. All the people I love or should've loved, all those I owe and will never be able to repay. I save Cristo's letter for last. His is the hardest to write and maybe the most important. I know he feels bad about moving out and leaving me all alone, so I start by saying it's okay, that I forgive him for taking off that night and for taking care of himself. But more than that, I tell him it was actually a good thing that he left. Not because I wanted him to go, but because I had to know that he was strong enough to do it. I didn't know I needed it, but walking out was a gift he gave me, and it makes me happy to know I taught him something, even if it meant leaving me behind.

I fold each letter and find envelopes for all of them, long white ones I stole from my case manager's desk. I address the few I know by heart and look up the ones I wrote down on the inside of matchbooks and gum wrappers. I leave the ones for my kids on the mantel, above the fireplace that no longer works, and put the rest in my pocket. I slip my sandals on and make the ten-minute walk to the post office on Weybossett, using my last three dollars to buy stamps with a picture of a black jazz musician on them. I drop them in the mailbox one by one, rereading the names and addresses one last time before I let it all go.

It's a beautiful spring day, sunny and not too hot. I walk with a smile on my face, something close to peace flowing through me. Folks here call this mud season—the weeks between winter and spring when the streets are covered with gravel and melting snow and the potholes are full of water. Near the high school I notice a row of lilac bushes just beginning to blossom. One bush has white flowers, but the others are covered with deep-purple buds that look just like candy. I walk over to the fence and pull a flower through the chain links. The metal feels warm against my fingertips. I breathe in the flower, feel its soft buds against my skin, but I can't smell anything. I twist the branch until it breaks off in my hand and hold it like a lollipop as I walk. When I get home I put it in a glass filled with water, hoping it will eventually bloom and fill the whole room with its scent.

◆ ❖ ◆

When I can't sleep I decide to clean the apartment. I wash the floors with a rag soaked in dish soap, getting on my hands and knees to pull out the furniture to dust behind it. I mix bleach in a bucket of hot water and disinfect everything in the bathroom. The smell makes me feel light-headed but I like it. I stand on a chair and wipe down the insides of each cupboard. I even climb on the kitchen table to wash the light fixture in the middle of the room. When I'm done I open all the windows to air out the smell. I'm sweating and my hands are sore from the work. It feels good to be tired in that way. The smell of bleach and lemon dish soap reminds me of my childhood, of Saturday mornings when my mother was still alive, how we would clean together in an empty house while she sang songs about broken people finding love.

I stay in the kitchen till the sun sets and the whole room fills with darkness. When I can't see the table or the color of my fingernail polish, I turn the lights on. I close the windows and pull all the shades. Now it feels too bright, like a classroom. I turn the lights back off and light a candle instead, watching the flame dance along the wall. The hunger is coming. I can feel it building inside me even though I can't find it yet. The first sensation—a tingle in the bottoms of my feet—feels really good, like an itch you're about to scratch. I try to remember that it won't always feel this good, that I'll start scratching and soon it will burn hot enough to take my breath away. But that don't matter right now.

I start yawning, even though I'm not tired. My nose starts to run. It's been a few hours since my last fix, but I'm already feeling the signs of withdrawal. I know I won't sleep without another hit, but Lucho is working an overnight and won't be back until the morning. I need a distraction. I need to do something with my body.

I search my bedroom for leftover food and find half a pizza under the bed. I eat a slice covered with shriveled green peppers and cheese that's hard like wax. A few seconds later I think I'm gonna throw up. I spend the next half hour lying on the bed telling myself not to. As soon as I stand up I walk straight to the toilet, lift the lid, and puke into the newly bleached bowl. Then I go outside to get some air.

It's completely dark by now and cold enough to empty the streets. It seems much later than it is. The pay phone at the corner store is busted, so I walk two more blocks and use the one outside the liquor store. I page Lucho and wait for her to call me back. Twenty minutes later she hasn't called so I page her again.

An old guy walks out of the liquor store with a paper bag wrapped tight around a bottle of whiskey. He stops on the street to open it and takes a long drink. His stubble is several days old but his hair is neatly combed. I recognize him from dinners at one of the soup kitchens and nod hello. He smiles, showing me all five of his teeth. Twenty years ago he might have been handsome, but now he's just pathetic. He offers me the bottle and I take it quickly. I don't even like whiskey but I drink as much as I think I can get away with.

"Lady's got a real thirst," he says.

"Sorry," I say, wiping my mouth. "You know how it is."

He keeps his eyes down as he buttons up his coat. "You thirsty for something else?"

I sneak another sip. "Like what, old man?"

He draws his hand out in a strange gesture, like he's about to take a bow. "Come with me and find out."

I give him back the bottle. "Thanks for the drink."

He tips an invisible hat in my direction. "And dance by the light of the moon," he sings. "Just like the song says."

I nod and let him walk away. A few minutes later my head is buzzing again and I wish I'd gone with him. I walk halfway down the block to see if he's still around. I don't find him, but I see a pack of teenagers smoking weed on somebody's porch. I wait until a girl's holding the joint and then ask her for a hit. She looks at the guy next to her first and when he shrugs she hands it to me. I take a long hit and pass it back, wishing that girls would pay to have sex as easily as guys will. I thank her and she smiles at me, pretty in exactly the same way I used to be. I wonder how many years she's got left.

I walk back to the liquor store and page Lucho 911. Even though she's working she knows what that means. If there's any way to get out, she will. My legs start to cramp so I walk in circles around the pay phone. I stretch them out one at a time, like I'm about to go for a run. I must look like a lunatic. A car drives by, music blaring. I feel the beat vibrating in my chest. My heart starts to ache. I want to go home and curl up on my bed and cry, but I can't risk missing Lucho's phone call. I curse the fact that I don't have a phone in my house or the money to pay for it. I want a different life. I want something—anything, everything—to change.

The phone finally rings. Lucho says two people called in sick and she can't leave until she's cleaned all the buses for the morning run. She says she'll get off by sunrise probably, and will make it worth the wait. I tell her I can't wait. She tells me to try, but if I get in a jam to call Charley. His shit is spotty but he'll come through in a pinch. She tells me to go home and try to sleep first, try to wait for her. I say I will, but as soon as I hang up the phone I call Charley. He isn't surprised to hear from me.

An hour later he meets me at the park and we drive down under the highway. I try to get away with just giving him a blow job but he says his shit is worth more than that so I have to fuck him. There are three good things about Charley: he comes real quick, he has a wife he wants to keep so he always uses a rubber, and he gives me a ride after, anywhere I want to go.

I snort half a bag while he drives us over to Federal Hill. A few minutes later it hits and life is suddenly good again. I feel normal. He buys me a spinach calzone and two cannolis, but I'm not that hungry by the time we find a parking spot on the bridge. After a few bites I give him the rest of the food. He don't eat it either.

I don't want to look at him, so I look out the window. I watch the city like it's a TV show I used to love. The sky is dark like the bottom of the ocean. There must be stars but I don't see any. Charley points to a construction site below us—a new mall going up by the freeway—and says it's the best gig in town cause they work so much overtime, nights and weekend at double pay. I watch the cranes lift huge steel spikes off the ground and place them gently on top of each other like they're toothpicks. It's hard to believe that one day those toothpicks will turn into a building that holds thousands of people. A building I might visit someday, if it's even open to people like me.

It's almost ten when Charley drops me back home. I snort the second half of the bag, since I don't feel like cleaning my rig. Then I take a long, hot bath. My arms and legs feel heavy in the water and I imagine that I'm an anchor falling to the bottom of the sea. As I start to fall asleep, the last thing I remember thinking is that this is the most comfortable tub I ever passed out in.

Javier

San Juan, 4 de abril

Querida Arcelia,

Tengo que admitir que tu carta ha sido una sorpresa. No la esperaba, y parte de ella ha sido dolorosa de leer. No es que haya pensado que nunca te volverías a comunicar conmigo; yo sabía que lo harías, pero no hubo nada que me indicara que sería ese día, este año. Imagino que no hay manera de prepararnos para algo así.

No importa cuanto tiempo haya pasado, tú sigues siendo mi esposa. Eso es algo de lo que estoy seguro. Eres la madre de mis hijos y la primera mujer que amé. Nada de eso va a cambiar. Pero muchas otras cosas han cambiado. Tanto tú como yo hemos hecho cosas malas, nos hemos herido mutuamente y algunas de esas heridas aún duelen. Sin embargo me hace feliz el saber que ahora estás mejor, que ya no bebes y que te estás cuidando. Quizás cuando salgas podrás ser la madre que siempre quisiste ser, la madre que antes fuiste. Recuerdo muy bien los primeros años, cuando Cristo apenas comenzaba a caminar y Luz colgaba de tu cadera como la alforja de un caballo, y aún me sorprende la cantidad de energía que tenías. Eras una mujer muy fuerte. Creo que nunca te lo dije, otro de mis muchos errores. Lo hacías todo por tus hijos, y es por eso que ellos eran felices y saludables. No sé cuándo cambiaron las cosas o por qué, pero se que tengo algo de culpa, quizás la mayor parte. No fui un buen padre y probablemente fui peor como esposo. Cuánto lo siento. Yo era tan solo un niño cuando nos casamos, y pensaba que el tener una esposa y un hijo a quienes cuidar, y un hogar, me haría hombre. Estaba equivocado, por supuesto. Aún no sé qué hace que un muchacho se convierta en hombre, tal vez las dificultades y las pérdidas, la desilusión y el simple acto de sobrevivir, pero hoy soy un hombre y he tenido que lidiar con todas estas cosas. Es por ello que puedo escribirte esta carta y decirte todo esto luego de tantos años de separación. Por muchos años tuve miedo de mis sentimientos: mi amor, mi odio, mi ira y mi alegría. Pero ya no le temo a esas cosas. Hay muchas otras cosas, cosas reales, a las que temer en este mundo. Temerle a los sentimientos es una pérdida de tiempo.

Tengo una buena vida ahora, un trabajo estable con un buen salario y un hogar acogedor en la parte trasera de la casa de mamá. No estoy feliz, pero estoy contento. Hay un par de ugujeros negros en mi vida, lugares donde perdí algo que una vez amé. Uno es por el béisbol, el otro es por mis hijos. Uno jamás podrá cerrarse, pero quiero hacer algo con respecto al otro: quiero ver a mis hijos. Cuando tenga el dinero quisiera comprarles billetes de avión para que puedan visitarme, y ver a sus abuelos y a todos sus primos que también los extrañan. Ya sé que ahora son norteamericanos, pero Puerto Rico simpre será su hogar, y siempre habrá un lugar para ellos cuando vengan de visita.

No sé qué decir acerca de nosotros. Sólo quiero lo mejor para tí, una buena vida, pero sé que en ella no estoy incluído. Tú y yo tuvimos nuestro momento, a veces bueno, a veces no tan bueno, y creo que cuando se trata de tu primer amor no hay una segunda oportunidad. Algo murió cuando te subiste en ese avión con rumbo a Nueva York, y yo lo enterré junto con el resto de nuestro pasado. Por el tono de tu carta imagino que también tú lo enterraste. Eso está bien, porque nuestro futuro no tiene nada que ver con nosotros, sólo con nuestros hijos. No podemos reparar lo que rompimos. Ya no los conozco, y ellos tampoco me conocen, pero no tiene por qué ser así. No he sido un padre para ellos, pero no quiero seguir siendo un fantasma. No sé que seré, pero creo que tenemos tiempo para decidirlo. Aún son jovenes y espero que puedan perdonarme por mi larga ausencia. Por favor, déjales saber que pienso en ellos a diario y que siempre los voy a amar. No quiero castigarlos por tus errores, y pienso que tú tampoco debes castigarlos por los mios. Ellos, no tú o yo, son los únicos inocentes.

En tu carta me pides que te perdone. Cuando comencé a escribir esta carta no sabía si ya lo había hecho, o si sería capaz de hacerlo. Pero ahora mismo siento que me he quitado un gran peso de encima. La furia depositada en la boca de mi estómago se ha liberado y se ha ido. Yo ni siquiera sabía que estaba allí. Así que ahí lo tienes. He hecho lo que me has pedido, te he perdonado, pero ¿qué hacemos ahora? Quizás ni tú ni yo somos quienes lo deciden o lo saben. Quizás está en las manos de Dios, y en los corazones de nuestros hijos. Preguntémosles qué quieren, a ellos que nunca tuvieron voz en nada de esto. Déjales decidir cómo quieren seguir adelante, cómo quieren vivir. Confío en que los has criado bien, tan bien como has podido, y sé que a lo sumo están en capacidad de hablar con franqueza. Una de las muchas cualidades que sacaron de tí. Siempre desde que eran muy niños podian pedir lo que querian, incluso cuando tú y yo no estabamos en capacidad de dárselos. Así que pregúntales ahora si quieren venir a Puerto Rico, si quieren verme. Ese poder es lo mínimo que podemos darles luego de haberles quitado tanto.

Escribe o llama cuando puedas y ya veremos cómo seguir adelante. Alguna vez me dijiste que el único lugar que te interesaba era el futuro. No se si aún crees en ello, pero en este caso es todo lo que nos queda. Sinceramente espero que éso sea suficiente.

Tu esposo,
Javier

Arcelia

I wake up not knowing where I am. I think it's morning, but it's still dark outside. The water in the tub is cold and my fingers are white with wrinkles. The back of my head is asleep. I try to add more hot water but it's all gone. I stand up and walk into my bedroom. A candle burns on the windowsill, smelling like jasmine. I dry myself off and put on my pajamas. Men's long-sleeved flannel, striped like an old prison uniform. The water from my hair makes a large wet patch on the back of my shirt. Goose bumps run down both arms. I find a decent vein in my hand and use that to boot the second bag. The rush is incredible. I feel it burst inside me like an orgasm. I sit there for a long time, just enjoying it.

When I finally get up, I walk into the kitchen. I bring the candle with me, so I don't have to turn on the light. The curtains are blowing in the wind. I know they are white, but they look yellow in the candlelight. I promise myself that I'll bleach them next time I do the wash. I used to like to wash clothes. As a girl it was my favorite chore. I liked to make things clean. Now I can't remember the last time I went to the Laundromat. The laundry basket is overflowing but I refuse to look at it. I stand in front of the window and look outside instead. There are no cars in the parking lot behind the house. I am alone. I close the window but the curtains keep blowing. There is no wind. My eyes are making them move. I reach out to grab them but touch only the air.

Suddenly I am in the bathroom again. I sit on the toilet

and use a vein in my thigh for the third bag. A lady from detox taught me how to use my toes if I want to hide the needle marks, but I don't care anymore. It's too late for me to hide anything. The pleasure hits me instantly, burning a path straight through my chest and out the top of my head. I close my eyes so I won't lose any of it. I don't want to share this high with anything, even the blank walls of the bathroom.

I sit in front of the TV but the images don't make sense. I find a magazine and read the same article again and again without remembering anything. Eventually, I throw it away. My bookshelf's empty except for the big book of Alcoholics Anonymous. It's the only book I own. I flip to random pages and read a few lines out loud. The sound of my voice makes me laugh. I put the book on the mantel, next to the letters I didn't mail. I turn it around so I don't have to read the title printed on the spine. I look at the lilacs. The buds are open but I still can't smell them. I start to cry. I bite off a few petals and put them in my mouth. I chew them into a paste and swallow. All I can taste is the snot in the back of my throat. I open my mouth to scream but bite my knuckles instead. I don't stop until I can taste the blood.

I pull a sweatshirt on over my pajamas and go outside in my bedroom slippers. The wind is strong and it dries my eyes in an instant. It's dark and quiet on the street. Somebody on a bicycle rides by, calling out "Be careful!" when I cross at the corner. I walk back to the pay phone and page Lucho again. I can't feel my fingers. I watch them punch in the numbers as if I'm watching someone else's hand. I want to call Chino but I can't remember his phone number. I try different combinations—patterns that seem familiar—but that horrible recording keeps screaming in my ear, telling me I've dialed a number that is no longer in service.

I feel a wave of nausea so strong I fall to the ground. Chills run through my body. I kneel on the sidewalk and puke into the gutter three times. My stomach keeps tightening, even when there's nothing left inside. I'm so cold and tired I can't imagine moving. I want to curl into a ball and sleep under a parked car, but I don't want the cops to find me here. No. The truth is I don't want Cristo to find me here. I look at my hands under the streetlight. My fingertips are almost blue. They look like the hands of a dead person. Fear floods my body. I touch the pavement, expecting to feel nothing. The gravel scrapes my skin. I can still feel pain. A voice in my head speaks softly. *You can't do this anymore.*

I pick up the phone and page Snowman. I don't even try to remember his phone number. It just comes to me. The voicemail picks up after two rings. His voice on the recording makes me want to cry. The sound of something familiar. I punch in the pay phone number and hang up. I close my eyes. The world tilts. I grab onto the phone to keep from falling. The coil's like a noose in my hand.

The pay phone rings. As loud as a siren. I answer it before it can ring again.

"Snowman?"

"What?" He sounds angry.

"I need help," I say. My voice sounds strange, like I'm talking under water.

"Who is this?"

"It's Arcelia." I clear my throat but my voice don't change. "I'm in trouble. I fucked up."

"Arcelia?" His voice softens. "I can't understand you. Slow down."

"I need help," I say again. My voice sounds wheezy, like an old lady who smoked two packs a day her whole life. "Help me." Tears are falling down my cheeks.

"Where are you?"

"At a pay phone." I close my eyes and lean into the phone booth. "By the liquor store near the Armory."

"Are you all right? What happened?"

I open my mouth to speak but no words come out. My tongue feels thick like a sock. I wonder if it's possible to forget how to speak.

"I'll be right there, okay?"

I nod my head, as if he can see me. I catch my reflection in the dingy Plexiglas of the phone booth. I don't recognize myself. I blink and the image disappears.

"Arcelia?" I hear something like panic in his voice. "Stay there, okay? Just don't leave."

I open my mouth again, to tell him I'll be okay. Instead, I watch my breath fog up the glass. It takes everything in me to speak.

"I'm dying, Snowman."

I hear the line go dead. The silence is deafening. I drop the phone and stumble down the sidewalk. The wind is against me, blowing garbage and leaves into my face. All I want is to go home. To be home.

I tuck my head to my chest and keep walking. I can't see anything. I stretch my arms out in front of me like a blind person. I don't want to be blind. My feet feel heavy like I'm walking through snow. I force myself to put one foot in front of the other, to keep going, even though all I want to do is give up. *All you have to do is make it home,* I tell myself, *and then you can rest.*

I see the house on Sophia Street—the dull yellow siding, the broken window, the toys scattered in the driveway. The last place I called home. I see my children inside. Cristo eating cold cereal straight from the box. Luz reading a book on the broken loveseat. Trini standing in her underwear over the hot-air vents on cold winter mornings, refusing to get dressed. I see my family. My home. Suddenly I know that's where I have to go. I walk past the park and turn onto Westminster, heading across the freeway to Olneyville Square. My legs ache, but I know I have to keep going. It's worth the pain, to be able to go home again.

I see the outline of Atlantic Mills in the distance. I'm almost there. I walk up Manton slowly. The wind is behind me now, pushing me up the hill. I can't even feel my body. Nothing hurts anymore. My eyes fill with tears. I squint to keep them from falling. Something's different about the old neighborhood. The sidewalks are empty, almost clean. And the houses seem bigger. They stand alone on vacant lots like they're waiting for something. The trees are taller, too. Some even higher than the buildings.

I try to read the street signs but I can't see the words. It's dark, and I wonder what time it is. It feels real late, like everybody in the city is asleep. A cat brushes my ankle. It stops on the corner to look at me, as if trying to remember my face. I want to smile but I can't figure out how. I nod my head instead, but the cat is already gone. I pass the liquor store and the church so I know I'm getting close. *You're almost home,* I tell myself. Again and again until I believe it. When I see the house I almost cry out with joy. *You're home now. Everything will be all right.*

I crawl up the steps on my hands and knees. I am thinking of my children. I picture all three sleeping safely inside. All three together. *You're almost there, Celie, just a few more steps.* I reach for the doorknob but it's locked. I try again. I try to push it open but I don't have the strength. I search my body for keys. My pockets are empty. I'm not carrying anything at all. I ring the doorbell. A pretty sound. I remember how it was always broken. I wonder if the bells are ringing in my head.

Wait. I see now. Other things are different. The porch was painted. The blanket is gone from the window. The broken glass was fixed. I touch the pane to make sure it's real. I knock hard on the glass, like it's made of wood. When I knock again, glass breaks under my knuckles. The sound is beautiful, like icicles falling from the roof.

I see blood on my hand but I can't feel any pain. All I feel is the heat from inside the house. I don't want to be cold anymore. I lean through the window and look into the dark room. There's nothing I recognize. I kick my leg over the windowsill and fall into the darkness. My knees hit the ground first, and then my face. The floors are cold and hard like ice. My cheek goes numb. I roll onto my back and stare at the ceiling. All the cracks have been fixed. This is not my home. I try to move but I can't remember how. It's too late anyway. I know I'll never stand up again.

I close my eyes. The world stops spinning. I hear a bird singing outside, calling my name. I hug the floor. It holds me like I'm floating inside it. I want to lie here forever, held by something that will never break. I feel my muscles twitch as I relax. As I give in. My breathing slows and I feel my body go limp. *You're done,* the voice says. *It's over.*

Now you can rest.

Trini

My mommy is gone, like the snow.

Miss Valentín

There is no funeral. They cremate her body and the kids decide to spread her ashes in the bay off Galilee. Cristo says he wants her in the water so she can go home again. With Snowman's help we charter a small passenger ferry, and on a bright Sunday morning in May we ride out to sea.

Every seat on the small boat is taken. Cristo, Luz, and Trini sit together in the front, Cristo planted between his sisters with an arm around each one. They sway as the boat rises up and down but he never lets go of them. Chino, Kim, and Sammy are seated along the bench that runs down one side of the boat, their legs touching because they have no extra room. César, Marco, and Graciela fill the opposite bench, all three looking at the floor. I sit in a chair along the back, right in front of the captain, while Scottie and Snowman stand beside me. My seat can rotate 360 degrees but I keep it facing forward. I watch the seagulls flying over the endless blue water, occasionally dipping down to feed.

Lucho is the final passenger. Lucky number thirteen. She stands away from the group, behind the captain, and faces the land as the boat pulls away from shore. She watches the lighthouse as we retreat, her eyes unwavering. She looks like she's in a trance, and like she hasn't slept in weeks.

After twenty minutes the captain turns off the engine. He drops the anchor but the boat still spins around, floating in circles. He taps me on the shoulder, assuming that I'm in charge, and tells me we can begin anytime now. There is no one to give the eulogy, so Cristo asked if he could read a poem instead. I told him he didn't have to but he said he wanted to. Needed to. I motion to him now and he stands up. He's wearing a tie and a button-down shirt with sleeves so long they cover his hands. His khaki pants, which I ironed this morning, still hold the crease down the center of each leg. He takes a book from under his seat and opens it to a marked page.

"Mami didn't read a lot of books. She always said she didn't have the patience. I understand that because I'm kind of like that, too." He looks up, squinting in the sunlight. "But she liked poems, if they were short, and she liked flowers. So I'm going to read a short poem about flowers."

He clears his throat and reads the poem, first in Spanish and then in English. It's a simple poem, but he reads it beautifully, pausing at all the right moments. His voice cracks a few times but he gets through it without breaking down. Tears well up in my eyes and I tip my head back, trying to keep them from spilling out. Chino has his hand over his face and every few seconds his entire body shakes. He doesn't make a sound. Kim holds a tissue in her hand but doesn't appear to be crying. When I lose the battle with my tears and they spill onto my face, she passes it to me. I smile at her, which makes more tears come out. None of the children are crying.

When he finishes reading, Cristo puts the book down. He picks up the bag containing his mother's ashes and carries it to the side of the boat, where the railing is low. The bag is made from heavy-duty plastic and he can't untie the knot. Luz tries to help him but her fingers aren't strong enough. Lucho eventually opens it, by tearing a hole in the plastic with her keys. She hands it back to Cristo as delicately as if she were handing over a newborn baby.

"Here goes," Cristo says in a whisper.

Everyone stands up, and we fall into a semicircle behind him. He holds the bag over the edge and slowly pours the contents into the water. At first it falls in a light sprinkle, but when the bag is half empty the remaining ashes pour out all at once, creating a dramatic splash that turns the water from dark blue to a bright emerald green. The sea lights up below, as if we had dropped a flashlight into the waves. No one takes a picture, but I'll never forget how the water seemed to glow as it filled with ash. I step to the edge to get closer, to see it one more time. It looks like a huge plume of smoke is floating right underneath the surface, as if a bomb had gone off on the ocean floor.

"Adios, Mami." Cristo speaks so softly I think I'm the only one who hears him say good-bye. I'm holding a bouquet of white roses, given to me on shore by the captain's wife, and without thinking I begin to break it apart. I pass each rose around the semicircle until everyone is holding a single flower. One at a time we walk to the edge of the boat and toss the flowers overboard. Lucho tears the head off hers and sprinkles the rose petals into the water one by one. When she finishes, she closes her eyes and stands at the railing like a statue. Tears fall from her eyes and she doesn't bother to wipe them away. She holds the stem of the rose in one hand and tosses it into the ocean like a javelin. When she opens her eyes she looks for it out in the waves, but a gull plucks it out of the water and flies away with it in its claws.

I say a short prayer as I drop my rose into the water. I try to follow it with my eyes, but soon it has blended in with the others and I can't tell which one is mine. The only person who keeps their flower is Trini. She holds it in her small fist like a torch. I watch her bring it to her nose and smell it several times. Every time she does I see a tiny smile flicker across her face.

On the ride back to shore I sit beside Luz. I put my arm around her and she rests her head on my shoulder. The wind pulls my hair away from my face and I feel like I did as a child riding the roller coasters at Coney Island. I put on my sunglasses and look out at the sparkling sea. A swimmer does laps along the breakwater, and I watch him pull his body through the waves as fast as a sailfish, jealous of the quickness of his flight. I wonder what it would feel like to be blessed with that type of agility, and if it's possible for me to lose the burden of my body in any environment.

As we pull into the dock Luz sits up straight, separating her body from mine. She looks back at the sea.

"Do you think she'll make it?" she asks.

"Make it where?"

"Back to Puerto Rico. That's where she always wanted to go."

I squeeze her shoulder, pulling her into my chest. I kiss the top of her head, right along the part where her hair splits into braids. "Yes. Of course she'll make it. I bet she's already there."

She nods, as if my opinion makes it fact, and turns away from the water. I never see her look back.

◆ ❖ ◆

I hold the dinner at my apartment later in the day. We eat stewed chicken with rice and beans that Graciela's mother spent all morning making. After I serve the food, Scottie corners me in the kitchen to thank me for handling all the preparations.

"It's good of you," he says. "Especially since you're not even family."

I smile to hide my contempt. He watches Cristo and Luz from across the room, gesturing at them with his beer.

"I thought about taking them, but it's just too much, you know? If they were mine, I'd have to...but since they're not—" He shakes his head. "I don't know."

"Have you thought about Trini?" I ask him.

"Course I have. She's my blood," he says, as if that makes everything clear. "She's my daughter, she needs to be with me."

I watch Trini stacking paper cups on the floor. She knocks down the tower she just built and then starts building it again.

"She's their sister," I say. "They need to see her."

"I know, I know." He sips his beer. "And I'm all right with that."

"Does that mean you'll help?"

He looks at me like I'm speaking another language.

"You know, just bring her around sometime, or invite them over. Just help make it possible." I lower my gaze. "I'm not saying you should raise them, but you can still make an effort to keep them close. It doesn't take that much extra."

He finishes his beer in one long swallow and places the empty can on the counter next to several others. He puts his hand on my shoulder.

"Sure, whatever you need," he says.

"It's not about me. I'm talking about what they need."

He nods and flashes a smile that looks just like Trini's. "Right," he says, "whatever *they* need." He slips behind me and disappears into the living room.

I'm still in the kitchen, cutting up lemon squares, when a hand touches my waist. I jump, knocking the dessert tray against the countertop. When I turn around Snowman is stepping away from me.

"Sorry, didn't mean to startle you."

"That's okay." I hold up the dessert tray. "I was just about to put these out."

"Here, let me help." He carries the tray into the dining room and walks around the room, offering lemon squares to everyone. Once he's circled the room twice he comes back to me with the tray, which now holds the two remaining squares.

"You could have just put it on the table."

"I didn't think of that," he says. "Sorry." He takes a piece, offering me the last one.

"No, thank you," I say, even though all I want is to taste the lemony sweetness in my mouth. But why even start, when I know that one won't be enough?

He puts the plate down and reaches into his jacket, pulling out a small dark-blue book. I can just make out the words *Alcoholics Anonymous* on the spine, the golden script raised like Braille. Tucked inside the cover are several long white envelopes.

"Maybe this isn't the time," he says, "but I don't know when would be."

He hands me the letters, his eyes focused on the floor like he doesn't want to embarrass me with eye contact. I flip through them slowly. One has my name written on the outside and the others are for Cristo, Luz, and Trini.

"I found them in Arcelia's apartment," he says. "The night she died."

"So it's true?" I take a step back. "You were there."

"I thought everyone knew," he says.

"I heard the rumors. But I didn't know what to believe."

"Yeah, well." He scratches the stubble on his face, so pale I can barely see it. "She paged me. She knew she used too much. But it was too late by the time I got there. I found her body lying in the middle of the floor." Instead of looking at me, he flips through the pages of the book.

"How'd you know to go to Sophia Street?"

He looks up. "I went to the new place first. When I didn't find her there I knew something was off. Especially when I saw those letters. The upstairs neighbor ended up calling me, said she heard noises that sounded like a break-in. Luckily the new tenants hadn't moved in yet."

I look around the kitchen, making sure no one else can hear us.

"You think it was suicide?"

"Who knows," he says. "What OD isn't suicide?"

I notice his hands, the knuckles spotted with brown and white like his skin is peeling from a burn. For some reason I want to reach out and touch them. Instead, I place my hand on his sleeve.

"It's not your fault," I say. "I hope you don't feel like you could have done something."

"I know," he says. "Not then, anyhow." He looks around the room, his eyes searching for something. "It might sound crazy, but I don't think she wanted me to do anything, to help her or whatever. I really think she just called so I would get there first. So Cristo wouldn't find the body. She was thinking about him in the end, not herself."

I look back at his hands, trying to process what he's telling me. I want to figure out which color is peeling off, the brown or the white, but I can't tell. Nothing makes sense anymore.

"I just thought I should tell you," he says. "That's everything I know."

"Thanks." I tuck the envelopes into the shallow pocket of my apron. When my hands are empty, he offers me the book.

"You can have this, too," he says. "Maybe the kids would want it."

I take it from his hand, wondering what I could learn about my own compulsion from a book like that. He picks up the last lemon square and eats it in one bite. Then he uses a napkin to clean off the powdered sugar around his mouth, even though it blends in perfectly with his skin and I hadn't even noticed it there.

"I've been thinking about what you said, back at the library," he says. "About what kind of influence I want to have on him. I'm not sure how much good I have to offer, but I know I don't want to be a bad influence. I know that much."

"Is he still working for you?"

Snowman shrugs. "I have him going to the library mostly, just getting books and copying articles for me. I took him off the street."

"That's good to hear. I appreciate that. But I don't think he needs to work anymore, not for anyone. He's a kid, he needs to play baseball and go to the movies."

"Understood," he says, nodding his head slightly. He turns to leave, but stops himself mid-step. "One more thing," he says. "I was thinking about the pool. He's a good swimmer, you know, and he loves it. I don't think you should take that away from him just because I introduced him to it."

"That's entirely up to him," I say. "I wouldn't make that decision for him."

"Okay, good," he says. "It's not a big thing, but it's good for him, you know, the discipline, the repetition." He tucks his hands into his pockets. "What I mean is, I think that's something I could give him, like going to church or something. We could make it a routine. Don't kids need that?"

I smile at him. "I'll ask him what he wants to do." I turn away, trying to end the conversation, but I can feel him step closer to me.

"And what about you," he says. "What do you want from all this?"

I turn around. "What do you mean?"

He gestures toward the living room. "Is this just temporary or are you going to keep them?"

I pick up a wet sponge and wring it out over the sink. "It's not all up to me. Even if I wanted to, the state might not let me. It's complicated. And in the end, I just want to do what's best for them."

He nods. "And do you know what that is?"

I let out a small, hard laugh and tell him I'm still trying to figure it out. He wishes me luck and tells me to reach out to him if I ever need anything. He says it in a way that makes me believe he really means it; he's not the type of guy to just say things to be polite.

I start to scrub the edges of the sink, even though I can't see any stains. All I want is to stop and rest, but I know I have to keep moving in order to get through this. The answers will come, I do believe that, but I can't control how and when. I have to give up control completely, and it's the most difficult thing I've ever tried to do.

◆ ❖ ◆

Later that night, after Cristo and Luz are asleep, I sit on my bed and read the letter from Arcelia. I haven't given them theirs, and sometimes I think I never will. But then again, is it my place to decide? Who am I to stand between a mother and her children?

I'm surprised by how well-spoken she is in the letter, especially compared to how she came off in person. They say that prison is a waste of time, but it seems to have helped her (at least for a little while), and who's to say how much more she could have done if it weren't so hard to navigate the system, and so easy to slip through the cracks. Her letter is the answer I've been waiting for, but I have to read it several times before the words really sink in.

> Dear Miss Valentín,
>
> I'm writing to thank you for all you did for my son. You been a better mother to him in the past year than I been his entire life. I used to hate you for that, but not anymore. If I still believed in God I'd thank Him for bringing you into our lives. Instead, I'll thank the Hartford Avenue School for putting you in his classroom, and your parents for putting you on this earth.
>
> You don't owe me anything, but I want to ask you a

favor. For me, but also for my children—if anything happens to me. I want you to take care of them if you can. Raise them as you would your own children, showing them all the good things I didn't see, but always wanted to believe in. I give you my blessing in this, and I hope no matter where I am you won't let them forget about me. Maybe they're Americans now, but we are all Boricuas on the inside, and I want them to be proud of that. They can only learn that from someone who is proud, too. From someone who has something to be proud of. I think that someone is you. I am ashamed of so many things I done in my life and I spent a lot of time hating myself for those things. I am finished with that now since I have run out of hate, even for myself.

I love my children, please believe that, and I wouldn't walk away unless I thought that someone else could do better. They deserve more than I can give them. That is why I brought them to this country, and I don't want to stand in the way of their success. A mother is supposed to teach her children things about the world, but my children taught me so much more than I ever taught them. Ain't that a strange twist? But I'm proud of what I learned from my children. I am so proud of them. Please make sure they know that. I don't have the time to list all the other things I want you to do, but I don't think I have to. You know what I want for them already, and I bet you know how to give it to them. There is not much that I could teach you, is there?

I will ask you one more thing, to pray for me and my children. If there is a God, we will all have to answer to Him in the end. And we never know when that will be.

With sincere and endless gratitude,
Arcelia Perez De La Cruz

After finishing the letter, I lie in bed all night but never fall asleep. In the morning I get up early and make breakfast for Cristo and Luz. I have no appetite so I make myself a pot of tea while I wait for them to wake up. When they stumble into the kitchen I serve them each a large plate of eggs and fried potatoes, and watch them eat from across the table, sipping my tea. Luz notices that I'm not eating and asks me what's wrong.

"I got a letter from your mother. They think she wrote it the night she died. Do you want to hear it?"

Luz looks at Cristo, who looks at me. After a few seconds, he nods. When I finish reading the letter Cristo asks if he can read it himself so I hand it to him. When he's done he looks at Luz and then back at me. He gives me back the letter, which I place in the space where my plate would be. I'm suddenly aware of how quickly my heart is beating.

"Did she leave us something?" Cristo asks.

"Yeah, did we get a letter?"

I reach into my bathrobe pocket for their letters. "You each got your own."

I place the letters on the table in front of them. Neither one moves, they just keep staring at me.

"There's a lot of paperwork to fill out, and we'd have to meet with social workers and get the state to approve it, but if it's okay with both of you, I'd like to do as your mother asked. I'd like you both to stay here permanently."

"You don't have to do that, Teacher."

"I know I don't. I want to."

Cristo looks at Luz.

"I want to stay," she says.

He looks at me. "I don't want you to offer because you think you have to."

Outside, I hear the roar of my neighbor's lawnmower, and a few moments later, the smell of gasoline and fresh-cut grass. I hear someone's radio, the slap of a basketball on the pavement, and farther away, the high-pitched laughter of young children. These smells and sounds are familiar, as is the sight across from me of Cristo and Luz at my kitchen table, eating what I've cooked for them; but something is fundamentally different about this moment, and I feel the reality of it like a throb in my chest.

"Listen to me, both of you." I lean forward in my chair, my eyes shifting between them. "This isn't about the letter, or guilt, or what your mother wants. This is about what we want.

What you want and what I want." I put my hands on the table to keep them from shaking. "I want you both to stay with me, to live with me, for as long as you want. Through high school or college or whatever. I don't want to replace your mother, please believe that. I would never try to take her away from you. But I do want to adopt you guys. I want us to be a family."

After a long silence Cristo places his hand on top of mine. We lace our fingers together.

"Okay, Teacher," he says.

Luz starts to laugh. "You can't keep calling her that, not if she becomes our mother."

I look at Cristo. "You can call me anything you want," I tell him.

"Even Vanessa?"

"That might be pushing it."

"What about 'Mom'?" Luz asks. "That's what American kids say."

"Mom is fine."

"Or Auntie? Auntie Vanessa?"

"How about Tia Vanessa?"

"There's no rush," I say. "We have a long time to figure this out."

They spend the rest of breakfast tossing around potential names, getting more creative as the game progresses. By the time we leave for school, they've cataloged at least a dozen options, some sincere, some silly. After the first bell rings, I leave them in the front stairwell, like we've done every day for the last month.

"See you guys after school." I wave at them from the bottom of the stairs.

"Bye, Miss Valentín," Luz says, same as always.

"Later, Teacher." Cristo runs up the stairs two at a time.

A smile breaks across my face that is still there when the second bell rings. I may not look any different, but I know I will be a different person from this day on, and probably a different teacher.

Certainly a different mother.

Cristo

A few weeks after my mother dies I find out I'm going to pass fifth grade. Mrs. Reed tells me I did much better than she thought I would and asks me if I want to take the test for Regular Ed over the summer. If I pass I can go into the same class as Luz. Graciela promises to help me study and Teacher promises not to be mad if I end up failing it, so I tell Mrs. Reed I'll try. I don't really want to do it, but I don't want to disappoint Teacher even more.

I still haven't opened the letter Mami left me from the night she died. I figure once I read it I'll have to really say good-bye so I keep putting it off. I carry it around with me, though, and pull it out to read my name on the outside of the envelope, just to see her handwriting and to imagine what it says inside. Some days I think I'll open it in a week or two, but sometimes I think it'll be a few years before I finally have the guts, and sometimes I think I'll never read it at all. I kind of like the mystery of wondering what else she wanted to say, something she had to write down and couldn't say to my face. But really, I just like knowing I have it waiting for me whenever I need it, and I don't want that feeling to ever disappear.

It's like when Graciela calls me at Teacher's place and I walk to the phone as slow as I can, just wanting to draw out that feeling of not knowing what's going to happen. Those moments between knowing I'm going to talk to her and actually hearing her voice are the best, when everything is about to happen and it's all still in our heads and it's all perfect. Sometimes I want to live my whole life in those moments, even though I know that's not the way life's supposed to be. It's messed up how things have to keep changing all the time, but I guess life is kinda like school—right when you start to like the grade you're in, you have to move up again.

César never comes back to school. There's a bunch of rumors going around—one that he's going to a school for blind kids, another that he's getting homeschooled by his grandmother—but the truth is he's just hanging around with his uncle Antonio playing card games and fixing cars all day. He got real good at both, especially poker, and now he says he wants to grow up to be a gambler. "I don't need to go to school for that," he tells me. "All I need is a lot of time." Teacher says all he's doing is wasting time, but I keep hoping he'll get better so he can stop taking all those pills and just come back to school and be a normal kid again.

I stop by to see him after school some days, even though it's not on my way home anymore. He's either playing cards in the back room, betting with M&Ms instead of poker chips, or sitting on the sidewalk while his uncle works on a car, dipping engine parts into gasoline to clean them. One time I see Charley outside talking to Antonio so I wait by the bus stop where they can't see me. They act like old friends, like how Charley was with Mami when we saw him at the soup kitchen. Charley jokes with him, punching him lightly in the arm every time César brings him a beer, and then tucking money into his front pocket as a tip, just like he used to do with me. I watch César sneak sips from the almost empty beer bottles and figure I should just keep on walking. The kid I'm looking for doesn't really exist anymore, and whenever I see this new César, it just reminds me how much has changed and how it's all going to keep on changing.

It's not official, but I guess Graciela's my girlfriend now. She saves me a seat at lunch and sometimes we walk home from school together. When she finds out my birthday's coming up she tells me she knows the perfect gift, a brand-new hardcover book that's never even been opened, but I tell her all I want from her is a thirty-second kiss. She says no way, but then she gives it to me when we're walking home one day—just stops short under the highway and plants one on me—and after, she says she's still going to get me that book. Girls always know how to get their way.

My birthday finally comes at the end of May but I don't want to celebrate. It's the first one without Mami and it seems wrong to celebrate anything now. But life doesn't stop just because someone you love is gone. I learned that when she went away last year, but also when I was a kid and we left Papi behind in Puerto Rico. My life didn't stop. It's like putting down a book—it still exists, even when you're not reading it.

I tell Teacher I don't want a birthday party, but she says all kids have to have one, at least until they're eighteen. Now that we're living with her I guess I have to follow her rules. We have the party on a Saturday so Trini can come, and a few kids from school come too. Scottie brings Trini late of course, but she stays to eat cake and play hide-and-seek in the backyard. She keeps calling my name from her hiding place, asking me if she's in a good spot. I finally tell her yes because I still can't find her, and then she comes running out with a panicked look, saying, "I'm right here, I'm not lost," over and over again until I pick her up and whisper into her ear, "I found you, I found you," which finally makes her laugh. She doesn't want to leave when Scottie comes to pick her up, but Luz and I tell her it's okay and she'll see us again real soon. I'm not sure I believe it myself, but I still keep on saying it.

After everyone leaves Teacher says I can open all the presents, but instead I tell her what I really want for my birthday is to learn how to make *pasteles*. It takes a while but I finally get her to agree. First we drive to the market to pick up the things she doesn't have, and then, when we get back home, she teaches us how to peel the vegetables without cutting up our knuckles, how to brown the meat without drying it out, and how to fold the banana leaves without losing any of the filling. She shows us how to knot the string around each package so they're tight now but easy to open later, and how to tell when they're done by how they float in the boiling water. I eat a couple straight out of the pot, even though I know I'm going to burn my mouth. Teacher sips on a bottle of water and won't even take a bite. I tell her it's funny that she doesn't eat a lot anymore and she says it's easier that way. "With some things, I'd rather have none," she says, putting the leftovers into the freezer. I don't tell Teacher, but that's exactly what Mami used to say about everything bad she was using, that it was easier to have nothing at all.

Snowman misses the party so he brings me a present when I see him at the pool a few days later. He gets me a mask with a snorkel attached and a set of flippers so I can swim laps as fast as he does. He says they're supposed to help me build my leg muscles, but I like using them to walk along the bottom of the pool like a duck. Sometimes he gets mad when I goof off like that, but most times he's cool with whatever, as long as I finish all my laps in under twenty minutes. He's big on people not wasting his time.

Tonight we're the last ones in the pool, still doing laps while the lifeguard sprays down the floors with bleach. In the locker room after we shower he lets me shave his head, saying now that I'm twelve I'm old enough to learn about shaving. He covers his head with this green gel that turns into a fluffy white cream as soon as he starts to rub it on. Then I stand on the bench behind him and run over it with the razor just like he taught me. It looks cool, like shoveling snow off a driveway, and afterwards it feels as smooth as a cue ball. I can't believe he trusts me enough to let me hold a blade to his head. "Either trust or stupidity," he says, laughing, but sometimes I think it might also be love.

I get home late from the pool and find Teacher in the kitchen waiting up for me. She says something came in the mail she wants me to have. "A letter you need to read," she says, handing me an already opened envelope, "from your father to your mother. He wrote it before she died, but sent it to the wrong address, so she never got it." She says more but I don't hear any of it, walking from the room with the letter shaking in my hands. When I was younger I always wanted him to write to us, but now that it's happened, I'm afraid of what he might say.

His handwriting is neat and small, not like I pictured, and he wrote in pencil like I used to when I worried about making a lot of mistakes. Before I know it, I'm translating it in my head, the English somehow easier to hear.

San Juan, April 4

Dear Arcelia,

I must admit that your letter came as a surprise. I was not expecting it, and parts of it were very difficult to read. I knew that I would hear from you again, but there was nothing to tell me it was going to be on that day, in this year. But I guess there is no way to prepare for something like this.

No matter how much time has passed, you are still my wife. This is one thing I'm certain of. You are the mother of my children, and you are the first woman I ever loved. None of that will change. But many other things have changed. We have both done bad things, we have each hurt the other, and some of those wounds are still fresh. But I am happy to hear that you are doing better now, that you are sober and taking care of yourself. Perhaps when you get out, you can be the mother you always wanted to be, the mother you used to be. I remember those first years well, when Cristo was just beginning to walk and Luz hung on your hip like a saddlebag, and I'm still surprised by how much energy you had. You were such a strong woman. I don't think I ever told you how strong I thought you were, another one of my many mistakes. You did everything for those kids, and they were happy and healthy because of it. I don't know when things changed or why, but I know that some of the blame is on me, perhaps most of it. I was not a very good father and I was probably a worse husband. I am sorry for that. I was still a boy when we got married, and I thought that having a wife and child to take care of, and having a home, would make me a man. I was wrong, of course. I still don't know what turns a boy into a man, perhaps struggle and loss, disappointment, and simply the act of surviving, but I am a man today, and I have dealt with all those things. That is why I can write you this letter, why I can say these things to you after all these years apart. For many years I was afraid of my feelings: my love, my hate, my anger, and my joy. But I'm not afraid of those things anymore. There are so many other things, real things, to be afraid of in this world, so it is a waste of time to fear emotions.

I have a good life here now, a steady job at the market with good pay and a nice home in back of my mother's place. I am not happy, but I am content. I have two black holes in my life, places where I lost something I once loved. One is for baseball and the other is for my children. One can never be fixed, but I want to do something about the other one. I want to see my children. When I have the money I would like to buy them plane tickets so they can visit me here and see their grandparents and the many cousins who also miss them. I know they are Americans now, but Puerto Rico will always be their home, and there will always be a place for them when they come to visit.

I don't know what to say about us. I want nothing but good things for you, a good life, but I know that it doesn't include me. We had our time, some good, some not so good, and I believe that there is no second chance when it comes to your first love. Something died when you got on that plane to New York and I buried it along with the rest of our life together. From the sound of your letter, you have buried it, too. That is a good thing, because our future doesn't have anything to do with us, it only has to do with our children. We cannot fix what we broke. I do not know them anymore, and they don't know me, but it doesn't have to stay like that. I have not been a father to them, but I no longer want to be a ghost. I don't know what I will be, but I think we have some time to figure that out. They are still young and hopefully they can forgive me for my absence. Please let them know that I think about them every day and that I will always love them. I don't want to punish them for your mistakes, and I don't think you should punish them for mine. They, not either one of us, are the only innocents.

In your letter you asked me to forgive you. When I began writing this letter, I didn't know if I had done that, *or if I ever could. But something has lifted out of me right now. An anger that was lodged in the pit of my stomach has broken free and flown away. I didn't even know that it was living there. So there you go. I have done as you asked, I have forgiven you, but where do we go from here? Perhaps that is not for us to answer or even know. Perhaps it is in God's hands, and in the hearts of our children. Let us ask them what they want, those who were never given a voice in any of this. Let them decide how they want to move on, how they want to live. I trust that you have raised them well, as well as you were able, and I know that if nothing else, they are capable of speaking their minds. One of the many traits they got from you. Even as little children, they could always ask for what they wanted, even if we were not able to give it to them. So ask them now if they want to visit Puerto Rico sometime, and if they want to see me. That choice is the least we can give them, after taking away so much.*

Write or call when you are able and we will move forward from there. You once told me that the only place you care about is the future. I don't know if you still believe that, but in this case it is all we have. I sincerely hope it will be enough.

Your husband,
Javier

I read the letter a few times, and when I'm done I feel Teacher walk up beside me. She puts her hand on my shoulder but I don't move or look up at her. I don't want to see her eyes, or have her see mine, filled with tears. She hugs me and I bury my face in her shirt, crying hard suddenly, as if the weight of everything just hit me, as if I just in this second began to understand all that's been lost.

Before, when she was just my teacher, she would have asked a lot of questions about how I was feeling and what I wanted to do, but now she has become something else, and we stand together for a very long time, both of us knowing that something else is what will keep us together, completely still, in the warmth of her living room, *our* living room, for as long as we need.

Later, she tells me we can talk in the morning if I want, but that I should go to bed now, since it's been a long day. "It's been a long year," I tell her. "I should be like fourteen by now." She smiles and tells me that day will come soon enough. She follows me into the hallway but I stop her at the bedroom door, telling her she doesn't have to tuck me in anymore, even though she's done it every other night since I moved in. She looks like she's going to argue with me, but then she leans forward and kisses my eyelids closed, tells me to have sweet dreams.

In the dark of my bedroom, I hear Luz breathing in her sleep. I slip under the covers slowly, careful not to wake her up. Most nights, when I lie in bed before falling asleep, I think about my mother and how I don't want to forget that her hair smelled like cigarettes and that her eyes closed when she laughed and how she hugged me so hard I could feel the bones in her chest. Tonight I think about my father too, things I thought I had forgotten, like the sound of his voice calling my name to wake me up, or the feel of his hands covering mine as he fixed my grip on a wooden bat. For years I didn't let myself remember any of that. But after reading his letter and hearing how he still thinks of us, I can now see the way they used to dance together in our kitchen to slow songs on the radio, both of them still moving, still in sync when the batteries eventually went dead, and I can remember how they would pick me up and hold me between them, singing the rest of the words without the music, sometimes making up their own lyrics to end each song.

Everybody thinks they know the story of their own life, but all we have are the pieces we remember. And what we remember is only one part of the story. I wanted to tell the whole truth, but the real story is bigger than the part I can tell by myself. And maybe that's okay. Maybe what matters is how we tell our stories, or just that we tell them at all.

Acknowledgments

For their love, support, friendship, and keen words of counsel over the many years I've worked on this book, I would like to thank the following people: Mike B., James Cañón, Jane Carroll, Tony Charuvastra, Shad Farrell, Graeme Fordyce, Alexandra Geis, Katherine Guyton, Daniel Alexander Jones, Maria Massie, Jim Radford, Brett Schneider, Ron Sharp, Ira Silverberg, Anjali Singh, Bobby Towns, Rebecca Walker, and Sam Zalutsky.

I would also like to thank my friends, students, and colleagues at Spalding University, who have given me a home for the last decade and who continue to inspire me daily. I wrote significant portions of this novel while in residency at Yaddo and the MacDowell Colony, and wish to thank the administration, staff, and fellow residents for making each stay so enjoyable. I have found respite in many libraries I wish to acknowledge, including: Brown University's Rockefeller Library, the Providence Public Library, the Providence Athenaeum, several branches of the Pasadena Public Library, USC's Doheny Memorial Library, and Art Center College of Design's Fogg Memorial Library.

My sincere gratitude goes out to the women at Prospect Park Books, Patty O'Sullivan and Colleen Dunn Bates, who have shown unwavering courage, loyalty, and grace during the process of preparing this novel for publication. They are true champions of the written word, and through their dedication and commitment to fulfilling our vision for this book, have shown themselves to be genuine and generous collaborators. A big shout out to Nicole Caputo for the gorgeous cover; she restored my faith in the power of an image to reflect something essential in even the most complex of stories.

Special appreciation goes to my family, for their listening ears and loving hearts, and for giving me the space one needs to create and complete a novel, with heartfelt thanks to my daughters, Auden and Braxton, for asking all the right questions.

And a final, boundless thank-you to the one who worked tirelessly as friend, partner, editor, and midwife through the long and arduous process of birthing this novel, and who taught me that it is only after such labors that the real work of living can begin.

About the Author

Rachel M. Harper's first novel, *Brass Ankle Blues*, was a Borders *Original Voices Award* finalist, and selected as a Target *Breakout Book*. She has received fellowships from Yaddo and the MacDowell Colony and is on the faculty at Spalding University's low-residency MFA in Writing Program. She lives in Los Angeles.